"LASHNER KEEPS THE READER SPELLBOUND."
Harlan Coben

"LASHNER IS AS IMPRESSIVE AS
ANYONE WRITING . . . THRILLERS TODAY."
Washington Post Book World

"[LASHNER] WILL KEEP YOU TURNING PAGES."
Philadelphia Daily News

"TIGHTLY PLOTTED . . . FIRST-RATE."
Deseret Morning News (Salt Lake City)

"REAL FUN."
Tucson Citizen

D0448732

The Bookworm
#62 Athabascan Ave.
Sherwood Pk, AB T8A 4E3
(780) 464-5522

6⁰⁰

2007

Praise for *New York Times* bestselling author
WILLIAM LASHNER's
MARKED MAN

"Chances are, if you met Victor Carl in a courtroom, you wouldn't like him . . . On the pages of William Lashner's books, however, Victor Carl is a pretty likable guy . . . [*Marked Man*] plays to the author's strengths—character development and gnarly, bizarre plots with multiple spikes that he manages to tie together in neat bundles."
PITTSBURGH TRIBUNE REVIEW

"Victor Carl is one of the mystery genre's most compelling, most morally ambiguous characters . . . Lashner thoroughly enjoys exploring the darker, seamier, grungier side of his lead character, and here he peels back a few more of Victor's layers. Genre fans will be reminded of George V. Higgins . . . and, more recently, John Lescroart."
BOOKLIST

"If there is a better opening scene out there, it must be a real corker . . . [Lashner's] close-to-the-edge attorney is every bit as great a read as Michael Connelly's flawed Harry Bosch."
MIAMI HERALD

"William Lashner's novel doesn't fall into the cottage variety of murder mystery. Indeed, *Marked Man* is as hard-boiled as an egg in a jar on a bar . . . One is left waiting eagerly for Lashner's next book."
HOME NEWS TRIBUNE (EAST BRUNSWICK, NJ)

"This yarn sets out to prove that it takes a deeply flawed lawyer to serve a perfect crime . . . Real fun."
TUCSON CITIZEN

Books by William Lashner

Marked Man
Falls the Shadow
Past Due
Fatal Flaw
Bitter Truth (Veritas)
Hostile Witness

Coming soon in hardcover

A Killer's Kiss

ATTENTION: ORGANIZATIONS AND CORPORATIONS
Most Harper paperbacks are available at special quantity discounts for bulk purchases for sales promotions, premiums, or fund raising. For information, please call or write:

Special Markets Department, HarperCollins Publishers, 10 East 53rd Street, New York, New York 10022-5299. Telephone: (212) 207-7528.   Fax: (212) 207-7222.

WILLIAM
LASHNER

Marked
Man

HARPER

An Imprint of HarperCollins*Publishers*

This is a work of fiction. Names, characters, places, and incidents are products of the author's imagination or are used fictitiously and are not to be construed as real. Any resemblance to actual events, locales, organizations, or persons, living or dead, is entirely coincidental.

HARPER

An Imprint of HarperCollins*Publishers*
10 East 53rd Street
New York, New York 10022-5299

Copyright © 2006 by William Lashner
ISBN: 978-0-06-072160-2
ISBN-10: 0-06-072160-X

All rights reserved. No part of this book may be used or reproduced in any manner whatsoever without written permission, except in the case of brief quotations embodied in critical articles and reviews. For information address Harper paperbacks, an Imprint of HarperCollins Publishers.

First Harper paperback printing: June 2007
First William Morrow hardcover printing: June 2006

HarperCollins® and Harper® are trademarks of HarperCollins Publishers.

Printed in the United States of America

Visit Harper paperbacks on the World Wide Web at
www.harpercollins.com

10 9 8 7 6 5 4 3 2 1

If you purchased this book without a cover, you should be aware that this book is stolen property. It was reported as "unsold and destroyed" to the publisher, and neither the author nor the publisher has received any payment for this "stripped book."

For my boy Jack,
hardball pitcher, blues guitarist,
King of the DDR

Marked
Man

CHAPTER

1

It must have been a hell of a night. One of those long, dangerous nights where the world shifts and doors open and you give yourself over to your more perilous instincts. A night of bad judgment and wrong turns, of weariness and hilarity and a hard sexual charge that both frightens and compels. A night where your life changes irrevocably, for better or for worse, but who the hell cares, so long as it changes. Batten down the hatches, boys, we're going deep.

It must have been a night just like that, yeah, if only I could remember it.

It started inauspiciously enough. The preceding few days I had been in the center of a media storm. The *New York Times* on line one, *Live at Five* on line two, *Action News* at six, details at eleven. Now, I am never one to shy from free publicity—the one thing, I always say, that money can't buy—but still, the exposure and the hubbub, the constant vigilance to make sure my name was spelled correctly, the crank calls and dire threats and importunings to my venality, all of it was taking a toll. So that night, after work, I took a detour over to Chaucer's, my usual dive, for a drink.

I sat at the bar, I ordered a Sea Breeze, I let the tang of alcohol, with its blithe promise of sweet ease, slide down my throat. There was an old man perched on the stool next to me who started talking. I nodded at his words, yeah yeah yeah, even as I looked around to see if there was anyone else of interest in the bar. A woman in the corner gave me the eye. I tossed it back. I finished my drink and ordered another.

My memory here sounds almost coherent, but don't be fooled. Even at the moment of which I write, it is starting to break apart. The old man, for example, I can't remember what he looked like. And in my memory I can't feel my feet.

John Lennon is singing from the jukebox, imagine that. The old man is talking about life and loss in the way old men in cheap bars always talk about life and loss. I finish my drink and order another.

The door opens and I turn to it with the great false hope one holds in bars that the next person to step inside will be the person to change your life. And what I see then is a beautiful face, broad and strong with a blond ponytail bobbing behind it. The face still lives in my memory, the one thing I remember clear. She looks like she has just climbed off her motorcycle, black leather jacket, jeans, a cowpuncher's bowlegged walk. The very sight of her gives me the urge to up and buy a Harley. She stops when she sees me, as if she had seen me before. And why wouldn't she have? I am famous, in the way you get famous for a minute and a half when they plaster your face on local TV. I give her a creepy smile, she walks past me and sits at the bar on the other side of the old man.

I finish my drink and order another. I order one for the woman. And, to be polite, I order one for the old man, too.

"I loved my wife, yes I did," the old man says. "Like a fat kid loves cake. We had all sorts of plans, enough plans to make a cherub weep. That was my first mistake."

I lean forward and look beyond him to the blonde. "Hi," I say.

"Thanks for the beer," she says as she taps her bottle of Rolling Rock.

I raise my glass. "Cheers."

"What's that you're drinking?"

"A Sea Breeze."

"I don't doubt it."

"I detect a note of scorn. I'm man enough to drink a prissy drink. Want to arm-wrestle?"

"I'd pop your elbow flat out of the socket."

"Oh, I bet you would."

"Let me try it," she says.

I smack my elbow onto the bar, twist my palm into a wrestling grip.

"Your drink," she says.

"See, you can't make plans," says the old man as I slide the drink past him to the woman. "Life don't let you. Wasn't long afore I found out she was sleeping outside our marriage bed. With my brother, Curt."

"You don't say," I say.

"I just did," says the old man. "But I could deal with that. Leastways she kept it in the family. No need to upset the apple cart and spill the milk."

"What do you think?" I say to the woman, whose pretty face is twisted sour after a sip of my drink.

"It tastes like hummingbird vomit," she says as she passes it back.

"My name's Victor. Victor Carl."

"What, they run out of last names when you were born?" she says. "Had to give you two first names instead?"

"Exactly that. So what do they call you?"

"Wouldn't you like to know."

"I'm just trying to be friendly here."

"I know what you're trying," she says, but a smile starts breaking out anyway.

"It was the cancer, finally did in all them plans," says the old man. "It tore up the throat. Curt's throat. When he died, she up and ran off with the night nurse. Happiest day of my life when she left. Now I miss her every minute of every hour. I loved her true, like a Hank Williams song, but what does that matter?"

I snatch down the rest of my drink, and that is apparently the moment my mental recorder decides to go seriously on the fritz. I remember Jim Morrison intoning sweet mystical nothings from the jukebox. I remember my drink tasting funny and me laughing at the joke. I remember the old man getting up for a moment and me slipping onto his warm stool so I could sit next to the woman. I remember ordering us another round.

She smelled of beer and gasoline and a clean sweat, that I remember, and I thought as I sat next to her that if I could bottle her scent right there, I could make a fortune in the perfume racket. At least I hope I only thought it, because if I said it that would be a truly lame line, which might explain what I seem to remember next, her giving me a strange, piteous look before pushing herself off her stool and starting out the door.

I don't remember if I followed her or not, though I assume I did. I assume I did because, in my memory, it is as if right then a door opens and I step through it and find myself inside a strange, muffled darkness.

This is the sum of what I remember of the night, and after that, nothing.

I awoke with a full-body cramp on a hard tile floor. My head was leaning awkwardly against a wall, my legs were sprawled at uncomfortable angles, one of my arms was missing.

An instant after I realized the arm was gone, I found it, dead to the world, pinned beneath my side. I rolled over to free it, sat up in a panic, flopped the appendage onto my chest. I slapped it, pinched it, let relief slide through me as, slowly, painfully, the nerves in my sleeping arm tingled to life.

I was now sitting, I realized, in the front vestibule of my building. The night I had passed through was gone. The gray light of dawn slipped softly in from the street, revealing the sorry state of my corporeal condition.

My suit was in tatters, my shirt untucked and torn, my tie untied but still looped within the buttons of my collar. My heavy black shoes were on, but my socks were missing. And I smelled like a mangy dog who had rolled in something. Physically, my neck was stiff, my hip was aching, my mouth was a cesspool, someone was chopping wood in my head, and there was a sharp, stinging pain in my chest, as if I had fallen smack into the middle of a heart attack.

Damn, I thought as I tried to rise on shaky legs and failed, plopping down again on the sore hip, it must have been a hell of a night. I tried to remember it all, but nothing came through, except for the image of a blonde in a leather jacket.

On my second try I staggered to my feet, fell with a clatter against the mailboxes, pushed myself back to standing. The small room stretched and contracted, the tiles in the floor spun. I sucked my teeth, they felt furry.

I tried the door into the building but it was locked. I patted my jacket, and then my pants, and was shocked to find my keys and wallet still in their rightful places. Okay, good, things were not totally out of control. I was home, I hadn't been mugged, this could all be handled. I unlocked the door, pushed it open, fell forward through the doorway.

My apartment, two flights up, was in as disastrous shape as was I. The cushions of the couch were slashed, the walls defaced, the shade of each lamp distended and torn. Atop a large television, with its screen smashed, sat another television, a small portable, with one of its rabbit-ear antennae bent like a defective straw. You might surmise that this was all fallout from my wild night, but you would be wrong. It had been like this for months, the by-product of a rage expressed toward me by an overzealous dental hygienist. The less said about her the better, yet the telling point is not that it happened but that, in the time since it happened, I hadn't done anything about it other than applying a few rolls of duct tape to the slashed fabric. What it said about the state of my life could fill volumes, but it wasn't volumes I was interested just then in filling as I burst through my door and staggered to the bathroom.

In front of the mirror, as the back of my hand wiped my dripping mouth, I recoiled from a ghastly sight. Lon Chaney was starring in the story of my life, and it was definitely a B movie. Turning my attention to my costume, I quickly realized that the only thing salvageable was my tie, an indestructible piece of red synthetic fabric that was a miracle of modern science. You want to know where all the money thrown at the space program went? It went into my tie.

As quickly as I could, I pulled off the tie, then my suit jacket, my shoes and my pants. But when I unbuttoned my shirt, something stopped me.

Taped to my left breast was a wide piece of gauze. The pain in my chest was apparently not just metaphysical. And, to my horror, I noticed that leaking through the gauze was blood.

My blood.

I ripped off the tape and slowly peeled away the gauze bandage. There was blood and an oily ointment, as if I had suffered through some sort of medical operation, and, beneath that, something strange seemingly pasted onto a patch of my skin just above the nipple.

I started wiping away the ooze, but it hurt too much, my

skin was for some reason too raw. With a little bit of water and soap, I gently washed away the ointment and blood. Gradually, bit by bit, the thing underneath became clear.

A heart, bright red, with two small flowers peeking out from behind either side and a fluttering banner across it all, a banner with a name inscribed that I had to read backward in the mirror: Chantal Adair.

I just stared at it for a moment, unable to process what it was. When it came to me, I started rubbing at it, I started scrubbing it, as hard as the pain would allow. But nothing happened. It wasn't pasted on at all. There it was, and there it would stay. For the rest of my life.

Damn. I had gotten myself tattooed.

After I showered and shaved, I put on a pair of jeans but no shirt. I sat on my ruined couch, with a lamp on and a mirror in my hand. Through the mirror I stared at the tattoo on my chest.

Chantal Adair.

I struggled to remember who she was and why I thought her important enough to inscribe her name atop my left breast for all eternity. I struggled to remember her and I failed. The entire night, after I stumbled out the door of Chaucer's, was a total blank. Anything could have happened. Was she the motorcycle blonde who had started my engine to running that evening? Most likely. But maybe she was someone else, some mysterious woman I met in the course of a long, bleary tour through the darkness. And was my attempt to immortalize her on the skin above my heart a terrible drunken mistake, or was it something else?

Chantal Adair.

The name tripped sweetly off my tongue. A pair of iambs bracketing a mystery.

Chantal Adair.

The tattoo itself was peculiar. There was something out-dated about it. The heart was boldly red, the flowers yellow and blue, the banner carefully shaded about the slope of its curves. It was not the type of tattoo you would see on the young students showing off their skin art in the parks on summer afternoons. It belonged instead on the forearm of an old sailor man called "Pappy," with the name of a prostitute in Shanghai scrawled across the banner. It was, to put a word on it, romantic.

Chantal Adair.

As I stared at the tattoo and said the name out loud, as I tried to dredge her image from the rubble of my memory, all I found was a sharp spurt of emotion that I was unable to identify. But the whole thing made me wonder. Sure, tattoo-ing a stranger's name on my breast was most likely the prod-uct of an inebriated whimsy I regretted even as the buzzing needle slid the ink between the layers of my skin. But I couldn't stop thinking, couldn't stop hoping, that maybe it was something else.

Maybe, in the course of the long night, I had slipped through my weariness and drunkenness into something ap-proaching a state of grace. Maybe only then, with my de-fenses down and my craven heart open to the full beauty of the world, had I been able to find a connection with a woman untainted by irony or calculation. And maybe I had chosen to scar my breast with her name so I wouldn't forget.

Chantal Adair.

Sure, she was most likely nothing more than a drunken folly, but maybe she was something else. Maybe, just maybe, she was the love of my life.

There I sat, in the wreckage of my apartment, in the wreck-age of my life—no love, no prospects, a gnawing sense of existential futility along with the certainty that a better life was being lived by everyone else—there I sat, staring at a name writ in ink within the skin of my chest and thinking the name might save me. The human capacity for self-delusion is beyond measure.

And yet there was no question but that with her name on my chest I was going to find her. The case that had me in the papers and on the news was a case of grand theft, of high stakes and lost souls, of an overbearing Greek matriarch, of a strange little man who smelled of flowers and spice, and of a Hollywood producer selling all the wrong fantasies. It was a case of failed dreams and great successes and murder, yes murder, more than one. And in the middle of that case, as it all swirled about me, there I sat, thinking that a name on my chest, thinking that Chantal Adair, could somehow save my life.

It might have been a pathetic fantasy of the lowest order, but in her own strange way she did.

2

The tattoo appeared on my chest at a rather inopportune time. I was just then in the middle of a delicate negotiation that had exploded in my face, hence the media storm and dire threats. But I should have known that trouble was brewing, what with the ominous way the whole thing started, a deathbed visit to an old Greek widow with gnarled hands and breath like pestilence itself.

"Come closer, Mr. Carl," said Zanita Kalakos, a withered stalk of a woman, propped up by the pillows on her bed, whose every raspy exhale held the real threat of being her last. Her skin was parchment thin, her accent thick as the stubble on her jaw.

"Call me Victor," I said.

"Victor, then. I can't see you. Come closer."

She couldn't see me because the lights were off in her small bedroom, the shades pulled, the curtains drawn. Only a candle flickering by her bedside and a glowing stick of incense provided illumination.

"Don't be afraid," she said. "Come to me."

Standing at the edge of the room, I took a step toward her.

"Closer," she said.

Another step.

"Closer still. Bring over chair. Let me touch your face, let me feel what is in your heart."

I brought a chair to the side of her bed, sat down, leaned forward. She pressed her fingers over my nose, my chin, my eyes. Her skin was rough and oily both. It was like being gummed by an eel.

"You have a strong face, Victor," she said. "A Greek face."

"Is that good?"

"Of course, what you think? I have secret to tell you." She glommed her hand over the side of my head and, with surprising strength, pulled me close so she could whisper. "I'm dying."

And I believed it, yes I did, what with the way her breath smelled of rot and decay, of little creatures burrowing into the heart of the earth, of desolation and death.

"I'm dying," she said as she pulled me closer, "and I need your help."

It was my father who had gotten me into this. He had asked me to pay a visit to Zanita Kalakos as a favor, which was curious in and of itself. My father didn't ask for favors. He was an old-school kind of guy, he didn't ask anyone for anything, not for directions if he was lost, not for a loan if he was short, not for help as he struggled still to recover from the lung operation that had saved his life. The last time my father asked me for a favor was during an Eagles game when I made a brilliant comment about the efficacy of the West Coast offense against a cover-two defense. "Do me a favor," he had said, "and shut up."

But there he was, on the phone to my office. "I need you to see someone. An old lady."

"What does she want?"

"I don't know," he said.

"Why does she want to see me?"

"I don't know."

"Dad?"

"Just do it, all right? For me." Pause. "As a favor."

"A favor?"

"Think you can handle that?"

"Sure, Dad," I said.

"Good."

"As a favor."

"Are you busting my chops?"

"Nah, it's just this is almost like a real father-and-son thing. Calls on the phone. Favors and stuff. Next thing you know, we'll be having a catch in the yard."

"Last time we had a catch I threw a high pop that hit you in the face. You ran off crying."

"I was eight."

"You want to try it again?"

"No."

"Good. Now that that's settled, go see the old lady."

The address he gave me was a small row house on the southern edge of the Northeast section of the city, my father's old neighborhood. A gray woman, round and slumped with age, cautiously opened the door and gave me the eye as I stood on the stoop and announced my presence. I assumed this was the old lady my father wanted me to see, but I was wrong. This was the old lady's daughter. She shook her head when she learned who I was, shook her head the whole time she led me up the creaky stairs that smelled of boiled vinegar and crushed cumin. Whatever the mother wanted with me, the daughter didn't approve.

"I knew your father when he was boy," said Zanita Kalakos in that crypt of a room. "He was good boy. Strong. And he remembers. When I called him, he said you would come."

"I'll do what I can, Mrs. Kalakos. So how can I help?"

"I am dying."

"I'm not a doctor."

"I know, Victor." She reached up and patted my cheek. "But it is too late for doctors. I've been poked, prodded, sliced like roasted pig. There is nothing more to be done."

She coughed, and her body heaved and contracted with a startling ferocity.

"Can I get you something?" I said. "Water?"

"No, but thank you, dear one," she said, her eyes closed to the pain. "It is too late for water, too late for everything. I am dying. Which is why I need you."

"Do you have an estate you want to settle? Do you want me to write you up a will?"

"No, please. I have nothing but a few bangles and this house, which is for Thalassa. Poor little girl. She wasted her life caring for me."

"Who is Thalassa?"

"She who brought you to my room."

Ah, I thought, the poor little girl of seventy.

"Are you married, Victor?"

"No, ma'am."

One of her closed eyes opened and focused on my face. "Thalassa, she available, and she comes with house. You like house?"

"It's a very nice house."

"Maybe you are interested? Maybe we can arrange things?"

"No, really, Mrs. Kalakos. I'm fine."

"Yes of course. A man with such a good Greek face, you find someone with bigger house. So we are back to problem. I am dying."

"So you said."

"In my village, when death it walked into your house on tiptoes and tapped you on shoulder, they rang church bell so everyone would know. Your neighbors, your friends, family, they all came to gather around. It was tradition. A final time to laugh and cry, to hug, to settle scores, to wipe off curses"—she rubbed her lips with two fingers and spat through them—"a final time to say good-bye before the blessed journey. For my grandparents it was like that, and for my mother, too. I went over on boat to say good-bye when it was her time. It wasn't choice, it was necessity. You understand?"

"I think so, ma'am."

"So now the bell it is chiming for me. All I have left in my life is to say good-bye. But time, it is running fast, like wind."

"I'm sure you have more time than you—"

Another wrenching, full-body cough silenced me like a shout. Her hands rose and shook in pain as her body contracted in on itself.

"How can I help?" I said.

"You are lawyer."

"That's right."

"You represent fools."

"I represent people accused of crimes."

"Fools."

"Some are, yes."

"Good. Then you are just man I need." She raised a finger and gestured me close, closer. "I have son," she said softly. "Charles. I love him very much, but he is great fool."

"Ah, yes," I said. "Now I see. Has Charles been accused of a crime?"

"Has been accused of everything."

"Is he in jail now?"

"No, Victor. He not in jail. Fifteen years ago he was arrested for things, too many things to even remember. Mostly stealing, but also threatening and extinction."

"Extortion?"

"Maybe that, too. And talking with others about doing it all."

"Conspiracy."

"He was going to trial. He needed money to stay out of jail."

"Bail?"

"Yes. So, like idiot, I put up house. The day after he left prison, he disappeared. My Charles, he ran away. It took me ten years to get back house for Thalassa. Ten years of breaking my back. And since he ran, I haven't once seen his face."

"What can I do to help him?"

"Bring him home. Bring him to his mother. Let him say good-bye."

"I'm sure he could come and say good-bye. It's been a long time. He's way off the authorities' radar."

"You think? Go to window, Victor. Look onto street."

I did as she told, gently opened the curtain, pulled the shade aside. Light streamed in as I peered outside.

"Do you see it, a van?"

"Yes." It was battered and white, with a raw brown streak of rust on its side. "I see it."

"FBI."

"It looks empty to me, Mrs. Kalakos."

"FBI, Victor. They are still hunting for my son."

"After all these years?"

"They know I am sick, they are expecting him to come. My phone, it is tapped. My mail, it is read. And the van, it is there every day."

"Let me check it out," I said.

Still standing by the window, I reached for my phone and dialed 911. Without giving my name, I reported a suspicious van parked on Mrs. Kalakos's street. I mentioned that there had been reports of a child molester using the same type of van and I asked if the police could investigate because I was afraid to let my children go outside to play. When Mrs. Kalakos tried to say something, I just stopped her and waited by the window. I expected the van to be empty, parked there by some neighbor, nothing more than an innocent vehicle left to inspire the wild paranoia of an old, ill woman.

We waited in quiet, the two of us, accompanied by the rasp of her breath. A few minutes later, one police car pulled up behind the van and then another arrived to block the van's escape. As the uniforms approached the car, a large man in horn-rimmed glasses, a flat-top chop, and a boxy suit came around from the other side. He showed a credential. While one cop examined it and another cop engaged him in a conversation, the man looked up at the window where I stood.

I watched all this as it played out, watched as the man in the boxy suit retreated back into his van and the two police cars pulled away. I closed the curtains and turned to the old woman, still propped up by the pillows, whose eyes, glistening with the light of the candle, were staring straight at me.

"What did your son do, Mrs. Kalakos?" I said.

"Only what I said."

"You haven't told me everything."

"They are hounding him for spite."

"Spite?"

"He was a thief, that is all."

"The FBI doesn't spend fifteen years searching for a common thief out of spite."

"Will you help me, Victor? Will you help my Charlie?"

"Mrs. Kalakos, I don't think I should get anywhere near this case. You're not telling me everything."

"You don't trust me?"

"Not after seeing that van."

"You sure you not Greek?"

"Pretty sure, ma'am."

"Okay, there may be something else. Charlie had four close friends from childhood. And maybe, long time ago, these friends, they pulled a little prank."

"What kind of prank?"

"Just meet him, meet my Charlie. He can't come into city no more, but he can be nearby. We set up meeting point for you already."

"A bit presumptuous, don't you think?"

"New Jersey. Ocean City boardwalk, Seventh Street. He be there tonight at nine."

"I don't know."

"At nine. Do for me, Victor. As favor."

"As favor, huh?"

"You do for me, Victor. Work it out, make deal, do something so my boy, he come home and say good-bye. To say good-bye, yes. And to fix his life, yes. You can work that?"

"I think that's beyond a lawyer's brief, Mrs. Kalakos."

"Bring him home, and you tell your father after this we're even."

I thought about why the FBI might be so interested still in Charlie Kalakos fifteen years after he fled his trial. Charlie was a thief, had said his mother. And long ago Charlie and his friends had pulled a little prank. That van outside told me it must have been a hell of a little prank. Maybe there was an angle in Charlie's long-ago prank and the FBI's strangely keen interest in it for me to find a profit.

"You know, Mrs. Kalakos," I said after I did all that thinking, "in cases like this, even when I take it on as a favor, I still require a retainer."

"What is this retainer?"

"Money up front."

"I see. It is like that, is it?"

"Yes, ma'am, it is."

"Not only a Greek face but a Greek heart."

"Thank you, I think."

"I have no money, Victor, none at all."

"I'm sorry to hear that."

"But I might have something to interest you."

Slowly, she rose from the bed, as if a corpse rising from her grave, and made her way creakily, painfully, to a bureau at the edge of the room. With all her strength, she opened a drawer. She tossed out a few oversized unmentionables and slid open what appeared to be a false bottom. She reached both hands in and pulled out two fistfuls of golden chains glinting in the candlelight, silver pendants, broaches filled with rubies, strings of pearls, two fistfuls of pirate's treasure.

"Where did you get that?" I said.

"It is from Charles," she said as she stumbled toward me with the jewelry dripping from her hands, falling from her hands. "What he gave me long ago. He said he found in street."

"I can't take that, Mrs. Kalakos."

"Here," she said, thrusting it at me. "You take. I have saved for years for Charlie, never touched. But now he needs me. So you take. Don't spend until he is back, that is all I ask, but take."

I let her drop it all into my hands. The jewelry was heavy and cold. It felt as if it held the weight of the past, yet I could feel its opulence. Like foie gras on thin pieces of buttered toast, like champagne sipped from black high heels, like tawdry nights and sunsets over the Pacific.

"Bring my son home to me," she said, grabbing hold of

my lapels with her hands and pulling me close so her foul, pestilential breath washed over me. "Bring my son home so he can kiss my old parched face and tell his mother good-bye."

CHAPTER

3

I walked to my office that afternoon with a light step, despite the pockets of my suit jacket being weighed down with plunder.

The offices of Derringer and Carl were on Twenty-first Street, just south of Chestnut, above the great shoe sign that hung over a first-floor repair shop. We were in a nondescript suite in a nondescript building with no décor to speak of and a support staff of one, our secretary, Ellie, who answered our phones and typed our briefs and kept our books. I trusted Ellie with our financials because she was a trustworthy woman with an honest face, the fine product of a strict Catholic upbringing, and because embezzling from our firm would sort of be like trying to cadge drinks at a Mormon meeting.

"Oh, Mr. Carl, you have a message," Ellie said as I passed by her desk. "Mr. Slocum called."

I stopped quickly, put a hand on one of my bulging jacket pockets, turned my head, and searched behind me as if I had been caught at something. "Did he say what he wanted?"

"Only that he needed to talk to you right away."

I thought about the FBI in the van outside the old woman's house and the inevitable phone call once they found out who I was. "That didn't take long," I said.

"He emphasized the right away part, Mr. Carl."

"Oh, I bet he did."

When I reached my own office, I closed the door behind me, sat at my desk, and carefully pulled out the chains and the broaches, the heavy mass of jewelry, letting it all slip deliciously through my fingers into a small, rich pile upon my desk. In the bright light of the fluorescents, it all seemed a little less brilliant, tarnished, even. I supposed the old lady wasn't into polishing her son's ill-gotten gains. Just then I had no idea how much it all was worth, and I wasn't intending to swiftly find out either. The last thing I needed to do was draw attention to the jewelry, being that my legal title to what was undoubtedly stolen property could only be considered dubious. No, I wasn't going to let anyone, not anyone, know about what the old lady had given me.

There was a light tap on my door. I quickly shoveled the swag into a desk drawer, closed the drawer with a thwack.

"Come in," I said.

It was my partner, Beth Derringer.

"What's up?" she said.

"Nothing."

She looked at me as if she could see right through my lie. She tilted her head. "Where were you this morning?"

"Doing a favor for my father."

"A favor for your father? That's a first."

"It surprised me, too. An old lady wants me to negotiate a plea deal for her son."

"Do you need any help?"

"Nah, it should be easy enough, or would be if the FBI wasn't suspiciously interested in the guy."

"Did we get a retainer?"

"Not yet."

"And you took it without a retainer? That's not like you."

"I'm doing a favor for my father."

"That's not like you either. What's in the drawer?"

"What drawer?"

"The one you slammed shut before I came in."

"Just papers."

She stared at me for a moment to figure out if it was worth pursuing, decided that it wasn't, which was a relief, and dropped down into one of the chairs in front of my desk.

Beth Derringer was my best friend and my partner and, as my partner, was rightfully entitled to one half of the retainer given me by Zanita Kalakos. I wasn't pulling a Fred C. Dobbs here, I had not been driven mad by the sight of gold and was intending to stiff Beth of her fair share. But Beth's ethics were less flexible than mine. If she knew what Mrs. Kalakos had given me, and the likelihood of from where it had come, she would have felt obligated to turn it all over to the rightful authorities. She was that kind of woman. I, on the other hand, figured the jewelry had been stolen long ago from the rich, who had already been reimbursed by their insurance companies, and so saw no reason to fight against my Robin Hood tendencies. Isn't that how he did it, take from the insurance companies and give to the lawyers? So the jewels and chains would stay safely and secretly in my desk drawer until I found a way to turn them into cash, and I already had an idea of just how to do that.

"I have a client coming in this afternoon that I'd like you to meet," she said.

"A paying client?"

"She paid what she could."

"Why don't I like the sound of that?"

"Should we maybe discuss the retainer we didn't get from your old lady?"

"No. Okay, go ahead. What's her story?"

"Her name is Theresa Wellman. She hit a bad patch and lost her daughter."

"Misplaced her, like under the bed or something?"

"Lost custody to the father."

"And this little bad patch that caused such an overreaction?"

"Alcohol, neglect."

"Ah, the daily double."

"But she's changed. She cleaned herself up and got a new job, a new house. I find her inspiring, actually. And now she wants at least partial custody of her daughter."

"What does the daughter want?"

"I don't know. The father won't let anyone talk to her."

"And we're involved why?"

"Because she is a woman who has changed her life and is now fighting for her daughter against a man with power and money. She needs someone on her side."

"And that someone has to be us?"

"Isn't this why we went to law school?"

I glanced down at my desk drawer. "No, actually."

"Victor, I told her I would do what I could to get her daughter back. I'd like your help."

I thought about it for a moment. I didn't like this case, didn't like it one bit. I mean, who the hell can tell which is the best parent for a kid? Let someone else take the responsibility. But Beth hadn't been happy in our practice for a while. She hadn't said anything directly to me, but I could see the discontent in her. I was increasingly worried that she would end the partnership, find something more fulfilling, leave me in the lurch. I didn't think I could keep the firm going all on my own, and, truthfully, I wasn't sure I wanted to. The only thing that would keep me trying was the utter lack of anyplace else to go. So if helping out in one of her pity cases was a way to keep my partner on board, then I didn't have much choice.

"Okay," I said. "I'll meet her."

"Thank you, Victor. You'll like her. I know it." She paused for a moment. "There's something else."

"That sounds ominous."

"It is." She looked away with embarrassment. "I'm being evicted."

"That is ominous. Playing your rock and roll too loud?"

"Yes, but that's not it."

"I'm sure we can scrape up a partnership distribution to get any back rent paid."

"It's nothing like that. I'm actually up-to-date in my rent, believe it or not. It's just that the real-estate market has picked up. The landlord wants to gut the building, redo each floor into luxury lofts, and sell them off at obscene prices. I'm in the way."

"What about your lease?"

"It's up in a month. He mailed me an eviction notice."

"When?"

"I got it a month or so ago."

"Why didn't you tell me about it then?"

"I don't know, I guess I hoped if I ignored the letter the whole thing would go away. Except it didn't go away, and the date's getting close."

"What about the other tenants?"

"They're all getting ready to leave. But I don't want to leave. I like my apartment, and I couldn't bear to move. Is there something I can do?"

"We can fight it. There are all kinds of screwy landlord-tenant laws on the books. We'll tie them up for months, bollix the whole condo deal, make their lives an utter misery. Making the lives of corporate types an utter misery is half the fun of being a lawyer."

"What's the other half?"

"I haven't found it yet. Give me the eviction letter and I'll file something."

"Thank you, Victor," she said as she stood. "I feel better already."

"Don't worry, Beth. It will be fine."

At the doorway she turned and gave me a wan smile. "I knew I could count on you."

Poor thing, I thought as she stood there with a hopeful expression on her face. She was going to have to find herself a new place.

When she closed the door behind her, I opened my desk drawer again, just to get another peek. Then I screwed up my courage and called Slocum.

"You have stepped in it now, Carl," said K. Lawrence Slocum, the chief of the Homicide Division at the district attorney's office.

"I don't know what you're talking about," I lied.

"The FBI called our office in a panic, trying to find out who you are. According to the FBI, you apparently visited a Mrs. Kalakos this morning."

"Did I?"

"Don't be cute, it's unbecoming."

"How are they so certain it was me?"

"How are they certain? Let me count the ways. First, they took a picture of you from the surveillance van. Then, while you were inside, they found your car and ran your license plate. Then they traced a cell-phone call that had sent a team of uniforms to check on their stakeout."

"Oh."

"What are you up to, Carl?"

"Nothing, really. I'm as innocent as a lamb."

"Why do I suspect that you are lying?"

"You had a difficult childhood, you never learned to trust."

"What did you and the old lady talk about?"

"Attorney-client privilege prohibits me from disclosing the details of my conversation with Mrs. Kalakos."

Pause. "That's what I was afraid of."

"But I would be interested in hearing what you know about her son."

"Charlie the Greek?"

"No need to start throwing around derogatory ethnic labels, Larry."

"That's his name in the gang. Charlie the Greek."

"Gang?"

"The Warrick Brothers Gang. You ever hear of it?"

"No."

"A local crew, named for its leaders, two psychopathic icemen."

"Icemen?"

"Jewel thieves. They were quite sophisticated, responsible for a plague of robberies and burglaries, including a series of spectacular jewelry heists from upscale mansions running from Newport, Rhode Island, to Miami Beach. They were stationed here and in Camden, which is why they were on our radar."

"They still around?"

"The brothers are out of commission, one is dead, the other in prison in Camden. But there are still some members floating around that are active in all kinds of criminal activities in the Northeast part of the city. We can't seem to put them away."

"But why is the file on homicide's desk?"

"It seems every time a witness shows up who might have something to say, the witness ends up floating in the river or dead in his car. One guy opened his trunk and got a faceful of steel from a rigged shotgun."

"Nasty."

"The whole investigation, including the murders, is still open."

"What was Charles Kalakos's connection?"

"He was one of the original gang members. He was arrested on a host of charges fifteen years ago, but he somehow made bail and disappeared before trial. We haven't heard a peep from him since."

"That doesn't explain why the FBI is so hot on his trail."

"There's a federal prosecutor name of Jenna Hathaway who is apparently out to clean up the Warrick gang once and for all and who believes Charlie the Greek is the key. But my sense is that this Hathaway, for some reason, is hot to get a hard charge on Charlie to squeeze something else out of him, something not related to the Warrick case at all."

"That's peculiar." The little prank? "Any idea what?"

"None, but she gives me an uneasy feeling. There's too much interest here for it to be small-time. Anyone caught between Charlie and this Jenna Hathaway is going to get crushed, trust me. You might want to think twice about taking up this loser's cause."

I thought about what he was saying. Then I opened the drawer and peeked in.

"To tell you the truth, Larry," I said, "I don't have much choice."

"Don't say I didn't warn you."

"I'm only doing this as a favor."

"A favor?"

"To my dad."

He laughed. "Now I know you're lying."

When he hung up, I took another look at the plunder in the drawer. Yowza. This must be how Trump feels when he stands at the window in his penthouse apartment, with his model wife by his side, and surveys all the buildings he owns. Maybe not, but to me it still felt pretty damn good. I now had a better idea of where the jewelry had come from: the mansions of Newport, seaside getaways in Miami Beach. Yeah, I knew where it had come from, and I knew where it was going, too. I searched my key chain for the desk key, found it, and locked the drawer tight.

Now all I had to do was figure out how to bring sweet Charlie home. Nothing I couldn't handle, I figured, which was not the last time in that case I would be very, very wrong.

4

"I've changed, Mr. Carl," said Theresa Wellman. "You have to believe that."

But why? Why did I have to believe that? Because she was pretty and well dressed and her print dress fit tight around her hips? Because her trim hands were wringing one another with sincerity? Because her eyes and voice were pleading with me to believe every last word out of her delicate little mouth? All very compelling, I must admit, but not enough to assuage my qualms.

I had grave doubts, just then, about the possibility of anyone past adolescence truly changing in this world. We were, all of us, prisoners of our character, unable to alter our true inner natures. When we said we had changed, what had only really changed was our luck. Put us in the same circumstances as our previous folly and suddenly we'd revert, all of us, to what we were. That's what I believed, which meant I didn't quite believe Theresa Wellman.

"I made mistakes in the past, I admit," she said. "But I have changed, and I am my child's mother, and she belongs with me."

We were in our rather ratty conference room. Beth was sitting beside Theresa Wellman at the table, leaning forward, offering support. I was standing in the corner with my arms unhappily folded. I suppose you could say we were playing good lawyer–bad lawyer, except we weren't really playing.

"Why don't we start at the beginning, Theresa," I said. "Tell us about your daughter's father."

"His name is Bradley Hewitt. I met him when I was twenty and I was working in a Toyota dealership. He came in looking for a Lexus, chatted with me while he waited for the salesman, and called me up that afternoon. I wasn't supposed to go out with a customer, but I couldn't say no. He was tall, handsome, he had money and liked to spend it. It was thrilling just to be with him."

"So it was his inner beauty that attracted you."

"I was young, Mr. Carl, and I had never before dated anyone like him. The way he spoke, the way he dressed, the way he touched me, both gentle and firm. He was older, he knew things, he wore suits as expensive as a car. At the time I was living at home, sheltered by my parents and fighting them tooth and nail. Bradley seemed like a way out. He set me up in a nice place, helped with the rent, and things were wonderful for a while, until they weren't anymore."

"That's usually how it goes," I said.

"We partied almost every night with his friends, drinking, dancing. We took fabulous vacations with his old college buddy. His crowd were all big spenders. Champagne and lobster and, yes, drugs, but not crazy drugs, nothing in excess. Just fun. Bradley was fun and charming, except when he was angry and violent. I didn't see much of that side of him at first, but after a while it became more and more apparent. Occasionally, angry at something, he would lash out, sometimes verbally in front of everybody and sometimes, when we were alone, with the back of his hand."

"Did anyone ever see him hit you?"

"No, Bradley was too careful for that. And he was always sorry afterward. He was quite charming when he apologized."

"What kind of business is he in?"

"He's in construction, but not like a construction worker. He wears suits and makes deals with the help of his college friend and gets projects off the floor. He earns a piece of the entire project for putting things together."

"Nice job if you can get it."

"It had its ups and downs. Whenever he had a business problem, I learned to stay away from him, or I'd be putting makeup over the bruises for a month. I was still having fun, living like I had never thought I could live, with a man I thought I loved even though he wasn't always good to me. And that's the way it was with us, calm and settled and a little dangerous, until I got pregnant."

"How did Bradley react?" said Beth.

"He didn't really react much at all. He just expected me to get an abortion. He set up the appointment, took care of the money. But I didn't want an abortion. I wanted the baby."

"Why?" I said.

"I don't know."

"To keep Bradley around? To keep his money flowing? Why did you want the baby, Theresa?"

"I don't know. It was a baby. I had always wanted a baby and wasn't willing to get rid of this one, like an old sweater or something."

"Okay," said Beth. "I understand."

I looked at my partner. Did she really understand that kind of longing? Was that the reason she looked despondent these days, or was I just being a jerk to think the explanation was that easy?

"Go ahead, Theresa," said Beth.

"He tried to convince me, he yelled and even hit me some, but I was determined, and there was nothing he could say. When he finally realized it, he just stopped."

"Stopped trying to convince you?"

"Yes, and stopped seeing me, too. He stepped out of my life. I was good, I quit drinking, I took care of myself, and with my family's help I had a beautiful baby girl, Belle. And for a while we were happy."

"Did Bradley pay child support?" I said.

"He used to give me some money for Belle now and then, when I called and complained, but it wasn't enough. I was still in my place, which was more than I could afford, and I had a hard time showing up at work while taking care of the baby. When they decided to let me go at the dealership, things got tougher. I didn't really have many skills. So I did the most desperate thing I could think to do."

"And what was that, Theresa?" I said.

"I hired a lawyer."

I involuntarily winced. "And how did that work out for you?"

"Not so good. We sued for child support. Bradley countersued for custody, which made me furious, because he never showed any interest in Belle before that. And then things took a bad turn."

"How?" I said.

"The fix was in. Yes, I had been having problems, drinking too much, a holdover from my time with Bradley, and I was using some recreational drugs with a fast crowd that Bradley had introduced me to. And yes, there were a few times when I left her alone for short periods where maybe I shouldn't have, but those weren't serious enough for them to take my baby."

"But they did," I said.

"They were going to. Before the hearing, my lawyer told me that things were looking bad, that criminal charges were being contemplated, that powerful forces were working against me. He urged me to work out a settlement."

"Powerful forces?"

"Bradley has influential friends."

"So you agreed to give up custody?"

"Outside the courtroom I went right up to Bradley and begged him to stop. In front of everyone, all of Bradley's crowd, I pleaded with him. But Bradley just stood there, stone-faced with anger. The possibility that my daughter, my Belle, would end up with such an angry, violent man seemed impossible. But the lawyer told me had I had no choice. The fix was in."

"With a family-court judge? Is that what you're saying?"

"Yes. I'm certain. It was his college friend who applied the pressure."

"So without a hearing you gave away your daughter."

"I was weak. I was ill."

"Did you get any money?"

"There was a financial settlement."

"And now, after selling your baby, you want to get her back."

"That's not what it was. And I've been in treatment, Mr. Carl. I've got a new job. I've worked hard to turn my life around. She should be with me."

"I filed a petition to alter the custody agreement," said Beth. "The hearing is scheduled for late next week."

"What exactly are you looking for, Theresa?"

"I just want to see my baby, have time with her."

"We're asking for some sort of joint custody," said Beth.

"Bradley hasn't been a bad father," said Theresa, "but a girl needs her mother, don't you think?"

"Who's Bradley's lawyer?"

"Remember Arthur Gullicksen from the Dubé case?" said Beth. "He's representing the father, and he's been adamant that Bradley won't share custody and won't let Theresa even see the child."

"What evidence do we have to present?"

"Theresa will testify," said Beth. "Theresa's new employer. Her drug tests from the treatment center have all come up clean. We can prove that she's changed."

"Can we?"

"You can," said Beth.

"Theresa, why did you come to Beth?" I asked.

"The woman's group I was seeing recommended her. They said Beth would come through for me."

"I bet they did." Once a sucker always a sucker, I thought. "But I'm sure there are plenty of attorneys with more experience in family court than Beth who would take your case."

"I tried. No one would accept it. They said I didn't have enough money. They said I didn't have a leg to stand on. But really, all the lawyers were simply afraid to go up against Bradley."

"Why?"

"Because of his friends."

"Especially his old college buddy."

"Right."

"The one who gets Bradley all those contracts, the one who had arranged to fix the custody case, the one who is intimidating half the bar. You mind telling me who it is, or am I just going to have to guess."

"Are you going to be intimidated, too, Mr. Carl?"

"Theresa, in the face of intimidation, I am like a herd of elephants: I can be stampeded by a mouse. And Bradley's old college buddy, I'm sure, is bigger than a mouse."

"It's the mayor," said Beth.

"Of course it is," I said. "Can I speak with you for a moment outside, Beth?"

In the hallway, with the door to the conference room closed, I gave Beth the look. You know the look, the one your mother gave you when you let the water in the tub run until it overflowed through the living room ceiling, warping the coffee table, staining the rug, that look.

"What are you doing?" I said.

"She needs someone."

"Of course she needs someone, she's in way over her head, but why does she need us?"

"Because no one else is foolish enough to take her case."

"So you're appealing to my innate stupidity, as opposed to my greed or low moral fiber."

"That's right."

"This is going to be a hornet's nest, you know that, don't you?"

"Yes," she said, with a sly smile.

"And it has nothing to do with your identification with a young girl torn from her parent?"

"I don't know, maybe I'm just a sucker for lost kids."

"She's with her father."

"He sounds like a jerk."

"He does, yes, if you can trust what our client says."

"I believe Theresa deserves another chance," said Beth. "We all deserve another chance, Victor. And she's changed."

"Has she?"

"I think so."

"I guess we'll find out. Okay, tell her we'll do what we can"—I glanced at my watch—"but right now I have to run."

"Hot date?"

"Sure," I said, "with a seagull."

CHAPTER
5

Charlie the Greek found me.

I was leaning on the railing of the boardwalk in Ocean City, New Jersey, across from the Kohr Bros. Frozen Custard stand at the Seventh Street ramp. The air was wet and salty, shot through with honky-tonk lights, the Ferris wheel spun, seagulls hovered. Little kids squealed as they pulled their parents to the amusement pier, boys bought skimmer boards at the surf shop. Taters Famous Fresh Cut Fries, Johnson's popcorn, Tee Time Golf, free live crabs with kit. Ah, summer at the shore, it can't help but stir sweet memories of an idyllic childhood, except not my memories and not my childhood.

"You Carl?" came a voice ragged and dry, with the flat accent of Northeast Philadelphia.

I turned to spot a short, old man with stubby arms who had sidled up beside me. His forehead came to my elbow. He looked to be in his sixties, and from the evidence they had been sixty hard years. His head was big and round and bald, his eyes were squinty, his plaid shorts were belted high on his waist. And then there were the white socks and sandals.

"I'm Carl," I said.

"You couldn't maybe have dressed to blend?"

"Would you have recognized me if I wasn't in my suit?"

"Maybe not, but jeez." The man's head swiveled, his eyes shifted. "Every mug on the boardwalk has you marked."

"Let me say this, Charlie. Even on the boardwalk, my suit is less conspicuous than those shorts."

"Bermudas," he said, hitching up his belt. "On sale at Kohl's."

"I bet they were."

"Was you followed? Did you check to make sure you wasn't followed?"

"Who would be following me?"

His head swiveled again. "Stop with the attitude and bark."

"I checked before I left the city and again when I pulled in to the rest stop on the expressway and surveyed the ramps. All clear."

"Good." Pause. "How's my mother?"

"She's dying."

"The old bat's been dying for years."

"She looked pretty bad."

"Ever seen her look good? Trust me, she'll end up spitting into my grave afore it's over."

He hiked up his shorts until they were just beneath his breasts, scanned the boards. "Want to know why I ran all them years ago? They wasn't going to send me away hard, it wasn't the time what had me worried. But she would have come in every visiting day to sit across from me and let me have it through the Plexiglas. I would have killed myself halfway through."

"She wants you to come home."

"I knows she does."

"So?"

"She tell you what I got facing me?"

"She told me some. From the D.A. I learned some more."

"Coming home for me, it ain't no luxury cruise. And not

just because of the time they're going to pound on my head. It would be a miracle I survive it."

"You're talking about the Warrick Brothers Gang?"

"Quiet, all right? Jeez, you want to get me capped right here?"

"It's funny, Charlie, but I don't see you as the gangster type."

"Hey, it ain't all rough stuff. I ain't so big, sure, but neither was that Meyer Lansky."

"Even Meyer Lansky was bigger than you."

"I was making a point, is all. I got some skills, don't think I don't."

"So why are the Warrick guys so mad at you?"

"I maybe said some things to some people. Hey, I could go for some soft-serve. You want to get me some soft-serve?"

I pressed my lips together for a moment and then said, "Sure. What flavor?"

"Vanilla. And don't forget the jimmies. I like all them different colors. It makes it festive. Like a party in your mouth."

"You got it."

"And make it a big one," he said.

I pushed away from the railing and got in line at the Kohr Bros. stand. I needed just then some time away from whiny little Charlie. Not that Charlie didn't have anything to whine about, what with the mother he had waiting for him. But if he decided to stay on the lam, I'd have to give back the pile of plunder sitting in my drawer. On the other hand, considering the FBI's keen interest, and what Charlie was intimating about his former running mates, it might be best for everybody if Charlie stayed out in the cold.

"You don't like custard?" said Charlie after I brought him a cone nearly half his size.

"Whenever I get soft-serve it ends up dripping on my shoes."

"You should buy a pair of sandals, that way it slips right through."

"Look, Charlie," I said. "What am I doing here? You sound like the last thing you want to do is to come home."

"Yeah, I knows, but you know."

"I know what?"

"It's my mother. She says she wants me to say good-bye. She says it would make up for everything, she could see me one last time."

"And what do you think?"

"I think I'm sick of running. And I ain't living the life of Riley, you know?"

"Who the heck is Riley anyway?"

"Some guy who ain't living in crappy week-to-week walk-ups and sweeping floors, who's actually looking forward to retirement because he's got Social Security coming, who ain't waiting for a knock that ain't about the rent or the rats, but about something worse."

A father took his three sons over to a bench by the rail to eat their cones. The kids' faces were smeared with chocolate, the youngest was crying about something, the middle was hitting the eldest, the father was ignoring them all and staring slack-jawed at the underage girls who strolled on by. Ah, fatherhood.

"Are you going to be able to take care of me?" said Charlie.

"I don't know."

"My mother said you could." He took a wet lick of his cone. "She said you would work it out."

"I don't know if I can. It's a little more complicated than she might have thought." I glanced at the family. "Let's take a walk on the beach," I said.

"I don't want to go to the beach," said Charlie. "I hate getting sand in the socks. It chafes my toes."

"A bit more privacy might be the ticket, don't you think?"

Charlie did his swivel-head thing, checked out the father and three boys on one side of us, a young couple on the other. "Oh, yeah," he said. "Sure."

We took the wooden stairs to the beach. On the way down, Charlie tripped and lurched forward. As he grabbed hold of the metal rail, the mound of vanilla atop his cone tumbled over and splattered onto the step.

"Ah, jeez," he said. "My ice cream. I hate when that happens."

He stood there, staring forlornly down at his now-empty cone and the white Rorschach blob at his feet. He looked right then, with the light streaming from the boardwalk behind and leaving him a round, bald, silhouette, like an overgrown toddler, about to break into tears.

"Want me to get you another one?"

"Would you? Really? Really?"

"I'll meet you at the water's edge."

Charlie was waiting for me just above the reach of the tide, in front of the stone jetty. The sea was black, with lines of phosphorescent foam rising and falling in the darkness. Behind us the sounds of the boardwalk turned tinny, as if being played from an old transistor radio.

"Why is the FBI still chasing you, Charlie?" I said after I gave him the cone and he sucked down half of it while staring at the ocean.

"Maybe something I done a long time ago."

"Something with the Warrick gang?"

"No," he said. "Something from before. When I was still legit and trying to prove myself to my mother. Something what I done with four of my pals I grew up with. Just something that we pulled."

"A little prank?"

"I guess yous could call it that."

"When?"

"Almost thirty years ago. It's a long story."

"I have time."

"I can't talk about it."

"Why not?"

"Because whatever I do, I won't rat out the old crew. The Warrick guys, they can rot in hell. But the old gang, they's more family than family, if you understand."

"Tell me about them."

"What's to tell? The five of us, we grew up together."

"Like brothers."

"Sure we was. One of them was Ralphie Meat, what lived just a few streets down from me. Bigger than anyone you ever saw, hard as tacks. And that rumor what gave him his name, it wasn't a rumor. He was the terror of his gym class. All those kids with their little weenies taking showers with this huge hairy thing waving in their faces. It was enough to put the whole class of them in therapy for years. Ralphie Meat."

"Is he still around?"

"Who knows? Who knows about any of them? There was also Hugo from Ralph's same street, a real troublemaker, one of those guys who was always scheming a way to slip a fiver out of the other guy's pocket. And Joey Pride, who lived in the border area between our neighborhood and Frankford. Joey was car crazy and certifiable—I guess you needed to be back then as a black kid hanging with a white crew. But it was Teddy Pravitz, the Jewish kid from across the alley, what made us more than we had any right to be. The thing that we done, it was him what convinced us we could."

"Could what?"

"Pull it off."

"Pull off what?"

"I can't talk about it," said Charlie.

"Come on, Charlie. What the hell did you pull?"

"Listen, it ain't important. I'm not spilling about any of this. I got loyalties, you know. And secrets, too, dark ones, if you catch the drift. Whatever they want, they don't get that."

"I talked with the D.A. They'd give you something for flipping on what's left of the Warrick gang, but the feds are apparently looking for something else."

"I bet they are. And let's just say whatever it is they're looking for, I can get my hands on it."

"On what?"

"Does the what matter? I knows where it is, the thing they's still looking for."

"If that's true, I might be able to work something out."

"Would it let me come home and say good-bye to my mother without getting my ass blown off or me dying in jail?"

"I could try to get you a deal and protection, if that's what you want. Maybe even set you up someplace in Arizona with a new life."

"Arizona?"

"It's nice there."

"Hot."

"But it's a dry heat."

"Clear up my sinuses."

"That it will."

"I miss her."

"Your mother?"

He turned to me, and it was strange, the way this old man could appear, in the shadows, like the youngest of children. The lights from the boardwalk collected in his eyes and then began to roll down one cheek.

"What do you think?" he said. "She's my mother."

"Okay," I said.

"She's dying. I'm too old to keep running. I'm tired. And I've changed."

"You too?"

"I'm not the hood that I was. Can you do it? Can you make that deal? Can you get me home again?"

That's when I felt it, that little spurt of emotion that trembled my jaw and left me helpless in the face of his want. If there's any part of being a lawyer that I can claim to be a natural at, it is the empathic connection to my clients. Yes, I had a retainer of riches that kept my imagination warm at night, and yes, I kept my billable hours with a banker's care, but it wasn't the money that drove me, at least not anymore. Frankly, the way my business was tanking, I could make more as a salesclerk in the tie department at Macy's. *Polyester is the new silk, trust me, and that red is just fabulous with your eyes.* But a client in desperate need, that was what really got my juices going, and that's what Charlie Kalakos surely was. A marked man, on the run, hunted by both sides of the law, desperate to make his peace with the dying mother who had tortured him all his life. And now he was asking me to bring him home.

"I can try," I said.

"Okay," he said, "then try."

"How do I get in touch with you?"

"You want to talk to me, talk to my mother. She's the only one I trust with a number."

"Okay. But I have to know more. You have to tell me what the FBI is looking for."

"Do I got a choice?"

"Not if you want me to have any leverage," I said.

"It was just a small job."

"Not so small if the FBI is still looking."

"Maybe it wasn't so small at that. Was a blonde I used to

hump when I still had some meat on my bones. Her name was Erma."

"The name alone gives me chills."

"She was big and beautiful, Erma was." The hint of a smile, a blush of pride, like one bright memory in a life of infantile failure. "And so was what we pulled."

I stared at his silhouette in the dim light of the dark beach, the excitement starting to build. "Tell me, Charlie. What the hell is it that you can get your hands on?"

"You ever hear," said Charlie, "of a guy named Rembrandt?"

CHAPTER

6

The Randolph Trust sits on a leafy suburban street in the heart of the Main Line. You'd expect to find a mansion or two on that street, sure, a few swimming pools and a tennis court, a purebred Dalmatian patrolling a front yard as big as a football field, and closets full of shoes you couldn't afford. You wouldn't expect to find one of the finest art galleries in the entire world. But there it sat, in a great granite building set down in that incongruous location by the iconoclastic real-estate magnate Wilfred Randolph. In a series of small galleries in that granite building were hung some of the finest paintings ever wrought by human hand, the fruit of Wilfred Randolph's maniacal passion for art, his entire collection except for two masterworks that went missing long ago.

I knocked on the great red doors of the granite building and waited. A few minutes later, one of the doors opened a crack and an old guard with a bulbous nose stuck out his head.

"No visitors today," he said. "The galleries are closed on Tuesdays. We allow visitors only on the second Monday of every month and alternating Wednesdays."

"No Thursdays?"

"We have classes on Thursdays."

"What about Fridays?"

"We're open on Good Friday only."

"Quite a schedule."

"It's all according to Mr. Randolph's will."

"Quite a will. But I'm not here to tour the galleries. I have an appointment with Mr. Spurlock."

He looked me over before examining a clipboard in his hand. "Are you Victor Carl?"

"Yes, I am."

"Why didn't you say so? Come on in, we're expecting you."

When I stepped inside, he closed the great door behind me with a gloomy thunk and locked it shut. Then he led me through a narrow foyer and into a large room with benches in the middle and paintings on the walls. It all sounds a little pedestrian, paintings on the walls, like nothing we haven't all seen hundreds of times before, but trust me when I tell you this was nothing like I had ever seen before. The artwork on the walls left me speechless.

"Mrs. LeComte wanted to personally escort you to Mr. Spurlock. She'll be with you shortly," the guard said before leaving me standing there alone, eyes wide with amazement.

Wilfred Randolph made his fortune the old-fashioned way, by buying up swampland and selling dreams. The Randolph Estates was the most exclusive residential development in Florida: What with the mangrove and mosquitoes, nobody lived there. But even so, plenty bought the dream and the sales made Wilfred Randolph a rich man. Newly wealthy and anxious to rise in the world, Randolph spied opportunity within the thorny thatches of high culture, and in that unlikely landscape he found his purpose in life. He would buy art. His brokers and his bankers descended like a plague of locusts on a Europe economically devastated in the aftermath of the First World War, and whole swaths of the Continent were denuded. He bought old masters and overlooked masterpieces at bargain rates and snatched up new works by struggling unknowns still fighting for recognition in their native countries. He had too much money and too many advisers not to make a hash of it, but he also had something else that made his collection different from anyone else's. Wilfred Randolph happened to have a golden eye, and those unknown artists whose paintings he bought for pennies turned out to be the giants of twentieth-century art, painters like Matisse and Renoir, Picasso and Degas, Monet. And there was the very fruit of their genius, hanging on the walls around me.

"It's quite astonishing, isn't it?" said a woman's voice from behind me.

"Is that a Seurat?" I said gesturing toward a huge pointillist piece raised above a door on the far wall.

"Very good, Mr. Carl."

"How come I've never seen that one before in any art books?"

The woman behind me sniffed. "We don't license photographs of our art. Mr. Randolph believed the only way to experience a work of art was to view it in the flesh."

I turned around and faced the woman. She was tall and straight and elegantly gray, a well-dressed and well-aged woman in her seventies. She had once been quite pretty, you could tell, with a narrow-face and dark features, but with time everything had pinched together.

"I am Mrs. LeComte," she said. "I'm to accompany you to Mr. Spurlock."

"Accompany away."

"Could you tell me first the purpose of your meeting with Mr. Spurlock?"

"I'm sorry," I said, "but I can't."

"You're a criminal lawyer, Mr. Carl, aren't you?"

"You make it sound like I'm more criminal than lawyer."

"I am just curious to know why a criminal lawyer is meeting with Mr. Spurlock here at the trust. It is quite unusual."

"I'm sure it's not that unusual. But as I've said, I can't talk about our meeting. It's a matter of privilege, you see."

Her eyes narrowed. "I am the chief administrator of the trust, have been for over forty years. I was appointed by Mr. Randolph himself to this post."

"Really? What was he like?"

"He was an extraordinary man, very fierce and very loyal. He gave me complete authority over all matters pertaining to the trust and its educational mission during his lifetime, and I've held that authority since. I'm sure I could help you with any inquiry."

"Maybe it's my mistake," I said. "I thought Mr. Spurlock was the president of the Randolph Trust."

"That is his title, yes. But, you see, I run things."

"I'd just as soon talk to the title. Is he waiting for me? I don't want to be late."

She fought to control the anger that was twisting her mouth into a thin, wriggly worm. "This way, please," she said.

Mrs. LeComte led me out of the ground-floor gallery, up a wide staircase, and through an upstairs gallery filled with giant canvas bouquets of wild color.

"Matisse," I said.

"Yes. We have five of his works in this room."

I stopped and spun around. "These are amazing."

"If you want to see the artwork, Mr. Carl, buy a ticket. We are open to the public the second Monday of each month and alternate Wednesdays."

"Let's not forget Good Friday."

"Mr. Spurlock is waiting in the boardroom," she said, her voice shivering with cold. There is nothing more bracing than a frigid blast of anger, though I couldn't help wondering where it was coming from and why it was directed at me.

"We should have coffee sometime, you and me," I said to her.

She stepped back, tilted her head, and gave me the once-over, not like I was a vile specimen in a jar, more like she was determining whether I was a man worth another slice of her time. Whatever she was now, Mrs. LeComte had surely been something once.

"Maybe we will," she said, "if you behave. Now, come along. It doesn't do to keep Mr. Spurlock waiting."

At the end of the hallway, Mrs. LeComte knocked lightly before pushing open one of the double wooden doors and leading me into the boardroom.

7

Two men waited for us at a great mahogany table in the dark, wood-paneled room. One I recognized as a fixture of the local bar association, Stanford Quick, tall and distinguished, with his gray suit and club tie. Quick was the managing partner of Talbott, Kittredge and Chase, one of the city's most respected law firms, as well as the trust's main counsel. He was the kind of old-school lawyer who had inherited his place at the table and seemed most concerned with his table manners. I had grown comfortable dealing with the type, their gentle condescension kept my inbred resentment at a peak. It was Quick whom I had called after my meeting with Charlie Kalakos and who had set up this appointment. The other man was shorter and younger and considerably better dressed, Jabari Spurlock, president and CEO of the Randolph Trust.

"Thank you, Mrs. LeComte," said Spurlock after she had introduced me.

"I thought I could be of assistance to the discussion," said Mrs. LeComte, her manner suddenly less imperious.

"Good-bye, Mrs. LeComte," said Spurlock. He stared at her until she backed out the door and closed it behind her. "Difficult woman, that, but she has been a fixture here from before I was born. Take a seat, Mr. Carl. We have much to discuss."

"Thank you," I said as I sat across from them at the long table. "Quite a place you got here."

"Have you never been to the trust before?"

"No," I said. "And it's no wonder, what with your screwy scheduling."

"Our visiting hours were all specified in Mr. Randolph's will," said Quick. He sat at ease at the table, long and languorous, leaning back, seemingly bored. "It is not up to us to change those terms, much as we would like to."

"We are merely the custodians of Mr. Randolph's passions and intentions," said Spurlock. "He believed his art was for the benefit of the working classes, not just the wealthy patrons who had time to tour museums at their leisure. To that end, the times for visitors to stroll the galleries are limited. Instead much of the calendar at the trust is reserved for teaching art appreciation to the less advantaged and the keenly interested, all based on Mr. Randolph's startling methods."

"It sounds so very noble."

"It is, Mr. Carl, and yet, even so, our methods and practices are constantly under attack by the privileged few."

"You've read, of course, Victor," said Stanford Quick, "of the trust's battles with its neighbors. And you've also read that there is a movement afoot to use the trust's current economic crisis to move the entire collection into the city and turn its control over to the art museum."

"It's been front-page news."

"Yes, Mr. Carl," said Spurlock, "unfortunately it has. Which brings us to your visit."

"I simply mentioned to Stanford that I might have information concerning a missing painting."

"No, Victor," said Quick. "You were more specific. You mentioned a missing Rembrandt. The only Rembrandt ever purchased by Mr. Randolph was a self-portrait painted in

1630 that was stolen from the trust twenty-eight years ago. Is that the painting you were referring to?"

"Was it a picture of some guy with a hat?"

"Do you have the painting in your possession, Mr. Carl?" said Spurlock.

"No," I said. "In fact, I've never seen it."

"But you know where it is," said Spurlock.

"No, I don't. I don't know anything about the whereabouts of the painting, about how it was stolen, or by whom."

"Then what are we doing here?" said Quick.

"The thing is, I have this client who claims he does."

"A client, you say," said Quick. "Who?"

"I need to find out some things first, like how the painting went missing in the first place."

"It was stolen," said Spurlock. "There was a robbery."

"A professional job by a crack group of the highest caliber," said Quick. "Most likely from out of town. Impeccably planned, flawlessly executed. Taken was Mr. Randolph's collection of religious icons, made of gold or silver, that he had purchased from all over the world, including Russia and Japan. None of those icons have been recovered, and it is assumed that they have been melted down for their precious metals. Also taken was an amount of currency and a large quantity of jewelry owned by Mr. Randolph's wife and kept at the trust because of its supposed tight security."

Thinking of the haul of jewels in my desk drawer, I tried to stop my eyes from widening with interest at that little nugget.

"Any idea of who was behind it?" I said.

"Not really. There appeared to be an inside contact, which was puzzling, because most employees of the trust had been hired by Mr. Randolph and were insanely loyal. A young curator was suspected of being involved, but there was never enough evidence collected to prosecute her. Still, of course, she was let go."

"What was her name?"

"Chicos, I think," said Quick. "Serena Chicos. But as for the Rembrandt, its inclusion in the robbery was always puzzling. It is a signal piece, not easily sold, and, in fact, from what we can gather, it has never appeared in the black markets that deal with stolen art. It simply vanished, along with a small Monet landscape taken at the same time. Both paintings disappeared without a trace."

"Until now," said Spurlock, "when you come to us claiming to have a client who can return the Rembrandt to us. For a fee, I assume. This is a shakedown, I assume."

"Why do you assume that?"

"Another part of your reputation precedes you, Mr. Carl."

"Whatever the circumstances," said Quick, "we cannot be involved in a shakedown."

"I would be appalled at the very suggestion," said Spurlock, "simply appalled. Except that the specific work in question is a very valuable piece to the trust, in more ways than you can imagine. One of the claims they are using in trying to wrest control of the trust is a supposed laxity in our security over the years, and the missing Rembrandt is Exhibit A. It would be very valuable to our cause to recover that painting. Unfortunately, Mr. Carl, our finances are at a difficult stage. To be frank, we are worse than broke, we are tragically in debt. We would not be able to pay near to what the painting is worth."

"How much is it worth?" I asked.

"It is priceless," said Quick.

"Everything is priceless until a price is placed upon it," I said.

"At auction," said Spurlock, "similar Rembrandts have fetched upwards of ten million dollars."

"Yowza," I said.

"But of course those paintings weren't stolen," said Quick. "The trust is the rightful owner of that painting. As such, the painting could not be sold at auction, it could not be sold to a legitimate collector, it could not be shown. It is ours. If we find it, we can simply take it."

"If you find it."

"How do we know your client isn't taking us for a ride?" said Quick. "The details of the robbery have been in all the papers. You wouldn't be the first person to come to us with supposed information about one or the other of the missing paintings. The other claims have proven to be fraudulent. Somehow I expect that this claim is fraudulent, too."

"There's an L," I said.

"Excuse me?" said Spurlock.

"On the back of the canvas. Apparently the work was damaged at one point. You can't tell from the front, but my client informed me there has been a restoration. From the back of the canvas it is clear. There is an L-shaped repair."

Spurlock looked at Quick, who opened a file. Slowly, he paged through the documents until he found what he was looking for. An old photograph of a browned piece of canvas. He fought to contain his excitement as he passed the photograph to Spurlock.

"Who is your client, Victor?" said Quick, leaning forward now. "And what does he want?"

"He simply wants to come home," I said.

"Go ahead, Mr. Carl," said Spurlock. "Explain what we can do?"

"My client is currently under indictment for crimes he committed long ago. He is actively being sought by both the district attorney's office and the FBI, as well as by his former gang, who would like to silence him. What he wants is a deal with the government that will give him protection

and allow him to avoid any jail time. It all seems fair enough
to me. But the feds have let it be known that the deal is not
acceptable to them. I was hoping someone with influence
would ask them nicely to change their minds. Isn't there a
congressman on your board? Isn't one of your benefactors
also a large contributor to the Republican Party?"

"You've done your homework, Mr. Carl. And you are telling me there is to be no money involved?"

"This is America," I said. "There's always money involved. My client would like to start a new life with a nice
stake, but his needs aren't excessive and the amount won't
be anything you'll have trouble meeting, even with your financial troubles. I'm sure we can work that out later."

"I'm sure we can," said Spurlock. "Yes, yes, I am sure."

"Whom in the public sector should we talk to?" asked
Quick.

"Do you know K. Lawrence Slocum in the D.A.'s office?"

"Larry? Sure. Head of homicide now, isn't he?"

"That he is. He's handling it for the D.A. On the federal
side, there's a prosecutor named Jenna Hathaway who has
taken charge of the case."

"Hathaway, you say?" said Quick.

"That's right. Apparently she's looking for a glory ride.
You want to apply pressure, you apply it to her."

"Good. So now, Victor," said Quick, "for us to do what we
need to do, you have to tell us: Who is your client?"

"His name is Kalakos. Charles Kalakos. Slocum will
know him as Charlie the Greek."

There was something in Stanford Quick's eyes just then,
a slight flinch that indicated he had heard the name before.
Interesting. Maybe Quick had done his homework, too.

"But I have to emphasize," I said, "that this all must be
done with the utmost of discretion. There are dangerous

people who will be very unhappy if Charlie comes home. Any leak of what we are trying to do here will destroy the possibility of a deal, put my client's life at risk, and end your chance at recovering the painting."

"We understand," said Spurlock.

"If it goes public, the deal is off."

"You can rest assured, Mr. Carl," said Jabari Spurlock, his hands clasped before him and his head nodding sagely, "that we will be the very souls of discretion."

Discretion lasted about twenty-four hours, and then all hell broke loose.

8

It had seemed a simple enough plan. I had one agenda for my client and Assistant U.S. Attorney Jenna Hathaway had another. The easiest way to get us all on the same page was to have someone else involved, hence my visit to the Randolph Trust. A few discreet phone calls from the powerful members of the board about a missing Rembrandt would have the FBI eating out of my hand.

I was so sure it would all work as planned, I hadn't even thought much about the strange questions raised by the visit, like why had Mrs. LeComte been so concerned about my meeting with Spurlock? Or why did Stanford Quick seem to recognize Charlie's name? Or even the strangest of all: How had a loser like Charles Kalakos and his ragtag neighborhood gang been able to pull an impeccably planned, brilliantly executed professional heist? Still, why should I care about any of that? I was a man out to make a deal, and it looked like a deal was at hand.

Until somebody let loose our laundry and hung my client's life on the line. And not just my client's life.

"I know you," said a man with a harsh strain of Philly in his accent. "You're that Victor Carl."

He had stopped me right after I left my office. I had been working late, it was after seven, and Twenty-first Street was pretty much deserted, the shoe-repair shop closed, the Korean grocery closing. There was plenty of traffic on Chestnut, but I was heading away from Chestnut, just past the alley at the edge of my building, when the man had stepped in my way.

"That's right," I said. "And you are?"

He raised a small digital camera and took a snap, the flash momentarily blinding me.

"Whoa," I said, blinking away the afterimage. "What are you, a reporter?"

"Not exactly," he said, and he wasn't exactly dressed as a reporter either, no ratty sport coat, no wrinkled shirt, no mustard stains on his tie, no air of bored disappointment with his life. Instead he was wearing shiny white sneakers, pressed jeans, a retro 76ers jersey over a white T-shirt, silver chains hanging down, and a white baseball cap with the Sixers logo embossed in cream. It was a strange look, stranger still on a guy with gray hair who was shaped like a pear.

"You mind turning your head a bit to the side, Victor, so's I can catch your profile?"

"What the hell are you doing?"

"Hey, pal, I'm just trying to snap some pictures here. No need to get hostile. Now, be a Joe and turn to the side."

"Go to hell," I said, and as soon as I said it, something hard clamped down on the back of my head, holding it stiffly in place.

I reached back and found a gnarled hand attached to an absurdly thick wrist. The hand turned my head to the side. From that angle I could see what had hold of me, a younger man in the very same outfit, except his retro jersey was green, for the Bucks, and his chains were gold. This second man was a foot shorter than me, but with the girth of a bull.

Camera guy took another photograph, checked the outcome on the camera's small screen.

"Jesus, I hope that isn't your good side," he said. "Turn him around, Louie."

Louie twisted his wrist and spun me around 180 degrees, like we were partners at a square dance.

Camera guy took another photograph.

"I think we've got enough here," he said. "I want to thank you, Victor, for your generous cooperation."

Louie let go of my head. I shook my neck, straightened my jacket, tried to restore some level of dignity.

"What the hell is going on?" I said.

"Louie and myself, we've come here to deliver a message."

"From who, the mayor?"

"The mayor? Now, why would the mayor be sending someone like you a message?"

"For his buddy Bradley. To threaten us off the Theresa Wellman case."

The guy in the Sixers jersey raised his eyebrows in sadness as he shook his head.

"Isn't that what this is about?" I said.

"Unfortunately for you, no," he said. "We didn't get dispatched from City Hall. But let me tell you something, Victor. If the mayor's irritated at you, too, maybe you ought to rethink your life. No, we're here with a message for your buddy Charlie."

"Charlie?"

"Yeah, Charlie. Your boy Charlie the Greek. And this is the message. You tell that bald piece of dick we haven't forgotten that he spilled last time he was in the stir. Fifteen years is but a snap of the fingers to us. You tell him painting or no painting, if he shows his face in this town, I'm going to personally rip it off his skull."

That's when Louie piped in. "Off his skull, boysy," he said, his voice soft and gravelly, like the crush of bones underfoot.

"We've picked a bog for him already. He'll understand. Tell him he'll be crapping cranberries into eternity."

"Cranberries," said Louie.

"And you tell Charlie, wherever he is right now, he ought to be running, because we've called in our friend from Allentown."

"Your friend from Allentown?" I said.

"Allentown, boysy," said Louie.

"Charlie will know who we're talking about," said the man with the camera. "He'll know enough to take it seriously."

"Who the hell are you guys?"

"The name's Fred. Charlie will remember me because I'm the very guy he was running from fifteen years ago. And you, Victor, let this be clear. If Charlie shows up, it won't be so good for your health neither."

"What makes you think I'm representing this Charlie?"

"Are you saying you don't?"

"I'm just saying—"

Fred pushed me. I started going backward and then flipped over some huge solid thing, which turned out to be Louie, bending at his waist. I hadn't fallen for that since grade school.

"You stupid little pisspot," said Fred, now standing above my prostrated body. "This thing with you and Charlie and that painting, it's all over the freaking news."

I was still on the ground when, side by side, they started walking away from me, south, toward Walnut. I sat up on the sidewalk, my legs spread before me, my arms behind, propping up my torso.

"Hey, guys," I said.

Fred and Louie turned together. In their twin outfits, they looked like part of a sanitized hip-hop dance troupe. Up with Hoods.

"What was with the photographs?" I said.

Fred took a couple steps forward until he was leaning

over me. "Our friend from Allentown," he said. "After what happened one time in West Philly, he let it be known from here on in we should take photographs. It cuts down on the mistakes. Very meticulous, our friend from Allentown."

"Why don't I find that comforting?" I said.

So much for dire threats. And I have to give him this, as far as I could tell, Fred hadn't been lying, because yes, I was a stupid little pisspot, and yes, Charlie's story was all over the freaking news.

9

I had missed the early wave of evening broadcasts, but I caught the eleven o'clock news, and there it was, on all three channels, narrated by each station's organized-crime reporter, the whole story of the missing painting. They broadcast shots of the Randolph Trust building, pictures of the painting itself—Rembrandt as a young man with his bulbous nose and sharp eyes and goofy hat—they had mug shots of a younger Charlie Kalakos squinting for the police camera, and they had file footage of me talking exuberantly to the press about one of my prior cases.

All in all a good night for a publicity hound, which I shamelessly admit to being, but a lousy night for a lawyer trying to keep his sensitive negotiations on the QT. Which was proved with the very next phone call.

"Carl, you make me so very weary," said Slocum.

"It wasn't me."

"First, this morning I get a call from some high-toned lawyer representing the Randolph Trust, barking in my ear about some missing Rembrandt. Then A.U.S.A. Hathaway calls up, irate as can be, complaining about sudden pressure from higher-ups concerning that selfsame painting. And, funny how it works, both conversations seemed to include your name."

"That I had something to do with."

"It was no small thing to calm Hathaway. Watch out for her, Victor, she's a hard case. But I worked it, yes I did, and just as I'm about to get a meeting set up, you leak the whole thing to the press to apply even more pressure."

"That's the part that wasn't me."

"You didn't talk to the press?"

"No, I did not."

"But you love talking to the press."

"Like Hoffa loves cement, true, but this time I refrained. And everyone I talked to understood that keeping the whole thing quiet was in everybody's interest."

"Obviously not everyone."

"So do we still have a meeting to work out a deal?"

"Not now, not after this. Hathaway called back and said if they deal now, it will look like stolen art was being used to buy off the righteous arm of justice."

"Which of course would be true."

"Of course. Except that when it's done behind closed doors it is one thing, and when it is headline news it is another. You should have kept it quiet."

"I tried."

"So who spilled?"

"I don't know. That Randolph Trust is a hornet's nest, with everyone holding their own agendas. There was an old lady there who wasn't included in the discussions, but I don't doubt that she knows every nook and cranny in the place and the best locations to eavesdrop. And then, of course, our friend in the U.S. Attorney's office could have leaked the information herself to give her an excuse to torpedo the deal."

"Are you accusing a federal law-enforcement official of using the press to further her own ends?"

"It's happened before."

"Yes, it has. Why didn't you just let me know about the painting right off?"

"I thought a little outside pressure would get the lard out of the FBI's ass."

"Well, you were right about that. The search for Charlie the Greek has been accelerated. All the field offices in New York, New Jersey, Delaware, and Maryland are in on the hunt."

"Crap."

"I knew you had stepped into it, yes I did."

"Hey, Larry, you ever hear anything about some hit man from Allentown?"

Pause. "Where'd you get that?"

"Just something I heard in the street."

"Oh, I bet you did. Remember all those murders through the years we're trying to link up to the Warrick Brothers Gang?"

"Yeah."

"Word is the finger man was some old pro from Allentown."

"Oh."

"Yeah."

"This isn't so good, is it?"

"No, it isn't. Sleep well, Victor, 'cause you'll be needing it."

It took me a while to figure it out, what I could do to salvage my client's chances to make it home, to give his dying mother his heartfelt good-byes, to let me cash in my pile of jewels and chains, and for both of us to survive it all without prison time or serious bodily harm. It had to be something that would push the feds to deal and something that would work fast enough to kick in before their revived manhunt pulled in Charlie, or the friend from Allentown mooted the issue. It took me a while to figure it out, because usually when a solution to a difficult problem congeals in your consciousness it ends up requiring sacrifice and daring, it ends up requiring you to transcend your baser instincts and rise to the occasion. But not this time. This time my baser instincts were spot-on.

I hadn't courted the wave of press attention that flowed like sewage into Charlie's messy life story, but now that it was here, I was going to ride it for all it was worth. Time for A.U.S.A. Jenna Hathaway to learn how low I could go.

The next morning at my office, the phone didn't stop ringing and I didn't stop answering. The television crews were lined up like rush-hour aircraft on the runway, waiting for their exclusive interviews.

"Channel Six, come on in, it's your turn. Channel Twenty-nine, we'll be with you next, and then Channel Three. But I might have to take a moment when the *New York Times* calls—don't want to keep the old gray lady waiting. And then I have a photo shoot with the *Inquirer* scheduled for two. Will that give us all enough time?"

And in each discussion about the painting and its whereabouts, because that's what the press all asked about, I talked about my client Charlie, who was simply trying to come home to say so long to his dying mother but was being stymied by the heartless autocrats at the FBI.

"My client wants to return this painting, not for his own benefit, or even for the benefit of Randolph Trust, but for the people of this great country and for all the generations to follow. He wants to return it for all the children who will someday find their lives enriched by this preeminent work of art. If only the FBI would show a little flexibility. If only the Bureau could stop thinking of its own selfish ends and consider the children. The children are what really matter."

And, of course, there was one key statement I made in all my interviews, the most important point I drove home that day and in the days to follow.

CHAPTER

10

"The name is Carl," I said to the reporter who sat across from me with her notepad out and her pencil sharpened. "Carl with a C."

"You said that already," she said. "Twice. Tell me about your client."

"He's a nice old guy," I said. "Harmless, really. My gosh, he's over sixty and not even five feet tall." I forced out a chuckle. "I'd hardly call him a threat to the community."

"Where is he now?"

"Still in hiding. It's a shame, really, with his mother deathly ill and praying to see her son one more time before she dies. I think the government is being quite unreasonable."

"So it appears."

"Can I get you something to drink? Water?"

"No, I'm fine, thank you."

The interview was being conducted in my office. My jacket was on, my tie tight, my feet were off my desktop. I was feigning a thoughtful, concerned manner, listening to the questions as if I hadn't heard them before, phrasing my answers as if I really cared. There were no cameras to explain my faultless etiquette, which could only mean that the reporter sitting on the other side of my desk was remarkably good-looking, which she was. Hair like scrubbed copper, green eyes, pale freckly skin, no longer young but far from too old. Her name was Rhonda Harris, and she was wearing a tight blue sweater and a green scarf. Occasionally, as she concentrated on her notebook, the pink tip of her tongue showed at the corner of her mouth.

"Could I possibly talk to Charlie?" she said.

"No, I'm sorry. That's not feasible."

"But it would really help me set the right tone. I'm trying to focus this article on whether it is possible to come home again, despite what Thomas Wolfe wrote."

"Ah, a literary twist. Good for you. Do you like Wolfe?"

"I adore him."

"Too many words for my taste."

"But that's what I love about him. All that ripe excess, the sensual pleasures of his long and twisting sentences. My God, sometimes his prose leaves me feeling ravished."

"People say I talk too much."

"But, see, if I could just speak to Charlie, even on the phone, it would help so. I think his sense of exile is at the heart of this story. Charlie Kalakos, like George Webber, trying to come home to a hostile city."

"That sounds very interesting, Rhonda. Can I call you Rhonda?"

"Of course." Nice smile, that, the way her eyes crinkled with warmth, the way the corners of her mouth curved down like a kitten's even as she showed her very white and very even teeth.

"And call me Victor, please. As I'm sure you understand, Rhonda, there are many people searching for Charlie, some more dangerous than others. His location must be kept a secret. I don't even know where he is or how to reach him."

"You have met with him, though, haven't you?"

"Yes."

"Where?"

"Now, now, Rhonda, really. I can't disclose that."

"How often do you meet him?"

"Who did you say you wrote for again?"

"Newsday."

"And you're their crime reporter?"

"I cover the art scene for them on a nonstaff basis."

"Ah, the Rembrandt."

"Yes, the famous Rembrandt." She leaned forward, tapped her pencil to her lip, opened wide her lovely eyes. "Have you seen it?"

"Just the photographs on television."

"Such a fabulous piece of work. It would be thrilling to behold it after all these years. I'd give anything to examine it up close."

"We're hoping you get that chance very soon." Pause. "At the Randolph."

"Of course," she said, leaning back again, tapping her notebook in disappointment. "Can I ask one thing more, Victor?"

"Shoot."

"I'm just on the art beat, so I might be missing something here, but is this whole thing fair? Do you really think that Charlie deserves a sweetheart deal simply because he somehow has possession of a valuable piece of stolen property? Isn't that just as bad as a rich man buying his way out of an indictment?"

I glanced at my watch. "Oh, I'm sorry, Rhonda, I have to cut this short. Maybe some other time we could talk in depth about fairness and the law. I have some very interesting theories about that." Smarmy smile. "Over drinks, perhaps."

"I'd like that, Victor. Very much."

I tastefully refrained from punching the air and letting out a whoop.

As I was escorting Rhonda through the hallway and toward the stairs, I caught a whiff of something precious in the air.

"Are you wearing a new fragrance, Ellie?" I said to my secretary as we stopped at her desk and I sniffed deeply. "Because I must say, whatever it is, it's lovely."

She didn't respond, she didn't even smile at the compliment. Instead she just let her eyes shift to her left. I followed her gaze.

He stood there, short and slight in a purple suit with lace shirt cuffs and very shiny, very small black shoes. "Mr. Carl, is it?" he said in a Southern drawl so thick it seemed to drip with kudzu.

"That's right."

"I wonder, sir, if I could have a smidgen of your time."

I glanced at Ellie, who was fighting to keep the smile off her face.

"I'm a little busy right now," I said. "Are you press?"

"Oh dear, no. Do I look reptilian to you? And if you see me in brown corduroy, please shoot me. This won't take but a moment, and I can assure you that our meeting will be very much worth your while. Oh so very, very much."

"You think?"

"Most assuredly."

I stared at him for a moment, tried to figure out what he was all about and failed. I turned to Rhonda Harris, who, surprisingly, wasn't smiling. I suppose some people just have no sense of humor about their profession.

"Thank you for coming, Rhonda," I said. "I hope we meet again sometime."

"Count on it, Victor," she said.

As Rhonda Harris passed the little man, she stared down at him and he stared back and I felt something spark between them, like the tension between two dogs circling a dead squirrel. I almost thought I heard a guttural growl.

Then Rhonda was off, heading for the door, and both the man and I stared at her as she walked away. Her skirt was as tight as her sweater, and her pumps were sturdy.

"Do you know her?" I asked the little man as she swung open the door and disappeared.

"Never saw her before in my life."

"You seemed to know her."

"I know the type."

"And what type is that?"

"Cold-blooded killer."

I turned my head to stare once more at the man, then I checked my watch. "I'm sorry, I really don't have much—"

"Just a pinch of time is all I need," he said, his voice flying high like a startled sparrow at the last word, "just the tiniest pinch."

"What exactly is this about?"

"Oh, let's just say I'm here to discuss the fine arts, one patron to another."

"I'm not really a patron of the arts."

"Oh, Mr. Carl, Mr. Carl. Don't slight yourself."

I thought about it for a bit. "All right, Mr. . . ."

"Hill," he said. "Lavender Hill."

"Of course it is. Why don't we go to my office?"

"Splendid," he said. "Simply splendid."

I gestured him down the hall and watched as he minced his way toward my office door. His walk wasn't so different from Rhonda's. I leaned over to Ellie.

"Any idea who he is?" I whispered.

"Not a pinch," she said.

"He give you a card?"

She took a card off her desk, passed it under her nose, and then handed it to me. It smelled as if he had dipped it in his perfume. I gave it a quick read. His name in a florid script, a phone number with an area code I didn't recognize, and the words "Procurer of the Sublime."

"What's a 'Procurer of the Sublime'?"

"I don't know, Mr. Carl," said Ellie. "Do you need me to stick around?"

"No, you can knock off for the day. I'll see you tomorrow."

"Thanks. But can you do me a favor?"

"What?"

"Can you find out what scent he uses?" she said. "Whatever it is, I like his better than mine."

CHAPTER

11

    "Such a charming office, Mr. Carl," mewed Lavender Hill as he settled into the chair across from my desk.

Not a promising start to our interview: one sentence, one lie. My office was officially a dump, scuffed walls, dented brown filing cabinet, a desk covered with useless papers that should have been tossed out weeks ago. It was utilitarian, maybe, it had an unsentimental personality, maybe, it suited me like a cheap, ill-fitting suit, maybe, but it was not charming.

"Thank you," I said. "I try."

His brown eyes filled with amusement at my counterlie. My God, they almost sparkled. He was quite a sight, I had to admit, with his legs daintily crossed, his paisley silk scarf around his neck, his black hair parted to the right and cut round, as if it had been styled in 1978. And he had the face of a jockey, anorexic, sharp, and corrupt. Lavender Hill.

"You are such a dear to see me on short notice," he said. "Normally I wouldn't barge in like a barbarian, but I felt our conversation just couldn't wait for the usual pleasantries. I'm sure the subject will be close to your heart."

"What exactly is the subject?"

"Art."

"So we're going to discuss aesthetics, is that it?"

"And money," he said as one small hand fussed with a purple lapel.

"Yes, now I see, Mr. Hill."

"Oh, call me Lav, everyone does. Do you know the Spencers of Society Hill? Simply the best people. They've called me Lav for years."

"No, I don't know the Spencers. We probably run in different circles."

"Oh, I suppose so, yes. They are horse people."

"The things they do with genes nowadays."

"One look at her, Victor, and you wouldn't doubt it. I can call you Victor, can't I?"

"You can call me anything you want, Lav, when we're talking about money."

"Oh, very good. You have a pleasing sort of directness I find quite . . . exhilarating. So let's get down to it, shall we? You have a client, Charles Kalakos."

"That's right."

"And he has access to a certain painting, from what I've been told."

"That seems to be the word on the street. What about it?"

"I represent, Victor, a collector, a man with impeccable tastes and a private collection of the most exquisite objets d'art."

"Objets d'art?"

"Oh, you're right. Good for you, Victor. Why put on all kinds of pretensions and airs when we're talking about stuff? He collects stuff, quite valuable stuff, but stuff all the same. What you buy when you already have everything. Still, his hunger for collecting can be quite lucrative for those of us in the position to feed it. Which is where we both now find ourselves."

"He wants the painting."

"Of course he does, you clever boy. A Rembrandt self-portrait would mark the pinnacle of his efforts. He is quite adamant about adding it to his collection."

"I'm sorry, Lav, but selling a stolen painting would be illegal. I couldn't possibly be part of such a transaction."

"Oh, Victor, I wouldn't suggest such a thing. You are a lawyer, bound by the boundless morality of your profession. Of course your selling the painting would be wrong, wrong, wrong. And yet"—a sly smile—"you are bargaining for the painting right now in a very public way, are you not? Trying to use it to get the best deal for your client."

"It's very different."

"Is it so different? Maybe the best deal for your client is not to turn himself into a gymnast for the prosecutors or return to Philadelphia and put his life at the mercy of his former gangland companions."

"How do you know about that?"

"Oh, Victor, you are a charmer, aren't you? Maybe the best deal for your client is something else. A new home, a new identity, a new fat bank account to keep him smelling clover for the rest of his days. These things could be arranged."

"In return for the painting."

"I must say, Victor, all the negative things I've heard about your intellect have been completely overstated. You are quite sharp for a lawyer. I approve. And rest assured those of us in the middle would be amply rewarded. You might even be able to afford a can of paint for your office. Ralph Lauren has some marvelous colors that would do wonders. Maybe a teal."

"You don't like beige?"

"The color of cheap coffins. So there we have it, Victor. The offer has been made. Your interest is apparent. All that is left is the details."

"Like how much money we're talking about."

"Yes, for one."

"How much money are we talking about?"

"Are we negotiating now?"

"No. I can't be part of the selling of stolen art."

"As I suspected you would say. But why talk money if we're not negotiating? This was only a preliminary meeting. Let me tell you how I believe things might proceed from here. You will tell your client about this meeting, keeping him informed of all developments in his case, as you are required by the bar association. He'll be interested, because he is a man with a healthy lust for money. You will give him my phone number. He will call. I will mention amounts in the six figures. And if there is a deal, we will take care of the transaction without your input. You, however, will still receive a healthy commission of, say, fifteen percent. It is so simple, really."

"I can't accept a commission."

"Of course not, that would be improper. But a retainer, from a new client, for a case that might never come to trial, maybe renewed for a couple of years, a substantial retainer, that you could accept. All the best law firms do. You have my card?"

"Yes, I have your card."

"Splendid. So our work here is done."

"Not quite, Lav. Before I do anything, I'll need to know who you represent."

"I represent a man with money who lives far away. You need know nothing more. An art collection of his sort, where provenance is not a concern, can be maintained only in absolute secrecy."

"Everything you tell me will be held in the strictest confidence."

"Your confidence doesn't impress him. All negotiations will go through me."

"I need a name."

"You need nothing of the sort," he said, the sparkle in his eye replaced with a flash of anger. "You have a job to do and you will do it and you will be paid for it. That is all that must concern you. And I have every faith that you will make the call."

"How are you so sure?"

"Because you are not representing Charles Kalakos only as a lawyer. He is a friend of the family. There is history that must be honored. You owe him the opportunity."

"I don't understand what you're talking about."

"Ask your father."

"My father?"

"This has been so pleasant," said Lavender Hill as he stood from the chair. "We should do this again. Maybe over a cocktail. I do adore a stiff cocktail."

"Why am I not surprised?"

"I can see myself out, Victor. Thank you for your hospitality."

Just as he stepped out my door, I said, "Six figures won't be enough."

He stopped, swiveled his hips to face me, put an expression of amusement on his face. "Are we negotiating now?"

"No," I said. "I can't negotiate such a deal. But, knowing the value of the painting, I couldn't advise my client to take anything less than seven."

"So we've both done our research. Very, very good. I'll discuss it with my client."

"And lawyers generally get a third."

"Yes, and auctioneers generally only get a tenth. Somewhere in the middle seems more than fair. But this is all so promising. I've made an offer, you've made a counteroffer, we're haggling over percentages. I know you can't be part of this, Victor, but already it feels like a negotiation to me.

Ciao, dear one. I'll be waiting for a call. But don't keep me waiting long."

When he vanished from the doorway, I was left with his lingering scent and the throb of my pulse that always accompanies the flash of big money. He hadn't even blinked when I told him six figures wasn't enough. Hadn't even blinked.

I sat at my desk, rubbing my hands together and thinking it through. To sell the painting would be illegal, and a lawyer really can't be involved in anything illegal. Really. And yet Lav might have been right when he said his offer would be the best for Charlie and maybe for Charlie's mother, too. I could imagine the tearful reunion on a lovely cay off the coast of Venezuela, mother and son, together again, under a bright Caribbean sky. And passing on a mere phone number surely wouldn't violate any of my legal oaths. Surely. And what about the law of either/or? If I wasn't going to be able to bank the retainer, I should at least get something out of this whole mess, don't you think? Either/or.

This favor for my father was getting more interesting by the moment, and more troubling, too. Who did this Lavender Hill represent, and how did he know so much about Charlie Kalakos and his situation? And what the hell did my father have to do with any of it? I needed some answers, and I knew who could get them for me. So I made a call and set up a meeting with Phil Skink, my private investigator, for the very next morning and then walked out of my office.

Beth was gone, Ellie was gone, the place was sadly deserted as dusk crept in. I was already dog tired, but I had no great desire to head to my ruined home. A drink, I decided, would be the perfect thing. Only one, maybe two, nothing much, just enough. And off I went, toward Chaucer's, my usual tavern, and toward what must have been a hell of a night, if only I could remember it.

12

"You look like a beaten dog," said Phil Skink, staring down on me as I lay on the old leather couch in his dusty outer office.

"I feel worse," I said.

"Impossible, mate. If you felt worse than you look, you'd be dead. I've eaten mutton what looked more alive than you. What the devil were you up to last night?"

"I don't know."

"Sounds like trouble, it does. A dame involved?"

"I think."

"Sounds like more than trouble. Next time you give me a call before it gets out of hand."

"And you'll pull me out?"

"Don't be daft," said Skink. "I'll be joining in. No reason you should be having all the fun."

Go to your butcher, ask for all the gristle and bone he can scrape off his floor. Pile it onto a roasting pan, dress it up in a natty brown suit with thick pinstripes, a brown fedora, a bright tie. Give it high cholesterol and pearly teeth. Add the brains of a mathematician, an irrational fear of canines, a weakness for wine-soaked women. Throw in a squeeze of violence and a dash of charm, season with sea salt, bake to hard-boiled, and right there you'd pretty much have cooked yourself Phil Skink, private eye.

I had set up a meeting in his office after my interview with Lavender Hill, and now I had arrived, late and limping from the night before, with my eyes still red and my jaw still slack.

"Your head hurt?" he asked.

"Is there a thunderstorm roiling through your office?"

"No."

"Then it hurts."

"You take anything?"

"Two Advil. Like shooting a woolly mammoth with a BB gun."

"Wait a minute," he said. "I'll take care of you."

I closed my eyes for a moment, and when I opened them again, there he stood, in one hand a glass with some thick brown sludge that was bubbling and belching, in the other a long green pickle.

"Sit up," he said. "Doctor's orders."

I did as he said and felt my consciousness slip as the blood drained from my swollen head.

"Drink this and eat this," said Skink. "A sip, a bite, a sip, a bite. You get the idea."

"I don't think so, Phil."

"Do as I say and you'll be good as new."

"Really, I'm okay."

"Look, mate, it hurts me just to look at you. Do it or I'll pour the drink down your throat and then stuff the pickle in after."

"Hell of a bedside manner," I said even as I grabbed hold of the drink and the pickle. With my eyes closed, I took a sip. Not terrible, actually, spicy and sour all at once, and with a bite of the pickle to chase it down, it was almost palatable. "What is it, hair of the dog?"

"The only thing you lose by chasing alcohol with alcohol is sobriety, and you lost enough of that already. Finish it up."

"All of it?"

"Well, hell, I don't want none of it."

"And if I throw it all up on the rug?"

"Be sure to miss my shoes."

I finished it all, closed my eyes, belched loudly, tasted it all again, and gagged twice. But strangely, when I opened my eyes, I did feel better, almost renewed.

"What's in that?" I said.

"A secret recipe taught me by a hostess name of Carlotta I was seeing in Salinas."

"Carlotta, huh?"

"She had tricks, she did."

"Oh, I bet."

"Hey, strictly management, she was. I still gots all my choppers. So what did you want to meet me about? This thing what's got you all over the news, this Charlie the Greek with the painting?"

"That's right," I said.

I handed him the card Lavender Hill had left with my secretary. He looked at it for a moment, brought it to his nose and took a sniff, raised his eyebrows.

"He came to me with an offer to buy the painting. But he knew enough about what was going on to leave me uncomfortable. Find out who he is and who he's working for."

"Lavender Hill."

"His friends call him Lav."

Skink took another sniff of the card. "Sweet guy?"

"Apparently, if a purple suit says anything anymore, although I got a sense not to take him lightly."

"He's got a Savannah area code." Skink took a notepad from a pocket, a pen from another, clicked the pen, started writing. "Anything else on him?"

"That's all I got."

"All right, mate," he said as he tapped the point of his pen on the pad. "Usual rates. It might necessitate a quick jaunt to Georgia to track down his story."

"Whatever you need to do. Oh, and Phil. He should know we're looking. Don't be too discreet. Let's rattle his chain a bit and see how he reacts."

"I'll be a regular bull in his china shop, I will. That it?"

"Something else," I said. "I want you to look into a guy name of Bradley Hewitt, a fixer of sorts. He has an in with the mayor and uses it for all sorts of business affairs. Find out what you can about him."

Skink again started scribbling on his pad. "Any details. Addresses? Phone numbers?"

"No, but it shouldn't be much of a trick to track him down. And also track down what you can about the life and history of a woman named Theresa Wellman. She and this Hewitt used to be an item. They have a kid together."

"Which one does you represent?"

"The woman."

"She have any money?"

"No."

"How'd you end up on the wrong side of that one?"

"Beth," I said with a shrug.

"Ah, that explains it." He tapped his pad with the point of his pen, clicked it shut. "That it?"

I sat there for a moment. Was that it, really, or did I have one more thing to ask my private eye? The brown gloop and the pickle had eased the pain in my head, but they hadn't done a thing for the burning on my chest. That morning I had made a quick check before I hobbled over to Skink's. Plenty of names in the Philadelphia phone book, but not the right name. I could have called each and every Adair and asked if there was a Chantal in the family, but that seemed fishy, especially when they started asking why? Why indeed? Because I might be in love if I could remember who she was?

And what if they said yes, they had a Chantal Adair, and I met her, and she had six teeth and looked like Moe from the Three Stooges, what then? I thought about it some more and decided. Skink was my PI, a hired hand, but he was also my friend and loyal as a Labrador.

"There's something else," I said. "Something personal."

"Personal, huh?"

"Billed to my home, not the office."

"Okay," said Skink, "I understands. Usual fees?"

"I don't get an insider discount?"

"My mother don't get an insider discount. Go ahead."

"Something happened last night."

"What?"

"I don't remember."

Skink cocked his head.

"But something happened, and I need you to find someone for me. Discreetly, you understand?"

"It's a woman, is it?"

"Isn't it always? But I don't want her to know I'm looking. Once you find her, let me know where she is and a little bit about her. Maybe take a picture. I'll decide what to do from there."

"You know, mate, it's a bad idea to get a private eye messed up in your personal affairs. It can't come to no good. In the end you never like what you find."

"Just do it, Phil."

"All right, then. What do you know about her?"

"I think she's blond and sturdy and rides a motorcycle."

"You think? You don't know?"

"If I knew, I wouldn't need you."

"Where'd you meet her?"

"I think at Chaucer's, but a lot of last night is a blank."

"How much is a blank?"

"Most all of it."

"You been drinking much lately, mate?"

"Some."

"Too much?"

"How much is too much?"

"The question is its own answer, innit? So's if you don't remember nothing, how do you knows something happened? How do you knows she wasn't just a girl what you eyed in a bar and who turned you down?"

"Because I know, damn it."

"All right, don't get all huffy on me. I'll do what I can. You got a name?"

"Yeah, I got a name."

"Well?"

I stood up, shucked off my jacket, undid my tie. Skink stared at me with a growing horror on his face, as if I intended on doing a striptease with grinding music and pompoms right there in the middle of his office. Gad, the very idea would fill me with horror, too. But it ended at the shirt. I unbuttoned it down to my belly, pushed the fabric aside to reveal my left breast.

Skink eyed my chest, raised his gaze to look into my eyes, eyed my chest again. "You get it last night?"

"I didn't have it yesterday."

"Nows I understand," he said as he stood to get a closer look. "Nice job, classic look."

"I don't want a critique, Phil, just find her."

He clicked his pen open. "Chantal Adair," he said as he wrote, and then he tapped his pad with the pen's point. "Piece of cake."

Wrong.

13

You can tell a lot about a lawyer by how she tries a case. If you saw Jenna Hathaway in the street, you'd think she was quite wholesome and sweet, with a round angelic face and haunting blue eyes. Long legs, honey brown hair, a nervous mouth, a figure not quite willowy but willowy enough, she seemed the kind of tall, good-natured woman you could imagine sharing an ice cream cone with while taking a long walk in a fine summer's mist. That was Jenna Hathaway in the street, or at a restaurant, or sitting on the porch swing drinking a tall glass of lemonade. But in court sweet Jenna Hathaway was an assassin.

I was sitting in the back of a federal courtroom watching as Jenna Hathaway cross-examined an accountant in a money-laundering prosecution. The accountant was impeccably dressed, what hair he had left was impeccably trimmed. He was obviously an important man with important clients who found refuge in the numbers that he used to define the world, but under the relentless assault of Jenna Hathaway's questioning he was turning into another creature before our very eyes. It was like a carnival freak show. An accusatory question from Hathaway, a feeble objection from the overmatched defense attorney, a sneering response from Hathaway, an admonition from the cowed judge compelling the witness to answer, and then we all watched in horror as the accountant devolved ever further into a pale, quivering, fishlike creature that gasped for oxygen and flopped like a beached carp on the stand.

"My God," I said to Slocum, who sat beside me on the bench as we both watched Hathaway work. "She should have been a gastrointestinal surgeon, the way she's giving that guy a second asshole."

"And he's not even the defendant," said Slocum.

"What's her story?"

"A born prosecutor, never even flirted with defense work. Her father was a cop."

"Here?"

"One of Philadelphia's finest. Homicide, retired now. His daughter's taken up the sword."

"I wouldn't want to be on her wrong side."

"You already are," said Slocum.

We must have been talking louder than we thought, because Hathaway stopped smack in the middle of a question and turned to stare at us. Her blue eyes focused on me, and I felt myself shrink beneath her gaze as if I had been dunked in an icy pond. She didn't quickly turn back either. She kept staring so that everyone else in the courtroom, judge, bailiff, defendant, jury, the whole kit and caboodle turned and stared at me, too. It was all quite intolerable enough on its own, and then Slocum started laughing.

K. Lawrence Slocum was a solid, starchy man with thick glasses and a deep laugh who took inordinate pleasure in my humiliations. We were not quite friends, not quite enemies, we were simply professionals who worked the opposite sides of the same street. But I could trust Larry to hew to the highest standards of his profession, and he could trust that I wouldn't even pretend to do the same, and with that understanding between us we got along surprisingly well. He had arranged a meeting between me and the intimidating Jenna

Hathaway, the federal prosecutor with the strange, abiding interest in Charlie Kalakos. Hathaway, in the middle of a trial, had asked us to meet her in court, and so we had.

After the judge called a recess, Hathaway packed up her oversize briefcase and started down the aisle toward the doorway. Without saying a word, she motioned with her head that we were to follow. Her heels clicked on the linoleum as she led us down the hallway and into one of the lawyer-client rooms, a dreary space with no windows, metal chairs, and a brown Formica table.

When she turned around and trained again her blue eyes on me, I put on my smarmiest smile and reached out a hand. "Victor Carl," I said.

Jenna Hathaway ignored the proffer and, while barely moving her tensed lips, said, "I know who you are."

"Good," I said. "I'm really glad we have this opportunity to get together and work out something on poor Charlie's behalf. I'm sure we're all looking for the same thing here, an outcome that will promote both the goal of justice and allow a wonderful work of art to regain its place in—"

"Could you just do us all a favor, Victor," she said, interrupting me in midsentence, "and shut up. Not just here, in this room, where your voice is grating beyond measure, but on the evening news and in the papers, too. You're in love with the sound of your own voice, and let me tell you, in your own best interest, you're no Caruso. So please, please, please, just shut up."

A little stunned, I looked over at Larry, who was fighting unsuccessfully to stifle his laughter, and then back at Jenna Hathaway. "Is that nice?" I said to her.

"I'm not trying to be nice."

"And good for you, you're succeeding. But whatever else all that talking did, it got your attention."

"What will it take to shut you up?"

"Cutting to the chase, are you? I admire that. Right to the bone of it. So often lawyers spend so much time talking around things that are essentially meaningless. They can go on and on, and it can get so—"

"You're doing it again," she said.

"Doing what?"

"Talking too much. Are you doing this on purpose, just to piss me off?"

"Actually, yes," I said.

She turned to Larry. "Is he a blathering idiot normally, or just a total jerk?"

"Oh, Victor can be a bit of both, but today he's being the latter."

She eyed me again, down and up, taking in the scuffs in my shoes, the railroad pleats in my pants, the wrinkled shirt, the weirdly glistening red tie. She rolled her eyes, sighed loudly, and dropped into one of the chairs. I sat across from her. "What can I do," she said, "to get you out of my life?"

"Make a deal."

"Terms?"

"We return the painting to its rightful place at the Randolph Trust and you drop all charges."

"We won't drop all charges," she said. "That's a nonstarter. And what about his testimony? He'd have to talk."

"With immunity?"

"Be serious."

"How long have you been going after the Warrick Brothers Gang, Larry?" I said.

"Years," he said.

"How you guys doing?"

"Not so well."

"And what's the life expectancy of those who agree to testify against them?"

"Short."

"We've already received a dire threat against my client's life and my own. The first is par for the course, but the second I take very seriously. Still, Charlie will talk about his time with the Warricks if you give him immunity and you agree to protect him. He'd be amenable to witness protection."

"Of course he would," said Hathaway. "Living his days off some golf course in a condo paid for by the government."

"And he mentioned something about a plasma TV."

"Is this clown for real?" she asked Slocum.

"Unfortunately, yes," he said.

"Then we have nothing more to talk about," said Hathaway. "The FBI tells me they're on the edge of finding your client anyway. As we speak, they are chasing down reliable leads."

"Even if true, it doesn't mean they'll find the painting," I said. "Did I mention the painting gets returned? Isn't that why you've been after him all this time? Isn't that why you had the FBI stationed outside his mother's house, so you could get back that painting?"

She looked at me coldly. "I don't give a good damn about the picture of some dead Dutch guy who painted himself."

I stared at her for a moment. None of this made any sense. If it wasn't the painting she was searching for, then what was it? I looked at Larry for help. He just shrugged.

"So what are you after?"

"I want to know how he got the painting."

"It was stolen," I said. "Thirty years ago. What more do you care about? There's nothing you can do to any of them now. The statute of limitations has run. They got away with it. Sometimes bad triumphs. Let's move on."

"I'm not moving on," she said. "If he comes in, he's going to have to talk not just about his old gang but about the

Randolph heist, too. Everything. And he's going to have to name names."

"He won't. He's already said."

"Then that is that, isn't it? You want to make a deal, make it with Larry."

"But he can only talk about the state charges. There's still a federal indictment against my client."

"Yes, there is."

"What are you really after?"

"Your client knows."

"Charlie knows?"

"Sure he does. That's it, those are the terms. If he comes back and talks truthfully about everything, and I mean everything, then we might be able to work something out."

"I'll talk to him."

"Good." She stood, hoisted her huge briefcase off the floor so that it thunked on the table. "Now I have to get back. There's still some flesh I haven't filleted off that accountant's back. But, Victor, hear this. If I see your face on the television again, or one of your obnoxious quips quoted in the newspaper, the next dire threat you'll be getting will be coming from me."

"Can I ask you something more personal?"

She tilted her head, tightened her lips.

"Do you like long walks in the misting summer rain?"

"With my dog," she said.

After she stalked out, her briefcase banging the doorjamb for emphasis, I remained seated at the table with Slocum.

"Do you have any idea what she's looking for?" I said.

"None."

"Don't you think you should find out? Maybe climb the chain of command to discover what's really going on?"

"You want to hear something puzzling, Carl? The attorney general of the United States doesn't return my calls."

"A shocking breach of decorum."

"Yes, it is. I would complain, but the vice president doesn't return my calls either."

"She's after something."

"Evidently."

"Did you notice that when she talks, she doesn't really move her lips? Like she's a ventriloquist."

"I noticed."

"It's a little frightening," I said.

"She's a frightening young lady."

"And, you know, from a distance she looks so sweet."

14

Rhonda Harris and her little notebook were waiting for me outside the courthouse. How she knew I was at the courthouse was a bit problematic, but the sight of her in her dark pants and white blouse, her green scarf, her long legs and red hair pulled back, brushed that niggling question aside. She looked oh, so Katharine Hepburn I half expected her to break into a quavering Yankee accent as she called me her knight in shining armor.

"Mr. Carl, I hope I'm not disturbing you."

"Not at all," I said. "It's gratifying to see the working press working. But unfortunately, right now, and for the foreseeable future, I have no further comment on anything."

"Really? That's so out of character."

"We all must change with the times. I know it's a grave disappointment."

"Not really. Your comments didn't quite grind the presses to a halt."

I checked my watch. "I have to get a move on. I'm due in landlord-tenant court."

"Can I walk with you a bit?"

"Only if what we say is off the record."

She put away her notebook, lifted her hands like a magician to show there was nothing here, nothing there, nothing up her sleeve.

"Come along, then," I said. "How's the story going?"

"Fine, sort of. My editor says he needs more detail and more human interest."

"I'm not an interesting enough human for your editor?"

"He told me I need to interview Charlie."

"That's a shame, isn't it? I really liked your Thomas Wolfe angle."

"How can we arrange an interview?"

"We can't."

"Oh, everything can be arranged somehow, can't it?"

"Not this."

"Give me a chance, Victor. I'll only write the most complimentary things. And I'll give you approval over your client's quotes if you want. I'm sure the public will find Charlie's story fascinating."

"It is, I assure you. But as of today the Victor Carl–Charlie Kalakos media machine has been shut down. And I wouldn't have let you interview Charlie in any event."

"But doesn't he have the right to have his say?"

"At the appropriate time, sure. This isn't it."

"You know, Victor, if I could have an exclusive interview with Charlie, I could get this thing splashed on the front page of *Newsday*. *Newsday*'s feature articles are picked up by papers all over the country. The publicity would be out of bounds. The morning shows would be calling. You could become the next Johnnie Cochran."

"I always admired Johnnie. Hardly anyone looks good in a black knit cap, but he pulled it off with style."

"Maybe after the article you could charge as much as he did."

"So now you're appealing to both my pathetic hunger for fame and my venality."

"Is it working?"

"Can I ask you a question? The man you saw in my office. Did you know him?"

"That little gnome? No, thank God."

"Why 'thank God'?"

"Didn't you sense it, the violence in him? I did. I've seen enough of that sort in my life. What did he want?"

"He was appealing to my venality, too. It seems to be a disturbing pattern."

"Then maybe there is something else I can appeal to."

"Rhonda, are you propositioning me?"

"Oh, Victor. Don't be silly. It's just a story."

"Too bad."

"What I meant is that maybe I could appeal to your sense of charity. I've been fighting to break through at my newspaper for a while. I fell into this business late, and it's hard being a stringer, but my editor said if I can make this story happen, he'd push to hire me full-time. All I need to make it happen is an interview with Charlie. In person if I can, by phone if I have to. You would be giving a huge break to a struggling reporter."

"We all have our jobs to do, Rhonda."

She gently took hold of my biceps, gave me a tug. "Please, Victor. I really need this."

I stopped, turned toward her, saw her green eyes swell with hope, and I felt an ache. It frightened me what I felt, an ache of wanting. She was a reporter—a life-form lower than a ferret, lower even than a lawyer—and I had no doubt but that she was trying to manipulate me for her own ends, anything for a story, but still I felt the ache. And yes, she was pretty, and yes, I liked her offhand manner, and yes, she treated me with an appealing lack of respect, but no, even then I could discern that my feelings had little to do with the truth of her inner being and everything to do with some pathetic need of my own.

I had felt the same ache for a bicyclist with long blond hair and pretty pink riding shoes who had asked for directions on the parkway. And before that I had felt it for a woman in a short black skirt whom I had spied across the street and who, without bending her legs, had leaned down to tighten the laces on her bulky black shoe. I could walk along the street during my lunch hour and fall in love a dozen times and feel the ache as each woman strode on through her life without me. And it was undoubtedly the same ache that had driven me, insensible with drink, to tattoo a stranger's name upon my chest in a declaration of love.

Either I was a wildly warm and openhearted person or my life was in serious trouble. And, unfortunately, I am not that warm and openhearted a guy.

Yet still, even if all those other supposed emotional connections were the result of some existential psychosis of the soul, who was to say that this emotion, the one I was feeling right now toward this woman with the blazing red hair and freckled face, might not be the real deal?

"Rhonda," I said with a slight stutter, "maybe we can go out sometime and get a drink."

She slipped on a sly smile. "Does that mean . . . ?"

"We'll talk about it over a drink. And maybe, if everything feels right and the circumstances allow it, maybe I'll talk to my client about you and your article."

"That would be just so great, Victor," she said. "Thank you, thank you so much. When?"

"I'll get back to you," I said. I glanced again at my watch. "But right now I have an eviction to fight."

CHAPTER

15

There are about fifty cases on the list each day in Courtroom 500 on South Eleventh Street, the city's housing court, yet only about three of those cases ever get tried. Instead most business is conducted, as in all courthouses, in the hallways, which is where Beth and I stood before our hearing when we were approached by a man with blond hair and a snappy green suit. About my age, but you could tell he had climbed higher on the legal ladder, which meant that I disliked him right off.

"Victor Carl?" he said.

"That's right."

"I thought so. Funny, you look younger on TV."

"And heavier, too, I suppose."

"No," he said. "Not really. Just younger and better dressed. Wait, please, I have something for you."

He balanced his briefcase on his palm as he unsnapped it open and pulled out an envelope, which he handed to me.

"A notice of eviction for your client, ordering her to depart her premises at the expiration of her lease," he said with a smile. "Personally delivered. Give it to Ms. Derringer for us, will you?"

I nodded and handed it over to Beth. "Here you go."

"Ah, so you are the recalcitrant Ms. Derringer," said the

man. "My name is Eugene Franks, of the law firm of Talbott, Kittredge and Chase, and I represent your landlord."

"Charmed, I'm sure," she said, her voice sounding neither charmed nor sure.

"I'm so sorry that your notice of eviction was only sent by mail and not personally delivered or nailed onto your door pursuant to the letter of the law, as your lawyer here pointed out in his rather voluminous brief. Actually, many of our tenants find mail delivery less embarrassing, not to mention less harsh on the front door, but from now on everything will be taken care of exactly by the book. We still expect you out when your lease expires."

"I don't think so, Eugene," I said. "Her original lease was in excess of one year, so your notice has to give her at least ninety days. From the date of notice. Which, based on this, is today."

"Aren't you being a little technical, Victor?"

"We're technicians, Eugene, you and I. Being nontechnical is akin to malpractice. When is construction scheduled to start at the building?"

"Next month."

"Ooh," I said as I winced dramatically. "That might be hard, with a tenant living in the building. Does your building permit allow knocking down walls and ripping up floors with a tenant still in residence? And the building is quite old. I wonder if there's any asbestos in the walls and ceilings. That would mess up the schedule even more than you already have, don't you think?"

He leaned toward me, lowered his voice. "Can we talk for a minute?"

"Sure," I said. I waved Beth over to one of the benches and then stepped with Eugene Franks to the far side of the hallway.

"Nice brief," he said.

"I try."

"We all had quite the laugh at the firm. Do you really think that the Fourteenth and Sixteenth Amendments to the United States Constitution really have any relevance here in housing court?"

"Maybe you should keep laughing in front of the judge. I'm sure she finds the badges and incidents of slavery hilarious."

"But your client isn't even black."

"Wait till you hear the argument."

"I'm on pins and needles." Eugene pursed his lips at me. "Weren't you the one who took down William Prescott a couple years ago?"

"I might have been."

"Prescott was the first lawyer at the firm I ever worked with. He was my mentor, he gave me my first big case, and you ruined his career."

"Prescott ruined his own career," I said. "I just pointed it out to the proper authorities."

Eugene Franks looked hard at me for a long moment and then turned away. "I never liked the son of a bitch. What can we do to make this disappear, Victor?"

"She doesn't want to move."

"It's just a move. She'll find a better place. It's no big deal."

"Not to her."

"We only want to spruce the place up, sell the new units, make some money. We're not bad guys here."

"I know."

"How much money are we talking about to get her out within the month?"

"Money's not the point. It never is with her."

"I find that distressing."

"Don't get me started."

"You know, Victor, it sounds a little Zen, but change happens. The building is going condo. Can you talk to her, please? Can you see what we can work out before we have to start arguing about the Sixteenth Amendment in front of the judge?"

"I'll try," I said.

Beth was sitting on a bench in a strangely passive position, hands on knees, head lolling slightly to the side. Normally before court she was a bundle of energy, sitting on the edge of her chair, her body in constant motion as she worked out the arguments in her head. But not today, not here, in the unusual position of litigant in the case of *Triad Investments, LP. v. Derringer*.

I sat down next to her. "I bought you some more time," I said.

"Thank you."

"I can try to string it out a little longer. I have some arguments for the judge."

"I read the brief. Your arguments are hopeless."

"I know, but I liked the way Franks there must have sputtered when he read them. And the judge can always take longer than expected to make a ruling. I could talk to the clerk. I think I know his brother."

"Okay. That might work."

"But you know, Beth, this Eugene Franks, he's not such a bad guy after all."

"In that suit he looks like a frog."

"And the people he represents are not evil. They're just businesspeople."

"They're kicking me out of my home."

"They're allowed. By law. You're eventually going to have to move."

"So they say."

"And fighting it isn't really the answer."

"But it sure feels good."

"Beth, what's going on, really?"

"I don't know, Victor. I feel . . . paralyzed. It's not that I even like my place so much. It's just that I can't face the idea of packing everything up, looking for a new apartment, moving, unpacking everything again, and it all being the same, the same bed, the same table, the same existence. Ever since that thing with François and the dredging up of the memories of my father, my life has taken on this weird momentum, just rolling along of its own accord toward nowhere. I don't find it particularly satisfying, and I don't seem to have the courage to direct it in any particular direction. But maybe, I think, if I can just stay in my stinking apartment for a few more stinking years, everything would be perfect."

"Your logic is impressive. But things aren't as bad as you make them out to be. Look at the firm. Business is better every day."

"We're getting by, and it seems like that's all we've been doing for years now. Getting by."

"We're fighting the good fight. What about Theresa Wellman? We're going to win her back her kid."

"You're going to win her back her kid. I feel like I'm just along for the ride. I need to do something, but I don't know what."

"What do you want to have happen here, today? How about getting some money?"

"Okay."

"Really?"

"Sure. Money's good. It would be fun to have a yacht, don't you think? Blue blazers, white pants."

"It's a good look for you."

"I should have been born a Pierpont."

"It won't be much, but I can get you something. Though you'll have to move out by the end of the month."

"All right."

"Really? I'm surprised. It's not like you to give in to the lure of easy cash."

"I'm sorry, Victor. This whole thing is stupid. I should never have dragged you into it, especially with Theresa's case coming to trial and you running around making a deal for Charlie Kalakos. I should have looked for a new place as soon as I got the notice. I guess I'm a little lost."

"We're lost together."

"I don't know, you've looked happier lately."

"It's because I'm in love. With a reporter."

"Really?"

"At least today. Yesterday it was a girl on a bike."

"I guess you're looking for something, too."

"Guess so. And remember when that dental hygienist tore up my apartment?"

"Sure."

"I haven't fixed it up yet."

"Victor?"

"It's still trashed."

"Victor." She laughed darkly. "That's pretty bad."

"Yeah."

"All it would take is one visit to IKEA."

"But I hate IKEA, all that blond wood and Swedish cheer. My name's not Sven, I'm not still in college, I don't even know what a loganberry is. An IKEA apartment would be the death of me."

"My God, Victor, you're in worse shape than I am."

I pressed my chest, felt the sting of the new tattoo still on my flesh. "And you don't know the half of it. Always remember, Beth, however much trouble you're in, I'm in more. Why don't I go now and see what kind of money I can get for you?"

"Okay."

I stood up and turned toward Eugene Franks, who was staring at us with hope on his face.

"How much are you looking for?" I said to her quietly.

"Whatever."

"I think that can be arranged."

I shook my head as I made my way over to Franks. He raised his eyebrows.

"No deal," I said. "Sorry. She absolutely, positively could not be bought. She intends to stay in her apartment until the very last hour. It's the principle of the thing, she said."

"I hate principles," said Franks. "They have no place in the practice of law."

"Tell me about it," I said. "But that's the kind of woman she is."

"There's nothing you can say?"

"I tried," I said. "I tried everything. Let's go in and stand in line, tell the judge we're going to trial. We're somewhere at the end of the list, so we should get called by mid-afternoon."

He looked at his watch. "I can't be here all day waiting for this stupid case. I have a meeting with the managing partner and a new client."

"Stanford Quick, right? The guy who represents the Randolph Trust."

"That's his pro bono client. The rest are all corporate giants."

"What's his story?"

"Typical bastard. Doesn't like to be kept waiting by mere associates."

"Sorry, Eugene, but she's adamant. If you want a continuance, I'd have no objection—"

"Do you have any idea how much we'll lose every day construction is delayed? I have to handle this today."

"Okay, then. I guess we have no choice but to take this to the judge."

We stepped together toward the courtroom doors, swung them open. The noise and smell hit us all at once. Housing court that day was like the Emma Lazarus poem at the base of the Statue of Liberty come alive: the tired, the poor, the huddled masses, the wretched refuse, homeless and tempest-tossed.

Franks sniffed and took one step back. "What about, Victor, if we come up with a figure that just out-and-out wows her?"

"Well, Eugene," I said, shaking my head with a sad certainty, "I doubt that will do it, but we could always try."

CHAPTER

16

The candle and incense, the darkness and thick, plague-infested air, the piled pillows at the head of the bed, the racking cough, the specter of death crouching like a gargoyle on the thin, aged chest.

"You want cup coffee, Victor?"

"No thank you, Mrs. Kalakos."

"I'll shout down to Thalassa, she brew pot. Insipid what she brews, more like spit than coffee, what with her using the grounds over and over, but still you can have."

"Really, I am fine."

"Come close, then. Sit. We need talk."

I came close, I sat. She reached her hand to my cheek. I tried not to flinch at the feel of her oily skin, the waft of her breath.

"You been on TV. My Charlie, he's become a celebrity because of painting. Which is funny, since my Charlie, he couldn't draw a dog."

"Someone else went to the press about the painting."

"Not you, Victor? You seem to enjoy it so. Then who?"

"I don't know, but once it was out, I thought giving the interviews was the best thing for Charlie. But it might not have worked out that way."

"What's matter, Victor? You have problem?"

"Charlie does, yes," I said. "I need you to get him in touch with me."

"Of course. But tell me first, what is trouble?"

"I really need to talk to Charlie about it," I said. "He's the client."

"But he's my son, Victor. I know what he needs. It always was such, and is no different now. None of us ever change, and Charlie, he changes less. You tell me his problem, I tell you how to solve."

"I'm not sure I can do that, ma'am."

She made some sort of hacking sound, and then the coughing began, great heaping coughs that brought her body into spasm. In the middle of it all, she raised her right hand, let it hover in the air for a moment, and then slapped my ear, hard.

"Ow."

Her coughing subsided as quickly as it began. "Don't tell me 'can't,' " she said. "You have obligation."

As I rubbed the side of my head, I said softly, "What obligation?"

"Whether you know or not, it wraps round your neck like snake and it is alive. So don't say 'can't' to me, Victor. You have good Greek face, but you not Greek enough down there to say 'can't' to me."

"What favor did you do for my father?"

"Why you ask me? Ask him. Or are you afraid of him, too?"

"Not afraid, exactly."

She barked out a laugh, bitter and understanding all at once. "I wouldn't want to have to call your father again. It upsets him so to hear from me."

"I bet it does."

"So now that this nonsense is finished with, tell me about my Charlie."

"There are a couple things. A reporter wants to interview Charlie. I thought it might help prod the government."

"No. What else?"

"This reporter seems sincere, and I'm not sure how it can hurt."

"It is reporter. They can always hurt. And remember what I tell you about my son? He's fool. You think anything he say can help, maybe you fool, too. What else you got?"

"It's not going to be as easy as we thought getting him home."

"Tell me."

"First, it appears, even after fifteen years, Charlie is still in danger. I received a visit from Charlie's old gang. The visitors roughed me up a little and then said worse would come Charlie's way if he came home."

"Okay, no problem. Lean close. This is what we do. We don't tell Charlie nothing about this."

"I can't do that, Mrs. Kalakos."

"You can and you will. Charlie is coward. He was afraid of bath, he was afraid of girls, he shakes in terror from his own shadow. It is why he ran so long ago. We tell him this, he disappear for good. You no tell him. Better we protect him when he comes."

"They're going to kill him if he comes home, Mrs. Kalakos."

"Pooh, Victor. They just talking. Big talkers, all of them. They want to come, they come to me, right? I'm reason for my Charlie to come home. And when they come, I show them something."

She sat up, reached over to a table by her bed, opened a drawer, pulled out an obscenely huge gun that glittered gaily in the candlelight.

"Gad, Mrs. Kalakos. That's a cannon."

"Let them come. I blow holes in them size of grapefruits. You hungry, Victor? You want grapefruit? I'll call down to Thalassa to bring you grapefruit."

"No thank you, ma'am, no grapefruit. Do you have a license for that?"

"I'm eighty-nine years old, what I need piece paper for?"

"You should get a license for the gun."

"Be like that, Victor, and I won't tell you what else I have for those *skatofatses*."

"Believe me, I don't want to know. I'm going to have to tell your son about the threats, Mrs. Kalakos."

She waved the gun a bit before shoving it back into the drawer. "Do what you must. But you tell him, too, that I take care of it for him, I protect him if police won't. What next?"

"There's a federal prosecutor who is causing problems. She's the key in allowing Charlie to come home without being thrown in jail, but she is refusing to do anything unless Charlie gives her what she wants."

"And what is it she wants?"

"She wants him to talk. To tell her everything."

"No problem. I make him talk."

"But she doesn't want him to just talk about the Warrick Brothers Gang. She wants him to talk about before that, about what went down when that painting was stolen thirty years ago."

She looked at me for a long moment, her moist eyes glittering in the sputtering candlelight. "Ah, yes," she said finally. "That might be problem. You have friends, Victor? Old friends, from when you were child, friends that are closer than brothers, closer than blood?"

"No, ma'am," I said.

"Too bad for you. I had friends like that in old country, and Charlie, despite himself, he found such friends here. When they was just toddlers, they ran around with each other in the blow-up pools. Five closest friends in all the world. My Charlie, and Hugo, always running around like a crazy boy, all legs, he was, and Ralph Ciulla, big like man already at twelve, and little Joey Pride. And then, of course, Teddy, Teddy Pravitz, who was leader. Five neighborhood boys, always together, always. Once—and I tell you this so you know what it was—once a group from the Oxford Circle—you know this place?"

"Down Cottman?"

"Yes, exactly. Once a group boys came into our neighborhood looking for trouble. This was when my son Charles was in high school. The Oxford boys found little Joey Pride. Joey was a nice boy, but black and with a mouth on him, and they beat him bloody. Just for the sport of it, Victor. Animals. The police threw up their hands. What was to do? But Teddy, he knew what to do."

"What was that, Mrs. Kalakos?"

"You want tea? I call down to Thalassa."

"No thank you, ma'am. Really, I'm fine."

"No, we need tea." She opened her mouth wide and shrieked, "Thalassa. Come now."

There was the sound of something dropping onto the floor below, a rustle, a sigh, weary footfalls rising up the stairs. The door creaked open, a withered face appeared.

"Victor, he wants tea," said Mrs. Kalakos.

Thalassa turned her head to me, stared with unalloyed hatred.

"He likes sugar with his tea," said Mrs. Kalakos. "And those round cookies."

"Really, I'm fine," I said.

The face slipped away, the door creaked closed.

"She good girl. Alas, her tea, it is thin like her blood. She saves her tea bags from cup to cup, as if tea were gold. We still have tea from when Clinton was president. Ah, Clinton, he was part Greek, he didn't know it, but I could tell."

"What did Teddy do after the beating?"

"Teddy, he was such a beautiful boy. So clever. He came to me, asked for keys to my car. I knew what he wanted, and so I gave to him. That boy was Greek where it counted. Off they went into the night, even Joey with his arm in sling, the five of them with their blood hot and their baseball bats, off they went. And they took care of it, Victor. It didn't even matter that he was wrong boy. Those animals from Oxford Circle, they not come round no more. The boys protected each other, you understand? Such bond survives the years."

"And these were the guys who pulled off the theft?"

She patted my cheek. "You smart boy. You sure you don't want to date my Thalassa?"

"No, ma'am. But this is what I don't understand, Mrs. Kalakos. I heard it was a crack team of professional thieves that robbed the Randolph Trust, not five schmoes from the neighborhood. So how did they do it?"

"They were not simply five schmoes from neighborhood, Victor. They were four schmoes and Teddy. That is difference."

Just then the door creaked open, and Thalassa, with gray body hunched and gray head bowed, brought in a tray. Mrs. Kalakos was right, the tea was weak, and musty, it tasted as old as Thalassa looked, but the cookies were surprisingly delicious. I was on my fourth cookie when my cell phone rang.

I stood up, slipped into the dark corner of the dark room, flipped it open. "Carl," I said.

"You free tonight, mate?" said the unmistakable voice of Phil Skink.

I looked at Mrs. Kalakos, sitting up now, her pale face bowed toward a porcelain teacup, steam rising around her sunken eyes. "Sure," I said. "I'm in a meeting, but it won't last much longer. What's up?"

"I gots someone I wants you to meet."

My heart skipped a beat. I could feel myself blushing in the darkness. "Did you find her?" I said. "Did you find Chantal Adair?"

"That's what I wants you to tell me."

CHAPTER
17

"Where are we going, Phil?" I said as I drove us down Spring Garden Street toward the eastern edge of the city.

"I just wants you to check someone out," he said.

"Is it her?"

"Don't know, does I? I put out the word, quietly like you asked, and this came back my way as a possibility. Things, they are not exactly as you'd expect in one way, and then"—he laughed—"in another way they's exactly as you'd expect."

"Did you take a picture? I might not want her to be the one, if you get my drift. Did I tell you I have a thing about mustaches? Big, thick mustaches? I don't like them on women. I don't like them on men either, actually, but on women they give me the creeps."

"Look, mate, if she's the one whose name you got scrawled on your chest, you'll like the looks of her, don't be worrying about that. But I gots some other pictures, too. You want to see them first?"

"Sure."

"All righty," he said. "Pull over there."

I edged the car to the side of the road, stopped behind a parked van, put it in neutral and left the engine running. Skink turned on the overhead light and took an envelope out of his suit pocket.

"There was no Chantal Adairs listed for Philly, South Jersey, or Delaware," he said, "but I found us a few C. Adairs, with no first name given. Usually an initial instead of a first name is a lady trying not to look like a lady in the book in case a predator is stalking, you got me? So I checked out thems that I could. Found one in Absecon, one in Horsham. Take a peek and see if a face rings a bell."

He passed me over the first of the photographs. A color shot, a little grainy and taken from pretty far away. It wasn't the clearest photograph, but right off I could tell that the woman in the picture was not whom I was looking for. She was older, much older, with steel gray hair that matched her walker.

"Is this a joke?" I said.

"Don't know what you are into these days, mate, now, do I?"

"Who else?"

The next photograph was of a younger woman, hugely pregnant, holding a young child on her ample hip. She had a pretty face, though, despite her evident maternity, and I squinted to see if it was familiar.

"I don't know," I said. "I don't think I ever saw her before."

"Don't think so neither, since her name is Catherine."

"Then what was the point of showing me the photograph?"

"I just wanted you to know they ain't too many of these Chantal Adairs out there. So you won't be sniffing up your nose at who we're seeing tonight." He switched off the light. "Let's get a move on."

I popped the car in gear, pulled out from behind the van, and continued heading east.

"What do you mean," I said, "that things aren't exactly like I would expect?"

"Well, her name ain't exactly what you got printed there on your chest."

"Then exactly why are we checking her out?"

"Because it's close enough."

"Close enough for what?"

"For you to tell me if she's the one. Turn there."

I turned. "What if I don't remember her?"

"Then maybe she'll remember you. Okay, take a right and then go under that bridge."

"What's that there?" I said, nodding toward a bright neon sign.

"Where we're headed, mate. Pull in to the lot."

The parking lot surrounded a one-story building wedged beneath a highway bridge. The lot held pickups and high-priced sedans, the building was painted black, the purple neon in the sign was blinking, alternately spelling out the name of the place in script and then showing a figure, a female figure, like the kind of thing you see on the mud flaps of a sixteen-wheeler. I stopped the car in the middle of the lot, felt my expectations deflate and my heart sicken. But I should never have been surprised. Whenever men head off into the limitless American night in search of true love, they more often than not end up at a strip joint.

"Club Lola?" I said, a tone of defeat in my voice.

"'At's it, all right."

"Isn't this the place where that guy met the stripper he killed his wife for?"

"'At's the one."

"And I suppose this Chantal Adair is one of the dancers here."

"'At's what we're here to find out."

"What's the point?" I said. "Of all the things I could have imagined for the tattoo on my chest, this is the absolute worst. What kind of loser gets drunk, ends up at a strip bar, falls in love with a stripper, and is determined to show her his undying devotion by tattooing her name on his chest?"

"We'll find out tonight, won't we?"

"Forget it. It's no mystery how this story turns out."

"You don't want to know for sure?"

"I've seen enough already to know the whole thing is a crushing mistake."

"If you give up now, mate, whenever you look in the mirror, you'll always think the worst," said Skink. "Not about the bird but about yourself. Park the car. Let's find out what's what."

"You just want an evening's entertainment."

"That, too, yes, and on your dime, which makes it all the sweeter."

I could feel the bass of the music even before I reached the entrance. My general rule is to never go into a place where the bouncer is dressed entirely in black and sports a ponytail, which conveniently keeps me out of all the places that don't want me inside, but I suppose this was an exception.

"You ever see me before?" I said to the bouncer as I paid the cover for the two of us.

Without looking up, he said, "I got a bad memory for faces."

"But this was just a few nights ago."

He lifted his head, sniffed like a Doberman. "If I didn't kick you out, I didn't know you was in. That's the way it is. Keeps me out of the courtroom, if you know what I mean."

"Yeah, I know," I said. "But was I in?"

"Like I said. And I'll tell the wife the same thing."

"Well," I said, taking my change, "that is a relief."

And off we went, into the fleshpot.

18

Club Lola was a wide, spotlit room, smoke-filled, dark-walled, with scores of tables and a long bar across the far side. There was a grand stage in the middle, on which a woman with a G-string and pasties and white high heels was hanging upside down. Her legs were hooked around a shiny pole, her hands were hooked around her breasts. The music was loud, the tables were small, the chairs were plush, the dancer was licking her own breast with a long, narrow tongue. Nice family entertainment.

The joint was half full, customers sitting with strange sated looks on their faces as a pack of she-wolves in high heels and sheer bikinis, their surgically enhanced bodies adorned with bracelets and tattoos, swarmed and socialized. What is it about high heels and bikinis that sings seductive songs straight to the masculine gut? And all it took was one look at the bikini tops to know that the air conditioner was definitely on.

Skink thumbed his fedora back on his head, took a cigar out of his jacket pocket, spread his arms wide, breathed deep the foul air. "My kind of place," he said.

"I bet," I said.

"Classy is what I mean. It's got ambience."

"It's got something, all right."

"Oh, quit your bellyaching. Let me buys you a drink."

"On the expense account you'll be charging back to me?"

"Victor, mate, what do you take me for?"

"That means yes."

"I'll see what kind of action we can rustle up. Now, take a seat, pop a smile, and enjoy yourself."

I sat, I smiled, but I didn't enjoy myself. And it wasn't just the mark of loserhood on my chest that was dampening my mood.

I know, I know, every woman believes that every man, in his secret heart, loves a strip club. But I, for one, don't. They give me the skives, and I think I know why. Every time I enter a joint like Club Lola, I feel squirrelly about the roles available to men in the little strip-club drama.

Am I the arrogant he-man who just assumes it is his due to have beautiful women wind their naked bodies into knots for my amusement? Am I the pitiable misfit who has to pay to get this close to a woman's bare flesh? Am I the bored husband who spends my nights getting angry at my life as I stare at the type of woman I should have married? Or, worst of all, am I the romantic sap who thinks that the dancer, there, that one, with the sweet eyes and full rack, really really likes me? No, really, she does. Really.

While I was having my existential strip-club crisis, Skink was having none of it. He knew exactly who he was and what he was doing there as he leaned back in his chair, a beer in one hand, his cigar in the other, and a dancer's wriggling J.Lo smack in his face.

"Oh, that's nice," said Skink, his gap-toothed grin broad and gleaming. "Just like that. Yes. Oh, that's just terrific."

"Anything else you want?" said the dancer, who had introduced herself as Scarlet.

"Why don't you turn around, sweetheart, and I'll slip in a little something just for you."

Scarlet did a spin, leaned forward with her back arched

dramatically, pulled down the bikini top with her thumbs, and shimmied. It was all so festive, even her pasties glistened brightly, like twin disco balls.

"Is Chantal in tonight?" said Skink as he slipped a bill into the side of her G-string.

"She's in back," said Scarlet. While she talked, she worked her shimmy as efficiently as a bank clerk counting bills.

"Can you send her over?"

"What, this isn't good enough for you?"

"Too good," said Skink. "You stick around much longer, my head is going to burst into flame." He slipped in another bill. "Be a honey and send over Chantal."

As Scarlet gathered up the cash and sauntered off toward the curtain beside the bar, Skink turned to me, his grin still in place. "This is why I became a PI."

"It's nice for you that you found your calling."

"You recognize anyone?"

I looked around at the women wandering the floor, talking to strange men or dancing on the stages in shifts, some good-looking, some great, all nearly naked, the sight of their bodies as available as the channels on a television set.

"Not a one," I said.

"How about her?" said Skink, gesturing toward a tall brunette who was walking toward us.

"I don't think so."

"You sure?"

"Her, I'd have remembered."

And I would have, too. She was like Fantasy Woman Version 2.0, new and improved, now with even longer legs and less clothing than before. What with her red heels, her thin hips, her high firm breasts, pale skin, green G-string, blue eyes, a mouth just irregular enough to trap your eye and get you thinking, it actually hurt to gaze upon her. It was as if she embodied in the flesh all the possibilities of your life that had never come true. No matter what doubts I might have had before about my role in that club, her very beauty defined it with utter definitiveness: She was what I could never have, I was the pathetic loser who had paid to stare.

"Hello, boys," she said in a silvery voice as she placed her right high heel on the little round table between our chairs. A red rose was tattooed on her ankle. "My name's Chantal."

She bent forward at the waist and then back in some twisty ballet move. The line in her calf tensed. I leaned close to smell the flower. I could see a scuff within the gleam of her high heel, and I had the strange urge to polish it with my tongue. Her black hair was straight and glossy, and when it whipped close to my nose I smelled lilac, in a field, with bees buzzing. Or was that just my blood?

It doesn't take much to break down my defenses, does it?

"Did you boys ask to see me?" she said.

"Uh, yes," said Skink in a suddenly weak voice. "Yes, we did."

She kept to her slow twisting, leaning her upper body over Skink as she said, "And what's your name?"

"Phil," he said. "The name's, uh, Phil."

"Just like that cute little groundhog," she said. "And you look like him, too, with that gap in your teeth. So what can I do for you, uh, Phil?" Her voice dripped with a promise more languid than lascivious. "What do you like?"

"Oh, I like everything," said Skink, "yes, I do." He shook his head, gathered himself. "But we're not here for me. We're here for my friend," he said, jabbing his thumb toward me.

"Oh," she said, "is this a bachelor party?"

"Of a sort," said Skink, "seeing as we're both bachelors."

With her foot still on the table, she faced away from me, showing off a tattooed shepherd's crook on her lower back, and then leaned backward, farther and farther, until her spine bent like a bow and her hands reached the far armrest of my chair. There was a white dove tattooed on her right shoulder. Her face was inches from mine.

"Hi," she said in that Tiffany voice as her body bent and surged to the rhythm of the music. "I'm Chantal."

The place suddenly grew hot, as if a furnace had sprung on.

"Hi, Chantal," I said.

"Do you like pinball? I like pinball, how the shiny little balls bounce around crazily. Just the way your eyes are bouncing around right now."

"Are they?"

"Oh, yes. Be careful not to tilt." She laughed, a sweet little girl's laugh. "And what's your name, honey?"

"Don't you recognize me?" I said.

A blankness washed across her face as she examined me before she forced a professional smile onto that gorgeous mouth. "Of course," she said. "How are you? It's so good to see you again. Thanks for coming back."

"You've never seen me before, have you?"

"No, I have, really. You're so sweet, and so good-looking, how could I not remember?"

"Then what's my name?" I said.

"Your name?"

She pushed herself off my chair and slowly straightened her long torso. She took her lovely shoe off the table, stepped back, stared at me for a moment like I was crazy, looked at Skink, then again at me.

"Is it Bob?" she said.

The humiliation of it all brought me back to my senses. I straightened my pants, stood up, closed my jacket as best I could. "Let's go, Phil."

"Wait just a second," said Skink. "No need to rush away when things is just getting interesting. Do us a favor, sweetheart, and tell us your name?"

"I told you already," she said, her voice suddenly not so silvery.

"But you only told us half. Chantal what?"

"Just Chantal," she said. "We only have first names here. Like Cher. And Beyoncé."

"Yeah," I said. "Just like. And I suppose Chantal's your real name."

"Sure," she said with a light laugh. "Just like Desirée is Desirée's real name and Scarlet is Scarlet's real name. And don't even get me started on Lola herself."

"Lola, huh?" said Skink. "Who is she really?"

Chantal leaned forward toward Skink, lowered her voice to a conspirator's whisper. "Sid," she said.

Skink burst out in appreciative laughter.

"What's this all about?" she said. "Why are you asking so many questions? Are you guys cops?"

"Do we look like cops?" I said.

"He does," she said, indicating Skink. "You look more like a high school guidance counselor."

"We're looking for someone," said Skink, "and we thought you might be her."

"Am I?"

"No," I said. "You're not. We're sorry to take up your time."

"So who is it you guys are looking for?"

"A girl name of Chantal," said Skink. "Just like you."

"Chantal who?"

"Chantal Adair."

She stared at us for a long moment, stared at us like we were specters from another world who were shimmering in and out of her reality. "Are you kidding me?"

"Why?" said Skink. "You know her?"

"Look," she said, backing away and crossing her arms

over her chest. "I have to dance, okay. It's my turn on the stage."

"Are you her?" I said.

"The farthest thing," she said.

"But you do know her."

I took a step forward, gently put a hand on her wrist. She looked down at my hand, then up at my face.

"What's your game?" she said.

"We're just looking for a dame, is all," said Skink.

"Well, if you're looking for her, you'll be looking for a long time," she said. "Chantal Adair was my sister. But she disappeared two years before I was born."

She smiled tightly, put her hand on my chest and pushed me away before she turned around and walked toward the bar. She leaned over it, arms still crossed, looking as if she had stomach cramps. She began talking to the bartender, talking about us, we could tell, because he was glancing our way. He gave her a drink, she downed it quickly.

"I guess she's not the one," I said.

"Worth a tattoo if she is, mate. Got to give her that."

"Yeah, but the name isn't hers."

"Her real name's Monica, Monica Adair," said Skink. "But it seemed worth a shot, what with the fake dance name and the real last name both matching the tattoo."

"Yeah, I suppose. It's a little weird, though, don't you think, using her missing sister's name to dance to?"

"She's a stripper, which explains a lot. I knew a girl out in Tucson—"

"I bet you did," I said, "but I don't really want to hear about it right now. I'm going home."

"I think I'll stay around a bit longer."

"I'm not surprised."

"Research, mate."

"Your enthusiasm for the job is heartwarming."

"I got a second possibility on the tattoo front. Since this didn't pan out, I'll set up that one."

"Another strip joint?"

"Nah, something a little more technical. I got me a guy what—"

Skink stopped in midsentence, which was a rare and wondrous feat. I followed his gaze, to see what had interrupted his chain of thought. It was Monica Adair, coming back our way, a strange smile on her face. She walked right up to me and put her hand on my arm.

"You never told me your name," she said to me.

"Victor," I said.

"Are you leaving, Victor? So soon?"

"I have to get home. Big day tomorrow. Big day."

"I'm up next on the stage, but then I can get out a little early. Sid owes me. Are you hungry?"

"It's kind of late, don't you think?"

"Oh, Victor, it's never too late to eat. And if you want, while we eat, we can talk about my sister."

19

It's not every day you sit in a diner with a stripper while she talks about a saint.

"Did you ever learn about St. Solange?" said Monica, her voice still silvery and childlike. Inside the confines of Club Lola, where every woman was there solely to satisfy a man's most puerile urges—long limbs to wrap you tight, abundant breasts to suckle—the voice fit in perfectly. But here, in the Melrose Diner on Passyunk Avenue in the hard heart of South Philly, it was more than passing strange.

"No, never," I said. "My people weren't much for saints."

"Not Catholic?"

"Jewish."

"That's too bad. Nothing is as comforting as a saint in times of stress."

"I prefer beer," I said.

She had taken the night off after her stint on the stage—a stint full of enough tricks and stunts to make even a politician blush—so she could talk about her sister. And I must say she cleaned up nice, did Monica Adair. Usually that expression refers to someone all dolled up for a change, but it was the opposite with her. In a pair of jeans and a T-shirt, sneakers, her makeup wiped off and her glossy hair pulled into a ponytail, she looked like the prettiest, most wholesome college kid you'd ever want to meet. But all it took was for her to open her mouth for you to realize she was also a total wack job.

"My mother is crazy for them," said Monica. "Saints, I mean. Saints and plates with paintings of clowns. My sister and I were each named after the saint on whose feast day we were born. Chantal was named for St. Jeanne de Chantal, the patron saint of parents separated from their children, which I suppose is a little sad, considering how things turned out."

"What about you?"

"August twenty-seventh, the feast day for St. Monica of Hippo. The patron saint of disappointing children. Are you going to eat that pickle?"

"No," I said. "Help yourself."

She reached over and plucked the long green sliver from my plate, snapped it between her teeth.

"It could be worse, though," she said. "We could have been named after the clowns. Could you do me a favor and straighten your tie?"

"My tie?"

"Yeah, it's a little off to the side. The other way, right. Stuff like that drives me crazy. Or untied shoelaces, or specks of dust on a lapel. And I wash my hands a lot. Is that weird?"

"If I worked where you worked, I'd wash my hands a lot, too."

"Why?"

"I'm just saying—"

"I think they keep it quite clean."

"I was just—"

"But St. Solange was always my favorite saint," said Monica. "She was this shepherdess in France who took a vow of chastity when she was, like, eight. Then, when she was twelve, the son of the count on whose land she grazed her sheep put the moves on her. She refused him, so he pulled her off her horse and chopped off her head."

"Nasty," I said.

"But then, and this is what I like, apparently she rose up after she was killed, picked her head off the ground, and carried it into the nearby town and started preaching. It was like nothing could stop her from getting out her message. She would have been perfect on the *Today* show. Could you imagine Katie Couric doing the interview?"

"Talking head to talking head."

"But the way St. Solange kept preaching even when she was gone, that's what I feel about my sister."

"I don't understand."

"She disappeared before I was born, but it's like she still talks to me. It's like she's been talking to me every day of my life."

I leaned closer, searched for a sign of insanity on her pretty face. "What does she say?"

"Are you going to eat the rest of that sandwich?"

"Probably not," I said.

"Can I have it?"

"Knock yourself out," I said, but even before I said it, she was reaching for the half of the corned beef special that was still on my plate.

"Mmm, that's good," she said after she took a bite. A shred of coleslaw hung from the corner of her mouth before she wiped it away with her finger. "I get so hungry after I work."

"Tell me about your sister?" I said.

"Oh, Chantal, she was like a saint herself. The darling of the neighborhood. She was only six when she disappeared, but she was already special. She loved church, loved animals, took in a bird with a broken wing, a stray dog. I have a dog. Luke. He's a shar-pei. The one with all the wrinkled skin?"

"I don't know it."

"From China. Not Luke, I picked him up in Scranton. The breed, I mean. Quite an aggressive sort. Don't mess with a shar-pei. Don't play accordion either. That's about the sum total of my advice on life."

"I'll remember that."

"And anchovies."

"What about them?"

"I don't know, I'm still up in the air about anchovies. A little too salty, don't you think? But they're not bad on pizza. Chantal liked pizza, and french fries. But especially she liked to dance. She was, like, great. My parents still have old movies of her in her outfit, doing her routines. They watch them all the time. She was on that *Al Alberts Showcase.* Do you know the one on TV on Sunday mornings? With all the local talent?"

"Yeah, I remember it."

"She did a dance solo on it once. The Amazing Chantal Adair. Tap, with little red shoes. I still have those shoes, like Dorothy's ruby slippers."

"What happened to her?"

"No one knows. One day she went out into the neighborhood to play, like she did every day, and never came back. It was in the papers for months. The police were all over it, but they never found anything. Not her body, not a ransom note, nothing. It's like she clicked her ruby tap shoes and disappeared."

"That's awful."

"Yeah, it is." She reached over to my plate and swiped a potato chip. I pushed the plate toward her, and she took another. "It destroyed my parents. They had me to try to make up for it, but I wasn't quite enough, so their disappointment was doubled. They've never recovered."

"What do they think happened?"

"Everyone just assumed she was murdered somehow.

There was an old rummy in the neighborhood that was acting weird, but they could never pin anything definite on him. And then a rumor had it that some guy in a white van had been trawling the neighborhood for kids."

"It's always a white van, isn't it?"

"Yeah, why is that? I have to remind myself that next time I rob a bank I should use the brown van. That's the second time you looked at your watch. Do you have someplace you need to be?"

"It's just late," I said. "And I have to be in court tomorrow."

"Something important?"

"No, just a custody thing."

"It sounds important to me. Who do you represent?"

"The mother."

"That's nice. I'm all for mothers. Do you know who the patron saint of mothers is?"

"No."

"St. Gerard. He was accused of getting a woman pregnant and refused to speak until he was cleared."

"He must have had a good lawyer."

"You ever shoot a gun, Victor?"

"Never."

"I have one. I've never used it, but one day someone's going to break into the wrong apartment and bam."

"What with the dog and the gun, Monica, I think I'll stay out of your neighborhood."

"Oh, Luke. Luke wouldn't hurt anyone. And that one guy in the park, well, he was smoking, and Luke has this thing about cigarettes. But I don't think she was murdered. My sister, I mean. I don't think she's dead at all. Remember the girl that was supposed to have been burned to ashes in a fire, but it turned out she was stolen and living somewhere in New Jersey?"

"I remember."

"I think that's what happened. I think Chantal was taken someplace, taken because she was so perfect, and given a perfect life."

"By who?"

"By someone who loved her very much."

"It's nice to think it, I guess."

"I feel her presence all the time, like she's close, looking over my shoulder, looking out for me. That's what I meant when I said she's my St. Solange. Gone but still preaching. Chantal guides my life. Because of her my life has a purpose. I was conceived to fill a gap. That it hasn't worked out so well is a little sad, but still, it's more than most people have. That's why I use her name at the club. As a tribute."

"I'm sure she'd be touched."

"Really?" she said, her smile blinding, as if I had complimented her on her hair. "I hope so, though I expect she'll let me know sooner or later."

"You think after all these years she'll just up and call?"

"Oh, Victor, I don't just think it. I'm certain of it. How about some pie? I could go for some pie. Do you think they make pie here?"

"I'm sure they do," I said.

It wasn't lost on me that she didn't ask anything about how I had come up with her sister's name. She had waited all her life for the word, I suppose she figured she could wait for it to come out on its own. And in any event I wasn't about to tell her of my tattoo. It was both too embarrassing and too bizarre to share that with her, especially as I observed her slightly deranged discussion of her sister. Her sister, Chantal, was a strange fire burning within her, she didn't need me to toss on a bucket of gasoline.

So we ordered pie. I had the peach, she had the blueberry, with a dollop of ice cream on top. Even with the blue streaks on her teeth, she was beautiful. And sad, too. Usually I can spot it right off, that streak of sadness that speaks to some primal part of my personality, but with her I didn't. It was only as she spoke that it became clear, how her life had been so sadly influenced by the missing girl who was the warp and woof of her existence.

But about one thing I was certain. All of it, the whole sad story of her missing sister, had nothing to do with me. The Chantal Adair she had been waiting her whole life to hear from was not the Chantal Adair whose name I had foolhardily tattooed onto my chest.

Sometimes my head is as dense as a solid block of ebony.

CHAPTER
20

I have a big red file folder that I keep for special occasions. Sometimes it's full of documents, sometimes it's empty, but either way what's inside is not as essential as the file folder itself. I clutch it close to my breast as if it contained nuclear launch codes, or the phone number of a decent Chinese restaurant, or anything else important enough to belong in a big red file folder.

"What's in the file?" said Beth as we waited in the hallway of family court for Theresa Wellman.

"Just some information Phil Skink unearthed."

"Did he get anything on Bradley Hewitt?"

"He's working on it."

"Then what's in the file?"

"Oh, look," I said. "Here comes our client."

Theresa Wellman, with her hair done and her dress subdued, approached us warily.

"Are we going on with it today?" she said.

"Of course we are," said Beth. "Now you've got the firm of Derringer and Carl on your side. Bucking the odds is what we do. You're the first witness. Are you ready?"

"Oh, I'm ready. I love my daughter more than anything in the world. I just want to see her and hug her and take her home."

"I'm going to be asking you the questions, Theresa," I said. "There might be some things you don't expect."

"Like what?" she said.

"Stuff about your past and how things are going now."

"What things?"

"It's best if we do it all in court. You don't want to seem rehearsed. But whatever happens, Theresa, you have to trust that I'm doing what I can to help you."

She eyed the big red file folder I held at my chest, bit the bottom corner of her lip. "Why should I trust you?"

"Who else do you have?"

"It will be fine, Theresa," said Beth. "As long as you can convince the judge that you've really changed, we have a great shot for some sort of joint custody."

"Can we trust the judge?"

"Judge Sistine is impeccably fair and absolutely fearless," I said. "She might be wrong, but never for the wrong reasons."

"Just tell the truth," said Beth. "If the judge thinks you're hiding anything, it can really hurt your cause."

"Okay. I'll try."

"Trying isn't good enough," I said. "Whatever happens in there, it's okay to show your anger, it's okay to show your sadness, it's okay to show the whole gamut of your emotions, but tell the truth."

"And you think the truth will get me back my daughter?"

"It's the only thing that can," I said.

There was a bustle in the hallway as a small crowd came our way. It was led by a tall gray man in an expensive suit. He was accompanied by a lovely younger woman who held on to his arm, three men with dark suits and briefcases, and a perfectly coiffed man swathed in sharkskin. This last I had dealt with before. His name was Arthur Gullicksen, and the material of his suit was entirely appropriate.

"Victor?" he said as he approached. "I'm surprised to see you here. I thought Beth was handling this case."

"She's my partner," I said, "which means we work together on everything. She asked me to help, and so here I am."

"That's just fine," said Gullicksen, letting his gaze stray from my eyes to the big red file folder. "Have you met Bradley Hewitt?"

"No, I haven't," I said.

After Gullicksen made the introductions, the tall gray man said, "I've heard about you, Mr. Carl." His voice was incredibly deep and rich, almost as rich as his suit.

"Nothing bad, I hope."

"So many of us, I suppose, hope in vain," he said. He didn't smile as he said it, and yet his expression wasn't unkind. It was as if all of us were together in an unpleasant situation that was not of our own making, all of us but one. When he turned his gaze upon Theresa, something shifted in his expression. Theresa seemed to wilt under his attention, until she turned and fled into the courtroom.

"She just wants to be able to spend time with Belle," said Beth.

"You think that's best for my daughter?" said Hewitt.

"A girl needs her mother," said Beth.

"But not that mother," said Bradley Hewitt.

"Do you have a second, Victor?" said Gullicksen.

I glanced at Beth, who nodded me on, and so Gullicksen and I huddled at the far end of the hallway, out of earshot of the rest of the crowd.

"You know, of course, that this is a mistake," he said. "I could understand a motion like this coming from Beth. She has a reputation for not worrying about political realities, but I'm surprised to see you involved."

"We are representing a woman who simply wants to

live with her daughter again. What political reality am I missing?"

"Mr. Hewitt is an intriguing man, with connections to the highest levels of government."

"And he used that power to force a mother to give up her child."

"He used that power to protect his daughter from a woman who didn't know how to care for her. All your client wants now is the money that comes with custody. Be aware that my client will continue to protect his daughter by any means necessary."

"Is that a threat? Because I've been expecting one, Arthur, from the moment I got involved."

"Not a threat at all, Victor," said Gullicksen. "Just a friendly piece of advice. Mr. Hewitt is willing to allow supervised visitations for your client."

"She already turned that down. We want joint custody, fifty-fifty."

"Too bad. I hate to keep a mother from at least seeing her child. What's in the file you so carefully clutch to your chest?"

"Oh, odds and ends," I said.

"I have a red file folder of my own. It's a neat trick. I couldn't help noticing that you're involved in a highly sensitive case involving a fugitive and a painting. I hope nothing that happens here will in any way interfere with your efforts on behalf of your other client."

"Now, that does sound like a threat."

"As I said, Mr. Hewitt has much influence and many friends. Including Mr. Spurlock of the Randolph Trust."

"Let's keep our focus on a mother trying to regain her daughter."

"Okay, Victor, then I must ask. What do you really know about Theresa Wellman?"

"She had a rough patch," I said, "but she says she's changed."

"Is that what she says?" Gullicksen smiled at me like I had just told an amusing little anecdote. "Tell me, Victor, when did you start believing in the Easter Bunny?"

CHAPTER

21

    Judge Sistine was a large, humorless woman with the forearms of a bear. She sat stone-faced on the bench, taking notes, as I questioned Theresa Wellman. I sneaked glances up at her every now and then to see how Theresa's story was playing, but Judge Sistine was too good a jurist to show her hand. Still, I had little doubt that the testimony was having an effect.

It was Theresa doing the telling, that's the way it is in direct examination, but it was my questions that created the setting, that decided where was the beginning, that maintained the pace, that ensured the telling details made it into the record, that slowed everything down at the most emotionally painful parts, giving Theresa the space she needed to break into tears. Nothing lubricates the wheels of justice like a few tears.

It was the classic story of a girl, sheltered and innocent, who is swept off her feet and into a fast and thrilling lifestyle by an older, wealthy man. Gullicksen objected from the start, claiming that none of this was relevant to the matter at hand, but I stated that the background was crucially important, and the judge agreed with me. So I put it all out there and on the record, the parties, the travel, the fine clothes, the luxury apartment, the important people who were suddenly paying attention. It was glamorous, it was exotic, it was simply too fabulous for a young girl from West Philly to turn down. A fantasy come true, with a darkness at the center, because at the center of it all was the unequal relationship between the young woman and the powerful, older man, Bradley Hewitt.

"Let's go into some details about these parties you mentioned, Theresa," I said. "Was there drinking?"

"Oh, yes. Wine at dinner, of course, Bradley liked his wine. Often champagne. Liqueurs after dinner and then more champagne or maybe really fine Scotch."

"Did you drink much before meeting Mr. Hewitt?"

"My parents weren't drinkers."

"But you drank with Mr. Hewitt."

"He developed my taste."

"Were there any other intoxicants at these parties?"

"Marihuana," she said. "Cocaine often. Pills."

"Did you have much experience with drugs before meeting Mr. Hewitt?"

"No, not really."

"You grew up in West Philly, isn't that right?"

"I went to a parochial school, Mr. Carl. The nuns were very strict."

"Did Bradley partake of drugs at these parties?"

"Not so much, but he encouraged the others. And he encouraged me. Strongly. He said he liked having sex when I was stoned."

"And you acquiesced to his requests."

"Yes."

Slowly, we went through the hints of violence, the cheating, the humiliations, the verbal abuse. I didn't have her go into the physical abuse, since there were no witnesses to it, Bradley Hewitt would just deny it, and I wasn't quite sure if I believed it anyway. Instead we focused on the pregnancy, Bradley Hewitt's demand that Theresa have an abortion, her refusal, the bitter end of the fantasy as the relationship died. The birth, the sporadic support from the new child's father, his complete lack of interest in the baby, her need for more child support, the petition, the response, the fear, the decision to give up her custodial rights in exchange for a financial settlement.

"Why would you do such a thing, Theresa? Why would you agree to give up custody?"

"I thought I had no choice."

"There's always a choice, isn't there?"

"He was too powerful. My lawyer said he would win. I made a mistake. What can I say, Mr. Carl? I think about it every day. I guess I was afraid."

"Afraid of what?"

"Afraid of what Bradley would do to me if I kept fighting."

"Are you sure it wasn't fear of what would come out at the hearing?"

"I admitted I was having some problems at the time."

"It was more than just a few problems, though, wasn't it?" I said as I picked up the big red file folder, opened it, looked inside.

"I was going through things," she said.

"What kind of things?"

"I was drinking."

"How much?"

"Too much."

"How often?"

"A lot."

"Every day, right? Day and night, even while you were caring for your daughter."

"I always cared for my daughter."

"Were you using drugs, too?"

"Not really."

"Theresa?" I said, waving the big red file folder.

"Some."

"How much?"

"What are you doing, Mr. Carl?"

"I'm trying to understand a crucial decision in your life. Not every mother agrees to give up the custody to her daughter. Were you addicted to drugs at the time you made that agreement?"

"I don't think I was addicted."

"What were you using?"

"Nothing much."

"Marihuana?"

"Yes."

"Cocaine?"

"Some."

"Crack?"

"Mr. Carl, stop this. What are you doing? I just want my daughter back."

"Were you using crack cocaine at the time you sued for child support?"

"I tried it."

"How often did you use it?"

"I don't know."

"Yes you do, Theresa. You were addicted to it, weren't you?"

"I don't know."

"But you do know, don't you? How much was a chunk of crack? Five bucks? And how often did you smoke it? How many times a day, Theresa?"

"I was having a hard time."

"Constantly, right? As much as you could, right?"

"It's a disease."

"So how did you pay for it all, the drinking and the drugs, the rent on your apartment?"

"I lost the apartment."

"Not right off. For a while you kept up with the rent. How did you pay for everything?"

"I had my job."

"Until you were fired, right? For coming in late too many times."

"I was a single mother."

"How did you pay for everything, Theresa?"

"I found a way."

I looked inside the file folder. "Do you know a man named Herbert Spenser?"

"No."

"Do you know a man named Rudolph Wayne? Do you know a man named Sal Pullata? Do you know a man—"

"Stop it. What are you doing?" This is when the tears started. "You're my attorney," she said. "What are you doing? Did they buy you off, too?"

"You sold yourself to those men, didn't you?"

"Mr. Carl, please stop."

"You sold yourself to those men and to others. Countless others."

"Stop."

"You sold yourself while you were still caring for your daughter. She was in the next room sometimes, wasn't she? When you drank with your clients and used drugs and sold yourself, she was right there."

"Please stop. I'm begging you."

"How could you do such a thing, Theresa?"

"I was out of control. There wasn't enough money. He left me with nothing."

"You knew you were endangering your daughter?"

"I was doing the best I could. I was sick."

"And when you signed away your custody, you didn't do it because the system was against you, or because your lawyer was bought off, or even for the money."

"No."

"You did it because you were scared."

"I needed help."

"You did it because at the time you couldn't take care of your daughter like she deserved."

"Mr. Carl, I love my Belle. More than anything."

"And you gave up your custody to Bradley Hewitt because, quite simply, it was the best thing for your daughter."

"I was lost."

"Of course you were."

"But that was before."

"And now you want her back."

"Yes."

"Why?"

"Because I love her."

"But why now?"

"Because she needs me."

"But why now?"

"Because now I know I can take care of her."

I looked up at the judge, who was staring down with something close to pity on her face as Theresa Wellman sobbed on the stand.

"What's next, Counselor?" said the judge.

"We're going to talk about the treatment Ms. Wellman has undertaken, about her new job, and how she has changed her life so that she can once again properly take care of her daughter."

"Would you like a moment to compose yourself before we go on, Ms. Wellman?" said the judge.

Theresa Wellman nodded.

"Fifteen minutes," said the judge.

When I sat down next to Beth, Theresa was still crying on the stand.

"You were a little tough on her," said Beth softly.

"How much of that did you know?"

"None of it is a surprise."

"Best thing she ever did was give up her daughter. It makes her look almost noble. It's going to be hard to prove she deserves her back, but that's what we'll try to do after the break."

"You think we still have a chance?"

"If I didn't bring out all that crap, Gullicksen would have, and he would have been ten times as tough. Now what's he going to do? Point his finger and call her a bad girl?"

Just then Gullicksen walked by on his way out to the hall. He nodded at me as he gestured at my red folder. "So it wasn't empty after all," he said.

"And if you think this one is thick," I said, with as broad a smile as I could muster, "wait until you see the one I've got on your client."

After Gullicksen had left the courtroom, shaken but not stirred, Beth looked at me with great hope on her face. "Do you have something on Bradley Hewitt?"

"Not yet," I said. "But give me time."

22

I had been putting it off, but I could put it off no longer. It was time to face the darkest of all my demons and to find some answers to questions that had been plaguing me from the start of the Charlie Kalakos case. It was time to visit my dad.

I didn't call ahead, there was no need. It was a Sunday afternoon, which meant my father would be home, alone, sitting in his La-Z-Boy watching the game, with a can of Iron City in one hand and a remote control in the other. It didn't much matter in what month the Sunday fell. In the fall and winter, he watched the Eagles. In the spring and summer, he watched the Phillies. And in the dead months of February and March, when baseball and football were both on hiatus, he watched whatever: beach volleyball, alpine skiing, *Battle of the Network Stars*. Just so long as he could sit and wince, drink his beer, grumble at the television. That's what Sundays were made for.

When I arrived at the little Spanish-style house in the little suburb of Hollywood, Pennsylvania, things didn't seem quite right. First, there was a beat-up old yellow taxicab parked right out front. Then, the front door was slightly ajar. It was not like my father to keep the front door slightly ajar. He kept his house like he kept his emotional life, buttoned up and locked tight, all to hold the world at bay. But even stranger was that I heard voices coming from his shabby little living room. It had to be the television, I figured, but it didn't sound like a couple of announcers discussing the offensive futility of the Phillies' lineup. It sounded almost like a friendly conversation. Between real people. In my father's house.

"Dad," I said. I opened the screen door, knocked on the slightly ajar front door. "Dad, are you there?"

"Who's that?" came my father's growl, which would have been a marginally acceptable response if I weren't an only child.

"Dad, it's me."

"What do you want?"

"I just came to say hello."

"Why didn't you call first?" said my father. "I'm busy."

"Dad?"

"What?"

"Can I come in?"

"No."

"Oh, don't be unsociable like, Jesse," came another voice, high and jaunty. "Even a crocodile don't turn away his own young. Invite the boy inside. This is a fortuitous treat, it is. Might liven up the conversation."

"I'm coming in," I said, suddenly apprehensive.

"Boy knows his mind," said the other voice. "I like that."

I pushed open the door, stepped into the living room, and there he was, my father, on his La-Z-Boy, beer in hand like every other Sunday, except the television wasn't on and he wasn't alone and there was a peculiar worry on his face. Two men sat side by side on the sofa, beers in their hands, both older even than my dad. One was huge, with big hands, a wide jaw, a mop of gray hair cut badly. The other was thin and dark, with a blue captain's hat cocked on his head. And somehow, in the geometry and atmosphere of the room, I tasted the acrid scent of latent danger.

"Let me guess," said the thin man with the captain's hat. "You the tiger cub, right? You that Victor, the one we all been seeing on the television."

"That's right," I said. "And who are you?"

"Old friends of your father," said the big man in a slow, deep voice.

"I didn't know my father had old friends," I said.

"Well, he do," said the thin man, before he took a swig of his beer. "And we is it."

"That's pleasant," I said, looking once again at my father's worried face. "Old friends getting together, drinking beer, talking old times. And the cab outside?"

"Mine," said the thin man.

"It's quite yellow."

"It's a Yellow Cab, fool."

"You fellows mind if I grab a beer, sit down and join you?"

"If you're going to the fridge," said the thin man, raising up his can, "fetch me another. All this reminiscing, it builds up a thirst."

I stole a look at my father once more before stepping into the kitchen and pulling two beers out of the refrigerator. I wasn't just then in the mood to drink, but I figured I'd join in. My father didn't seem so happy to see his old friends, and less happy that I had stopped by at the same time. And I had a strong sense of why. I had never seen the two men before in the entirety of my life, never in the flesh and never in a photograph, but I recognized them all the same.

"So how do you guys all know each other?" I said when I returned with the beers.

"From the old neighborhood," said the big man.

"Your daddy was younger than we was," said the thin

man. "But we still remember when he went into the army. All spit and polish, with his feathers preened. From the snappy side of town, he was."

"That's enough of that," said my father. "We don't need no more old stories."

"Sure we do," I said. "I love old stories."

"He wore his hair all swept up and back, shiny black, it was, and a little wavy. That was the Jewish in him. And he always had a tube of grease and comb with him. Always getting that hair just right."

"And good with the girls," said the big man.

"Course he was," said the thin man. "Take a lesson, boy. Never underestimate the power of a good head of hair."

We all laughed at that, all but my father, whose hair wasn't anymore black and shiny.

"So what brings you here this afternoon?" I said.

The two men on the couch glanced at each other. "Just visiting," said the big man.

"Really? Just visiting, out of the blue?"

"Well, Joey did have some business to talk about."

"We was talking with your father," said the thin man, "about a moneymaking proposition. Ralph and me was discussing it together, this opportunity, and we thought we'd give our old friend Jesse here a taste."

"Why, that is so nice of you," I said. "Isn't that nice, Dad?"

"I already told them to keep me the hell out of it," he said.

"Oh, Jesse's just not seeing the possibilities," said Joey. "He's always been like that, so busy looking down at the sidewalk so he won't trip over those feets of his that he can't see what's up there to be grabbed."

"I see it all right," he said. "I just don't want anything to do with it. And neither does Victor."

"My dad's a little shortsighted when it comes to money," I said, which was something I believed all my life but knew now to be untrue. "Though I myself might be interested."

"What do you say there, Ralph," said the thin man. "Think we ought to let the kid in?"

"I guess we don't have a choice, do we?" said Ralph.

"Not no more," said the thin man. "Being as you showed up when you did, smack in the middle of our discussions."

"Good for me, huh?" I said, my grin so wide it hurt my cheeks.

Joey took a long drink of his beer, nodded his head. "So this is it, Victor. We have received an offer, a very generous offer. Something that could change all our lives, and let me tell you, speaking for Ralph and myself, our lives could use some changing."

"Mine, too," I said.

"It's an opportunity to take advantage of, don't you think?"

"He don't want nothing to do with it," said my father.

"Let the boy decide for himself," said thin Joey, tilting back his cap, leaning forward. "We have an offer from a certain party to purchase an object that belongs to us. It's simple enough, and the terms couldn't be more generous."

"Oh, terms could always be more generous. Getting them more generous is my specialty. Tell me who it is you're talking with, and I'll give him a ring."

"We don't need you negotiating for us, fool," said Joey. "I didn't spend thirty years driving a cab without learning how to negotiate the fare."

"But if you like the deal as it is, then sell the damn thing by yourselves and be done with it. You don't need me or my dad. That's capitalism."

"Yes, yes it is. Precisely put."

"But there's a problem," said the big man.

"There always is, isn't there, Ralph? Let me guess." I closed my eyes, rubbed my hands over my face as if trying to pull an idea out of the air. "Something makes me think you don't know where this object is."

"Jesse, why didn't you tell us your boy here was an Einstein?" said Joey. "Why didn't you brag on him? I had a boy like that, I'd tell the world."

"He's not as smart as he thinks," grumbled my father.

"Actually, Joey, since my father isn't really interested, we don't need to involve him in these discussions any further, do we?"

"This is the deal of a lifetime, and you want to cut out your own dear dad?" said Joey. "I admire the hell out of that."

"My father and I have learned never to mix business with blood. Why don't we go someplace to talk?"

"How about a bar?" said Joey, smacking his lips. "All this talk about money builds up a thirst."

"I bet a lot of things build up a thirst for you, Joey."

"Don't never trust a man who don't drink or don't laugh," said Joey. "That's what my daddy taught me. That and not to trust nobody named Earl." He swallowed the rest of his beer. "Which was, unfortunately, my daddy's name."

"Then let's go," I said. "The drinks are on me when we get where we're going."

"Why, that is most generous of you, squire. Most generous. Let's be on our way, then. I'm sure your dad's got better things to do than waste his time talking to old friends."

"I'm sure he does. Just give me a minute with him, won't you, for some family stuff?"

As soon as they left to wait for me outside in the taxicab, I sidled over to my father, still in his chair. He roughly grabbed my sleeve. "Do you know who they are?" he said.

"Yeah, I know. They're two of the guys who used to hang out with Charlie the Greek thirty years ago."

"Then why are you getting involved with them?"

"To remove them from your house, for one thing. They only came to you to get to me, and you didn't seem so happy to have them here."

"It's Sunday. The Phils are on."

"And you wouldn't want to miss that."

"What are you doing here anyways?"

"I wanted to see how you are. And maybe also to ask a few questions. Like why you owe that old witch Kalakos a favor."

He turned away. "None of your business."

"It is now, since she's using it to rope me deeper into her son's cesspool. You're going to have to tell me sometime before I get submerged. But not now. Now I have to share a pitcher with Big Ralph and Little Joey."

"Be careful."

"Oh, I think I can handle a pair of sweet old guys like that."

"They're not that old, and they're not that sweet."

I looked at the still-open front door and the Yellow Cab waiting outside for me.

"When they were boys, they roamed the neighborhood like wolves," said my father. "They beat some kid to near death with a baseball bat."

"You got me into this."

"I made a mistake."

"I don't think they'd let me ditch them now, do you? Besides, I have a question they might be able to answer."

"Like what?"

"Like who the hell knew enough to make those two old crooks an offer."

23

"So we saw on the TV you're representing that Charlie Kalakos," said Joey Pride, the froth of a beer on his upper lip.

We were sitting in the back booth in the Hollywood Tavern, just down the road from my father's house. There was a half-filled pitcher of beer between us, rough-hewn glass mugs, a bowl of little pretzels. I took a handful of pretzels from the basket on the table, shook them like dice, popped one into my mouth. "Yes, I do."

"And there was something about some painting by some dead guy that was stolen from some museum," said Joey.

"Yes, there was."

"So we was just wondering"—he glanced at Ralph—"the way guys, they wonder about things, what this Charlie was planning to do with the painting?"

"Give it back," I said.

"Give it back, huh?" said Joey. "Aw, that's nice. Isn't that nice, Ralph?"

Ralph nodded, his huge face devoid of any appreciation of Charlie's selfless gesture. "Nice," said Ralph.

"It's an underrated virtue, don't you think?" said Joey Pride. "Everyone wants to be tough or ruthless, everyone wants to be king of the world, don't they? But nice is, well, nice. And that Charlie is a hell of a nice guy."

"You guys know Charlie?" I said with unbridled disingenuousness.

"Who, Charlie Kalakos?" said Joey. "Sure we know Charlie. We grew up with the boy. Little Charlie, nice Charlie, dumb-ass Charlie Kalakos, trying to rip off his oldest and dearest friends."

"What do you mean by rip off?"

"Well, that painting, it don't just belong to Charlie, now, does it?"

"You're right. Legally, it still belongs to the museum."

"But we're not talking legally here, are we, Victor? Legally is only for when lawyers and cops gather around to sniff each other's butts, like dogs at the hydrant. We're talking now about what's right. And what's right is that those that did the job with Charlie all those years ago, they should get their fair share."

"Maybe," I said. "But that's going to be hard to work out, because Charlie refuses to talk about the heist and who was involved in it with him."

"See what I told you, Ralph? The boy wants to keep it all to himself."

"So it appears," said Ralph.

"It's not that simple," I said. "There's a federal prosecutor very keen on finding out who else was involved with Charlie in that robbery thirty years ago. She wants Charlie to spill to her all the details, and he's refusing."

"There's a fed still hunting them what pulled that job?" said Ralph. "That don't make no sense."

"You're right, it doesn't, since the statute of limitations has already run. But still, she's hunting. I thought she was simply looking for the painting, but it's not that. She's got some other reason to be looking hard into that robbery."

The two men glanced at each other as if they knew exactly what Jenna Hathaway was looking for. Interesting.

"I want you boys to understand that Charlie, by keeping his mouth shut, is not trying to stiff his fellow thieves, he's trying to protect them."

"Protect them out of their money," said Ralph morosely.

I leaned forward, looked first at one and then the other. "Let's cut to the chase. Them is you, right?"

Joey gave the bar a quick scan before leaning forward and lowering his voice. "Them is us."

"Damn, I knew it," I said. "It must have been a hell of a thing to be in on that."

"Greatest thing we ever done," said Joey, and from the self-satisfied smirks that slipped onto his and Ralph's faces, I knew they were bursting to talk about it.

"But I'm confused, guys. I heard it was pulled by a bunch of professionals."

"That's what we wanted them to think," said Joey.

"But it was just us," said Ralph.

"So how did five guys from the neighborhood fall into the biggest heist in the city's history?"

Joey picked up his beer, downed it, poured himself another mugful from the pitcher. He glanced at Ralph, Ralph nodded back.

"You can't tell nobody."

"I'm a lawyer, Joey. If you can't trust a lawyer, who can you trust?"

"Like everything else in the city," said Joey, "it started in a bar."

There they were the four of them, sitting in a bar, Joey Pride told me, not this bar but one just like it. Ralph, with his hands still black from the metal at the shop. And Hugo Farr, splatters of concrete on the legs of his jeans and work boots, something haunted and thirsty in his eyes. And Charlie Kalakos, whining away about his mother. And Joey Pride, on his second pitcher already when the others came in, just starting to feel the sweetness of oblivion that he fled to every evening after running his shift in the cab. They were no longer youths, they were at that stage in life when things should be happening. But things for them had stalled.

There's a line that you pass, Joey told me, it's hard to see, a bit blurry, but there for sure. On one side of the line, all the dreams in your life are still possible. On the other side they've become fantasies you only pretend to believe, because having nothing to believe is too close to death. Fool's dreams, Joey called them, sad little lies. There's that line, and the four of them, they had blown past that line years before, never looking back.

Ralph was then bending metal for Karlov, that Russian son of a bitch. What he wanted was his own shop, nothing much, not Standard Press Steel or anything, just something of his own. But Ralph was a fool for love, there was always a pair of tits to throw his money at, and the dream of his own shop, being his own boss, was now as empty as his bank account.

Same with Hugo, who was always talking about college and business school. Wanted to be a mogul. He had started at Temple but took a semester off when his dad got sick. Thought he'd earn some cash to help his mother before getting back to it, but for some reason he never got back to it. He ended up working construction, laying cement, taking the up-front payoff and drinking beer late into the night to forget where he wasn't headed.

All Charlie wanted was to get away from that mother of his, to find a girl and buy a house and live a life on his own. That was his fool's dream, a pallid little thing, but to Charlie it was such a grand idea it was painful for him to even imagine it. So at nights he sat with the rest of them and drank and watched the years tick, tick away.

Truth was, Joey was the sanest of them all, and he was the one officially certified as crazy. He was sent away twice. Once for stealing a car and then a few years later when they found him wandering the streets in a daze with a gun and a huge wooden cross, spouting off about Jimi Hendrix being crucified for our sins. He had always loved cars, wanted to build hot rods and race along the boulevards, but when they finally released him from the state mental hospital high up on that suburban hill, the only work he could find was driving a cab. A short-term job to get him back on his feet, but the term was already longer than the one he had served in prison, and the time felt just as dead.

So there they were, the four of them, in that bar, cursing their luck and settling into failure like it was their most comfortable pair of ratty jeans, watching the pathetic embers of their fool's dreams grow dimmer each day, when they got the word. Teddy Pravitz was back in town.

Teddy was the slick one who got out from under it all, who left Philly for the far coast and was making his life happen. He had become something of a legend among them, less flesh and blood, more avatar of the success that had eluded them. They never had gone west to find him, never were certain exactly what he was up to, but they all were sure he had done better than had they. And now he was back. They figured he had come home to toss off a quick hello, for old times' sake, had only returned for a shot and a beer and a howdy doody, glad we knew you. But they were wrong.

He strode into the bar like a foreign potentate. There were heys and hurrahs, slapped backs and spilt beer. Teddy Pravitz was back in town. He bought them a round and then another, he flashed that smile, flashed a wad, he preened. There was something shaggy about him, something California, like the Philly had been burned out of him by the West Coast sun. You half expected he'd be surfing down Broad Street, what with the smile and the colorful hippie vest. He had come through a portal from another place entirely, a place with lights and banners, with a mystique he brought back with him. He was blinding.

They slid together into a booth in the rear, the five of them, together again. And the four that had gotten stuck in the city of their birth, well, they had their questions, but he was short with his answers.

Where you been, Teddy? Around. *You married?* Nah. *Working?* Hardly. *Getting any?* More than I can handle. *You back for good?* Just for a while. *Any reason?* Sure. *Another round, Teddy, my man?* On me. *So come on, tell us. Why are you back?*

"Boys," he said, finally, his eyes shining. "Boys, I'm back for one reason and one reason only. To give you all one last chance to save your lives, one last chance at redemption."

"Funny," I said, "you guys don't look redeemed."

"That's the point," said Joey. "Thirty years later we're still here, busted like a fat lip, still trying to make it happen."

"But the painting was only a part of the haul taken from the Randolph Trust. There was plenty of other stuff taken, jewels and gold and even some cash. You guys must have done pretty damn well."

They didn't answer, Little Joey and Big Ralph, instead they stared mournfully at their beer mugs. With a quick snatch, Joey downed the rest of his beer and emptied the pitcher into his mug and snatched that down, too.

"What happened to it all?" I said.

"We got some," said Joey. "Our piece of the cash."

"And the rest?"

"Disappeared," said Ralph.

"How?"

"Does it matter?"

"What we're here to talk about now," said Joey, "is making it back. Fish comes up to us. He knows we know Charlie from way back. He knows we might have some influence on him, being we are old friends and all of us were once thick as weasels."

"Who made the offer?" I said.

"Does it matter?" said Ralph.

"Yeah, it does."

"Fish wants it confidential. But the offer is enough to get us interested. And let me say it's enough to get us a little pissed if it don't come off like the fish, he says."

"A little pissed, huh?"

"Yeah. So that's the story. Tell Charlie we got ourselves a fish on the line and we all want a share of the eating. Tell him fair is fair. Tell him that the baseball bats are out."

"Is that a threat, Joey?" I said.

"No, no, you got me all wrong," said Joey. "I'm just like Charlie: nice. Aren't I nice, Ralph?"

"He's nice."

"It's just that we haven't played ball in a while and we want to get us up another game. Like old times. You tell Charlie about the baseball bats, and he'll understand."

"Okay, I got the message," I said. "You hear again from your fish, you give me a call." I handed each of them one of my cards. "Did you tell anyone else about the offer?"

"Just a few interested parties."

"Like?"

"Your father."

"Okay. From here on in, you keep him out of it. Anyone else?"

"Charlie's mom."

I closed my eyes, shook my head. "You guys are more stupid than you let on."

"We're covering our bases here, Victor."

"More like you're covering your graves. Now, before I do anything, I need to know this fish you have on the line is the real thing and not just blowing little bubbles out his butt."

"Oh, he's the real thing," said Joey.

"How do you know?"

"He gave us a taste. A clean pair of Bens to each of us just for talking."

"You mind if I take a look?"

"Mine, unfortunately, are already gone. Expenses and such. I had a tab, you see."

"Oh, I bet you did. How about you, Ralph? You got any of those bills left?"

Ralph reached into his pants pocket, pulled out a gold money clip with some sort of a medallion on it, drew out the wad, unfolded it.

"Aw, man," said Joey, "you been holding out on me. Didn't I just ask you for a tenner?"

"I didn't say I didn't have it," said Ralph as he plucked from the wad two hundred-dollar bills.

The bills he handed me were new and crisp, like they had been dealt from a thick stack fresh from the mint. I waved them below my nose, taking in the newly printed scent of the inks. And something else. I sniffed them again, more deeply this time. Something flowery, something precious. Son of a bitch.

Lavender Hill.

24

"Victor Carl here."

"Hello, Victor. How pleasant to hear your sweet voice. You left a message on my cell?"

"Lavender?"

" 'Tis I."

"Lav, dude, you're killing me."

"Oh, Victor, let's be clear about a few things. First of all, I am not and never have been a dude. Put the skateboard away and remember that you are on the far side of sixteen. As for the second part of your execrable sentence, the part about my killing you, rest assured it could be arranged."

"Not amusing."

"How gratifying, because it is not my goal in life to amuse you. Those we find amusing are not taken seriously, and let me caution you, Victor, I may twitter and chirp, but you need to take me, my offer, and my concerns, very seriously. There have been inquiries about my person in the city of my current residence. I find that quite distasteful."

"You didn't think I'd check you out?"

"I had hoped you'd show a bit more discretion. But it was almost as if your man doing the inquiries wanted word to get out that I was being looked at. Victor, there is an element of public humiliation in such an inquiry that sets my teeth to grinding. Tell your investigator to cut it out, boy, or I'll find something else to cut."

"You know, Lav, you're a lot less genial over the phone."

"I am not happy with you, and it is too much of strain to be genial when one is not happy. Bad for the skin."

"Well, color me unhappy, too, Lav, dude. Because I met up with Joey and Ralph today. Remember them? The two old guys you collared one night and gave a couple hundred each, in hard cash that smells suspiciously of your precious scent?"

"How impolitic of them to show you the bills, and how clever of you to notice. I suppose I'll have to do something about that."

"The two old men left me with the impression that you were trying to bypass my client and buy the painting from them."

"What did you expect, Victor? I've been pining for you, and yet there was no word, no message, nothing. I have been feeling ever so unrequited."

"I haven't been able to talk to my client since our meeting. He's on the run, he's not easily accessible."

"Try harder."

"You're making everything more difficult."

"Making life harder on lawyers is nothing I trouble myself about. As for your client, I'm merely giving him options. He can decide to take the money himself or to share it with his friends. And if those old comrades put pressure on him to make the right decision, so much the better."

"What you've done is made it more difficult for him to return the painting to the museum."

"Exactly, dear boy."

"Making you the more attractive landing place for Mr. Rembrandt."

"Yes, yes, you have seen through me like a ghost."

"You negotiate like a shark."

"I negotiate like a hyena, Victor, with a modicum of hilarity. But I close like a shark."

"I bet you do, Lav. How did you find those guys anyway?"

"Are you underestimating me, Victor? I hope so. It makes everything easier. Now, be advised that I have many virtues, a certain compassion for small animals and a talent for the rumba among them, but patience, I'm afraid, is not included. I am not a patient man, and neither is the man I represent. Move quickly, Victor, or I'll be forced to move myself."

"To Cleveland?"

"No, to Plan B."

"What's Plan B?"

"Staggeringly unpleasant."

"Victor Carl here."

"Hi, Victor, it's me."

"You?"

"Yes, me. And I was just sitting here thinking about you."

"About me?"

"Of course you, silly, and I thought I'd give you a call."

"That's nice, I suppose."

"So how are you doing?"

"Fine, I guess."

"Did you see the game? The Phillies lost today. I'm always a little depressed when the Phils lose."

"I don't think they make enough Prozac."

"I used to date a Phillie. A middle reliever."

"With the state of the bullpen the last couple of years, that must have been hard."

"God, yes. Every time he blew a lead, I'd hear about it

from everyone at the club. 'Yo, your boyfriend sucks.' Like it was my fault his slider didn't slide. But then they traded him to Seattle, so that was that."

"Too bad."

"Well, he really wasn't very good. On the other hand, he signed a two-year, $4.7 million contract, so he had that going for him."

"Can I ask you something?"

"Sure."

"Who are you?"

"Mon."

"Excuse me?"

"Monica. Monica Adair. Remember?"

"Oh, yes, of course. Monica. Yes. Right. Monica. From Lola's whatever. The one with the missing sister. Okay, now I get it. How's it going?"

"Well, the Phils lost."

"And why did you call?"

"Most guys, when they take me out on a date and it goes well, the next night they show up at the club. At least to get another look. So I expected to see you sometime soon, but you haven't been back."

"We didn't have a date, Monica."

"We ate together."

"You did most of the eating."

"At a restaurant."

"A diner."

"And you paid."

"I was being mannerly."

"That wasn't a date?"

"No."

"Wow. I kind of missed those signals, didn't I?"

"Sorry about that. We were just discussing your sister. You seemed to want to talk about her, so I agreed to listen."

"You brought her up."

"No, just the name. It was obvious pretty early on that we were talking about two different people. The Chantal Adair I'm looking for is not your sister."

"You sure?"

"Oh, yes."

"Why are you looking for her anyway? You never told me."

"It's not important."

"You want to keep it private, I understand."

"It's no big deal. But, Monica, really, though it's nice to talk to you and all, I have to go."

"Is your girlfriend calling for you?"

"I don't have a girlfriend."

"So you're married?"

"No."

"Oh." Pause. "I see. It's like that, is it?"

"Like what?"

"You don't date strippers."

"Well, I haven't as of yet."

"Don't worry, we get that a lot. You'd be surprised how many men go to the club to let us rub their bald little heads with our breasts but wouldn't think of dating one of us."

"I'm not one of those guys."

"Like you'd have no problem taking a stripper home to Mommy."

"With my mother, actually, no. Pump enough vodka into her and she'd join you on the pole. But that's not what I meant. I meant I don't go to those kinds of clubs."

"But you went to Club Lola that night."

"To see you, to ask about the name, that's all."

"Why again did you ask about the name?"

"Really, Monica, I have to go."

"So you don't want to have drinks one night?"

"No, not really."

"Men always say they want a woman who is willing to take the initiative, but then when we do, they think we're pushy and desperate. Do you think I'm pushy and desperate?"

"Not desperate, no."

"Then what is it? Are my breasts too small?"

"God, no."

"You don't like brunettes?"

"I like brunettes fine. Listen, Monica, this is too odd for words. I'm about to self-immolate from awkwardness. Really, I have to go."

"Then just tell me."

"Your breasts are fine. Better than fine."

"No. Tell me why you're looking for Chantal."

"If I tell you, will you hang up and not call again?"

"I promise."

"Okay. It's weird and embarrassing. One night, not too long ago, I must have gotten so drunk that I don't remember anything about what happened. But when I woke up, I had a tattoo on my chest. And on the tattoo was a name."

"What name, Victor?"

"Chantal Adair. I don't know how it got there, or why, but I was just trying to find her."

"That is weird."

"And with the juxtaposition of your stage name and last name, we thought you might be a possibility. But seeing as you've never seen me before and I never saw you before, then it's pretty certain that my tattoo has absolutely nothing to do with you or your sister who went missing decades ago."

"No, it doesn't. Unless . . ."

"Thanks for calling, Monica, but I'm going to hang up now."

"Hey, Victor, can I ask one more thing?"

"No."

"Do you want to meet my parents?"

"Absolutely not."

"They'd really like you. I'm going to set it up. I'll let you know when."

"Monica, don't."

"Bye-bye."

"Monica? Are you there? Monica? Monica? Crap."

"Victor Carl here."

"Hi, Victor, it's me."

"Beth, hi. Gad, it's been a bad night. The phone is ringing off the hook, and every call is worse than the last."

"And here I am, right on cue. What's going on?"

"Just stuff. The Kalakos case is getting a bit hairy. Still, I must say it's nice for once having a case without any dead bodies floating around, you know what I mean?"

"Yes, I do. This whole murder business you fell into is creepy. Not what I signed up for in law school."

"Theresa Wellman is what you signed up for, I suppose."

"That's right."

"Did she recover from the ordeal of my direct examination?"

"Quite well, actually. And the part after the break, when you had her discuss her treatment and her new job and the new house her parents bought for her, that was fabulous."

"See, Beth, we work well together."

"We do, but that's never been the problem, has it? Are you busy tomorrow at about noon?"

"Not especially."

"Can you meet me?"

"At the office?"

"No, someplace else."

"What's up?"

"I've been doing some thinking."

"Oh, Beth, don't."

"About my life."

"Gad, Beth, whatever you do, don't do that. Wouldn't you just rather change the channel and see what else is on?"

"I'm taking stock, Victor."

"Why am I suddenly terrified? This whole thinking thing, Beth, can only lead to disaster."

"So we'll leave together from the office, say eleven-thirty, is that okay?"

"You never said where we are going?"

"I know. See you tomorrow."

"Victor Carl here."

"Carl, you slimy son of a bitch. You busy?"

"Busy enough."

"Too busy to take a drive out to meet me?"

"I guess it depends."

"On what?"

"On who the hell you are."

"You don't recognize the voice?"

"Oh, it's a game, is it? Let me guess. You sound like some sort of rutting rhino. Is it Barry White?"

"Close enough. It's McDeiss."

"That McDeiss?"

"Yeah."

"Crap."

25

There are hosts of people you don't want to hear from late on a Sunday night. Your oncologist, maybe, or the girl you had sex with six months ago and haven't called back since, definitely, or the highway patrol, or the marines, or your mother . . . well, my mother. But a homicide detective might just be tops on the list.

Detective McDeiss of the Philadelphia Police Department Homicide Unit had directed me to a street on the south edge of the Great Northeast, not far from the Tacony-Palmyra Bridge and just a few blocks east of the Kalakos house. The location itself offered a clue as to what it was all about, which was more than McDeiss had given me. McDeiss was a big man with a small capacity for trust when it came to me, which made some sense, since his job was to bang away my clients and my job was to frustrate him at every turn. He hadn't given me any details, just the address, but once I found the street, it wasn't hard to pick out the right house, what with the crowd, the cops, the flashing lights and yellow tape, the satellite trucks parked with the reporters waiting for their close-ups. I was surprised they weren't selling T-shirts.

I parked two blocks down the street from the carnival. I had slipped on a suit—nothing more faceless than a guy in a plain blue suit—and slowly made my way toward the center of all the activity, a nondescript brick row house with an open cement porch and a small plot of scraggly grass. In front of the house, I spotted the coroner's van, the back doors open, something dark and shapeless on a gurney inside. As I approached, the doors slammed shut. I let out a sigh of relief as the van drove off. I'd been to enough crime scenes by now to know that my stomach much prefers I show up after the corpse is taken away to the morgue.

At the edge of the yellow tape, I subtly gestured one of the uniforms over. I leaned toward him when he arrived and pitched my voice as low as I could while still being heard. "McDeiss asked me to come on by."

"Are you the lawyer we were told to look out for?" he said a little too loudly.

"Can we keep this quiet? No need for the press to find out I'm here."

"Sure, I understand," he said softly, with a wink.

"I'm the lawyer, yes. Victor Carl."

"Go on in."

"Thanks."

I ducked under the tape as unobtrusively as I could. Just as I reached the second step of the stoop, I heard something harsh and loud from behind me.

"Yo, Joe," hollered the uniform. "Tell McDeiss that creep Victor Carl, you know, the scumbucket lawyer what we were told to look out for? Tell McDeiss he finally showed."

Instinctively I turned toward the crowd of press. Flashbulbs popped. My name was called out, questions were shouted, questions about Charlie and Rembrandt and whether the murder here was somehow connected to the sudden emergence of the painting. So much for slipping in unnoticed.

I turned to the uniform. "Thanks, pal."

"We aim to serve," he said with a grin.

I turned again toward the pack of press and spotted a flash

of red hair surrounding a pale freckled face before I ignored the shouting and headed into the house.

It was a crime scene, all right. Cops were wandering around with notepads out, technicians were testing, walls and doorknobs were being dusted, photographs were being snapped, jokes were being laughed at, hoagies were being eaten.

I started into the living room and was stopped by a uniform and told to wait while he found McDeiss.

The house was one of those places that had been decorated decades before and then left to age. I suppose if you lived there day by day you didn't notice it so much, but coming in fresh you could see the unalloyed weight of time on the décor and the lives inside. The walls were dark where they had once been bright, the furniture was greasy, the rug was worn, and everything had a tinge of brown to it and smelled as if it had been marinating in nicotine for an untold number of years. And there was another smell, something repulsive yet faintly familiar, like rot and decay and death, like pestilence itself. It took me a moment to make the connection. It smelled like Mrs. Kalakos's breath. And with good reason. Littered across the rug were little placards with numbers on them, next to circles drawn in chalk. And there, on the edge of the rug, in front of a fully stocked liquor cart, was the taped outline of a sprawled figure and an ugly dark stain.

Across the living room and through the dining room, I could see the doorway to the bright lights of the kitchen. McDeiss, large and round, with his brown suit and black hat, was in the kitchen talking with K. Lawrence Slocum. As the uniform approached the two of them, their heads swiveled at the same moment to stare. McDeiss shook his head at me in that way he had, in the manner of the parent of a problem child, as if my ending up in the middle of a god-awful mess was a disappointment but not a surprise. Slocum stared for just a moment before looking away in disgust.

"Who is it?" I said, when the three of us were cliqued together.

"A man by the name of Ciulla," said McDeiss.

"Do I know him?"

"I expect you do," he said, "seeing as your card was in his wallet."

"Oh." I suddenly remembered now where I'd heard that name before. Old Mrs. Kalakos had given it to me. "Is the victim perhaps a Ralph Ciulla?"

"There you go, Carl," said McDeiss. "I knew you'd come up with it."

"How did he get it?"

"One in the knee, two in the head."

"When?"

"A few hours ago."

"Who did it?"

"If we knew that, we wouldn't need you, now, would we?"

"Big Ralph."

"He was big, all right."

"Can I have a minute, guys?"

"I didn't think it was possible for you to get any paler," said McDeiss, "but once again I am proven wrong."

"Just a minute," I said as I heaved myself over to a big old easy chair and plopped down into it, put my head in my hands. It took me a while to catch my breath, a longer while to settle the fear that rippled through my stomach like a bout of gastrointestinal distress. Big Ralph, murdered, just a few hours after we had a beer together at the Hollywood Tavern. Whatever was really going on in the Charlie Kalakos case, it had just taken a turn. I peered through my fingers onto the darkened carpet. Between my shoes was a placard with the number seven on it, and a circle of chalk, and in the middle of the circle a dark black stain. Somehow that didn't help.

I glanced up at McDeiss and Slocum. The two were ignoring me as they tried to piece together what had happened. They would have questions, and they'd want some answers. Some things I was forbidden by law to disclose, and some things could get in the way of what I had once thought to be an easy payday. As I considered my options, the pile of jewels and gold ensconced in my desk drawer dissolved in my mind's eye. But along with that fading image was another, the shapeless sack of flesh and bones I had glimpsed in the coroner's van. A man was dead, murdered in the coldest of blood, and something needed to be done.

I started thinking about who might have killed Ralph Ciulla. There were probably a lot of guys over the years who had wanted to pop Big Ralph, not that old and not that sweet, had said my father, but the timing was pretty damn definitive. It couldn't be a coincidence that Ralph and Joey had thrust themselves into the middle of Charlie's case and immediately thereafter Ralph had ended up dead. But who would have known about Ralph's interest? Lavender Hill, who had made him a far-too-generous offer for the painting? Joey Pride, who was his partner in the endeavor? Mrs. Kalakos with her big gun, whom the two men had gone to first before approaching my dad? Or even Charlie Kalakos, clued about his old friend's intentions by his witch of a mother. All of them yes, and so all of them were possibilities, but not possibilities that made much sense.

From the chair I said, "So how do you fellows figure it happened?"

"You ready to talk?" said McDeiss.

"I'm ready to listen," I said. "And then I'll talk."

McDeiss shook his head in exasperation, but Slocum gave him a nod.

"This Ralph Ciulla had been married twice, divorced twice," said McDeiss. "His mother died five years ago, and after that he lived here alone. He apparently let the shooter inside, closed the door behind him. Best we could tell, there was no struggle. The shooter was standing there, the victim was here. The victim turned toward the liquor cart, maybe to fix some drinks. First shot went into the knee from behind, shattered it. A lot of bleeding. None of the neighbors heard the shot, so it was probably an automatic with a silencer, though no shells were found. Ballistics will tell us the caliber, but it looked medium-sized, like a thirty-eight. After he was on the ground, the shooter put two in the right side of the skull."

"Left-handed?"

"That would be my guess."

"How long between the knee shot and the head shots?" I said.

"Impossible to tell. Maybe the coroner can give an estimate. But the knee was wrapped with a towel from the kitchen, which was a little strange."

"Was there a trail of blood into the kitchen?" I asked.

"No."

"Then the shooter wrapped the wound," I said.

"That's what we figure," said McDeiss. "Maybe he was looking for something and hoped the victim would tell him where it was. That's why we were so intrigued when we found your card. We hoped you could tell us what might have been going on with the victim."

"Who called the murder in?"

"A 911 call from a pay phone not far from here. Panicky voice, didn't identify himself, but he knew the victim's name."

"The shooter?"

"Whoever did this doesn't seem the panicky type. In any

event we dusted the handset and the change in the box for prints."

"Anybody see anything?"

"We have a squad going door-to-door. Nothing yet."

"Anything taken?"

"Doesn't look like it. A valuable ring still on his finger, a watch, and his wallet was still in his pocket, with your card inside and a credit card, but no cash."

"What about his money clip?"

"A money clip?"

I lifted up my head, looked out a window onto the street, thought I saw a flash of yellow slipping by. "That's what he had on him today," I said. "Gold, with some sort of a medallion on it, clipped around a pretty thick wad."

McDeiss looked at Slocum, who shrugged.

"You were with this Ralph Ciulla today?" said McDeiss.

"I was."

"What were you boys talking about?"

I stood up from the chair, closed my eyes for a moment, fought to regain my stomach.

"Go ahead, Victor," said Slocum.

"Ralph Ciulla was an old friend of Charlie Kalakos," I said.

Slocum didn't even blink, he already knew.

"Ralph was trying to inject himself in the negotiations for the missing Rembrandt. He and another old friend, Joey Pride, believed they could sell the painting to some high roller, and they met with me in an attempt to get Charlie to go along."

"How'd they get in touch with you?" said Slocum.

"By phone."

"Where did you meet?"

"Hollywood Tavern."

"That's near where your father lives, isn't it?"

"Is it?"

"When did you meet?"

"About two."

"Anyone else?"

"Just Ralph and Joey Pride and myself."

"You know where this Joey Pride lives?"

"Nope."

"What he looks like?"

"Same age as Ralph. Thin, nervous, talks a lot. African-American. Drives a Yellow Cab. That's it."

"If he gets in touch with you, you'll get in touch with us?"

"Count on it."

"They say who the high roller is who wants to buy the painting?"

"No, but Ralph showed me a couple hundred-dollar bills he received up front. That's how I knew about the money clip."

"And now they're gone. What did you tell them?"

"I told them the painting legally belonged to the museum."

"And?"

"And I wasn't going to be involved in anything illegal."

Slocum looked at me impassively, withholding judgment as to whether I was being only partially insincere or was flat-out lying.

"Spare us the act," said McDeiss, not withholding anything. "We've both known you too long."

"How'd they take your rejection of their deal?" said Slocum.

"Not so well."

"But you gave him your card," said McDeiss.

"I'm a businessman," I said. "I give my card out to panhandlers and delivery boys, to babies in strollers."

"Why did this Ralph Ciulla fellow and that Joey Pride

think they had the right to get a piece of that painting?" said McDeiss.

"From what they told me, it was because they were in on the theft."

Slocum and McDeiss turned toward each other, as if the theory had already been discussed.

"What does your client say about it?" said Slocum.

"Whatever he says is privileged," I said.

"But as far as you know, the only people who knew about the hundreds were you, the guy who gave them to Ciulla, and this Joey Pride."

"Do you really think Ralph was killed for a couple hundred bucks?"

"You been in this job as long as I have, Carl, you'd be amazed at how cheap a life can be measured by a guy on the trigger side of a gun."

"We'd like to talk to your client," said Slocum.

"You want to talk to my client, you get Hathaway to get off of her high white horse. It's getting dangerous here, and she's not helping."

"I'll talk to her."

"Good."

"What are you going to tell Charlie?" said Slocum.

"When I get hold of him finally," I said, "I'm going to tell him the truth. That things have escalated in a very bad way, that murder is afoot, and maybe his best bet is to bury the damn painting and stay the hell out of Dodge."

26

She was waiting for us by the front door, long and lean, pretty and hard, blond hair, black roots, hoop earrings dangling, bracelets jangling, lips painted bright red, the darting, vicious eyes of a middle linebacker. Her portfolio was brown leather, her heels were black and high, her silver Escalade was parked out front. When she saw us approach, she glanced at her watch and tapped her toe, and she terrified the hell out of me, just standing there. But of course she did.

She was a Realtor.

"I think you'll adore this one, Beth," she said in a tight, energized voice as we climbed the cement steps in front of the narrow row house. "I know it was a little sudden, but I wanted to get a jump on some other buyers who are coming to look this afternoon. The interest in this house is through the roof. It won't be available much longer."

"Thanks, Sheila," said Beth.

"And is this your boyfriend?"

"Just my partner, Victor," said Beth.

"Just," I said.

"Nice to meet you, Victor. Are you life partners or something like that? It's so hard to keep the nomenclature straight."

"Legal partners," I said.

"Oh," she said, placing a hand lightly on my forearm. She smelled edgy and dangerous, like she had doused herself in a new perfume from Revlon called Barracuda. "It's nice of you to come and provide support. So are we ready?"

"I think," said Beth.

"Now, use your imagination, Beth," said Sheila as she fiddled with her keys. "The buyers haven't prepped it for sale, so it will look a little dingy, but that's to our advantage, because it will keep the price down. You have to envision it with fresh paint, sanded floors, new fixtures throughout, especially the sconces."

"The sconces?" I said.

"Oh, the things they have now are simply beastly. But with something a little art deco and bright, maybe some frosted glass, the walls will look fabulous." She found a key that fit, twisted it, shouldered open the door. "Let's take a look."

A blast of must hit us from the open door, as if the place hadn't been inhabited in years. I was ready to duck in case a bat flew out.

Sheila the Realtor walked in with authority, switched on the lights, opened a window. Beth and I followed warily, stepping directly into a living room. There was a ridge running across the dirty wooden floor, the walls were scuffed, the fixtures hung by frayed wires, the windowsills were rotting, the ceiling had a great crack tearing through it.

"Isn't it wonderful?" said Sheila. "Isn't it thrilling? Varnished floors, maybe some flocked wallpaper. A leather couch, something bright on the wall. The potential here is outrageous. And you should see the kitchen—it's bigger than some condos I sell."

There was an archway to a small grimy dining area devoid of windows and then another arch leading to the kitchen, which was big but sparse, too, with just a few counters, a stove collapsing on itself, and a refrigerator with rounded edges that belonged in a museum. The linoleum floor, a filthy brown, was coming apart at the seams.

"Lovely, just lovely," said Sheila, admiring the wreck of a kitchen. "It gets morning light, which is really a fabulous feature. You have enough room for an island and a breakfast nook. This is the house's single best feature."

"This?" I said.

"Oh, yes, Victor," said Sheila. "I have clients in half-million-dollar homes who would kill for a kitchen like this. The possibilities are endless. And whatever you put into a kitchen, you will get out twice when you sell, especially a kitchen as big as this."

"It does have potential," said Beth.

"You see, Victor, Beth has vision. Beth can see beyond the current condition to what this kitchen can be. State of the art. A Viking stove, a glass-fronted refrigerator, granite countertops, walnut cabinets."

"I like walnut," said Beth.

"You could do the whole thing in walnut, with pin lighting from the ceiling. I could see this kitchen in *Philadelphia* magazine."

"Really?"

"Absolutely. Now, there are two floors above us. Three bedrooms on the second and a bedroom and an attic space on the third. Plus a full basement," she said, gesturing to a door in the kitchen.

"Finished?" said Beth.

"You could," said Sheila. "Why don't we take a look upstairs first? I thought, for you, the third-floor bedroom could be a home office. It gets a tremendous amount of light, and there's a view of City Hall. Oh, Beth, I think this place is perfect for you, just perfect. And I know there's some leeway on the price."

"You want to come up with me, Victor?" said Beth.

"In a minute."

I stood with Sheila as Beth wandered back through the dining area and toward the stairs in the living room. As she climbed them, the stairs creaked like an arthritic old man trying to straighten his back.

"It's a little run-down," I said to Sheila the Realtor.

"It admittedly needs some work," she said, the manic edge gone from her voice.

"It's a pit."

"Her price range was limited."

"Are there really people coming to look at it this afternoon?"

"There are always people coming to look in the afternoon. What's your situation, Victor?"

"Single," I said.

She laughed, leaned back, flicked her hair. "I meant housing," she said.

"Oh, right. I rent."

"You could just throw your money out the window, it would be more efficient. Do you ever think of buying?"

"No, not really."

"It's a good time, Victor, while interest rates are still low."

"I guess you're right."

"I have some places that would be perfect for you." She whipped a card out of her portfolio, offered it to me. "If you're interested, give me a call."

"I don't think I really want to buy something right now."

"Still, give me a call. I'm sure we could work out something. Now, why don't you go up and see how your partner's getting along."

I found Beth leaning on a sill, peering out a window in a small, closetlike room with a sloped ceiling on the third floor. There was enough room for a chair or a desk, maybe, but not enough room for both.

"Nice home office," I said.

"Look at the view," she said.

"What view?"

"If you lean forward and look left and bend your neck just so, you can see the tip of Billy Penn's hat."

"Oh, that view."

"What do you think?"

"I think I don't have the imagination for this place."

"I like it."

"You always had a thing for reclamation projects. That's why you're with me."

"This would be quite a cozy office," she said.

"Cozy being the operative word."

"And did you see the rooms on the second floor? A nice master bedroom, a guest room, and then the small room that could be a nursery."

"A nursery?"

"Paint it pale blue, put in a cradle, a nice rocking chair."

"Doesn't a nursery need a baby first?"

"And the kitchen is marvelous, isn't it? You heard what Sheila said. *Philadelphia* magazine."

"Yeah, I heard."

"I love walnut."

"There's not a stick of walnut in this entire house."

"With the settlement you wheedled out of Eugene Franks and some help from my dad, I bet I can swing this."

"Beth, do you really think this is the answer to whatever existential disquiet you're feeling, to buy a house and saddle yourself with a thirty-year mortgage and a limitless future of home repair?"

She turned from the window and stared right at me, her

lips flat with seriousness, her eyes impassive. "What would you suggest?" she said in a calm, soft voice.

I thought about it, but not for long, because the very calm of her voice let me know that she didn't really want an answer.

"I represented a home inspector in a DUI once," I said.

"Is he an incompetent drunk?"

"Only when he drives."

"Perfect. Thanks, Victor," she said, looking up to the sloped ceiling. "I think I'm going to be really happy here."

"Can I make one piece of decorating advice?"

"Sure."

"For the home office, get a laptop."

27

I wasn't long back from our visit with Sheila the Realtor when I was summoned from on high.

Talbott, Kittredge and Chase was one of the firms that had rejected me out of law school. There were many firms that had rejected me out of law school, a glorious fellowship of discretion and good taste. Yet Talbott was the bluest of the blue chips, and its rejection, all these years later, still irked. Whenever I spied a Talbott lawyer, the bitter strands of resentment and envy rose like bile in my throat. By now I had realized that my big-firm dreams were a chimera, I was congenitally unfit for working for anyone except myself, but if there was a spot I still secretly pined for, it was among the brilliant successes at Talbott, Kittredge and Chase, one of whom was Stanford Quick.

"Can I get you something to drink, Mr. Carl?" said the very attractive paralegal who had escorted me into the conference room of Talbott, Kittredge and Chase on the fifty-fourth floor of One Liberty Place. The paralegal's name was Jennifer, the conference table was marble, the chairs were upholstered in real leather. The conference room's windows stretched from the ceiling to the floor, and the view of the city as it rolled to the Delaware River was breathtaking.

I sat in one of the leather chairs and sank in as if sitting on a cloud. "Water would be fine," I said.

"Sparkling or mineral?" said Jennifer. "We have San Pellegrino and Perrier, we have Evian, we have Fiji, and we have a wonderful artesian water from Norway called Voss."

"That sounds refreshing," I said.

"Very good."

"Do you do general paralegal work here, Jennifer?"

"Oh, no, Mr. Carl. I work exclusively for Mr. Quick."

"How nice for him."

I was sipping the Voss, admiring the view, remembering an old joke—*How do you get laid on Capitol Hill? Step out of your office and call, "Oh, Jennifer."*—when Jabari Spurlock and the tall, elegant Stanford Quick entered the room. They didn't seem so happy to see me. They seemed, in fact, quite peeved.

"Thank you for coming, Victor," said Stanford Quick as the two men sat themselves across from me at the table with somber expressions and parched eyes.

"You didn't give me much choice," I said. "I've heard more temperate demands from the IRS."

"Well, as you can imagine," said Spurlock, his hands clasped on the table, his head leaning forward aggressively, "we are quite concerned about the events of the last few days and their effect on the reputation of the Randolph Trust. That is why I insisted on this meeting and why I insisted it not be at the trust but in this office. It was alarming enough when our supposedly secret negotiations were splashed across the newspapers and television screens, but it is totally appalling for the trust to be in any way connected to a murder."

"I didn't make any such connection," I said.

"You were spotted entering the scene of the crime," said Spurlock. "Questions were asked and broadcast over the air. The connection was made."

"Let's be clear about something from the start," I said. "It wasn't I who leaked our original discussions to the press. I told no one about it, not even my partner, and next thing I know, it's on the television, so look to yourselves for that."

Spurlock glanced inquiringly at Quick, who simply shrugged. "We didn't leak it," said Spurlock.

"Well, somebody did, and the disclosure put my client and my own health at risk. Why don't you guys find out who spilled the beans and get back to me."

"Nobody forced you to appear like a publicity hound on every news show for a week," said Quick.

"I simply continued the story's play in the media in an effort to bring the situation to a head more quickly. As for the murder, I showed up at the scene at the request of the homicide detective in charge of the case. It was the media itself that drew the connection."

"Is there a connection?" said Stanford Quick. "Is there any link between our painting and this victim, whom the papers identified as one"—he opened a file, examined some papers for the name—"Ralph Ciulla?"

"I'm not certain yet. There is certainly a connection between the victim and my client. They are old friends. That's as much as I can be definite about. But it also appears the victim may have been involved with my client in stealing the painting many years ago."

"That hardly seems possible," said Quick, rather quickly. "There was nothing to indicate that the dead man, or even your client, had the wherewithal to be involved in a crime of that sophistication. From all accounts, the robbery was pulled off by a team of experts from out of town."

"Why do you keep saying they were from out of town?"

"No city has looser lips than Philadelphia, but there was never even a whisper about the crime from the city's underworld. No thief ever crowed about stealing the works, no fence ever owned up to selling the metal and jewels."

"Neither of us was with the trust at the time of the robbery," said Spurlock, "and so we know little more than was disclosed in the papers. Mrs. LeComte would know more of the details."

"Would you mind if I spoke to her?"

"Not at all. I'll tell her to expect your call. But even if, as you say, this Ralph Ciulla was involved in the theft, why would he be killed now?"

"My best guess," I said, "is that the murder was a warning to Charles to stay away."

"Is he going to heed the warning?" said Quick.

"I'll have to ask him that, won't I? Much will depend, I'm sure, on you."

"What are you talking about?" said Spurlock. "How are we involved in the decision?"

I poured myself more of the sparkling water, took a drink to keep them waiting. The meeting was about to shift from their purpose, to upbraid me for the media frenzy, to my own purposes, and I was using the pause to make the point.

"I'm afraid to say, gentlemen, that you are not the only ones interested in the painting. Because of the unwanted publicity, our Rembrandt self-portrait is suddenly in play."

"In play?"

"An offer has been made, a very generous offer."

"But it is legally ours," sputtered Spurlock. "It cannot be legally sold."

"This is all true, and I will so inform my client. But he has not been much concerned with legal niceties in the past and I don't expect the legal situation will have a great deal of impact on him now."

"What are you suggesting we do?" said Spurlock.

"Two things. First, increase the pressure on the government to come up with a deal that will bring Charlie home. The federal prosecutor I mentioned before, Jenna Hathaway, is for some unknown reason standing in the way of what

I believe would be a fair resolution of Charlie's criminal matters. Someone needs to strip her of the case and take responsibility, someone perhaps more amenable to negotiation. Second, you had mentioned that a cash payment might be arranged. It might be a provident time to come up with a specific figure that I can relay to my client."

"We will not bid against a criminal element for what rightfully belongs to the trust," said Quick in his usual languid manner.

"Don't consider it a bid. Consider it a conciliatory gesture to a man who desperately wants a reason to come home and happens to have control over a valuable piece of your property."

"It is out of the question," said Quick.

Spurlock turned to Quick and said, sharply, "All avenues remain open until the board closes them off, Stanford. We will decide what to do; your job is to bend the law to make sure our decision stays within its bounds." He focused his eyes on me, clasped his hands together. "How much is he seeking?"

"He hasn't given me a number," I said. "But it appears to be in your interest to wow him."

"We understand. I will take this to the board, and we will be in touch with you when we have a more definite response."

"Don't wait too long. Now, Mr. Spurlock, I have a question on a not entirely unrelated matter. I believe you're acquainted with a Bradley Hewitt?"

"I know Bradley."

"I am involved in a domestic matter in which he is on the other side. His attorney used your name to threaten me."

"How so?"

"He intimated that if I continued to press my client's claim against him, you might scotch any deal with Charles."

"That's preposterous," said Spurlock. "Bradley is a personal acquaintance, that is all. To think I would abridge my responsibilities to the Randolph Trust on his behalf in some sort of domestic dispute is insulting. And with the ongoing federal investigation, you can be sure I want nothing more to do with that foul-mouthed liar."

"Federal investigation?"

"Mr. Spurlock has perhaps said too much," said Stanford Quick.

"Federal investigation?"

"Our discussion of Mr. Hewitt is at an end," said Quick curtly. "Now, Victor, I want you to listen closely." Quick leaned forward, sharpened his gaze until it nearly pierced my forehead. "You say that the murder of Mr. Ciulla was possibly a warning to your client. Have you considered that the warning might not have been meant for Charlie but instead meant for you?"

His stare was so pointed, and his voice suddenly so cutting, that I jerked back as if indeed I had been stabbed in the head. Where did that come from? I wondered. And when I looked at Jabari Spurlock, it seemed as if he were wondering the very same thing.

28

"**I don't know** what you're going on about so much," said Skink. "It ain't like you're the only one what ever got hisself inked."

"But I might be the only one who didn't remember getting it," I said.

"Oh, don't give yourself so much credit, mate. If it weren't for the mind-numbing effects of alcohol, half these joints would be out of business."

By these joints, he meant tattoo parlors, because that's where we were, in a tattoo parlor, or, to be more precise, a tattoo emporium, Beppo's Tattoo Emporium. Tacked onto the walls of the cramped and dark waiting room were Beppo's original designs: dragons and griffins, swords and daggers, religious icons, movie stars, insects and guns, dancing spark plugs, frogs and scorpions, skeletons and clowns, geisha dancers, samurai warriors, naked women in all manner of lascivious pose. Scattered about the waiting room were a few plastic chairs, a ragged coffee table with loose-leaf notebooks filled with art. The place smelled of ammonia and rubbing alcohol, of cigarettes smoked to the filter. From behind the curtain that covered the doorway came a steady buzz punctuated here and there by a whimper of pain.

"You find anything on that Lavender Hill yet?"

"I've been asking around."

"And making noise about it, too. He is not happy."

"It's how you wanted it, mate. Apparently he has a hand in many pots and just as many names."

"No surprise there."

"Those what know him some think of him as a harmless fop with impeccable taste. But those what know him better are too scared to talk."

"That's troubling." I thought of the outline of Ralph's body on the carpet of his house. "Any reputation for heartless violence?"

"Heartless and otherwise."

A yelp erupted from the back room. The buzz stopped for a moment. There was a loud slap, and then the buzzing started again.

"I had a friend once," said Skink, "what got a tattoo of a rooster on his shin. The rooster had a noose round its neck. He said that way he could always tell the dolls he had a cock what hung below his knee."

"He sounds like quite the ladies' man. Anything yet on the federal investigation involving Bradley Hewitt?"

"I'm working on it," said Skink. "We might have an errand to run in a few days that you'll enjoy."

There was another yelp and a falsetto curse, followed by a harsh "Calm your tools, we almost done," before the buzzing started up again.

"You think this Beppo can help?"

"Oh, Beppo's a pro, he is. The other artists in the city, they call him the dean. We've had no luck tracing the name, so we might as well trace the tattoo. He's our best bet to pick who did the what on your chest. We find him that did it, we might find us some answers."

"What's there to find? I stumbled in drunk as a skunk and immortalized on my chest the name of a woman I hardly knew and can't remember."

"Well, mate, all that might be true. But the needle boy might remember who you was with and might be able to tell us how he was paid. Interesting, isn't it, that your money was intact and nothing came up on your credit card?"

"Maybe she paid," I said.

"Maybe she did, unusual as that might sound, and if she did, and paid with something other than cash, we might be able to trace her that way."

"It's worth a try, I guess."

The buzzing stopped, replaced by a quiet, pathetic whimpering.

"How do you know this guy?" I said.

"I did him a favor once. While you're in the chair, you want I tell Beppo to put a rooster on your shin?"

"No thanks, Phil."

"It might help your social life."

"My social life's fine."

"Oh, is it, now? You go out with that girl again?"

"What girl?"

"The one from the club, the one with the sister."

"Monica? No, please. I didn't go out with her in the first place."

"You bought her dinner."

"I paid the check at a diner. It didn't mean we were dating."

"What, you too good to date a stripper?"

"It's not that."

"I dated a stripper once. In Fresno. Nice girl, name of Shawna. Pious."

"Pious?"

"For a stripper."

Just then the curtain across the doorway swung open and a young kid in a T-shirt came out, his left arm hanging limply, a long white gauze patch covering his entire upper arm. His face was red and swollen, but it held a wide, helpless smile, like he was stepping out of his first whorehouse.

As the kid passed us by, a stocky older man came through the doorway, pulling rubber gloves off his hands. He had dark hair and big ears, a jutting jaw, the short, bow-shaped legs of a longshoreman. His thick arms were covered in tattoos from his wrists until they disappeared under his T-shirt. A cigarette dangled out of his mouth. He smiled when he saw Skink.

"You been waiting all this time?" he said. His voice had been burned rough by life and tobacco, and as he spoke, his cigarette stayed miraculously in place, as if glued to his lower lip. "I'da kicked it into third, I knew you was here."

"Didn't want to disturb the artist at work," said Skink. "How's business, Beppo?"

"I'm grinding them out."

"What's up with Tommy?"

"After you bailed out his ass, he up and joined the marines."

"How's he doing?"

"His second tour in Iraq. Maybe you should have left him where he was. So you the guy?"

"I'm the guy."

"This is Victor," said Skink.

"Where's the piece, Victor?" said Beppo.

"On my chest."

"All right, then," he said as he held aside the curtain. "Strip to the waist and hop in the chair so I can get a look-see."

The room behind the curtain was small and bright, with an overhead light and a chair in the middle that looked suspiciously like a dentist's chair. I took off my jacket, my tie and shirt, and as I did, I had the uncomfortable sensation that I was exposing more than mere flesh, I was exposing a part of my inner life.

"Don't be shy, Victor," said Beppo. "I seen it all before, good art and bad art, the vile and the sublime."

"You think you can identify the ink slinger?" said Skink.

"If he's from around here, I can make an educated guess," said Beppo. "I've seen the work of pretty much every shop in town. A big piece of my day is fixing up the mistakes of everyone else. If it's an original, I'll be able to ID it. Up in the chair you go."

My shirt off, I slid into the dentist's chair and leaned back. My jaw instinctively lowered.

"Close your mouth, I ain't pulling molars," he said as he slipped on a pair of thick glasses and leaned his head close to my chest. "Let's take a look." The ash of his cigarette teetered, he rubbed his fingers over my breast. His touch was strangely gentle. He made a sound like a failing carburetor as he looked over the work.

"No skin scratcher here," he said. "This is nice work, made with a first-class iron. Classic design. Solid fill, the colors bright and even. Keep it clean, use the goo, and stay out of the sun. The sun fades everything. You look after that piece, Victor, it'll stay sharp for years."

"That's comforting."

"This Chantal lady, she must be very special to you."

"Oh, she's special, all right."

"Any ideas?" said Skink.

"Not right off. The quality is high, and I think I seen the design before, but I don't recognize it as from one of the local artists. Haven't seen one exactly like this in years." He leaned closer, peered through his glasses, pawed at the skin. "Wait a second. Wait a freaking second. I'll be right back."

He skittered through a bead curtain at the back of the

room. We could hear him climbing a set of stairs, then footsteps and voices above us.

"He lives up top," said Skink.

"Handy."

"That's his girlfriend he's talking with," said Skink. "She's
sixty-eight. The girl he cheats on her with is fifty-four. And
then there's a piece what he keeps on the side."

When Beppo came back down, he had a fresh cigarette
dangling from a victorious smile and he carried a big black
book cracked open.

"I know the puncher what created the design on your
chest," he said.

"Who's our boy?" said Skink, rubbing his hands.

"A fellow name of Les Skuse."

"Skuse?"

"Yeah, with a *k*. Skuse. I knew I had seen that exact tat
before. I been keeping a record of all the designs I seen
since I started in this business. And I have a couple of
pages of original Les Skuse designs. Let me show you.
Right here."

I sat up in the chair as he dropped his book on my lap. The
pages were encased in vinyl covers. One page held a dozen
designs of coiled snakes and dripping swords, of spiders
and birds and skulls. The other page had hearts, all kinds of
hearts, hearts with daggers through them, hearts being held
aloft by fresh-cheeked cherubs, hearts with flowers, with ar-
rows, with kissing figures above a banner reading TRUE LOVE.
And then, in the corner, a familiar design, my design, a heart
with flowers peeking out of either side and a flowing banner
with the words ANY NAME.

"There it is," I said.

"That's the one," said Beppo. "See how even the colors
on the flowers match? Yellow and red on the one, blue and
yellow on the other."

"So Les Skuse is our guy," said Skink. "Give me a where, Beppo."

"Bristol."

"Bristol, Pennsylvania?"

"Nope. The other Bristol."

"England?" I said.

"Exactly so. Les Skuse was the self-labeled champion tattoo artist of all Britain. I met the man once. Quite a brute." Beppo rolled up his sleeve, pointed to an eagle spreading its wings amidst a veritable zoo on his arm. "He did this. He's a legend, all right. But even if you go out that way, you'd have a hard time finding him. He up and died a good long while ago."

"I don't understand how that's possible," I said.

"Well, he was getting up there in years. He was already old when he did my eagle, and being by the sea, he spent a lot of time in the sun."

"No, what I'm asking is how—"

"I knows what you're asking, Victor," said Beppo, letting out a raspy laugh. "You should get out more, lighten up. You got a girl?"

"No."

"Walk around without your shirt, you'll find one. Nothing draws the girls like a tattoo."

"But how did this design end up on my chest?"

"Somebody swiped the design, is how. It's no crime. I done it myself."

"Any idea why he'd pick that one?" said Skink.

"Sure," said Beppo. "You see, every artist got his own style. It can't help but come out, even on something as simple as a heart. Little telltale things like shading and shape, the way the barbed wire winds around it. As identifiable as a fingerprint."

"Unless you copy someone else's heart," said Skink.

"There you go, Phil. The slinger who inked your tattoo, Victor, he picked this design because it's the kind of thing you ink if you don't want anyone to know who it was that done the inking."

"He didn't want me to find him," I said.

"That's right, and I suppose that means he knew you'd be looking, too."

"Why would he want to hide?" I said.

"How the hell would I know?" said Beppo. "Ask Chantal."

CHAPTER

29

I don't normally take a taxi to work, being that my office is only a few blocks from my apartment and that I am so tight with a buck, my wallet squeaks when I walk. So on the morning after my disturbing visit to Beppo's Tattoo Emporium, I didn't take much notice of the battered old taxi passing down my street. When the taxi stopped and backed up toward me, I figured the cabbie needed some directions. I stepped off the curb, leaned into the window, and felt a shiver of fear when I saw Joey Pride, his right hand on the wheel, his blue captain's hat pulled low over his brow.

"Get in," he said.

"That's sweet of you, Joey, really, and I appreciate the offer, but my office is only a few blocks—"

"Shut up and get in."

I took a step back. "I don't think so," I said.

"You're right to be scared, Victor," he said as he turned his face in my direction, "but however scared you are, you not half as scared as me."

His eyes, peering out from beneath the brim of his cap, were moist and red. Fear, like pain pure, rippled the flesh between his eyes. He was right, he was more scared than I, at least he was until he showed me the gun, held unsteadily in his left hand. A revolver, small and shiny, aimed through the open taxi window smack at my forehead.

"Get in the back. I got something to show you, something that will get you scared good and proper."

"Is that the gun you killed Ralph with?"

"Don't be a donkey. I didn't kill Ralph. I loved the man. That's what we need to talk about. Now, get the hell in the cab. I got something to show you. Something it's worth your boy Charlie's life to see."

I thought about it a moment, considered running to get the hell out of there. In a split second, I imagined it all—my briefcase flying, the soles of my shoes hammering the pavement, my suit jacket fluttering behind me like a cape—the whole scene came clear. But something was missing. And I suddenly knew what it was and why. Joey Pride wasn't shooting at me in my imagining because Joey Pride wasn't out to kill me in real life. The gun, too small and of the wrong caliber to have killed Ralph Ciulla, was just another element of his fear, not of mine.

"All right," I said. "Put the gun away and I'll get in."

The gun disappeared. I looked around before slipping into the rear of the taxi. The cab slowly drove off and turned left.

"I'm the other way," I said.

"I know."

"Then where are we going?"

"Around," he said, as he snatched a small silver flask to his lips.

"Shouldn't there be a Plexiglas barrier between the passenger and the driver?" I said. "I'd feel more comfortable with a Plexiglas barrier."

"Shut up."

"Okay."

However beat the cab was on the outside, on the inside it was worse. The vinyl of my seat was mended with silver duct tape, the walls of the doors were stained with the sweat and grime of thousands of indifferent passengers. The cab smelled of gasoline and grease, of smoke and bleach and boredom. It had the pinched feel of a soul that had been waiting too long for not nearly enough.

"The cops called you out to Ralph's house the night he got hit," said Joey.

"That's right."

"What they want with you?"

"They found my card in Ralph's wallet. They wanted to know what I knew."

"What'd you tell them?"

"Just that the three of us had met that afternoon."

"You gave them my name?"

"Yes, I did."

"Thank you for that, you little snake. What they say about me?"

"They want to talk to you, to ask some questions. A detective named McDeiss. He'll give you a square deal."

"He'll get me killed, is what he'll do."

"Who's after you, Joey?"

"I told Ralph to be careful, that we were stepping back into it all. But he always thought he couldn't be touched." He snatched another drink from the flask. "You should have seen him play football for good old Northeast High. He played huge."

"I'm sorry about your friend."

"Yeah. We're all sorry, but that's not helping Ralph none, is it? Who'd them cops think done it?"

"They don't know. But it looks like Ralph knew who killed him."

"Of course he did. The ghosts have come back, boy. Avenging ghosts from Nightmare Alley."

"And you think a bullet from that little gun will stop a ghost?"

"Don't know, never shot one before."

He took a drink from his flask, wiped his mouth with his sleeve. The car swerved before righting itself. The drinking didn't seem to be helping his fear or his driving.

"You spend all of Ralph's cash yet?" I said.

"How you know that was me?"

"Nothing else was stolen but the money clip. No ring, no watch. You were the only one who had seen the cash in the money clip."

"I took the money 'cause I knew I'd be running and I'd need it. Ralph would have understood. But I didn't shoot him."

"Of course you didn't. You were old, easy friends. You finished each other's sentences. You couldn't have hurt him."

"He was more a brother than my own brothers."

"You came to his house after the murder, saw him dead on the floor, panicked, took the money and ran. A few minutes later, you stopped at a pay phone and called it in to the police. But what I don't understand, Joey, is why you ran. Why not call from the house, wait for the cops, tell them what you knew, save yourself from being on the run?"

"You just don't get it. I ain't running from the cops, fool. That's what I wanted to tell you. There's something after me."

"The ghosts?"

"Laugh all you want, but they're after me, they are. And it ain't just me that needs to be running. When I took the money, I took this, too."

He reached a hand back and handed me a piece of notebook paper, folded in half, badly creased and spotted with blood. Carefully, using only my fingertips, I unfolded it, read what was scrawled in a thick black marker.

"Where did you get this?" I said when I had started breathing again.

"It was right on top of Ralph when I found him."

"Left by the guy who killed him," I said.

"You catching on," said Joey.

I looked again at the sheet and the rough printing on its face, among the creases and spatters of blood:

WHO'S NEXT?

"Can I take this to the police so they can get it processed for prints?" I said.

"Do what you want, boy. I done my duty to Charlie by giving you the warning. Rest is up to you. But the killing won't stop with Ralph. We're cursed, all of us."

"All of who?"

"You know, the five of us. That's who the message is for. Ralph and me, Charlie, too, and the others."

"Hugo and Teddy?"

He didn't answer, he just took another swig.

"What did you guys do that's got you so spooked? What happened thirty years ago? Do you think the painting is cursed?"

"Not the painting, just us. Teddy was giving us a way to save our lives, that's what we thought. That's what he said."

"In the bar, when he came back into town?"

"That's right."

"What happened in the bar that night, Joey?"

"He rubbed our faces in our own damn crap, that's what happened," said Joey. "He told us he was ashamed of us. That we had let life happen to us in the worst possible way. Right there, in that back booth, he told us we was a bunch of losers going nowhere but to the corner tap in hopes of drinking enough to forget all we hadn't done with our lives."

"That was pretty harsh," I said.

"But it was the truth. We were failures, all of us. We told him we had our reasons for the way things had turned out, but he didn't want to hear it. Told us that nothing consumed a man's soul more than the easy excuse. And then he put the lie to them excuses, Teddy did, starting with Charlie."

"What about Charlie?"

"He said Charlie let his mother rule his life like a dictator because it was easier than stepping out and making decisions on his own. He told Ralph he threw his money away on women so that he wouldn't have to see if he could really make it on his own. And that Hugo quit school not to take care of his family but because no matter how hard it was hauling those sacks of cement, it was easier than matching his brain up against the suburban kids who thought a college education was a birthright."

"What about you, Joey?"

"Said that me going crazy and getting myself hauled up to Haverford State was a ready-made excuse for not even trying. Called me crazy as a coward."

"What did you guys do?" I said.

"We went after him, we all did. I even tried to slug him, but not because the son of a bitch was insulting my integrity. I wanted to slug him because he was right. We were, the four of us, drowning in our excuses, even as we drowned our sorrows in our beer. When it all calmed down, he said he had learned something out there in California. He had learned that we had to do anything necessary to take hold of our dreams, and sometimes that meant taking hold of our lives and becoming something new."

"Something new?"

"That's what he said, and then he started talking crazy talk. About ropes and apes and supermen. He said we were hovering over some great hole—an abyss, he called it—and we could either go back to the failures we was or go forward and become something new. He said the only answer was to cross that abyss with a rope. But not any rope. He said we was the rope. He said we had to climb over the losers we had become in order to get to the other side. I didn't understand a word of it, but it felt true, you know what I mean? It was like a part of the Bible I never heard before."

"And what was there on the other side?"

"Our fool's dreams, made real."

"Someplace over the rainbow."

"Sure, but then he described them to us in a way that made us believe it all could happen. Hugo was a business school graduate, running some huge company, flying about in the corporate jets, letting the congressmen and senators wait for him in his outer office while some lackey shined his shoes. And Ralph had his own shop, taking orders from all over the country, never touching the metal himself. And his secretary was way hot, and Ralph was banging her on his desktop every lunch hour. And Charlie was running free like a feral cat, doing whatever the hell he wanted, and his mother was happy about it, because he had finally become a man."

"What about you, Joey? What were you doing on the other side?"

"I was driving the fastest rod on the East Coast, going town to town, racing and winning on makeshift tracks, with my own garage and a staff of forty mechanics to keep my baby humming. And, you know, the way he was telling it, he made it come alive. I could see it there, my future, shimmering in the distance. It was dazzling. I could see it clear, just there, beyond the horizon. I still can."

"And all you needed was a way to get there."

"That's right. And then Teddy, he gave us the way. He said we needed something that purified and burned at the same time, an opportunity clean enough and hard enough to transform our lives. And he said he might have the right opportunity in mind." Joey took a long drink from his flask. "And he did, didn't he?"

"The Randolph Trust job."

"Had it all worked out from the start. And when he was through preaching to us, we was converts, all of us. It didn't take too much convincing after that to get us on board."

"The power of Nietzsche."

"Who?" said Joey.

"Some German philosopher. All that stuff about the abyss and the rope, it came from him. Friedrich Nietzsche, the patron saint of disaffected adolescents who want to cast off their chains and become supermen."

"How'd it work out for that Nietzsche fellow?"

"Not too well. He declared God dead, had sex with his sister, went insane."

"Was she hot, at least, his sister?"

"She looked like a turnip. How did Teddy light on the Randolph Trust as the means to perfection?"

"Never knew. This your spot here?"

I looked up. We were on Twenty-first Street now, my street, pulling up to the front of my building. And there was someone waiting by the door. Someone familiar. I squinted at her for a moment before I recognized her.

"Damn," I said.

"That's the word for it."

I shook my head, tried to move from the next crisis back to the current one. "Joey," I said, "I have to go. Thanks for the ride."

I opened the door, slid out of the taxi, leaned in the cab window. "You never said why you were cursed?"

"And I never will neither."

"You see them around, Hugo and Teddy?"

"Hugo left the city a long time ago, I haven't seen him in the flesh since. And Teddy, that sweet-talking son of a bitch disappeared right after the robbery."

"Disappeared?"

Joey let out a soft whistle, like the wind flying across a plain.

"You should turn yourself in, Joey, answer their questions."

"No, sir. I'll end up just like Ralph, I do that."

"When I give them the note you found with Ralph's body, I'm going to tell them how you showed up, took the money, made the 911 call. They'll still be looking for you, but you won't be a suspect."

"Do what you gotta do."

"What are you going to do?"

"Drive around, pick up fares, support myself like I always done, and sleep in the cab until it blows over."

"Get rid of the gun."

"Right," he said as he took another swig.

"And that's not helping either. Listen, how can I get in touch with you?"

"Call your father."

"My father?"

"I'll check in with him now and again. We could always trust your father."

"Be careful."

"You, too, Victor."

"Joey, one thing more. What was Teddy's dream? Did he ever say?"

"He was heading for the other side of the world, he was. Said there was a girl he was going to chase. And about that note. Tell the cops they won't find nothing of interest on it."

"Why is that?"

"Because ghosts don't leave no prints."

CHAPTER

30

Ghosts. I was surrounded by ghosts, or at least those plagued by them, because when the haunted man in the cab drove away, I turned to face the haunted woman waiting for me in front of my office. She was wearing the classic Philly combo: red high heels, blue jeans, tight black shirt. My first thought was how damn pretty she was, so pretty it was hard to tear my gaze away. My second thought was how the hell I was going to get rid of her.

"You promised," I said.

"I promised I wouldn't call," said Monica Adair.

"This is worse. Monica, it wasn't a date. Really. It wasn't."

"Okay, I buy that now. It wasn't a date."

"I didn't mean to lead you on."

"I know."

"Good, I'm glad that's clear. Then what are you doing here?"

"Can we talk, like, privately?"

I looked around. Pedestrians were sparse. "This isn't private enough?"

"Not really. I have a legal question."

"Monica, this is crazy. Stop it now. I feel like I'm being stalked."

"Maybe I'm a little confused. You are a lawyer, right?"

"Yes, I'm a lawyer."

"Then why won't you talk to me about an important legal matter?"

I closed my eyes. "What kind of matter?"

"Do you always talk about important legal matters on the street?"

"With people who aren't clients, sure."

"How do I become a client?"

"Pay a retainer."

"How much?"

"Depends on the case."

She opened her bag and reached in, and as she searched, she said, "Do you take small bills?"

"What kind of legal matter is this, Monica?"

"Can we discuss this upstairs, in your office? Please?"

Beaten, finally, and wanting to get the spectacle off the street, I led her through the dirty glass door, up the wide stairs, past the accountants' office and the graphic-design office, and into our suite.

Ellie smiled warmly at Monica. "I see you found him, Miss Adair."

"Yes, Ellie, thank you," said Monica.

"Good luck."

I gave my secretary a wary look as I led Monica into my office. When I had her seated, I stepped back out.

"Ellie, do me a favor and call Detective McDeiss. I need to hand over some evidence to him as soon as possible."

"Sure thing, Mr. Carl."

"And ask him if he could set up a meeting with Mr. Slocum and that fed, Jenna Hathaway, for this afternoon, okay?" I paused, thought about something. "Ellie, why did you wish our Miss Adair good luck?"

"She said she's looking for her sister. I hope she finds her."

"Right," I said.

"Are you going to help her, Mr. Carl?"

"I think she's a little beyond my help, Ellie. Thank you, and let me know right away when you hear back from Mc-Deiss."

When I returned to the office, Monica was standing behind my desk, leaning back, arms crossed, examining the framed photograph of Ulysses S. Grant hanging crookedly on the wall. "He looks like my Uncle Rupert," she said.

"He looks like everybody's Uncle Rupert," I said. "Can we get started? I have a busy day and it's already taken a turn for the worse."

She winced at that, slightly, nothing big, but a wince just the same. I watched her as she moved away from the photograph and sat in the client chair in front of my desk. She was twisting her lips, as if she were trying to figure out why I was being such a jerk. Good luck to her. I wasn't quite sure why myself, though there was no doubt that I was.

"All right, Ms. Adair," I said.

"Oh, we're all formal now, are we?" she said with a slight smile.

"Yes, that is what we are," I said. "So what can I do for you?"

"I want to hire you."

"To do what?"

"To find my sister."

I sighed for effect. "This sister who disappeared before you were born."

"That's right. I want you to find Chantal."

"I'm not a private detective, Ms. Adair. I can refer you to one if you'd like."

"I want you."

"I'm sorry, but I can't. It's not what I do."

"What do you do, Victor?"

"I primarily defend people accused of crimes."

"And that's more important than finding a missing girl?"

"No, and it's not more important than being a teacher or a doctor, or even dancing with my clothes off, but it is what I do."

"Why are you so mean to me?"

"I'm not trying to be mean. I'm just trying to be honest."

"But you're being mean."

"What do you want from me, Monica?"

"I want to see it."

"See what?"

"The tattoo."

"Gad, no. Forget it. There is no way."

"Please."

"Absolutely not. I'm starting to get very uncomfortable here. I'm sorry I can't help you with your sister, but right now this meeting is over."

"Every place I go, I check the phone book," she said. "Every day I look her up on the Internet. Just to see if there's anything going on with a Chantal Adair. I know it's silly, she won't have the same name if she was taken, but I do it. There are a couple Chantal Adairs out there. I keep track of them all. They're not the right ages, but still I feel close to them, as close as family."

"Monica, you're starting to weird me out."

"Is that so weird?"

"Yes."

"Maybe it is. You know those guys who sit all alone in some laboratory, listening in on the static, waiting for a message from outer space?" she said. "That's me, that's my life. I'm all alone with my dog and my gun, waiting for a message from my sister. And there's been nothing. Nothing." Pause. "Until last week."

I leaned forward, my interest suddenly piqued. "Really? What happened last week?"

"You," she said.

It was only then that it dawned on me, with heartbreaking clarity, that I was dealing with a higher level of insanity than I had heretofore previously thought. And I sensed its root cause, too.

We all suffer, from time to time, the spiritual unease that flickers like a faint flame before being doused by a nice chardonnay or a ball game on the tube. What is our purpose? What is our destiny? Is there more to life than this bland string of continuous sensation? We try to stifle our questions with money or love, with sex or politics or God, we try to plaster over the hole as best we can until the very end, when the light dims and the plaster shatters and we're left alone to wrestle with our doubts through to our final, painful breath. But hey, that's half the fun of being human.

Yet here, sitting across from me, was a woman who had no existential hole to fill. She had been taught, from her earliest moments on earth, that her life contained a singular purpose. She was conceived and raised and carefully trained to fill the gap created by the loss of her sister. And she had succeeded in her own strange way. Chantal was a precocious little dancer with a pair of ruby slippers, and so Monica became a dancer herself, using her sister's name as she strutted in red shoes of her own. Chantal loved animals, so Monica owned a maniacal guard dog with a taste for smoked flesh. Chantal had been killed or abducted, and so Monica guarded Chantal's replacement with a dog and a gun and a series of locks, no doubt, on her door and her heart. No word had been heard from Chantal in decades, and so Monica dedicated herself to listening for a voice in the ether. If you think it's tough being born without a purpose in your life, imagine how tragic it must be being born with one.

"Monica, you must know that I am not a message from your sister."

"You don't know that."

"But I do. This is all just a sad misunderstanding. The tattoo was a mistake, and telling you about it was even worse. I'm sorry."

"Can I see it?"

"No."

"Please?"

She stared at me with her big blue eyes, the simple, faithful eyes of a baby or a pilgrim. I think maybe those eyes were the reason I had been treating her so badly. They seemed to need too much of me, pleading for me to fill a want I could neither fathom nor satisfy. Her parents must really have done a job on poor Monica. And, in turn, I had been a jerk. I felt ashamed.

"If that's what you want," I said. "If that will end all this."

"Yes, it is what I want."

I stood up from my desk, walked around it, closed the door and pressed the button on the knob. I sat on the front of my desk and shucked off my jacket. I stuck my finger above the knot of my tie. When I gave it a tug, it slipped down a bit. I tugged it again.

With the tie completely undone and hanging loosely from my collar, I unbuttoned my shirt, slowly, all while she was closely watching. It must have been a strange reversal for her. Now she was in the small locked room, waiting with bated breath as someone else stripped. I had the urge to warn her against being handsy, but the seriousness of her expression stopped me. She was not a drunken frat boy urging the girls on the balcony to lift their shirts, she was the devout, waiting for a glimpse of the miraculous.

I pushed away the edge of my white shirt. She leaned forward, her eyes widened, she tilted her head. "I thought it would be bigger," she said.

"I get that a lot," I said.

As she leaned her head still closer to get a better look, she reached out her hand and gently traced the name with her finger.

I pulled back a bit and thought about stopping her, but it felt so strange and comforting, her soft flesh brushing my still-wounded skin, that I let it go on. And when she leaned yet more forward and drew her face closer to the tattooed heart, I found myself waiting, expectantly, for the soft kiss of devotion.

A sharp knock at the door.

She pulled back. I almost clocked her with my elbow as I hastily clutched the front of my shirt together.

I jumped off the desk and said loudly, in a voice strangely high-pitched, "Yes?"

"Mr. Carl," said Ellie from the other side of the door. "Detective McDeiss called and said he was sending an officer over to pick up the evidence and take a statement. He also said that Mr. Slocum is in court today, and A.U.S.A. Hathaway told him—and this is a quote—'I never want to see his ugly face again.'"

"Ouch," I said. "Okay, thank you, Ellie."

"Do you need anything else?"

"No, that's it."

We looked at each other, Monica and I, and then we both turned our heads away in embarrassment. We had let something go a bit too far, and we both knew it. I started buttoning my shirt. She leaned back in her chair and crossed her arms.

"Well, that's that, then," I said as I went to sit behind my desk and started retying my tie. "You can see it's just a silly tattoo and it has nothing to do with your sister."

"I suppose."

"It was actually nice meeting you, Monica, and I wish you luck in the future."

"That means you're not taking the case."

"That's right," I said. "Finding a missing person, especially one missing for decades, is not really my thing."

"And you won't be coming back to the club?"

"No, it's not my kind of thing either."

"So no more dates."

"It wasn't a date."

"Oh, right. I guess that's it, then," she said, standing. "By the way, the Hathaway you're meeting with today, is that the police detective?"

"No, she's a prosecutor. Why?"

"Because it was weird hearing the name. The police detective who was investigating Chantal's disappearance was a Detective Hathaway."

My hands suddenly grew clumsy and the knot I was tying disintegrated.

"My parents still speak very highly of him. Detective Hathaway spent years looking for Chantal. He and my parents became very close. It was like he was one of the family."

"You don't say."

"We haven't seen him in a while."

"How old are you, Monica?"

"Twenty-six."

"And your sister disappeared how many years before you were born?"

"Two. Why?"

"Just thinking, is all."

"Thank you for showing me the tattoo, Victor. I don't know what it means, but I won't annoy you anymore, I promise."

I watched as she turned around, as she turned the knob,

as the button popped and the door opened. I watched and I thought and I tried to make sense of everything.

"Monica," I said before she was out the door. She turned around again, and she had that look of need and expectation on her face. "Maybe I ought to meet your parents. What do you think?"

My God, she had a beautiful smile.

31

"It wasn't any trick to find your boy Bradley Hewitt," said Skink. "A guy like that, he needs to let it be known that he's a player. Lunch at the Palm, dinner at Morton's, doing the stroll among the well-heeled and the powerful, and always accompanied by his three guys with their suits and their briefcases."

"He's got an entourage," I said.

"That he does."

"I want an entourage."

"You couldn't handle an entourage. And why is it the power joints all serve steak?"

"Like in the days of the dinosaur, the most feared are always carnivores."

"You wants to know why the cemeteries are filled with indispensable men? Because they all eats steak."

We were walking north, on Front Street, quiet and cobblestoned, with a few cars slipping back and forth looking for parking. Most of the city action was to the west, Old City and Society Hill, the bright lights, the bars. Front Street was staid and dark, close to the river and its mist, a street for the cozy rendezvous or the quiet conversation, a place to walk and talk unobserved.

"That was the public face of your Bradley Hewitt. Nothing of interest there," said Skink. "But I don't give up, it's not in my nature. I keep following. And then, on a quiet Tuesday night, just like this one, I follows him down to the river, away from the crowds."

"Entourage in tow?"

"It's an entourage, so of course it is. Down toward the river, right here to Front Street, and then up a few blocks until he finds hisself a swanky little chew-and-choke just off Market. They all pop inside. A few minutes later, I slip close and scan the dining room. Nice, truly, red walls, marble floors, old school. And chowing down at a table is the entourage, enjoying the hell out of themselves. But no Bradley."

"He was in the men's room?"

"No extra plate at their table. He was somewhere else, and they weren't invited."

"Interesting."

Skink slipped across to the east side of the street, and I followed. We began walking on the sidewalk behind a line of parked cars.

"So I find me a comfortable place and keep my eyes open and sees what I can see. It wasn't long afore limos started disgorging their occupants on the curb like a string of Bowery drunks disgorging their stomachs, one after the other, *splat, splat, splat.*"

"That's an image I could do without."

"First a hot-shot developer what has been in the news, then a councilman what has been railing about developers, and then, wouldn't you know it, His Honor hisself."

"The mayor."

"That's right. I check again through the window, careful now with a cop standing outside. Not a one of them showing."

"There's a private dining room."

"Of course there is. I waits until the night is over and everyone has left the joint, first the mayor and the councilman, then the developer, then Bradley and his entourage. I wait for the last of the fat cats to clear and the door to be locked. I keep waiting until the waitstaff starts slipping out, one by one. It's no real trick to find the one I'm looking for. Someone with a hop in the step, the furtive glance, the twitchy fingers, the one that can barely wait to start spending the tips. And it's a she, and not a bad looker."

"Convenient."

"I start following, but it doesn't take long. She heads north, turns left on Market, slips into the Continental, the upscale joint in that old diner, finds herself a place at the bar. It isn't long afore I find myself a place next to her."

"What was she drinking?"

"Blue martinis. What is that all about? Looks like antifreeze, tastes like nothing. But they gets her in a jovial enough mood. Name is Jillian. Nice girl. She's going through a phase. A few years she'll be back in college where she belongs."

"And what does sweet Jillian say?"

"She says there's a private dining room in the wine cellar of that restaurant, a fancy room with frescoes on the ceilings and bare tatas on the frescoes. And every Tuesday night the mayor meets with his friends to conduct private business."

"Making deals."

"It's the way the city works, right?" says Skink. "He's not even shy about it. Pay to play. The mayor's always running for something, always needs a little cash for the upcoming campaign."

"Jillian tell you this?"

"Jillian didn't know the details, of course she didn't. When she was in the room, pouring the wine, they talked only about golf and the Islands."

"But she knew the players."

"Yes she did. And it seemed every Tuesday night Bradley

was there with some other money boy looking to enter the game."

"So Bradley Hewitt is the middleman, bringing together the mayor and the money for a nice little meal."

"She said our Bradley was partial to the *nodino di vitello all'aglio*."

"What the hell's that, Phil?"

"Veal chop in garlic."

"And he's probably sawing through one right this second. Fabulous. Now all we have to do is figure how to get in, listen to what they're saying, and get it all on tape to use it against him in court. I assume you have a plan to do just that?"

"You assume wrong."

"No plan?"

"No plan."

"You always have a plan."

"Not tonight, mate."

"Then what good is all this?"

"I just thought you'd be interested."

"But I won't be able to use any of this in the Theresa Wellman case."

"Well, maybe not directly."

"What are you talking about, Phil?"

"Something else Jillian let slip. This was after the fourth martini, when she was trying quite hard not to fall off her stool."

"Go ahead."

Phil Skink stepped behind a large black SUV, and I did the same. He pointed across the street to the blue awning and quiet front entrance of an upscale, family-owned Italian joint with one of the best wine lists in the city. There was a limo parked out front and a plainclothes cop leaning against the entrance, looking at his nails.

"I happened to mention to Jillian some sort of federal investigation I had heard tale of, and she nodded. Like she knew what I was talking about. And then she put her finger up to her pretty lips, like it was a secret."

"Like what was a secret?"

"You're a smart cookie, you figure it out."

I looked at Phil, looked at the restaurant and the plain-clothes cop, who now was flicking a piece of lint off his lapel. I tried to put it all together, what he was getting at, and I flashed back again on pretty Jillian, her eyes lidded from drinking, leaning forward with that drunken sexiness as she puts her finger to her lips. *Sssshhh,* it says, that gesture. *Don't let anybody know.* Know what? That someone is listening. To whom? To Jillian and Skink at the Continental? No way. The whole point of the Continental is to act so cool as to ignore everyone else.

A car was coming from the left. As it came at us, I ducked. Skink laughed. After it passed, I scanned the street, back and forth. To our left I spied a row of cars parked nose first, facing the river. I hadn't given it much notice when I passed it before, but this time I gave it a good scan. And there I saw it. How could I have missed it?

A battered white van with a raw brown streak of rust on its side. A van I had seen before.

"Son of a bitch," I said. "Someone is listening in for us."

"You happen to know anyone in the Department of Justice who might give you a hand?"

"It just so happens I might at that, except she hates my guts."

"Charm her, mate."

"I'd have better luck with a cobra," I said, "and probably a better time, too."

CHAPTER

32

"I don't think it's going to happen," I said to Rhonda Harris over drinks at a swank pickup joint on South Street.

"That's too bad," she said with a rather saucy smile. "It would have been sensational."

"Oh, I bet it would."

We were sitting across from each other in a small booth upstairs at the Monaco Living Room, among swarms of the young and the beautiful looking for the quick and the nasty. It was a dark, intimate space with small tables, a mirrored dance floor, and a balcony set back from the main room for those private moments. Not my normal type of beer joint, but she had picked it, and I must say I liked the way the flame of the candle flickered in her green eyes.

"What's the problem?" she said. "Is there anything I can do to make it happen?"

"Not really. We just don't think it's quite the right time for Charlie to talk."

"Who doesn't think that? Charlie?"

"I haven't been in direct contact with my client lately."

"So it's someone else calling the shots."

"In a way, yes. You want another round?"

She was drinking Cosmopolitans, which was very cosmopolitan of her. I was drinking my usual Sea Breeze, which was not. I spun my finger at the beautiful black-clad waitress, asking for another round. Truth was, if I wasn't falling in love with Rhonda Harris, I would have been falling in love with the waitress.

"Doesn't Charlie himself have a say?" she said. "Some people are thrilled to see their names in the newspaper."

"Really?" I said. "I hadn't heard that."

"I could get your picture in the article along with his."

"My good side?"

"Is there a bad one?"

"Now I know you'll say anything to get the interview."

"Busted. Are you going to give Charlie a chance to make up his own mind?"

"When the time's right, maybe." I lifted up my drink and snatched what was left of it just as the waitress came with our next round. They were quick with the drinks at the Monaco Living Room. I smiled like a buffoon at the waitress. She ignored me.

"Do you like being a lawyer, Victor?" said Rhonda as she swirled her rose-colored drink.

"Lawyers rank in job dissatisfaction second only to proctologists."

"Well, then," she said. "I guess things could always be worse."

"But the rubber gloves are so cool, don't you think? That's why everyone uses them now. Lunch ladies, cops. Remember the good old days when dentists stuck their hands in your mouth after just a quick wash?"

"Do we have to talk about dentists?"

"So let's talk about another despised profession, newspaper reporters."

"Are we despised?"

"Oh, yes. More than lawyers, even."

"I doubt that."

"The things I've heard. Do you like writing?"

"Not writing, really. That's the chore at the end of the chase. But I'm a very goal-oriented person and my job fits right in with that. When I need to find a story or get an interview, I usually find a way. Sometimes I ambush the target, sometimes I use my charm."

"Like now."

"I'm trying, although it doesn't seem to be swaying you much."

"Try harder."

"You'd like that, wouldn't you?" She dropped her hand casually on my forearm, looked at me straight with her captivating eyes. "But either way, Victor, know that I will get it done. I'll find Charlie, with or without you, because it is what I do."

"Take it easy, Rhonda. It's just a story."

"It's more than that, Victor. People aren't adjectives. You can think of yourself as kind and sweet and funny, but how you think of yourself doesn't mean a thing. People are verbs."

"What verb are you?"

"I eliminate. Distractions, obstacles, impediments to my success. I'm someone who gets what she's after, no matter who or what gets in the way."

"My God, you sound ruthless."

"Does it excite you, Victor?"

"Oddly, yes. You seem so sure of things. No doubts?"

"What's the point of doubt? You make a decision, go down a certain road, and there you are. You can whine and dither, or you can keep going and get it done. I'm not sure how I ended up here, but I'm not backtracking. Pick a path, do your job with neither fear nor hesitation, that's the only way I know."

"So if you never let anything get in your way, how come you're still just a stringer?"

"I started late, switched careers in midstream."

"What did you do before?"

"Animal control."

"You're kidding."

"No, I'm not. Dogs and cats. Ferrets and snakes and squirrels. Lots of squirrels. You'd be surprised how dangerous they can be."

"Squirrels?"

"After alcohol and lawyers, they're the number one health threat in America."

"Really?"

"No, but don't ever mess with an angry squirrel."

"I bet you looked hot in your uniform."

"I still have it."

"Yowza."

"So what verb are you, Victor?"

"I question, I suppose. I trust uncertainty. I've found out that whenever I'm sure of something, I'm dead wrong."

"What are you sure about right now?"

"That you talk tougher than you really are."

She pursed her lips, sipped her drink. "Maybe you're right."

"You're not so tough?"

"No, that's not it," she said, leaning close enough so I could smell the triple sec on her breath. "You're right about being dead wrong."

CHAPTER

33

Later that night she lay naked beneath me, facedown on the bed. I was naked atop her, my thumbs gently kneading the taut muscles of her back and neck. She was purring like a lioness stretched out in the noonday sun, I was vibrating like a hyena over a freshly felled giraffe. But it was not mere animal lust that was driving me, though I freely admit to lusting like an animal. No, I was filled with some sharp emotion as I stroked and massaged.

I leaned down, kissed the knife's edge of her clavicle. She reached up with her hand to rub the nape of my neck. I nuzzled her earlobe and with my tongue flicked lightly the flesh beneath it.

I have heard tell that the capacity to love is a sign of mental health, which meant, I suppose, that I was just then the healthiest man in the city, mentally wise at least, seeing as I was falling in love with every woman I laid my gaze upon. I pined for them, I felt lost without them, I was sure that each of them, the woman beneath me being no exception, could save my life.

I kissed her again. Her bracelets jangled lightly as she rubbed my neck harder than before. I wasn't even sure who she was, really, in her soul, but the raw emotion she coaxed out of me with every purr and every touch cut like a jagged shiv through my heart.

But even in my besotted state, I knew I couldn't be feeling true love so indiscriminately. No, what was flooding my blood that night, along with the lust, was a potent cocktail of fear and desperation, of loneliness and need, of a pathetic yearning for the merest breath of salvation. What I was searching for, in my deepest soul, was someone to pull me out of a bottomless hole whose dimensions I couldn't fathom.

I nibbled her flesh. Her fingernails dug into my scalp with a lovely pain.

Yet even as I recognized the fallacy of my emotions, I couldn't give up the hope that maybe, just maybe, this woman, this one, here, now, not womanhood in general but this specific woman in particular, could actually be my savior. The others might have been counterfeit totems to a false hope, but maybe this one, here, was actually the true answer to my questing heart.

Suddenly she arched her back, lifted her torso out of the bed, bent her legs back and locked them around my own, like a breaststroker doing a scissor kick. I felt myself being pulled under.

"Wait," I said. "What are you doing? Whoa. Whoooa."

She was laughing as we fell into a rhythm, and I started laughing, too. My God, maybe it was the real thing, maybe I had found it after all.

You are the one, no you, no no you are the one, beneath me, right now, you.

"Right there," she said. "That feels good. Oh, yes."

I wanted to kiss her just then, not on the shoulder or on the back of the neck but on her mouth, hard and clean, as we gazed at each other eye to eye.

I slid down and out, rose onto my knees, reached under her arm, gently spun her around until I was staring with a longing heart straight into the face of Sheila the Realtor.

*   *   *

I am as appalled writing this as you must be reading it. But there is a simple explanation. Really.

So I was drinking with Rhonda Harris upstairs at the Monaco Living Room, feeling the love, so to speak, and hoping that things might actually lead somewhere with someone this time, when she glanced at her watch and leaped out of her seat. "Got to go," she said.

"Really?" I said, trying to keep my crest from falling.

"Sorry, Victor."

"I was thinking maybe dinner. Maybe Italian."

"Can't. Not tonight at least. Will you talk to Charlie for me, please?"

"I guess."

"I'll call you."

"I'll be waiting," I said, like a puppy.

I was sitting forlornly, alone with my drink, when the pretty young waitress brought another round that I had optimistically ordered a few moments before.

"She coming back?" she said, indicating Rhonda's spot.

"Not tonight," I said.

"Too bad," said the waitress, cleaning Rhonda's side of the table. She was lean and athletic, with long black hair and big eyes. "I guess you won't be needing the Cosmo, then," she said. She had a fresh rosy complexion that said soy milk and yoga. I didn't know about the soy milk, but I could learn yoga.

"Since the drink's already ordered," I said, "you want to join me?"

"Can't. Against the rules."

"When do you get off?"

"December," she said.

I lifted up my new Sea Breeze. "Merry Christmas."

By then I was a little too comfortable in my seat and couldn't quite face going home to my ruined apartment to flop down on my ruined couch and spend another night watching the reception flicker on my cableless portable television. So I reached for the phone in my jacket pocket. I was going to call Beth, whom I hadn't spent enough time with lately, or maybe Skink, who could cheerfully turn the evening in a more sinister direction, or anyone in the directory who could provide a little company. But with my phone I inadvertently pulled out a card that had been sitting in the same pocket. Sheila the Realtor's card. And I remembered the way her eyes had shone when she told me to give her a call.

So I did.

And I'll say this for her, she was all business, was Sheila the Realtor, and she knew how to close the deal.

"I'm so glad you called," she said after, as we lay in bed together while she smoked. She used her cupped left hand as an ashtray. "This was such an unexpected treat. Want a cigarette?"

"No thank you," I said. "I'm nauseated enough already from the sex and the drinking."

"I smoke to keep thin."

"I throw up," I said.

"I do that, too. So who is Chantal?"

"Excuse me?"

"The name on your tattoo. Is she your girlfriend?"

I looked down at the heart on my chest. "Not really."

"An old girlfriend, then?"

"Something like that."

"Not too old, since it looks fresh enough. What do you do when you tattoo a lover's name on your chest and then you break up?"

"Look for someone with the same name."

"Sort of limits your options."

"Maybe that's why I don't get out much."

"They can remove tattoos with lasers now. You can lose the tattoo and have a peel all at once."

"Convenient," I said.

"It's important to keep your facial skin fresh. Your partner Beth made an offer on that house."

"Are the sellers going to accept?"

"I think so. It's lower than they want, but the place has been vacant for a while now. She's getting a tremendous deal."

"Yeah, what's up with that? Why has the house been vacant for so long?"

"Ghosts," she said.

"No, seriously."

"I'm perfectly serious. There was a suicide there. It was about fifty years ago, but the most recent tenants complained about strange noises and creaking floorboards before they moved out in a panic. They've had a hard time finding a buyer since."

"Does Beth know?"

"Not from me."

"You didn't tell her?"

"Beth looks lost, Victor, don't you think?"

"She's doing okay."

"No she's not. She clearly needs something in her life, and what I've found is that real estate fills so many gaps. I didn't want a silly piece of nonsense to get in the way of a fabulous opportunity. She won't find anything near as wonderful within her price range."

"Are you always selling?"

"Oh, come on, Victor. We're talking ghosts. And you saw the size of the kitchen."

"With the morning light."

"Well, some mornings. It's there for the first few weeks of April, maybe. After that it sort of slides into the house next door." She sat up, the sheet fell from her breasts. "This was fun, but I have a big day tomorrow, appointments lined up back-to-back, and then my fiancé is flying home from Milan."

"Your fiancé?"

She turned to me, leaned close, brushed my cheek with her right hand. The smoke of her cigarette floated into my eye, and I started blinking it away.

"You're sweet," she said. "Are you sure you're a lawyer?"

"I'm not very successful."

"Call me again sometime." She tossed off the rest of the sheets, kicked her long legs off the bed, and stood, stretched, headed to the bathroom. "Got to be going."

"Going? Isn't this your place?"

"Please. This is right on South Street. Why would anyone in her right mind live here? This condo is one of my listings. You can stay as long as you want, but please make the bed before you leave. I'm showing it tomorrow."

"It's sort of nice."

She stopped, twisted around, stared at me with her cigarette held elegantly to the side of her face and a renewed interest in her eye. Was there a real connection between us after all? I found myself, against all reason, hoping so.

"If you're serious, Victor," she said, "I could get you a fabulous deal."

I suppose that was it, right there, the moment when I fully realized how much trouble I really was in. I was lying in a bed that was not my own, blinking wildly still from the smoke, tearing, staring at a naked woman who was affianced to someone else, and feeling strangely deflated because all the time she was trying to close a deal. If I was capable of sleeping with a Realtor, was it possible to fall any lower?

I needed something, anything, to pull me out of this hole, but I couldn't for the life of me figure out what, even when the answer was in front of me from the very start.

34

"Can you do me a small favor?" said Monica Adair as we drove north on I-95.

"Sure," I said.

"This might sound a little weird, but my mom and dad worry about me so much, and you might be able to put their minds at ease."

"Whatever I can do."

"Great, then you'll, like, tell them we're dating, right?"

"Excuse me?"

"They're afraid I'm too often alone. They'll be so reassured to know I have a boyfriend who's a lawyer."

"Monica, is that a good idea?"

"I know they might not be so happy about the lawyer part, but they'll get over it."

"That's not what I meant."

"You can say you met me at work."

"At the club?"

"No, silly. They think I'm a legal secretary. And your being a lawyer and my fake job being a legal secretary, it makes perfect sense that we would have a fake relationship."

"Should I call you Hillary, too?"

"Why would you call me Hillary?"

"To be consistent."

"I knew a girl named Hillary, once," said Monica. "She

wasn't a legal secretary, but she had a very nice figure. Not too smart, though. Thought Canada was a foreign country."

"It is a foreign country."

"That's good, teasing me like that, just like a boyfriend would."

"Monica, I'm not so comfortable lying to your parents."

"Are you sure you're a lawyer?"

"Pretty sure, though a lot of people seem to be doubting it lately. But if you're so ashamed of your life, don't lie about it, change it."

"I'm not ashamed of what I do, I just have secrets. You don't have any secrets, Victor? You tell everything about your personal affairs to your parents?"

I thought of the escapade with Sheila the night before. "Well, no."

"There you go. Their life has been hard enough already, they don't need to be burdened with the truth about mine. So the story is we met at the office and we've been dating for only a few weeks, but things are going really well."

"What do we do together?"

"See movies, take walks. I cook you dinner. Veal parmesan."

"Do you really?"

"No."

"But I like veal parmesan."

"I'll fake-cook it."

"Do I have a fake dog?"

"You did, but it died."

"That's a shame."

"You'll see, Victor, this is going to work out famously."

I doubted very much that it would.

I was visiting Monica's parents to learn what I could about the disappearance of Chantal Adair and its connection to Charlie Kalakos's Rembrandt. That there should be a connection at all was too strange for words, but both girl and painting went missing almost thirty years ago, and each seemed to be of great concern to the family Hathaway, father and daughter. None of it made any sense, but I was not naïve enough to assume it was all a coincidence. I could no longer believe that the tattoo was evidence of a deep and abiding love found during my missing night. There was something else going on, something dark and as of yet inexplicable. But I was going to figure it out, yes I was, and when I found who the hell had induced me to tattoo the name on my chest, a price would be paid.

"And you're sure they won't mind talking about your sister?" I said to Monica as I parked the car in front of a small, tidy house.

"Don't worry."

"It must be difficult for them to discuss."

"Not at all," she said. "Chantal is their favorite topic of conversation."

There are canyons of loss among us, chasms of pain hidden behind well-tended lawns and freshly painted exteriors. Drive by a seemingly innocuous house and you can feel the tug, like a deep, swirling ache reaching out to pull you in, and all you want to do is keep driving until you slide into shallower, more placid waters. These are churches of sadness and doom, where voices remain hushed and candles burn in sad remembrance. Lower your gaze, speak with soft reverence, hunch your shoulders, stifle your joy. Such was the Adair household on a narrow residential street not far from the western mouth of the Tacony-Palmyra Bridge, just a stone's throw from where Ralph Ciulla had been murdered.

"Mommy, Daddy," said Monica, suddenly hugging my arm as the door opened, not giving me the chance to step away. "This is my new boyfriend, Victor."

"Hi," I said, trying and failing to take back my arm.

Mr. Adair was lean and gray, stoop-shouldered, parched by life, looking like a dried-out seventy even though still in his fifties. His smile was pained, his handshake thin, his averted eyes glassy, as if he had been throttled just moments before I arrived.

"So you're the young man Monica has told us about," he said.

I glared at Monica. "That would be me."

"Come in, please," said Mrs. Adair, a wraith with black eyes and nervous hands. "I put out some Chex Mix. I hope you like Chex Mix."

"It's my favorite."

"And you simply must meet Richard."

"My brother," said Monica.

"Of course," I said. "Your brother, Richard. The whole family."

"Not quite the whole family," said Mr. Adair.

"But Richard so enjoys guests," said Mrs. Adair, "and he's especially looking forward to meeting you."

"I bet," I said.

He didn't get up when first he spied me. Richard Adair looked like he wouldn't get up for a tornado. His heavy hips spread out on the couch as if planted there. Sweatpants, Eagles jersey, stocking feet propped on the coffee table with the tips of his socks flopping over his toes. He was about a decade older than me, big and balding, with a round face and graying mustache. A bunch of billboards were roaring around some oval piece of asphalt on the television, and Richard kept staring at the tube as if, instead of the current running order, the secret of the universe was about to be broadcast and he was just waiting to sneer at it.

"Richard," said Mrs. Adair as if to a spoiled child. "Monica's brought her friend to the house."

"I'm watching here," said Richard. "What do you think?"

"Richard loves his television," said Mrs. Adair. "When he's not on the computer, you can always find him in front of the television."

"We got a big one from Best Buy," said Mr. Adair. "What is it, Richard, the thin-screen thing?"

"LCD."

"It was on sale."

"Can you keep it down?" said Richard. "I'm watching."

The living room had that closed-in, windows-painted-shut feel, stifling and hot. We set ourselves on the various pieces of furniture, Monica still clutching my arm, as if she were the one in foreign territory. There were pictures of saints clustered on one of the walls, and plates painted with clowns with their big sad eyes on another. Chex Mix was scattered about in various bowls. I wasn't lying, I always liked Chex Mix, and Mrs. Adair didn't just open the boxes and stir, she did the whole margarine and Worcestershire sauce baking thing, which filled the house with a savory scent while imparting to the Chex Mix a nice garlicky crunch.

"Lovely Chex Mix, Mrs. Adair," I said.

"Thank you. Richard, dear, Victor is a lawyer, did you know that?"

No answer from Richard. I guess he knew.

"NASCAR is on," said Mr. Adair in explanation. "The racing cars."

"Yes, I know," I said. "Who among us doesn't love NAS-CAR?"

Mrs. Adair clapped her hands together and rubbed. "So how long have you two kids been an item?"

"Not too long," I said.

"When Monica called and said she had a date with a young man she met at work, we were just so thrilled. You would think someone as pretty as our Monica wouldn't have trouble finding a young man, but she is very particular."

"Oh, Mommy, stop it."

"She works all day and then just stays at home all night, poor thing. She needs to get out more. Don't you think so, Victor?"

"Oh, you'd be surprised," I said.

"What kind of law do you do?" asked Mr. Adair.

"All kinds, but mostly criminal law."

"We don't like criminals in this family."

"Well, they're not as popular as NASCAR, I give you that, but they still have rights."

"What about the rights of the victims?"

"Stop it, Daddy," said Monica. "Daddy's been watching too much cable news. He thinks he's O'Reilly."

"The man makes good points. He's a pillar."

"So was Lot's wife," I said.

"I hate lawyers," said Richard, without looking away from the television. "Greedy little buggers, all of them."

"I suppose we are," I said. "But it's a capitalist country, right? Where would we be without greedy little buggers?"

"What's it like making money off other people's heart-break?" said Richard, still without turning his head in my direction. "I mean, a guy breaks his leg, you make money. A guy breaks his head, you make more money. No matter how crippled the victim, you make out like a thief. It must sicken your heart."

"But the cardiologists these days can do wonders," I said. "What do you do, Richard?"

"Richard is between things," said Mrs. Adair. "More Chex Mix, Victor?"

"No, ma'am, I'm fine. Thank you."

"You bagging my sister yet?" said Richard.

"Excuse me?"

"Richard, shut up," said Monica.

"I'm just asking," said Richard. "I'm allowed to ask."

"Something to drink, everyone?" said Mrs. Adair. "Tea?"

"Tea would be lovely," I said. "Thank you."

"Monica, why don't you help me in the kitchen? There's another batch of Chex Mix in the oven. It's especially nice hot out of the oven, don't you think, Victor?"

"Oh, absolutely. What kind of margarine do you use?"

"Oh, heavens, I wouldn't use margarine. Only real butter in my Chex Mix."

"It shows."

The two women departed for the kitchen, and the three men were left with nothing but the sound of engines roaring out of the television set. The announcers got excited about something, Richard belched, Mr. Adair pushed himself out of his chair to hit the head. I swirled some Chex Mix in my fist.

"Who's winning?" I said to be friendly.

"Some guy with a hat," said Richard. "Do you care?"

"No."

"Neither do I. Can I be frank?"

"Sure, and I'll be Sam."

"We both know Monica isn't the brightest bulb in the shed. We both know you're not dating her for her taste in literature. So I figure you got to be bagging her. I mean, if you're not, and I'm talking about bagging her steady, giving her the old heave-ho night and day and night and day, then really, what's the point?"

"Nice mouth on you, Richard."

"I'm just saying."

"She's your sister."

"Yeah, sure, I know, but my God, look at her. Have you seen those legs? They go up to her chin. And her breasts are, like, perfect."

"How do you know that?"

"Sometimes she sunbathes in the back and loosens her top. I just sit up in my room and stare out the window."

"Richard, you're being creepy."

"Listen. There are girls on the Internet not half as hot as Monica making a fortune just by spreading their legs and lifting their shirts for the camera. With the package she's carrying, she could make double, triple, but she's wasting it all in that stupid law office."

"She does good work in that office," I said.

"Maybe you could talk to her for me."

"About what?"

"I've got this idea of opening a Web site. 'Monicaland dot com,' we'd call it. I've already reserved the domain name. I'd do all the work, all the designing and maintenance, answer all the e-mails for her. I'd even pretend to be her in the Monicaland chat room. All she has to do is let me take some pictures. We could make a fortune."

"I don't think so."

"I'd be doing all the work, and the money we make could set her up for life. I'd give you a cut, too, if you convince her."

"You'll have to dress better, Richard, if you're going to be a pimp."

"Hey, I'm just looking out for my sister. I just want to build her up a nest egg. That's the way my family is—we look out for each other. And let me tell you, if you want to keep bagging my sister day and night, like you're doing now, you'll go along."

"Or else what?"

"I knew it was you as soon as you walked in the room. I seen you on the TV. You're the guy representing that Charlie Kalakos guy with the painting."

"What about it?"

"Here's the deal. You talk to Monica about our Web site and I won't tell my parents who you are."

"Why would I care if you tell? What does one have to do with the other? I'm a little lost here, Richard."

"There's a connection, trust me."

"Oh, is there?" I got up, stepped over the television, stood right in front of it, the vroom vroom going on behind me. Richard craned his neck to try to see around me, found it futile, looked at me for the first time and then away. His eyes were yellow, his skin flabby and white like an overworked dough.

"You want to tell me about it?" I said.

"I'm trying to watch," he said.

"Okay, I wouldn't want to get in the way of your NAS-CAR." I moved from in front of the television, around the coffee table, and sat smack on the couch, so close our hips were rubbing.

He tried to slide away, but I slid with him. He watched the racing, I watched him, watched him wilt under my gaze. I knuckled his head, twice, and he just shrank away, like a slug shrinking away from salt.

"What's the connection, Richard?"

"Forget about it."

"No, I want to hear."

"It's not important."

"Sure it is."

"What are you doing here? Get the hell out of here. Leave me alone, or I'm going to tell Monica you hit me."

"You'll do nothing of the kind," I said. I leaned close, so close my lips were almost touching his ear. "Here's a lesson for you, boy. There are two types of people in the world, users and tools. You want to be a user, you want to turn your sister into a whore, but you'll always be just a tool. And you want to know why? Because you have to be able to read people to be a user, and you are functionally illiterate. See, here's the thing, Richard: You thought I came here because I have the hots for Monica, that I have her name tattooed on my lustful little heart, but you're wrong. She's not the Adair whose name I have tattooed on my heart. How do you like them apples?"

He turned and stared at me, and there was fear on his doughy face and in his yellow eyes. The couch shifted as his butt muscles clenched.

Just then the toilet flushed. Richard's head swiveled. Mr. Adair stepped out of the downstairs powder room. Monica and Mrs. Adair appeared from the kitchen with a tray.

"I have the tea and a fresh batch of Chex Mix," said Mrs. Adair. "Oh, look at you two, getting along so nicely. What are you boys talking about?"

"Chantal," I said.

CHAPTER

35

It was the movies that finally determined it for me. The home movies, Super 8s unspooling on a projector Mr. Adair pulled out of the closet, the images splashed upon one of the living room walls. After I brought her name up, the Adairs seemed only too willing to talk about Chantal. They reminisced about her sparkling personality, told fond stories, recounted again the great day when Chantal danced on television on the *Al Alberts Showcase*. It was all sweet enough to make of me a disbeliever. Is there anything more dubious than someone else's happy childhood? But then at one point, Mrs. Adair clapped her nervous hands and said, "Let's see the movies," and only a moment passed before the projector was whirring and the memories were flickering.

It took me a moment to get my bearings as the past unreeled for me on the living room wall. That young woman with the short black hair and sexy smile, with a body lithe enough to get me to thinking, the woman clapping her hands in delight at her children, oh yes, that must be Mrs. Adair. You could see now where Monica got her beauty. And that arrogant young buck with the muscles bursting proudly from beneath his tight shirt, that was Mr. Adair, when life still was full of electric promise. And that kid there, laughing and tossing leaves into the air, towheaded and pink-cheeked. Richard? It couldn't be, could it? Yes it could. Richard. Gad.

I looked away from the images and scanned the room, the parents staring raptly at a time when life was perfect, Richard with his arms crossed, unhappy to be there but unable to look away. And Monica, sitting next to me, leaning forward, her face suffused with some strange nostalgia for an era that ended brutally before she was born. Something had turned the past of the film into the withered present, something more vicious than the mere passage of time.

"She just never came home," said Mrs. Adair. "Went out one day to play and never came home."

"We went door-to-door," said Mr. Adair. "Had the police out, put up posters, walked every inch of the parks. The whole neighborhood came out."

"Her picture was on the news for a solid week."

"Nothing. And it's the not-knowing that's the worst of it, like we're still in the middle of it. The ache, it never leaves. It started in my chest before creeping into my bones. My doctor says it's arthritis, because he doesn't know."

"Did she have friends?" I asked.

"She was very popular," said Mrs. Adair. "Miss Personality. But none of her friends had seen her that day."

"Who saw her last?"

"Richard saw her leave," said Mr. Adair. "But it's not his fault, it's our fault. We let her go out, always. We trusted her, and we trusted everyone else."

"Any idea where she was going, Richard?" I said.

"I told the police everything," he said.

"Detective Hathaway," said Mrs. Adair. "What a wonderful man, what a sweet man. He did everything he could."

"He kept the case open for years," said Mr. Adair. "Never gave up."

"What did you tell him, Richard?"

"That I didn't know where she went. Can we get back to the race?"

"Sometimes still, I get so angry," said Mr. Adair, "angry at myself, at the world, at my own helplessness. Sometimes I still try to put my hand through the wall."

Chantal Adair. My breath caught in my throat the first time she showed up on the screen, my chest throbbed. The name had been scrawled into my flesh and engraved deep in my consciousness, and now there, in front of me, in light and color and shadow, there she was, oblivious to the tragedy rising already behind her, moving to some jerky, otherworldly rhythm. To see her on that wall was to see a legend, a mythic hero come to life, like watching old movies of Babe Ruth or Jack Dempsey, of a young Willie Mays loping like a leopard in the outfield.

"Oh, my sweet Chantal," said Mrs. Adair.

Whether she was sweet or not, little Chantal, you couldn't tell from the sun-drenched images in the movies. Her dark hair, flashing eyes, the glittery dance shoes she loved, the way she laughed, hugged, mugged for the lens. Already there was something self-conscious in her pose, something of the ingenue in her movements, like she knew already at age six how to turn and twist for the camera.

There was a little blond girl in many of the shots, about the same age as Chantal, throwing snowballs and laughing as she roughhoused. She marched and ran while Chantal pranced.

"My cousin Ronnie," said Monica. "Uncle Rupert's daughter."

"Uncle Rupert. He's the guy who looks like Grant."

"Who's Grant?"

"The guy with the beard in the picture in my office."

"That's the one. My mother's brother."

"Was Ronnie close to Chantal?"

"They were like sisters," she said.

"Thick as thieves," said Mrs. Adair. "They were nothing alike, but they were together all the time. The loss really hit Ronnie hard."

"Did Detective Hathaway have any ideas about what happened to Chantal?" I said.

"He had ideas," said Mr. Adair. "Nothing that amounted to nothing, but he sure had ideas. And most of them centered on something he found in Chantal's room."

"What was that?"

"Strangest damn thing. A lighter. How she got hold of it, none of us could figure it out, but there it was, hidden in one of her drawers."

"Do you still have it?"

"No, he took it as evidence, but I still remember it," he said. "A gold lighter, well worn, with the initials W.R. engraved on its case."

"Do you have a picture of Chantal I might be able to take with me?"

"We printed up tons for the search. A head shot. We still have them somewhere." Mr. Adair pushed himself out of his chair with a soft moan. "Wait a minute and I'll get one for you."

And that was what I had in my pocket, that photograph, as Monica and I drove away from her girlhood home. The lighter with Wilfred Randolph's initials was evidence of a possible connection between the disappearance of Chantal Adair and the robbery of the Randolph Trust. And if a connection really existed, then my client, definitely involved in one, most likely knew something of the other. Next time I saw him, I'd have to give him the third degree. But something else was tugging at my sleeve.

"That was nice of you to come to my parents' house," said Monica. "It seems to help them to talk about it. It's almost like when they talk about her, or watch the movies, she's still there."

"I liked your parents."

"And they liked you, I could tell."

"Your father scowled at me."

"Only at the beginning. Later he warmed up. You're the best fake boyfriend I've ever had."

"There have been others?"

"Usually they're gay."

"Which must lessen the complication."

"You would think. But my parents don't show the movies to just anybody."

"Are you sure? I got the sense they corral Mormon missionaries and Fuller Brush men to see the movies and hear the tale."

"Not true. And my mother told me approvingly that you sure do know your Chex Mix."

"You're going to have to tell them eventually that we're not dating."

"We aren't?"

"No, Monica. This wasn't a date."

"I brought you home, you met my parents."

"You're kidding, right?"

"Yes, I'm kidding. Oh, my mom will ask about you for a while, and then I'll say we broke up, and that will be the end of it. Maybe I'll fake-date a doctor next. They always liked doctors."

"Why don't you date someone for real?"

"Fake dating is so much easier. You should try it, Victor."

"Why not? I've faked everything else. Tell me about your brother, Richard."

"What's to tell? He's a little sad, a little lonely, but he's very smart. He's my older brother. I used to idolize him."

"What kind of work does he do?"

"He doesn't. He just plays on the computer or watches TV."

"No friends?"

"It's hard to find a friend when you haven't stepped outside the house in twenty-five years."

"Excuse me?"

"He doesn't leave the house. He can't step through the doorway. He's stuck, and he's been that way since before I was born. He has that thing."

"Agoraphobia?"

"That's it. First time I heard it, I thought he was afraid of sweaters. But what it really means is he can't go outside or to public places."

I thought then of the home movie projected onto the wall, not the parts with Chantal posing or playing with her cousin Ronnie, not the parts that held the rest of the family in thrall, and not the images of the parents either, at the start of their lives when the world held nothing but hope. No, I thought of the boy, laughing and tossing leaves into the air, towheaded and pink-cheeked and full of promise. The palpable sadness in that house had burrowed like a parasite into his heart, turning him into some grotesque creature. I had come on all hard-boiled with him, and maybe he had asked for it, but it wasn't right, and I felt ashamed. He had deserved better from me, better out of life. Whatever evil had happened to Chantal had happened to him, too, it had happened to all of them. And my client's involvement was enough for me not to be able to ignore it.

"I'm going to find out what happened to your sister, Monica," I said.

"You're taking the case?"

"No, I can't take it on as a case. No retainer, no fees, no expenses. And believe me, it hurts to say that, more than you can imagine. But I have a conflict with another case I'm involved in, so I can't take it on professionally. But I'm going to find out all the same."

"For me?"

"Not really."

"Then why, Victor?"

"I don't know. Because her name somehow got tattooed on my chest and I'll be staring at it in the mirror for the rest of my life. Because what happened to her was dead wrong and it pisses me off. Because of your brother."

"My brother? I didn't think you liked him."

"It doesn't matter."

"I don't understand."

"Maybe neither do I, but still. My apartment is trashed, my partnership is cracking up, I'm drinking too much, flirting with reporters, sleeping with Realtors. Frankly, I'm in desperate need of something hard and clean in my life, and finding what happened to Chantal is all I have."

"That is so . . . Victor, that is so . . . so . . ." She leaned over in the car and kissed me on the cheek.

"We're still not dating," I said.

"I know. I'm just so happy. It was a message, wasn't it? The tattoo, I mean."

"Maybe it was."

"From her."

"From someone. Let me ask you, is anyone in your family a tattoo artist?"

"No."

"I'm still trying to figure out who gave it to me."

"She did. You're fighting hard not to admit the truth, but it will come to you. So when do we start?"

"We?"

"Sure."

"No."

"You're not going to let me help you?"

"Monica," I said, "I work best alone."

"But I want to help. Can't I help? Please, Victor. I need to do this."

"Monica, there is no way that—" And then I stopped.

My first impulse is always to be a lone wolf. One of the reasons Beth might have been dissatisfied at the firm was my penchant for pushing her away and going it by myself. And here was Monica, whose life had been as altered and bruised as anyone's by Chantal's disappearance, asking me if she could help find out what happened to her sister. I didn't know what aid she could give, but maybe I was being selfish, maybe she more than anyone deserved the opportunity to be involved in the search. Or maybe I was kidding myself and simply still felt the soft touch of her finger on my chest.

"Okay," I said. "You can help."

"Really? You mean it?"

"Sure. We'll start in a couple days. Maybe you and I, we'll go together to visit an old friend of your parents'."

"Why don't we start right away? Oh, Victor, this is so fabulous. I'll take a few days off from the club, buy some black leather pants, clean the gun."

"No gun."

"But, Victor, I like my gun."

"No dog, no gun, no heels sharp enough to penetrate flesh. That's not the way I do things, at least not professionally."

"All right, all right, don't get your tie into a twist. What about the black leather pants, are they okay at least?"

"Why black leather pants?"

"Emma Peel, from *The Avengers*."

"Sure, the black leather pants are fine."

"But why aren't we getting started right away?"

"Because first I have to meet someone in New Jersey, and that I have to do alone."

CHAPTER

36

This time I was dressed to blend: sneakers and jeans, red baseball cap, a garish yellow Hawaiian number hanging open over a white T-shirt. I had thought of wearing shorts, but my legs were so white they glowed, which didn't quite fit the image of a sun-worshipping Jersey boy, so jeans it was. When I reached my perch at Seventh Street on the Ocean City boardwalk, the sun was setting and the sky over the ocean was turning Kodachrome. I did a quick peruse. No Charlie, no goons who might have followed me, just the usual crowd swarming and laughing in the thick salt air, flirting and ignoring the flirts, whining, strolling, dripping soft ice cream onto their shoes. I thought some ice cream might fit my disguise.

I was standing in line at the Kohr Bros. Frozen Custard stand when I heard a hiss from the T-shirts in the store next door. Behind a scrim of shirts, I could spy the top of a round bald head, ugly plaid shorts, sandals over socks.

"I'll have a small vanilla," I said to the pretty Russian woman behind the stand. "And a large vanilla with rainbow sprinkles."

With the ice creams in hand, I sauntered over to the T-shirt store and held out the large sprinkled cone. Through a collection of shirts and sweats, a hand reached out.

"Thanks," said Charlie. "I love the custard."

"Who doesn't? You want to talk here?"

"I'll meet you at the waterline in five minutes."

"Just don't spill your custard on the steps this time."

I waited on the beach, breathing deep the salt air. A wide stone jetty was just ahead of me. The evening was breezy and clear, the sea glinted orange, the surf was angry. I stood at the crest of the sand, where the shoreline started slanting toward the sea, and watched the waves swell and froth before pounding themselves into oblivion. Quite a show. They ought to sell tickets. The fate of the universe in six-second tableaux. Appearing nightly. Try the veal, and don't forget to tip your waitresses.

The beach was open to the left, closed in by a music pier on the right. In the reddening light, I could spot a few silhouettes climbing along the jetty or strolling across the sand. I kept track of them all, checking to see if any were a little too interested in anything I was doing. As usual I was being completely ignored, which was, as usual, fine by me. Especially when I was meeting with a client who was wanted by a bunch of gangsters, a hit man from Allentown, and the FBI all at once. I turned toward the boardwalk, spotted a giant toddler with an oversized head and splayed legs coming my way.

"You alone?" said Charlie Kalakos.

"Sadly, that's my condition in the world."

"Were you followed?"

"No."

"How do you know?"

"Because I drove slowly with one eye on my rearview mirror. Because I stopped on the side of the highway twice, and no one else stopped. Because I parked on Seventeenth and walked the ten blocks on back streets and spotted nothing. But I'm just a lawyer, Charlie, not a spy. My training is in torts, not tails. I'm doing my best."

"Your best might get me capped. How's my mom?"

"She's fine. She's even seemed to perk up a bit."

"So am I heading home?"

"Before we talk about the negotiations, I've got some news for you. Remember you told me about your friends, and one of them was a Ralph?"

"Why?"

"He was shot in the head a few days ago."

"Ralphie Meat? My God. How'd it happen? He get caught with someone's wife?"

"It looks like a professional hit. The killer got inside his house, popped him in the leg, wrapped it up and asked him some questions before shooting him in the head."

"Questions about what?"

"The questions were probably about you, Charlie. Right after our negotiation hit the papers, I got a visit from some of your old friends in the Warrick Brothers Gang. One of them said he was chasing you fifteen years ago, a hood named Fred."

"That fat bastard still around?"

"In the flesh," I said. "And he's got some homunculus helping him out. He told me to give you a warning. Apparently they put some hit man on your tail, someone from Allentown."

Suddenly Charlie's head swiveled and his eyes widened.

"You know this guy from Allentown?"

"I saw him once," said Charlie slowly. "An old bull with a flattop, cold eyes, and huge, gnarled hands. He was a soldier who was trained too good and learned he liked the killing."

"What war? Vietnam?"

"Korea, from what I heard."

"What, that makes him well over seventy."

"You didn't see them eyes, Victor."

"He left a note as a warning. It read 'Who's next?' "

Charlie seemed to shrink at the words. I scanned what I could of the beach. Nothing out of the ordinary, the same uninterested runoff from the boardwalk, a group of kids at the far end of the jetty, laughing.

"Charlie, do you still want to come out of hiding?"

"I don't know. You tell this to my mother?"

"About the threat, yeah, I did. About Ralph, I didn't need to, it was front page in all the papers."

"What did she say?"

"She didn't want me to tell you. She says she'll take care of you."

"She show you her gun?"

"Yeah, she did."

"Crazy old bat. She used to point that thing at my head when I acted up, scared the hell out of me."

"Charlie, I'm not supposed to tell you this, but the way things are going, I think I have no choice. There's some guy in town offering a lot of money for that painting. I can't make a deal for you, you'd have to make it yourself, but he says he could give you enough to get lost for a good long time."

"How much?"

"Enough. High six figures at least. And you should also know that he's approached a few other people about it, including Ralph before he was murdered and your old friend Joey Pride. They both seemed to think they deserved a piece of the price."

"High six figures, huh? You think you can get more?"

"I know I could, but I have to advise you that the sale of stolen property is illegal."

"You tell my mother?"

"No. I was afraid she'd point the gun at me." I reached into my jacket, pulled out an envelope. "Here's his card. Just so you know."

"Are you advising that I sell to this guy and lam off?"

"I'm thinking that maybe Philadelphia isn't the safest place for you right now."

"What about witness protection? I thought you was going to make a deal."

"That's gotten a little complicated. I'm having a hard time making a deal with the government. The federal prosecutor I told you about, she's still got a stick up her butt."

"What the hell about?"

"I was hoping you could tell me."

"I ain't no proctologist."

"She wants you to tell her everything about how you got the painting. No immunity and no protection unless you agree. She seems to have some ulterior motive behind her demands, and I think I know what it is."

"What?"

"You ever hear of a detective named Hathaway?"

"What does that bastard have to do with anything?"

"The fed is his daughter."

"Oh, jeez."

"How do you know Hathaway?"

"He was sniffing around after the robbery. Asking about some girl what went missing about the time we took the painting."

"A girl named Chantal Adair?"

"Who the hell remembers a name?"

"I do," I said, and there must have been something in my voice, because Charlie backed up a bit. I took a breath to calm myself, checked the beach once again. The kids were still laughing. A couple of overweight joggers in baseball caps had just made their way around the music pier. A family grouping had formed at the ocean's edge, the youngest throwing handfuls of sand into the sea.

"I'm going to show you a picture," I said, pulling the shot

of Chantal Adair from out of my jacket pocket. "Do you recognize her?"

He glanced at it, shook his head. "It's too dark. I can't see."

"Tell me about Hathaway."

"I don't know," said Charlie. "Some girl went missing, and Hathaway, he thought it was all connected to the robbery. Somehow he connected the robbery to us."

"Any idea how?"

"Who knows? But the thing was, he couldn't finger us for either charge, no matter how hard he looked. See, we never spent nothing, we never slipped up. Our lives didn't change one bit."

"No mink coats, no Cadillacs? How'd you pull that off?"

"It was easier than you think, seeing as we never got our cuts in the first place."

"I don't understand."

"We got stiffed," said Charlie.

I looked at Charlie's silhouette, looked down the shoreline, trying to figure out what I was hearing. Joey had said something about the money disappearing, and now Charlie was talking about getting stiffed. The family was heading back for the boardwalk, the joggers were getting closer. Two men, one shaped like a pear, the other short and wider than a truck. Funny shapes to see in joggers. The moonlight glinted off their chains, and my head shook with the slap of recognition. Fred and Louie. Up with Hoods.

"Crap," I said softly. "We have company."

"Who?" said Charlie, his head swiveling. "What?"

"Turn and walk slowly toward the boardwalk like nothing is wrong."

"What?"

"Just do it, Charlie. Now."

Charlie's swiveling head stopped in the direction of the two joggers. He coolly let out a yelp and then, suave as could be, ran the hell away, toward the little path between the fences that led to the boardwalk. He was sprinting as fast as he could, which was not fast at all, arms and legs akimbo, like a cartoon character running in midair and going nowhere.

I caught up to Charlie Kalakos in a flash, grabbed hold of his arm, and started lugging him toward the stairway. The hoods were shouting as they ran for us, the seagulls were squawking, Charlie was whining.

"Stop pulling me. You're going to tear off my arm."

"How'd you get here?"

"Car."

"Where is it?"

"You're hurting my arm."

"Where's your car?"

"Down Seventh."

When we reached the stairs, I pushed him ahead of me. I glanced back quickly. The hoods were about thirty yards away, sprinting toward us, sand flying behind them. I leaped up the wooden steps, two at a time, pulled Charlie up the last. At the boardwalk we charged into the crowd and then stopped, looked around.

"Here," I said, grabbing Charlie and pulling him now to the right, away from Seventh. "This way."

"My car's that way," he said.

"I know, but the crowd will be thickest in here."

I was pulling him toward the Turkish arches of a small amusement park, with its carousel and roller coaster and great Ferris wheel rising over the boards. On the way I saw an overweight kid with a huge tub of caramel popcorn.

"You might not realize it," I told the kid as I grabbed the tub smack out of his chubby hands and threw it as hard as I could, high in the air, over the crowd, toward the stairs, "but I'm doing you and your arteries a favor."

The kid screamed like a siren, the popcorn spun out in a cloud.

An onslaught of seagulls descended upon the flying popcorn like a ravenous army, viciously pecking pedestrians and each other in their frantic quest for each loosed kernel. The two hoods from the beach, rushing up the stairs toward us, fell back when faced with the fluttering, vulturous cloud.

Charlie and I plunged into Gillian's Wonderland Pier.

CHAPTER

37

The sound of the calliope puffing away, the smell of the popcorn popping, the crush of the crowd moving thick and slow in the narrow gap between two kiddie rides. We tried to force our way but were swallowed whole and carried leisurely along by the viscous mass. Kids wiped their noses, grandfathers rubbed their backs. To our left was a balloon race. To our right a mini-NASCAR raceway.

"They'll come after us in here," said Charlie.

"It won't be so easy to find us in the crowd."

"Which way?" said Charlie.

"Down there," I said, pointing to a ramp that led toward the rear of the park.

We made our way, bobbing and weaving through the family groups, grandparents and grandkids, teenagers looking flushed and bored at the same time. We didn't even glance back until we reached a fence at the entrance to Canyon River log flume. We took a moment to survey the whole of the crowd.

"You see them?" said Charlie.

"Not yet."

"Maybe they went the other way."

"Sure," I said, "and maybe cigarettes are good exercise for the lungs." I stopped jabbering for a moment and thought. "How do you think they found us?"

"They didn't follow me," he said, and he was right about that. And being as this had been a two-man meeting, that left one dope to take the blame.

"I didn't spot them," I said.

"How long you think they been following you?"

"I don't know," I said, and then I thought about Ralph Ciulla and I felt a great gaping dread.

They had been following me from the start, the sons of bitches, waiting for me to lead them to their targets. And like the stupid pisspot I was, I did exactly that. When Ralph and Joey found me, they found them, and, putting it together, Fred probably took a picture and sent it to Allentown so that the killer would know exactly whom to ask his bloody questions and with whom to leave his bloody message. Son of a bitch. So first I had led them to Ralph, and now I had led them to Charlie.

"We have to get out of here," I said.

"No kidding."

For a second I looked at Charlie, short and heavy, sweating with effort and fear, still haunted by his mother, as threatening as a koala bear. Charlie was as unlikely a hood as ever I saw, and it got me to wondering.

"Joey Pride was telling me about that time in the bar that Teddy Pravitz first brought up the idea of hitting the Randolph Trust."

"Yeah, I remember it. Teddy promised the whole thing would make men of us, change our lives forever."

"Did it?"

"Sure," he said. "Look at me now."

"But here's my question. Teddy obviously had the plan to do the Randolph heist before he ever walked into that bar. So why did he need you guys?"

"Manpower."

"He could have latched onto professional hoods if he wanted."

"He didn't want hoods, he wanted guys he could trust. And besides, it wasn't like the four of us, we didn't have skills."

"Skills, huh? Like what?"

"Well, Joey Pride was a genius with engines and electricity. Whatever alarm system the place had, he could disarm it, and take care of the lights and the phones, too. And Ralphie Meat, besides being huge and strong, was a metal guy. Could bend anything, solder anything, melt anything."

"Like the golden chains and statues?"

"Sure."

"And Hugo?"

"Hugo had his own little skill. He used to sit in the back of the room and imitate all the teachers to a tee, crack us all the hell up. He did my mother better than she did. *'Charles, I need you now. You come here this instant.'* He could become anyone he wanted."

"And what about you, Charlie?"

"Well, you know I worked with my dad at the time."

"And what did he do?"

"Dad was a locksmith," said Charlie. "Wasn't a lock made that he couldn't open in a heartbeat. And he taught me what he knew."

"Locks, huh?"

"And safes. Later, with the Warricks, safes became my specialty."

"Must have come in handy up in Newport. Let me show you the picture of that little girl again now that the light's better."

"I don't want to see the picture."

"Sure you do." I took the photograph of Chantal Adair out of my pocket, showed it to him again. "You recognize her?"

He glanced at it and pulled back. It was a small movement, as quick as an inhale, but there it was.

"Never seen her before," he said.

"You're lying to me."

"You don't trust me?"

"I have to represent you, Charlie, but I don't have to trust you. Oh, crap."

"What?"

"They're here, or at least one of them."

Just at the edge of the arcade, with his white baseball cap and a retro Celtics jersey, chains glistening, stood Fred, the older, pear-shaped hood who had roughed me up outside my office. He had a phone to his ear. He stepped forward, peered into the crowd, scanned our direction without registering our presence.

"What do we do?"

"Let's get to the rear exit," I said. "But slowly. You see the little guy?"

"What little guy?"

"He'll be in the same outfit, just a different jersey. He's shorter than you, wider than a Buick. My guess is he's on the phone, too."

"You mean that guy?" said Charlie.

"Yikes."

Louie was standing right at the exit. He was also on the phone, standing on tiptoe, trying to see over the shoulders of a pack of tweens. It didn't look like he had spotted us yet.

"This way," I said, pulling Charlie away from Louie toward a narrow ramp that led up and to the right. As we ascended, I glanced back at the entrance. Fred was staring right at us, talking into his phone.

There were younger kids now on the ramp, strollers,

grandparents moving slowly, mothers shouting. We pushed our way past as many as we could until we reached the upper level, and then we made a beeline as far from the ramp as possible, past the tykes' jungle gym and the Glass House, past the little roller coaster and the Safari Adventure. At the far end was a set of stairs that led right back to the lower level, where Louie waited.

I spun around in frustration. The rides on the deck were all for toddlers, there was no place for us to hide. I could see the head of Fred bobbing up the ramp. Louie was coming for us from the other direction. There was no place to go. Except maybe . . .

"We need three tickets," I said.

"I don't got no tickets," said Charlie.

I ran up to a father with a big block of tickets. He was watching his kids on the spinning teacups. I grabbed my wallet, took out a ten. "Ten dollars for three tickets," I said.

He looked up at me, down at the waving ten-dollar bill, back up at me. "They're only seventy-five cents a ticket."

"I don't care."

"There's a booth right at the bottom of the ramp."

"I don't care. Ten bucks for three tickets. Now."

"I could give you change."

"No change, no nothing. Please."

He looked at me strangely, took three tickets off his block. "Just take them," he said.

I wasn't going to argue. I grabbed the tickets, grabbed Charlie, headed back to the middle of the Fun Deck where stood the Glass House, a strange maze of smudged glass panels. I gave the tickets to the lady, pushed Charlie inside.

"Go to the back, turn away from the crowd, and wait," I said.

"But—"

"Just go, and keep your hands in front of you."

Charlie swiveled his head, spotted something that spooked him, and charged inside. He banged into one of the panels, turned and banged into another, and then, with his hands in front of him, made his way through to the rear of the maze.

I ran toward the ramp until Fred spotted me. I did a little pump with my elbows and then charged away from him, past the Glass House without a glance, toward the rear stairs and down, right smack into Louie, who grabbed me by the belt and held me close.

"Hello, boysy," he said.

I won't go into a blow-by-blow description of our encounter after the two hoods dragged me outside the park. Fred asked the questions. I made snarky, nonresponsive comments. Louie drilled me in the stomach with his fists. I fell to my knees and dry-heaved. All rather unpleasant. And it might have gone far worse if a cop hadn't turned the corner just as I was struggling back up to my feet for the second time. The cop was young, his hat was tilted low over his eyes.

"Oh, look," I said, standing a little straighter. "A nice policeman. Why don't you boys ask him to help you find Charlie?"

"Don't even try," said Fred.

Louie grabbed the collar of my shirt and pulled me down to his level. "Don't even try, boysy."

"Should I call the nice policeman over?"

Fred looked behind him, did a double take, then tapped Louie on the shoulder. Louie turned, went wide-eyed. Without taking his eyes off the cop, he let go of my collar and started smoothing it out with his hand.

As the cop approached, giving us a nod, Fred injected a false heartiness into his voice. "It was nice talking to you,

Victor. What about your friend Charlie? We'd like to say hello to him, too."

I thought about grabbing the cop as he passed by, but if I did, I'd have to tell him the story, and that meant telling him about Charlie, which might be as much trouble for Charlie as were these goons. So I let him pass with a nod and a smile and then said, "Really, guys, it was nice chatting, but I have to go."

Yet even as I said it, I glanced at the giant Ferris wheel turning slowly in the middle of the park.

Fred caught my glance, followed its line to the high, spinning ride.

"We're not finished with you yet," he said, looking once more at the cop's back before starting toward the Ferris wheel, nodding at Louie to follow. Fred took a few steps and then stopped, came back, leaned close so he was whispering in my ear.

"If we don't find him, you should give Charlie this advice. Tell your pal to take the cash and run, or both of you are dead, understand?"

"What do you mean, take the cash?"

"You heard me," he said. "Remember, our friend from Allentown has your picture too." And then he was gone, along with Louie, headed for a ride on the Ferris wheel.

I waited a bit until they were out of my sight, and then I hurried back into the park, back to the right, and up the stairs to the Fun Deck. I expected to see a toddler-shaped figure shaking with fear in the rear of the Glass House, but there were only a couple of kids and a father comforting his daughter who had banged her head.

I looked around for Charlie: nothing. I went to the rear of the deck. There was a low fence surrounding the whole of the upper level and, on the ground below, a number of small spruce trees. One of the trees was strangely bent, its tip hanging limp. I looked at it for a moment and then turned my gaze to the street, following it south. In the distance I could see a squat figure in plaid shorts running, not moving very fast, but running, running away, running for his life.

He had been running for fifteen years. It was time for me to bring him home. But first I had to learn exactly what he was running from, and then I had to figure out why figures as disparate as the high-priced lawyer for the Randolph Trust and the two knuckleheads of Up with Hoods all seemed ever so determined to make sure that I failed.

38

"I'm sorry, Mr. Carl, but you're not on the list."

"What do you mean, I'm not on the list?" I said, my voice filled with a false indignation, false because in the whole of my life I have never been on the list. "Of course I'm on the list."

"No, I've looked twice, and you're not," said the large, bald-headed guard at the reception desk. "As a general rule, we don't allow visitors who are not on the list."

And as a general rule, I thought, I don't feel bound by general rules. "But he's my Uncle Max. Of course he'll want to see me. My sister's in town for only a few days and she was always his favorite niece."

The guard turned his stare toward Monica, standing behind me with her gas-station bouquet of flowers. His gaze swooned at the sight of her loose white shirt and tight black leather pants.

"I haven't seen my dear Uncle Max in years," said Monica in her little girl's voice. "I doubt he'd even recognize me anymore."

"But I'm sure she'd cheer him up, don't you think?" I said.

Monica smiled, the guard's eye twitched.

"Please," she mouthed, without a sound coming through her lips.

"Well, seeing that there are no special restrictions on his sheet," said the guard, "and seeing that you all are related—"

"On our mother's side, twice removed," I said.

"I don't suppose there'd be any harm."

"Oh, thank you," said Monica. "What's your name?"

"Pete."

"Thank you, Pete," she said.

"Uh, yeah. Okay. Let me see some ID, sign in, and I'll take you guys to him personally."

The Sheldon Himmelfarb Convalescent Home for the Aged was a cheerful little warehouse in the northern suburbs, not far from where I went to junior high school, so I was familiar with the landscape of its despair. There was a small lawn, a big parking lot, and a host of bright, processed smiles to go along with the processed hospital smell that was pumped out of the vents. We had never before actually met Uncle Max, who wasn't actually our uncle, but word was that Uncle Max's visitors weren't strictly restricted, that he didn't quite remember as much as he used to, and that he sure would appreciate the visit.

Pete stood in the doorway watching as I entered the room and spread my arms wide. "Uncle Max," I said in a loud voice with a great deal of enthusiasm. The unshaven old man in the bed sat upright at my entrance, a puzzled expression on his long, grizzled face. "It's me, Victor."

"Victor?"

"I'm your second cousin Sandra's son. You remember Sandra, don't you?"

"Sandra?" he said, with a sadness that indicated there were many people now whom he was forgetting.

"Of course you remember Sandra. Big hips, small hands, and she made that great three-bean salad."

"Three-bean salad?"

"Oh, Mom made the best three-bean salad. It was the waxed beans. She always used fresh, boiled in salt water. It made all the difference. And then a good wine vinegar and basil from our garden. Don't you just love a good three-bean salad?"

"I don't think I know a Sandra," said Max.

"And, Uncle Max, you must remember my younger sister, Monica. You were always so close. She came, too." I yanked Monica so that she stumbled forward until she regained her balance right in front of Max. "Say hello, Monica."

"Hello, Uncle Max," she cooed, leaning over the old man, flowers held out before her. "These are for you."

Max's jaw trembled for a moment at the sight of her. "Oh, yeah," he said finally. "That Sandra. How is she?"

"Dead," I said.

"It happens," said Max with a shrug of resignation. Then he patted the side of his bed. "Monica, tell me how goes life with you?"

"Fine, Uncle Max," she said, sitting down beside him. From that position she waved her fingers at Pete, who smiled back before heading down the hall to return to his desk.

"Where are you now, Monica?" said Uncle Max.

"San Francisco."

"And you have a boyfriend?"

"Oh, yes. He's an accountant."

"Good for you," said Uncle Max, growing livelier by the second, leaning toward Monica in the bed. "You know, I was an accountant, too."

"Really?" said Monica. "I find numbers so alluring."

"You mind if I turn up the music?" I said, indicating the small clock radio on the little table beside Max's bed.

"Go ahead," said Max.

A somber big-band ballad was wrenching its way out of

the tiny speaker. I found a station playing good old-fashioned rock 'n' roll, pumped up the volume, started strumming a little air guitar.

"Is that Bob Seger?" I said.

"Who?" said Max.

"No, but a good guess."

Monica laughed. Max raised his eyebrows and opened a drawer beside his bed, pulled out a pint of rum and a small stack of plastic cups.

"You won't tell?" said Max.

"Cheers," said Monica.

And so we had a nice visit with Uncle Max, with the music and the rum, talking about our fake mother, our fake family, about Monica's fake life and fake boyfriend in San Francisco. It wasn't too hard to figure out that Monica was much happier in her fake life than in the real thing. And I must say, with the way he was laughing and patting Monica's arm, with the way his eyes rolled when he sipped the rum, Max seemed pretty happy with his fake relatives, too.

It was small, the room Uncle Max shared with his roommate, just enough space for the two beds, a door to the bathroom, a couple bureaus and chairs, a pair of televisions bolted to the wall, and a drawn curtain that divided the space in two. We weren't hearing a peep from the other side, just the low murmur of the television on some insipid talk show flitting over the music. Even so, while Max was telling Monica one of his more interesting accounting stories, I took the opportunity to slip around the loose white fabric and visit the man behind the curtain.

He had once been fearsome, you could tell, big jaw, big hands, his feet reached from under the blanket and over the far edge of the bed, but age takes its bitter toll on us all. Now he lay slack, his jaw shaking, his watery eyes open but unfocused. He turned his head slowly toward me as I stepped close to his bed, registered my presence, and then turned away again. I took the chair, pulled it close to him, sat down, leaned my arms on the edge of his bed.

"Detective Hathaway," I said. "My name is Victor Carl. I'm a lawyer, and I have a few questions to ask you."

When I stepped out from behind the curtain, I was in for a second nasty surprise. Jenna Hathaway and Pete the guard were standing in the doorway of the room, glowering. And Pete had his hand on his gun.

"Hello, Jenna," I said as calmly as I could. "It is so nice to see you."

"What the hell are you doing, you son of a bitch?" she said.

"Just paying a sick call."

"I'm going to put you in jail for this."

"For visiting my Uncle Max?"

"For trespassing, for fraudulent misrepresentation, for harassment." She stared angrily at me for a long moment, and then, without taking her hard gaze from me, she said, "Could you turn off the music, Mr. Myerson?"

Max shut off the radio and, without much guile, slipped the bottle of rum back into the drawer and closed it.

"I'm sorry these people have been bothering you," said Jenna.

"These aren't people, and there is no bother," said Max as he patted Monica's forearm. "They were just checking in with their old Uncle Max. They're my cousin Sandra's children."

"Your cousin?"

"Second cousin, twice removed," I said.

"What does that mean, exactly?" said Jenna.

"I don't know," I said, "but it sounds about right."

Jenna sighed wearily. "You don't have a cousin Sandra, Mr. Myerson."

"Of course I do," said Max. "Or did. She died. Which is sad for all of us, since she made a very nice three-bean salad."

"I need to stop you there, Max," I said. "Mom made a fabulous three-bean salad. And who among us doesn't love a three-bean salad?"

"I want you out of here, Victor," said Jenna Hathaway.

"We're still visiting."

"Now," she said, and there was something in her eyes, both angry and fearful, that stopped me from prevaricating further.

"I'm sorry, Uncle Max," I said, "but I suppose we have to go."

"It was so nice seeing you," said Monica.

"You'll come again?" said Max.

"When I'm in town," said Monica.

"Good luck, then, in San Francisco and with your boyfriend. Tell him I give my regards, one numbers man to another."

"I will," she said, standing now.

"And next time you come," said Max, "bring a *bissel* of that three-bean salad."

When we were out in the hallway, Jenna stared at us both as she clasped and unclasped her fists. "We'll go to the office now and call the police."

"Are you sure that's necessary?" I said.

"Oh, yes, I am. I'm going to pull your ticket for this." She turned her head toward Monica. "And who the hell are you?"

"Now, where are my manners?" I said. "Let me introduce you to each other. Monica, this is Jenna Hathaway. Her father, the former Detective Hathaway, is Uncle Max's roommate. And Jenna Hathaway, please say hello to Monica Adair."

Jenna stared at Monica for a moment with an expression of awe mixed with disbelief, before surprising the hell out of us all by grasping hold of Monica like a long-lost sister and bursting into tears.

39

"It's been like this for about a year," said Jenna Hathaway as we stood in a sorrowful group beneath the bright sun in the parking lot outside the Sheldon Himmelfarb Convalescent Home for the Aged. She was fiddling with her keys, her head was bowed, she seemed younger somehow as she talked about her father.

"It's been like what?" said Monica.

"My father doesn't recognize anyone anymore. Not my mother, not his old friends. I'm just the woman who comes in every other day to say hello. It's as if all the names in his life have slipped away from him, all but one."

"Your sister," I said to Monica.

Monica nodded without surprise, as if obsession with her sister Chantal were only to be expected, and, seeing the company she was in, maybe she had a point.

"Each detective has an unsolved case that haunts him," said Jenna. "For my father it was your sister's disappearance. He couldn't abide the idea that a girl that young, so full of life, could simply vanish. He never put the case to sleep when he was still at the department, and when he retired, he took the file to keep working on it. That was going to be his hobby. But somewhere along the line, his mind latched onto the whole affair with something beyond obsession. Every day and every night he would stare at the file, at the pictures, the clippings, the strange lighter he found in your sister's drawer. It was as if the rest of the world had ceased to matter and all that was left was the one thing that didn't exist anymore—Chantal."

I could see it right off during my brief visit behind the curtain. That was the first unpleasant surprise I mentioned before. I had come to Detective Hathaway with a series of questions, but he was the only one who did the asking. *Have you seen her? Do you know what happened to her? She was just here, and then she was gone.* His eyes were unfocused, his jaw trembling. *Chantal. Where is Chantal?*

"I don't know," I said.

"I have to get out of here. I have to find her. Will you help me?"

"I don't think I can, Detective."

"You have to, you must. I need to find her."

"We all need to find her," I had said.

"After a while my mother couldn't take it anymore," said Jenna Hathaway in that parking lot. "She grabbed the file, everything he had about Chantal, and burned it all. She hoped that would free his mind of the missing girl. But it didn't work out that way, it only drove him deeper into himself. We wanted to believe he had willfully shut us out of his life. Somehow that was easier for us to handle than the truth, that his fixation with Chantal was an indication of something going awry in his brain. By then it was too late to do anything."

"But you're still trying, aren't you?" I said.

Something changed in her just then. Her back straightened, her eyes flashed anger, she was no longer Jenna Hathaway, bereaved daughter. Instead she was now Jenna Hathaway, self-righteous federal prosecutor. It didn't last but for a moment, before she deflated again.

"I thought maybe learning the truth might help," she

said. "Maybe if he found out what really happened to Chantal, he'd find another name to replace hers in his memory."

Monica reached over and took hold of Jenna Hathaway's hand. "I understand," she said, and they looked at each other with the sad knowledge of their secret bond: They both had parents obsessed with the same missing girl.

"So how'd you light on Charlie?" I said.

"There was a task force formed to try to deal once and for all with the remnants of the Warrick gang. It wasn't my usual turf, but they brought me in to see if there were any tax charges that could be leveled at the leaders."

"The Al Capone strategy," I said. Despite all his thieving and murders, it was a tax charge that finally sent old Scarface to Alcatraz.

"During one of the meetings," said Jenna, "Charlie Kalakos's name popped up. There were rumors that he wanted to come home. He had once before given information against the Warricks, and his testimony could be the linchpin of a RICO charge that could wipe out the gang once and for all. But I also remembered my father telling me of his suspicions about a connection between Charlie Kalakos, the Randolph Trust heist, and the missing girl. So I asked to be assigned to deal with Charlie, and I pressed the FBI to find him. That's why they were outside Charlie's mother's house when you went visiting."

"And why you've been such a hard-ass about giving him a deal."

"I just want to find out what he knows."

"But you're not willing to give him immunity."

"If he's responsible for what happened to that girl, he has to pay a price. And if you have a problem with that, maybe you should ask Monica."

We both looked at Monica.

"I'm with her," she said, edging closer to Jenna.

"Thanks for the support," I said. "Okay, how about this? Why don't I draft up a cooperation agreement for my client? I'll send it to you, and you can put in the provisions you want regarding Chantal's disappearance. I'll give a look-see to what you have in mind."

She stared at me for a moment and then turned her head with suspicion. "That sounds almost reasonable. What's the catch?"

"No catch. But I'd appreciate you hand-delivering it to me so we can talk it over. I'll be running around the next couple of days, but I'll be in family court on Wednesday morning. The child involved in my case is not at risk, so the judge has been letting the proceeding drag, delaying the trial to deal with more pressing matters. I could be waiting there for hours. That would be a good time to talk. And there might actually be something in my case you'd be interested in."

"What?"

"I'll tell you then. But you won't be disappointed."

She looked at me again, trying to figure what the hell I was doing, and then she looked at Monica. "How did you guys end up together, anyway?" said Jenna.

"I began looking into the Chantal situation myself," I said, "and found Monica. Let me ask you, before he drifted away, what did your father tell you about the case?"

"Just that he was sure there was a connection between the robbery and the disappearance, and he was focusing on five neighborhood guys. Charlie was one of them."

"What about at the trust? Did he think anyone there was part of it all?"

"There were two women at the trust who were apparently in some sort of death fight. One was a young Latin woman, the other was an old lady who my father said he never trusted. I forget her name."

"LeComte?"

She looked at me, surprised. "That's it, yes. Tell me, why are you so interested, Victor? Why did you start looking into Chantal's disappearance in the first place?"

"You don't know?"

"No. How would I know?"

"Because somebody knows. Somebody made sure that the missing girl's name was tattooed onto my brain, and I thought you might be the one."

"I have no idea what you are talking about."

"No idea, huh?"

"None."

I stared hard at her. Not a smile, not so much as a twitch. Damn, I thought I had figured it out.

"Nice girl," said Monica after Jenna Hathaway had shaken her keys for the last time and left the parking lot.

"You two seemed to hit it off."

"Remember how she said I should call her for coffee sometime? I think I will. We have a few things in common."

"You going to tell her what you do for a living?"

"Shut up."

"Well, I noticed that you seem more comfortable with a fake job and a fake relationship. So maybe you should lie to Jenna and start up a fake friendship."

"Victor, if you want to psychoanalyze me, get a degree."

"Exception noted."

"What?"

"That's lawyer talk for you're right and I'm sorry."

"Did you really think that Jenna was responsible for the tattoo?"

"It was a thought."

"You still don't get it, do you? So where do we go now?"

"I suppose to Mrs. LeComte at the Randolph Trust."

"Let's do it."

"I think I'll do this one alone, Monica. Mrs. LeComte, despite being on the far side of seventy, is a woman to be reckoned with. She'll want to use all her charms and wiles on me, and I think I'll let her."

40

"Why, you're a regular Sammy Glick, aren't you?" said Agnes LeComte, leaning forward, her legs crossed, her elbows on the table as she slowly stirred her iced tea with a long silver spoon.

We were sitting at an outside table at a café just east of Rittenhouse Square. The sun was bright, her sunglasses were big, pedestrians passed by, their arms swinging. Women smiled down at me, assuming I was lunching with my grandmother.

"I knew another Sammy Glick just like you," she said, "but that was a long time ago."

"Sammy Glick?" I said.

"You are young, aren't you? Do you have a mentor, Victor?"

"Not really. I've had a few people who helped me along the way, but generally I've muddled through the thickets of the law on my own."

"I don't mean in the law—what do I know of the law?—I mean in other ways. There is so much in life one can learn from a more mature viewpoint." She pursed her wrinkled lips, demurely lowered her chin. "Trust me, I know."

"While I would never deny the need of a more mature viewpoint in my life, Mrs. LeComte, what I really wanted to discuss was the Randolph Trust robbery thirty years ago."

"Why would you ask me?" she said, her silver teaspoon still stirring her tea. "Why wouldn't you ask your client? He knows far more about it than I, I'm sure."

"I'm sure you're right," I said. "But my client is not as available to me as I would like, seeing as he is on the run. And I would like to know the way the trust saw it."

"Oh, I don't want to talk about that silly old robbery. Don't we have other things to talk about?"

"Okay, then," I said. "Who is this Sammy Glick person you mentioned?"

"Are you jealous of another man?" She laughed. "Sammy Glick is a character in a novel written decades ago. He is a young Jewish boy with a sharp ferret face who rides his ambition to unimaginable heights."

I put a hand to my jaw. "You think I have a ferret face?"

"From firsthand knowledge, Victor, I have learned that certain intimate relationships of diverse ages can be a glorious opportunity for both parties. One learns from experience, the other is inspired by youth. Have you ever read Colette?"

"No, actually. Is she any good?"

"She's yummy, and she has much to say on the benefits of ripened wisdom handed down to the young."

Gad, could this have turned any weirder? "Can we talk about the heist?" I said.

"I would prefer not to."

"Mr. Spurlock himself suggested I talk to you about the robbery. He'd be disappointed if he discovers that you refused to answer my questions."

Her face soured at the name of the trust's president. "I was at the trust before he was born, and I will be at the trust long after he is thrown out of his post." She took the lemon from the rim of her glass, bit into it with yellow teeth. Her lips curled like an old movie queen. "What would you wish to know, Victor?"

I leaned forward, lowered my voice. "How did they do it?"

"No one is certain," she said. "You've seen the trust's building. It is a fortress, impregnable, impossible to break into even with a battering ram, and there was no evidence of a battering. The doors were all locked tight, the windows intact. But, like the Greeks at Troy, they found a way inside. How they did so is the enduring mystery. Once inside, they were able to immobilize the guards, silence the alarms, and open the locked cabinets and safes where the most valuable objects were stored."

"Could they have just snuck in?"

"There are only two entrances into the building and each was constantly guarded. No one was ever allowed in without authorization and without signing the book. Even I was required to sign in and out."

"Maybe they came in as visitors and never left."

"Impossible," she said. "From the earliest days of the trust, Mr. Randolph feared that someone would either steal or vandalize the artwork. And just a few years before the robbery, when that madman took a hammer to Michelangelo's *Pietà* in Rome, Mr. Randolph himself tightened all procedures. Visitors were required to put their names into a log, and a complete search of the building was conducted each night after visiting hours. In any event, the day of the robbery was not a sanctioned visiting day and there were no educational events scheduled."

"Could someone have let them in? Maybe left a window unlocked?"

"Everything that night was checked and double-checked. The records are clear. Still, there were some irregularities. Miss Chicos had signed out some blueprints of the building and her fingerprints were found on the file jacket containing diagrams of the alarm system. None of that information was in the purview of her employment, which made her an obvious suspect. She was a young curator just out of graduate school. Nothing could be proved, but still, the suspicion was enough to force her to forfeit her position. I never thought much of her in the first place. Her tastes were slightly vulgar and her neck was too long."

"Too long for what?"

"Is there really a chance that your client will return the Rembrandt to the trust?"

"There's a chance."

"What about the missing Monet? It was a small work, but so lovely. Does your client have anything to say about that?" Her chin rose, the lines outside the dark circles of her glasses deepened.

"No," I said. "Just the Rembrandt."

"Pity. It was one of my favorites."

"Can I show you something, Mrs. LeComte?" I pulled out the photograph of Chantal Adair. "Have you ever seen this girl before?"

She took the photograph, examined it carefully. "No, never. Lovely girl, though. Is she somebody I should know?"

"Probably not. Do you know where that Miss Chicos is now?"

"I heard Rochester. Just the place for her, don't you think?"

"Why's that?"

"I've heard things about Rochester."

"You mentioned you met another Sammy Glick once? Who was the other?"

"Oh, Victor, we all have our lost loves, don't we? Some dwell on the past, others move forward. This was fun. We should do it again. Maybe someplace more intimate than an outdoor café. And maybe after you've read Colette. You know, those of us who have been on the younger side of one of those special relationships want nothing more than to pass on all we've learned. There is so much I could do for you if you would let me."

And I knew exactly what she had in mind.

CHAPTER

41

    "It was tough, what happened to Ralphie Ciulla," said my father, rooted in position on his Naugahyde lounge chair. He sipped his beer, belched softly. However tough it was on Big Ralph, my father wasn't taking it personally. "He didn't deserve to get it that way, a bullet in his head in his mother's house."

"No one does."

"Any idea who did it?"

"It looks like it was an enforcer for the Warrick Brothers Gang."

"I didn't know Ralph was involved with those clowns."

"He was involved with Charlie Kalakos, which was apparently enough for them."

"Who else they after?"

"Joey Pride, Charlie, the other two also, I would suppose. For some reason it looks like they're going after everyone involved in the Randolph heist."

"It could be a bloodbath."

"It's shaping up to be."

"That's tough."

"Yeah."

"Real tough." Pause. You could see him think it over, my father, not so much working out the intimations of all our varied fates in the grisly death of Big Ralph, but more wondering at the appropriate period for remaining somber in the face of such news. I suppose, after due deliberation, he decided it wasn't that long. "You want to get me another beer?"

"Sure, Dad."

"And while you're up, some chips, maybe."

When I came in from the kitchen with the Lay's and two Iron City Beers, the television was on. My dad had been itching to press the power button on his remote from the moment I stepped into his little house in Hollywood, PA. As proof of my theory that he would watch anything so long as it was on, there he was, staring at a little white dot hurtling across an impossibly blue sky.

"Golf?"

"The Phils are in L.A."

"But you hate golf."

"Except when they hit the ball into water and get the whiny face. I love the whiny face. 'Ooh, I'm making six mil a year plus endorsements, but I just hit the ball in the water. Ooh.'"

I handed him his beer and the chips and then walked to the television and turned down the sound. He looked at me with the startled expression of a little kid who'd just had a candy bar snatched from his hand.

"What the hell are you doing?" he said as he pressed the volume-up button on his remote.

I killed it again. "We need to talk," I said.

"What, are you breaking up with me?" He turned up the volume once more. "Just close the door on your way out."

"Dad, do you really need for Johnny Miller to tell you that the guy should have made the putt he just missed?"

"It adds ambience."

"We need to talk," I said, "about why you owe a favor to that Mrs. Kalakos. She's roped it around my neck like a horse collar."

He looked at me for a moment, thought about it, and then let the volume bleed out until it died. He flipped open his beer, took a sip. I sat down in the chair catercorner to his and opened my own.

"It was my mother," he said.

"My mother was an artist," my father told me as golfers moved grimly and silently across the television screen. "Or at least she thought she was."

"I don't remember Grandma Gilda painting."

"This was before you were born. Our house was filled with her paintings. She was also a poet, and she liked to sing. This was all when I was still young, after we left North Philly and were living in Mayfair."

"Near the Kalakoses?"

"That's right. There was an art class at the community center, and every Tuesday and Thursday night my mother would pack up her paints and brushes in her wooden artist's box and go to class. And in that same class was guess who?"

"Mrs. Kalakos?"

"Right. One night I was hanging outside the community center with my pals when the class was breaking up. My mother came out with her little wooden box and her smock draped over her arm. But the strange thing was that she was laughing, which was not a usual thing for her. And next to her, laughing also, was a tall, ungainly man, stooped, with a shiny bald head and a pipe in his girlish lips. Not much to look at, but the son of a bitch was making my mother laugh. His name was Guernsey."

"Guernsey?"

"Like the cow. And after that, I noticed my mother was distracted at home. Before, she was always telling my father what to do, complaining about all the stuff I wasn't accomplishing with my life. But now she just stopped, as if she had other things on her mind. It was kind of peaceful and nice, until the night she went off to art class and didn't return."

"Guernsey."

"She called my father so he wouldn't worry. She was leaving him, moving in with Guernsey, becoming an artist. She was still young, in her thirties, and she said she needed to break out before she was swallowed whole by the narrow life of a cobbler's wife."

"How'd Grandpop take it?"

"Not well. The next Thursday night, I stood with him as he waited silently outside the community center. When the students came outside after the art class was over, he confronted her. He begged her to come home. She refused. He spit out some words in Yiddish, and she spit them back. Enraged, he went after Guernsey with his little fists. I held my father back as the tall, stooped man recoiled in fear and then ran away. I remember the holes in the bottom of his big shoes as he ran. My mother pushed my father down before she went after Guernsey. It was all quite the scene. And when it was finished—the scene, the marriage, everything—Mrs. Kalakos, who had seen it all, came over to my father.

"'Don't you worry,' she said in her thick Greek accent. My father, still on the ground, looked up at her with a pathetic hope in his eyes. 'A wife and mother, she belong in her own house. I bring her back to you.'

"And she did. A week later Mrs. Kalakos marched into our living room with my mother following meekly behind, a suitcase in her hand. And the three of them, sitting across from one another, worked it out."

"How?" I said.

"I don't know. They sent me away. When I came back, it was as if none of it had happened. My mother kept house, my father hummed, my mother complained about my father, my father took it with a little smile. That was it. And it was never talked about again."

"Grandma Gilda."

"My mother, I think, always had a sadness in her eyes after that. No more painting or poetry or singing. But my father was always grateful to Mrs. Kalakos. Whenever he saw her, he would remind me what she had done and that I should never forget it."

"Grandma Gilda. I didn't think she had it in her."

"That's why I owe the old lady a favor. Can I turn up the volume now?"

"You don't want to talk about it? How it made you feel?"

"Bewildered, abandoned, desperate for a hug."

"Really?"

"Get out of here. It was just something that happened. But I'll tell you this. First chance I had, I up and joined the army. Anything to get the hell out of that house."

"I don't blame you."

"Good, now that's settled." He aimed the remote, the golf commentators started yapping.

We sat and watched the golf for a while, until the sun started slanting and the baseball came on. Whatever you can say about baseball on the tube, it's better than golf. I got us both a couple more beers, and as I drank my Iron City, I began to think about my grandmother.

I remembered her as old and complaining, never happy, never satisfied with how anything in her life had turned out. But there was a moment when she had made that move to change her life, was living in sin with that big lug Guernsey, devoting herself to her painting. It was almost romantic, a woman abandoning her placid domestic life for love and art. Like Helen leaving Menelaus for Paris, or Louise Bryant leaving her middle-class life for John Reed, or Pattie Harrison leaving George for Eric Clapton. These were the heroines of epic poems, Oscar-winning films, classic rock ballads. And in that immortal group, at least for a few weeks, was my Grandma Gilda.

I wonder if it would have worked out for her, if a life with Guernsey would have been richer, truer than the one she fell back into. More likely, after a few brief weeks she would have started nagging Guernsey about the dishes in the sink and the clothes on the floor, about his lack of ambition, about the way he never took her out dancing. But she never would know, would she, my Grandma Gilda, because Mrs. Kalakos had taken charge.

The Furies of Greek mythology were three sisters who scoured the earth for sinners to torment. One of them, Megaera, was a shriveled crone with bat wings and a dog's head. Her harping often drove her victims to suicide. I bet she also drank old tea and kept her shades drawn. I bet she burned incense to hide the scent of death on her breath. I bet she inveighed against freedom and risk, against free will, against any chance to rise and become something other than that which fate had decreed.

"By the way, I got a message for you," said my father.

I grew suddenly nervous. "From Mrs. Kalakos?"

"No, from that Joey Pride. He wants to talk. He said he'll pick you up tomorrow morning same time outside your apartment house."

"He can't. Call him and tell him he can't."

"Tell him yourself. I don't call him, he calls me."

"Dad, I'm being followed all the time. I think they followed me to Ralph. And they're looking for Joey, too. If he picks me up outside my apartment, they're going to find him."

"Tough for Joey."

"Dad."

"If he calls, I'll tell him."

"This is bad."

"For Joey maybe."

"Your sympathy for those guys is overwhelming."

"They were punks," he said. "Always were, always will be. If they was involved with that robbery, like you said, then they stepped out of their league, and now they're paying for it. That's always the way of it. You got to know your limitations."

"Like your mother."

"Yeah, that's right. You know, after she came back like she did, she threw out all her paintings. Never touched a brush again."

"Were the paintings any good?"

"Nah. But she sure was happy painting them."

42

I got to the office early the next morning, fiddled with some paperwork, made some phone calls. Then I headed off to City Hall.

Philadelphia's City Hall is a grand monstrosity of a building set smack in the very center of William Penn's plan for the city. Four and a half acres of masonry in the ornate style of the French Second Empire, the building is bigger than any other city hall in the country, but that doesn't say enough. It is bigger than the United States Capitol. The granite walls on the bottom floor are twenty-two feet thick, the bronze of Billy Penn is the tallest statue atop any building in the world. You want to get an idea of the size of the thing? About ten years ago, they removed thirty-seven tons of pigeon droppings from its roofs and statuary. Seventy-four thousand pounds. Think on that for a moment. That's a load of guano, even for a building designed for politicians. If you can't get lost in Philadelphia's City Hall, you're not trying very hard.

I entered the doors at the southwest quadrant, climbed the wide granite steps to the second floor, where I headed toward the prothonotary's office. Prothonotary is our local term for clerk, like cheese steak is our local term for health food and councilman is our local term for crook. I ducked in, looked around, ducked out again, spotted no one suspicious in the hallway. I proceeded to make a grand tour of the building, starting with the mayor's office. A cop was stationed at the door, to keep the FBI from sneaking inside and bugging it again, no doubt. I took an elevator to the fourth floor and walked past the Marriage License Bureau and the Orphans' Court, two locales still thankfully foreign to me. I climbed down another huge stairwell to the third floor, walked past City Council offices, felt my sense of morality disappearing into some strange vortex. At the elevator I looked around and went back down to the second floor.

The cop in front of the mayor's office eyed me as I passed by. "You looking for something, pal?" he said.

"Yeah," I said, "but fortunately I'm not finding it."

I entered another of the wide stairwells and climbed down to the ground floor again. I was now at the northeast corner of the building, the exact opposite of where I had entered. I slipped out of the building and quickly raised my hand.

A battered old Yellow Cab with its top light off pulled up beside me. I opened the door and slid inside. The cab veered around a few lanes and then headed north on Broad.

"I expect there's a reason for all this subterfuge and flim-flam," said Joey Pride from behind the wheel.

"Just trying to keep the body count down," I said.

"Whose body you talking about?"

"Yours."

"Well, then, boy, flimflam away. And at least you sent me a messenger easy on the eyes."

"Yes, I did," I said, smiling at Monica Adair sitting beside me on the backseat, her hair back in a ponytail, her face freshly scrubbed. While I was staying busy at my office, I had sent Monica to intercept Joey in front of my apartment and direct him to our rendezvous. I hadn't been able to spot who was following me—I was no Phil Skink, who could spy the tail of a mouse at fifty yards—but after what happened with Charlie at Ocean City, I had begun to take precautions.

"So, Joey," I said, "you wanted to see me?"

"Your boy's trying to screw my ass," said Joey Pride, "and I just wanted you to tell him it's not worthy of our past together."

"Do I have any idea what you are talking about?"

"Maybe we ought to drop her off before we keep talking."

"Oh, Monica's fine," I said. "Anything I can hear, she can hear, too. Her profession is all about secrets."

"Okay, then. Remember that fish we was discussing before Ralph got it in the head, the one handing out the Benjamins?"

Lavender Hill. Damn. "Yes, I remember."

"He got hold of me once again. Said he was close to working out a deal with Chuckles the Clown, and that Chuckles, out of the generosity of his shriveled Greek heart, had decided what my share will be when the deal goes down."

"And what share is that?"

"Well, he figured, since there was five of us in that long-ago escapade, that I should get a fifth."

"That makes some sense."

"Did thirty years ago, don't make that kind of sense now. Ralph is dead, Teddy has been missing since the painting was took, and considering what he ended up with, he don't deserve nothing more, and Hugo ain't going to be begging for his share, I can tell you that."

"What does that mean?"

"It don't matter. What matters is that, the way I see it, the split should be fifty-fifty."

"Fine, but leave me out. I can't be part of any negotiation."

"You part of it already, Victor. You the one who set this up."

"You don't know that."

"No other way it could have played out, so don't pretend you're wearing a white suit here and glowing like an angel.

You get back to our boy and tell him it's fifty-fifty or there will be trouble."

"What kind of trouble, Joey?"

"He's still got a mother and sister, don't he? They still got a house, don't they? It ain't smart business to trifle with a desperate man on the run from ghosts."

"Did you hear that, Monica?"

"I heard that."

"That is a threat, which is absolutely against the law. As an officer of the court, I have a duty to report any crimes I see."

"I have a cell phone," she said.

"You ain't making no call."

"I don't need to," I said. "Let me give you a piece of advice, Joey. Don't mess with Mrs. Kalakos. She'll carve you proper and then make soup from your bones."

He thought about it for a while, driving north on Broad, toward her territory and his past. "She's old."

"Not old enough. Your concern about the shares is duly noted and, all the time remembering my responsibilities, I'll see what I can do to make your grievance understood."

"Am I going to get any more than that lame assurance from your skinny ass?"

"No."

"Then I guess it will have to do."

"Good. Now I have some questions for you." I leaned forward, took a photograph out of my pocket, shoved it in front of him. As he drove, he glanced down at it, looked up, glanced down again.

The taxi swerved left, a horn honked, the taxi swerved right again.

"Mind your own damn lane," Joey yelled out the window.

"You recognize her?" I said.

"No."

"So says your words, but the steering wheel gave you away."

"Take another look," said Monica. "Please."

He glanced nervously up to the rearview mirror.

"Her name was Chantal Adair," said Monica. "She was my sister."

"Your sister?"

"She disappeared twenty-eight years ago," said Monica. "Could you please take another look?"

He glanced again at the photograph. "Never saw her before."

"That's what Charlie said, too," I told him, "but he was lying, just like you."

"Who you calling a liar?"

"Calm down. Let's talk a little bit about what happened after Teddy gave you his speech in that bar. When did he tell you that the opportunity he had in mind for all of you to save your miserable lives was to rip off the Randolph Trust?"

"That very night. He laid it out, and then he left us to chew it over. I had already been in the pen, didn't want to go back, ever. Ralph never had a larcenous bone in his body and Charlie was not the type. But with Teddy gone, it was Hugo who went about convincing us. Said all that talk about changing our lives didn't have to be only talk, that we could do it. We just needed the balls to step up and take what was ours."

"He was in on it from the start."

"Hugo?"

"Sure," I said. "How else did Teddy know so much about what was going on in your lives? From what you told me before, I figured one of you was recruited before Teddy ever stepped into that bar."

"Hugo. Damn."

"So the four of you signed on."

"All that talk of becoming something new, it was more intoxicating than the booze we were swilling. So we were in, and Teddy, he had a plan for each of us."

"You took care of the burglar alarm."

"That was my job, that's right, that and the driving. Teddy, somehow he got the electrical drawings for me. The setup was complicated, the drawings looked like a plate of spaghetti, but I eventually figured a way to beat the thing. A wire's just a wire, a current's a current, it ain't too hard to make them electrons dance the way you want."

"What was Ralph's job?"

"Muscle during the operation. And all the while we was preparing, he was quietly setting up a shop in his mother's basement to take charge of whatever gold and silver we brought in. He was going to melt it into something we could sell without it being traced."

"What happened to all the equipment after?"

"We buried it, right there in the basement. Cracked the cement floor with a sledge, buried it in the dirt, along with our clothes and the guns we used to keep the guards quiet. We poured homemade concrete right on top. It's all still there, best I know."

"Buried in the basement so that nothing could be traced." I made a mental note to give Sheila the Realtor a call. "And Charlie was there to take care of the safe, right?"

"If he could. If not, Teddy said they'd blow the damn thing. When he laid out his plan, it was all 'if this, then that, if not that, then this.'"

"How did you guys get inside?"

"That was Hugo's department. Hugo was hard and sly, like a fox with brass knuckles."

"How did he get in?"

"I'm not talking about Hugo."

"Why not?"

"Remember what I said about ghosts? Some of them are more dangerous than others. More solid, too."

"Then just tell us how the girl got mixed up in everything."

"What girl?"

"The girl in the picture, Joey. Chantal Adair."

"I never saw her."

"Joey?"

"No, I admit, I recognize her picture. I seen that picture before, in all the papers. About the same time as the heist, this girl went missing. It was that girl, right?"

"That's right," said Monica.

"But it wasn't her who was hanging around all the time as we were making our preparations."

"What are you talking about?" I said. "Who was hanging around?"

"Teddy was a real pied piper. All the kids took to him. Always had a piece of candy or a little toy. It was just the way he was. And there was one kid who was hanging around all the time, flitting around like a moth. A boy. Towheaded dude."

"What was his name?" said Monica.

"Who the hell remembers?" said Joey. "Who the hell knows?"

"I do," I said.

43

Sometimes it's a chore to find someone, sometimes it can take days, years, an entire bureau of detectives. Whole investigations have stalled because one key witness couldn't be found. Sometimes it's a chore, and sometimes it's the easiest thing in the world.

"What are you doing here?" he shouted.

The room was an airless filthy mess, the floor covered with clothes and crumbs, the bed an unmade tumble of creased sheets and blankets. It smelled of the sickly-sweet scent of contained sweat. The screen of the computer in front of which he was sitting suddenly transformed from a lurid mix of flesh tones and red to a photograph of a gently rolling hill of green beneath a lightly clouded sky.

"No one's allowed in here," he said. "Get the hell out. Both of you."

He was wearing a grimy T-shirt and ripped briefs, a pair of black socks, a pair of glasses. His arms were flabby, his jaw unshaven, the hair on his legs bristly. And when he turned to stare at us, his expression was one of horrified indignation, the holy imam whose mosque had been invaded by gaunt crusaders.

"Hello, Richard," I said. "How's tricks?"

"Monica," he whined, "get him out of my room."

She looked around at the mess, shook her head, and then

leaned forward to pick up a wrinkled pair of sweatpants. She tossed the pants to her brother. "Put these on," she said.

He clutched them to his groin. "Go away. Please."

"I don't think so," I said. "We have business to discuss."

"Monica."

"Put on your pants, Richard dear," she said.

He looked at his sister, then at me, then back at his sister before standing and turning around. His skin was the color of hard-boiled eggs, his ass was saggy, the back of his neck was pimpled. Until looking at Richard Adair in his underwear, I had never realized the health benefits of simply walking outside. With his back to us, he climbed into the sweatpants and then turned around again.

"Now will you go?"

I stepped to his desk, littered with half-eaten food, empty soda cans, scraps of paper, magazines, rolled-up panties. Panties? I fiddled with his mouse until the verdant hill was transformed once again into the mass of lurid colors. I tilted my head and stared at the colors for a moment until the array of limbs and breasts and lips and cocks all came clear.

"Yowza," I said. "Doing research for our Web site, Richard?"

He reached over and pressed a button on the screen, turning the cathode-ray tube to a deep, empty green.

"What do you want?"

"Like I said, we have business to discuss."

"What kind of business?"

I pointed at the now-dead computer screen. He stared at it for a moment and then turned to his sister. She shrugged.

"Really?"

"Sure," I said. "Let's talk."

"Monica?"

"We discussed it," she said. "I'm ready to listen."

"Okay, then. Great." He rubbed his hands. "I knew I'd get

you on board, Victor. This will work out, I'm sure of it. Why don't you guys take a seat."

"Where?" I said, looking around at the room.

"Here," he said, grabbing a bedspread and pulling it over the mess of his sheets and blankets. "Just sit down here."

I looked at the filthy spread now covering his bed, shook my head, and leaned against the doorjamb. "I'll stand."

"Monica, go ahead," he said, gesturing to the bed.

Tentatively, she sat, her hands safely in her lap.

"Good," said Richard, turning around his chair and sitting, leaning forward like a copier salesman making a pitch. "Now, I have some experience with these sites, and I know this will be huge. We'll start with just photographs and a chat room, small like, you know. I'll take care of all the chatting. I know what these guys want to hear, how to make them depart with the cash. And I'll answer all the e-mails. Later we might want to do a Web camera, but that's way down the line, when you're more comfortable with things. Right now we should start small. A few pictures, a few advertisements, a minimal access fee to talk to Monica online, and a very few items to sell."

"Items?" I said.

"You know, underwear and things that Monica has worn."

"Doesn't it bother you, Richard, to put me up on a site like that?" said Monica.

"It's just pictures, just digital dots and dashes. It's not real. Trust me, Mon. And half the girls with sites that are bringing in real cash are like little rodent girls compared to you. It's all attitude, you know. You just got to work it."

"What about the photographs?" I said.

"I'll take them. I got a camera. We can set up something in the basement, a few sheets for a background. Or"—he lifted up his hands—"if you want to take care of that, Victor, that's fine."

"What kind of pictures will I be taking?"

"Look, I'm not talking anything hard-core. Yet. Just show some ass, some tit, those long legs, pout a bit. Give the shirt a lift. It's all just a come-on to get them to open up their wallets."

"And you really want me to do this?" said Monica.

"We're just talking about pictures," he said. "And the money will be great, better than you're making slaving for those asshole lawyers. Nothing you're not comfortable with, Mon. And we can use a different name if you want."

"Why don't we call her Chantal?" I said.

He turned his head to me with a jerk, as if I had hit him smack across the face, and the enthusiasm visibly ebbed from his features.

"I mean, if we're going to be consistent," I said, "we might as well keep the name the same as the sister you sold out before."

"What are you talking about? What's he talking about, Mon?"

"We're talking about Teddy," I said. "We're taking about how your special friend Teddy ended up with Chantal."

"Monica?"

"I don't blame you, Richard. You were as much a victim as she was. We just want to know what happened."

"Nothing. I don't know nothing. I told you that before. I told them all."

"Nothing," he said, but the quiver in his lip said something else.

"Oh, Richard, sweetie." She left the bed and walked over to her brother and knelt before him, putting her head on his leg. "You've been holding it in all this time, and it's been killing you."

Richard tried to respond, but the shaking of his lower lip grew progressively worse and his eyes began to leak and all he could get out was a weak, tearful "Mon."

"Look around, Richard," she said. "Look at what has happened to you. Look at this room. You're my big brother, my hero, but look at you. Keeping it in and staying like this can't be worse than telling someone the truth about what happened."

"What about the Web site?" he said.

"We don't want to hear about the Web site," I said. "We want to hear about Chantal."

He was crying now, the tears falling in big droplets onto her cheek. "But I don't know what happened," he said through the sobs. "I don't."

She raised up on her knees, took his ugly wet face in her hands, hugged him close. She was crying now, too.

"Just tell us what you know, baby," she said.

"No."

"It's okay. Everything's okay."

"It's not."

"It will be," she said. "We're going to find her. I know it, I can feel it, she has spoken to me. But we need your help."

"I can't."

"Sweetie, yes, yes you can. Just tell us what you know."

And then, through sobs and tears and the racking breaths of a ruined life, he did just that.

He had been a wanderer, Ricky Adair, a loner who floated through the neighborhood, the streets, the back alleys, the narrow stretch of Disston Park running after the squirrels. In those days the neighborhood was safe, and mothers let their children off on their own. *Go out and play. Go out and get some fresh air.* And that was what he had done, roaming wild over a landscape that was rooted in both the urban reality and the fluid fantasy of his imagination. The haunted house on Ditman, the troll who terrorized Algard Street, the witch that flew with the bats in the dusky sky above Our Lady of Consolation on Tulip. And it was on one of his wanderings that he met the Halloween Man, who was sitting on the stoop of an alleyway smoking a cigarette.

"Hey, kid," he called out to him as he spied Richard walking down the alley. "You live around here?"

"Not too far," said Ricky, keeping his distance. He had never seen the man before.

"You want a cigarette? Of course you do."

Ricky took a step back. Though his mother and father both smoked, no one had ever offered him a cigarette before, and the thought thrilled him. He was nine. "No thank you."

"You sure?"

"I'm not allowed."

"How about some gum?"

"Okay."

"Come on over," said the man, reaching into his pocket.

When Ricky approached, the man beckoned him closer and told him to reach out his hand. Ricky did as he said, and the man slapped his own hand down atop Ricky's and held it for a moment, like he was doing a trick. When the man lifted his hand, there, in Richard's palm, was a stick of gum, with its green-and-silver wrapper, and a cigarette.

"Keep it quiet," said the man with a warm laugh. "This will be our secret."

"Okay."

"Come back tomorrow and I'll pull a pack of matches out of your ear."

"I'm not allowed matches either."

"Don't worry, kid. I won't tell if you don't."

"Deal," said Ricky before running off down the alley with his gum and his cigarette and his secret.

He came back the next day for the matches and a jaw-breaker, huge and yellow, that took him all day to lick down to the spicy red center. The day after, the Halloween Man gave him a Hershey bar and a magic slide that could make a quarter disappear. He amazed Ricky twice with the trick before showing him how to do it. The day after that, he gave him a Three Musketeers bar and a whistle.

"Hey, kid," said the Halloween Man. "You got any friends?"

"Not really," which was a sad truth. Not an athlete, not a musician, not much of a conversationalist, not much of anything, Ricky had no friends. "But I got a sister."

"Really, now? How old?"

"Six."

The lopsided grin grew a little more lopsided. "Bring her along tomorrow and I'll have something for her, too."

The next day Ricky brought along his little sister, Chantal. He had thought it through, considered all the angles, and it had seemed like a sharp enough move at the time. Chantal agreed to give Ricky half of any candy bar she received from the nice man who acted like every day was Halloween. And Ricky was pretty certain there wasn't any danger.

He could sense danger, that was his talent, like he had a special radar in the back of his head. A little too much interest from the weird, gray-haired man in the library or the quiet snarl of a dog waiting for Ricky to slip within the ambit of his chain. He could sense danger, and he sensed nothing from the Halloween Man. Each time Ricky came by, the man would be sitting on the step out back in the alley, sometimes alone and sometimes with his four friends, a huge guy with a giant's jaw or a small black guy or a round, soft guy or a handsome guy in jeans. And when Ricky would show up, the men would stop talking, suddenly, like everything was a secret. The Halloween Man would say, "Hey, kid," and pull out the candy, pat his head, and send him on his way. Nothing to it. Nothing to be worried about. Just free candy and free toys and that lopsided smile. And so one day he brought along Chantal to increase the haul. He took Chantal to the Halloween Man, and everything changed.

"Hey, kid," said the Halloween Man, standing now, looking not at Ricky but at the little girl by his side. "So who is this?"

"My sister," said Ricky. "Chantal."

"What a pretty name." The Halloween Man reached out his hand and bent forward. "Hello, Chantal. My name is Teddy, and it sure is nice to meet you. What do you like to do, Chantal?"

"I dance," she said.

"I don't doubt it."

"I've been on television."

"How exciting is that?"

"Are you the man with the candy?" said Chantal.

"That's me," he said. "What's your favorite, Chantal? Chocolate? Nuts? Marshmallows?"

"Nougat," she said.

"Nougat? I don't even know what nougat is," said the Halloween Man, laughing.

"Neither do I," said Chantal, "but the commercial says it's good."

"So nougat it will be next time. You'll come back next time, won't you?"

Chantal shrugged.

"Hold out your hand," said the Halloween Man.

Chantal did, and the Halloween Man surrounded her little hand with his two big ones and kept them there for a long moment, before slowly removing them, leaving a Milky Way and a dollar in her palm.

Chantal's eyes glowed with delight.

"Here you go, kid," said the Halloween Man, tossing Ricky another Milky Way before heading back inside.

If you want to blame anything on what happened later, blame the dollar. The Halloween Man had never given Ricky a dollar.

"I get half of that, too," said Ricky.

"It's mine."

"But we had a deal."

"I only agreed to split the candy bar."

"That's not fair."

"He gave it to me," said Chantal, a sly, superior smile breaking out on her pretty face. "Get your own dollar."

That was so like Chantal.

She was a selfish little brat, with her red shoes and her bright dimples. Darling Chantal. Sweet Chantal. Everybody's favorite dancing doll, Chantal. She was the star of the family, the little girl who could sway hearts with a slide step and a wink. In the presence of adults, she was the ideal child, smiling and pliant and soft, aching to please, with her little-girl's voice. *Yes, Mommy. No, Mommy. Please, Mommy. I love you, Mommy.* But when no one was looking except her brother, she was the sneakiest little witch on the face of the earth, stealing what was his and sharing not a whit of anything that she had been given. He resented all the attention she garnered, all the praise lavished upon her, the gifts and toys, the hugs and kisses and exclamations of joy, the way she soaked up the energy in a room and left nothing for him, nothing but annoyance and orders. *Be quiet, Richard, and sit still. Chantal is dancing. Go ahead, Chantal, sweetheart. Try it again.*

And now the Halloween Man had pulled it, too, giving her all his attention, giving her a dollar, just tossing him a stupid Milky Way like tossing a scrap of gristle to a dog.

Ricky was too angry, too full of jealousy and resentment to sense the danger in the Halloween Man's strange sudden interest in little Chantal, the way he used her name over and over, the way he told her his name when he had never told it to Ricky, the way he held her hand in his a little too long. Ricky should have sensed the danger, but his radar was overwhelmed with the bitterness, all of it purchased with a single dollar. Or maybe, to be truthful, filled to overflowing with the acid of resentment, he did sense the danger and just didn't care.

"For some reason," said Richard, wiping his eyes with his forearm, "it wasn't so much fun going to the Halloween Man anymore. And then, once, when we were there together, he told me to stay put while he took Chantal inside the basement to see something. When she came back outside, she was beaming, like she had just gotten the greatest gift in the world, and she wasn't, she wasn't, she wasn't going to share. She never wanted to share."

"What did he give her?" I said.

"A lighter. Gold, heavy. She wouldn't even let me try it. After that, I didn't feel like going back, so I didn't."

"But Chantal did?"

"She used to show me the candy he gave her and laugh at me because I wasn't going anymore. And there was also the lighter, which she hid in her drawer and played with in the house whenever Mom wasn't around."

"The gold lighter the detective found."

"That's right."

"What happened when she went missing?"

"I don't know exactly what happened. But as soon as it happened, I knew it was the Halloween Man, that Teddy."

"Did you tell anybody?"

"Not right then. How could I? I had taken her to him. I was responsible. Mom and Dad would have killed me, would have thrown me away."

"You were nine," said Monica. "You didn't know."

"But I did, didn't I? And suddenly, with Chantal gone, things changed at home. It was no longer, 'Keep still, Richard. Keep quiet, Chantal is dancing.' It was, 'Oh, Richard, our sweet Richard, stay home, Richard, stay safe.' They kept hugging me and showering me with attention. They wouldn't let me go out anymore, which was fine, really, because with Chantal gone, it was my home again and I was the star. Me. And you know the truth? I didn't want her to come back."

"Did you hate her so much?" said Monica.

"No. Yes. I don't know."

"You said you didn't tell anyone right when she disappeared. Did you ever tell anyone?"

"The detective. He took me aside and promised not to tell Mom and Dad anything I said, and I told him."

"Detective Hathaway."

"That's right. And he was good about it. He never told that it was all my fault. He said he would find the Halloween Man for me, but he never could."

"Okay, Richard," I said. "I think that will do."

"That's all?" he said.

"That's all. Thanks."

He looked at his sister, a desperate fear etched on his face. "Are you going to tell Mom?"

"Oh, sweetheart," she said, still kneeling. "You were nine years old."

"Don't tell Mom."

"You can't keep living like this, you just can't. We have to clean up this room, we have to get you out of this house."

"I like it here."

"You can't stay like this. You just can't."

"I want to."

"Oh, sweetheart, Richard, sweetheart. Look what he did to you. Look what he did to all of us."

I left them there, brother and sister, agoraphobe and shadow dancer, left them in that room, in tears, in tatters. And Monica was right, he did do this to them, to all of them. Not to mention what he did to Chantal, or was doing. Because I was thinking that maybe Monica had been right after all. Maybe when that bastard left with all the stolen money, he left with Chantal, too. Just taken her, taken her to his new life, to do with her as he would, with no concern and no consequences. At least not yet, not until now.

Because I was going to find him. I was going to track him down and find him. And find Chantal, too. As sure as that tattoo was on my chest, I was going to find him and make him pay. And I knew just where to start.

But first it was time to deliver a message.

CHAPTER

44

I picked the most unlikely place possible. Dirty Frank's. The name says it all. And you should see the bathrooms. Yeesh.

Squatting on the corner of Thirteenth and Pine, Dirty Frank's was what was officially known as a dive. An ancient refuge for bearded bikers and frail, chain-smoking art students, it had low ceilings, ratty booths, a steady surly clientele, and a brilliant jukebox that still spun classic 45s. The place was always thick with smoke and the alluring scent of poor hygiene and spilt beer.

I was late on purpose, to let the ambience sink into his pale, soft skin. I found him sitting between two drunken bikers at the bar, a glass of wine in front of him.

"I didn't know they served red wine in this joint," I said.

Lavender Hill, in violet velvet, sniffed with disgust. "They don't," he said. "This is ox piss mixed with lamb's blood, flavored with iodine."

"The house specialty," I said.

"Charming place you picked."

"Only the best for you, Lav. I thought this was a nice anonymous place for conducting our underhanded business."

"Anonymous maybe for you, Victor, in that suit—burlap, is it?—but I don't quite fit here, or haven't you noticed. If you had clued me in to the type of establishment you were directing me to, I would have worn my black leather catsuit."

"I hate to admit it, but I'm sorry I missed that."

"Oh, you would have been charmed, I'm sure. Meanwhile I'm drinking this awful concoction, the smoke is making my eyes tear, which is hell on the mascara, and the Neanderthals on either side of me are preparing to get into a puking contest."

One of the bikers, the man behind Lav's back, lifted his head up off his arms at the comment. "What'd you say?"

"I wasn't addressing my comment to you, sir," said Lavender Hill. "Be a dear and crawl back into your beer. One thing this establishment has going for it, Victor, is the very real possibility of a barroom brawl. Nothing gets the blood stirring like a good barroom brawl."

"I'm not a barroom-brawl kind of guy."

"I figured that out."

"But I wouldn't take you for a brawler either."

"You wouldn't take me at all, trust me. Maybe we should find ourselves someplace more private to talk? Ah, there's an empty booth." He slid off his barstool. "Care to order us a round of beers? The swill they call wine, I'm afraid, is too vile for imbibition."

I watched him mince his way to a booth with a filthy table and torn seats. The bartender came over and watched along with me. It was quite a show. When he reached the booth, Lav looked down, his head shaking with sorrow. He took out a handkerchief and dropped it onto the seat before finally easing himself down upon it.

"A friend of yours?" said the bartender, a nice-looking woman in a black shirt.

"A business acquaintance."

She eyed the still-full glass. "He didn't like the wine."

"Not especially."

"I can't imagine why. It's fresh out of the box."

"His tastes are a bit too refined for his own good."

"Maybe yes," she said, "but he sure smells nice."

"A pitcher of Yuengling and two glasses," I said as I slipped a ten onto the bar.

Lavender was sitting at the booth, trying to find a spot upon the table clean enough for him to rest his elbows, trying and failing. He looked up at me, exasperation writ clear on his face, and then dropped his little hands into his lap. I sat across from him and leaned forward over the table.

"I understand you've been in touch with my client."

"There has been communication. I don't know how he got my number"—wink—"but he did, and as of late we have been in frequent contact. Has he spoken to you about our discussions?"

"No."

"Then how did you learn of it?"

"Joey Pride."

"Ah, yes, the recalcitrant Mr. Pride. It was quite difficult to find him after what happened to his friend."

"How did you track him down?"

"I have my ways."

"Did you talk with him in person or on the phone?"

"He was not willing to meet me face-to-face after the unfortunate death of his friend."

"It wasn't unfortunate," I said. "It was a murder."

"Are the authorities certain of that?"

"He was shot in the head."

"Ah, quite gruesome. Not a suicide, perhaps?"

"Shot in the head twice. After being shot in the knee. And there was no gun at the scene."

"Oh, I see. Sloppy technique, that, but the training they give out today is simply appalling. So I guess murder indeed is the likely cause of death. Well, that is truly regrettable, though perhaps not as regrettable as this establishment."

"Joey told me he's not happy with the deal Charlie is proposing. He doesn't want a fifth, he wants half."

"How unsurprising. But I fear he might be looking for half of nothing. Your client's initial enthusiasm for my offering has seemed to diminish."

"He's wavering?"

"Yes, unfortunately he is. This could be so clean, so beneficial to all involved, but the pathetic sap keeps on babbling about his mother."

"He's quite attached."

"An unfortunate condition. Are you close to your mother, Victor?"

"Not really."

"That means you are still too close for comfort. Come back to me when you resent her with a murderous passion that still boils your blood decades after they buried her bones in the foul, swampy earth, and then we can talk. Oh, my, we have an uninvited visitor."

"Where?" My head swiveled. All I saw was the bartender coming our way with a tray and our pitcher. "No, she's just bringing the beer I ordered."

"Not her. On the table."

There it was, darting for my elbow. I pulled back quickly as a cockroach, fat and brown and quick, sprinted to the edge of the table, spun in a circle, and then stopped, its antennae waving slightly in the air. It started again, sprinting back the way it had come, when a pitcher of beer fell out of the sky and squashed the arthropod flat as toast. Two foamy drops of beer flew out of the pitcher and flopped onto the table.

"Here's your Yuengling," said the bartender. Thump, thump. Two glasses appeared. "You want another pitcher, just give me a holler."

Lavender Hill stared at me with an amused glint in his eye. The brown in his irises pretty well matched the brown thing that had been scurrying around our table just an instant before. Lav laughed as he grabbed the pitcher by the handle and poured us each a glassful. As he poured, I could still see, through the beer, the lifeless blob adhering to the glass bottom.

"Sometimes you're the pitcher," said Lav, "and sometimes you're the bug. I'd like you to talk to your client for me. Convince him that the deal is in his best interests."

"Convince him to commit a crime, you mean. No thank you." I took a long draft of beer. Funny, it tasted great, cool and crisp. Maybe they should squash a roach at the bottom of every pitcher of beer, sort of like the worm in the tequila.

"I have an idea," said Lav with a disingenuous ingeniousness in his voice, as if he had just come up with the idea. "You could talk to the mother. I understand you've been in touch. You could advise her as to what you believe to be the most profitable, and safest, course of action for her son. You wouldn't be advising Charlie to commit a crime, but you would be doing something that could quite possibly save his life."

"If you want to lobby Charlie's mother, be my guest, but it won't do any good. She wants her boy to come home, that's what this is really all about. And trust me, Lav, you don't want to get in her way."

"Oh." A little smile played out on his pouty lips. "I think I can handle her."

"Bring an army with you when you try, because you'll need it." I finished off my beer, slammed the glass back on the table, lowered my voice. "Who are you working for?"

"One of the things I get paid for is discretion, something you should learn."

"Oh, I can be discreet when I want to, but things keep

puzzling me. There were two paintings stolen from the Randolph Trust, the Rembrandt and a Monet. You've only asked about the Rembrandt. Why?"

"It was only the Rembrandt that was mentioned in the news."

"Ah, but a smart guy like you, Lav, one who, as you've repeatedly told me, does his homework, would know enough to at least ask about both."

"My collector is not interested in the other work."

"I find that hard to believe. If he is as you described, then nothing would delight him more than scoring two masterworks in one illicit deal."

"Who can plumb the fathomless depths of the obscenely rich? Fitzgerald was right, they are different from you and me."

"Sure they are, they pay less taxes. But it was a little queer, your not asking about the second painting. It was as if your collector already knew that Charlie only had access to the one. How would he know that?"

"What he knows doesn't concern me."

"And how did you know to contact Ralph and Joey when it seemed your offer to me had gone nowhere? Why those two?"

"Old friends of Charlie's."

"But they were more than that, weren't they? They had a claim on the painting, too, and you knew it. And somehow you also knew about my father."

"What is your point?"

"I think you're working for someone who was involved in what went down thirty years ago. I think you're working for someone who doesn't give a damn about the painting but is more interested in buying silence. And maybe it's not enough to pay off Charlie. Maybe you're required to silence the others. Like Ralph? And Joey, if you could only deal with him in person and not on the phone? Buy the witnesses or kill them off, either/or, just so that everything stays quiet."

Lav clapped his hands sarcastically. "Aren't you the clever boy! It is a rather cute theory, except that it is completely and slanderously wrong. If I had killed Ralph, it would have been quickly ruled a suicide, mark my words on that. And as for the painting's not being of prime importance, false false false. All I care about, I assure you, is getting hold of that Rembrandt. That's how I get paid, and I will get paid. Finally, as for silence being my client's main goal here, I can't tell what is in the recesses of my client's mind, but I must ask why? I'm no lawyer, but I know enough to know that the statute of limitations has run on the robbery. Why would it be worth a couple of lives for the story to go away?"

I took a photograph out of my suit jacket, tossed it toward him. He picked it up, squinted at it, handed it back. "I never cared for children," he said.

"Her name is Chantal Adair. The picture's from thirty years ago. She went missing the same time as the Rembrandt. Never heard from since."

He looked again at the photograph, bit his lip as he tried to figure it out.

"That's what your client wants to keep quiet," I said.

"Is she dead?"

"Maybe, or maybe just kept illicitly, like a stolen painting, kept in a locked room, looked at sparingly. Who knows?"

"But you're going to find out, is that it?"

"That's it."

"Until the money is good enough for you to turn your back."

"There's not enough."

"There's always enough, Victor, you should know that by now."

"I don't think so," I said as I loosened my tie and started unbuttoning my shirt.

Lavender Hill's eyes darted around to check out the scene in the bar before he leaned forward. He watched as each button slipped out of its slit. When I showed him the tattoo, his eyes widened, he read the name, and then a huge smile cracked his hardened face.

"My, aren't we full of surprises!"

"Why don't we make a deal, Lav, you and I?"

"Oh, yes, let's." He rubbed his hands hungrily. "I've been wondering when we would start our delicate negotiations. We are of a like mind, I believe. I sensed that from the start. So, Victor, what are your terms?"

"I will mention your offer to Mrs. Kalakos, which is as far as I can go down that street, but she's a smart enough cracker to get my drift and independent enough that she would make her own decision in any event."

"Fabulous. You will also have to escort Charles and the painting to me if an agreement is finally reached."

"I can only take him and the painting to the police."

"I don't trust him. For some reason I trust you. If a deal is reached, you will ensure that the painting and I get together like lost lovers. And, of course, by doing so, you'll also protect your client from my murderous intentions."

I thought on that a bit. Whatever Charlie decided to do with the painting, I realized, I would have to be part of it. He was just as likely to get himself killed as to get himself a big payday. I had promised Mrs. Kalakos I would deliver him home alive, and I couldn't renege on that, partly because she terrified me and partly because there was a family obligation.

"Okay," I said. "If that's what he decides, I will help effectuate the transfer, but only for the purposes of protecting Charlie."

"Splendid. And in return?"

"You will go to your client immediately and give him a message for me."

"And what would that be, Victor?"

"You tell him I'm coming."

Lavender Hill tilted his head for a moment and then let out a huge, acrid laugh. There was a warning in the laugh, but a real delight, too, and it was loud enough to draw attention, which he never seemed to mind. After his laughter had subsided, the smile remained, even as he shook his head at me as if I were a naughty boy and he was amused at my naughtiness.

"I was completely wrong about you," said Lavender Hill. "You are a barroom brawler after all."

45

Family court, that last bastion of civility, where mothers and fathers work unceasingly, with good-will and decorum, to find custodial arrangements in the best interests of their children. Sure, and hockey is played by dainty men with fabulous teeth.

We were in family court, waiting for Judge Sistine to show up, sitting around and killing time. Much of a trial lawyer's day is spent killing time, which just then suited me fine. It was Bradley Hewitt's day to testify in his custody suit with Theresa Wellman, and I was a bit short on material.

After Theresa Wellman stepped down from the stand, Beth had spent the intermittent trial days granted us by Judge Sistine putting on a torrent of evidence about Theresa's rehabilitation, her new job, her new house, her new life. We had shown, about as well as could be shown, that letting Belle live part-time with her mother might not be a total disaster. But the judge would have to decide more than simply whether Theresa could take care of her daughter. She would have to decide whether joint custody, as opposed to keeping Belle with Bradley full-time, was in the child's best interests. Bradley Hewitt, with his suit and manners, his fine house and his high-paying job, would certainly put on a good show. And, to be honest, I didn't quite know how to prove joint custody a better solution. But I had a plan, and killing time was part of it.

Bradley Hewitt, self-satisfied and self-assured, was sitting beside his attorney, Arthur Gullicksen, at the counsel table. His entourage was lined up like black-suited ducks on the bench behind them. Gullicksen passed me a confident smile just as the courtroom doors opened.

We all turned and looked. It was Jenna Hathaway.

I turned back and checked out Gullicksen. His face took on a puzzled expression. He knew her, of course he did. I would have told him all about her, except I checked and found out I didn't need to. One of his clients, an upper-crust Main Liner from an old, distinguished family, had been hiding assets from his wife, which was bad enough, but he had also been hiding them from the IRS. Jenna Hathaway had descended like an avenging angel and banged him into the Federal Correctional Institution at Morgantown for a good seven years. I let Gullicksen sit there and puzzle it out for a moment before I stood and walked toward Jenna.

"Thanks for coming," I said quietly.

"Are you sure this is a good place to talk?" she said.

"No problem. The judge is forever handling some emergency child-care issue. This case has been held over longer than *Cats*. Did you look at the cooperation agreement?"

"Totally insufficient, and you have some gall to even try to pass this off as complete. I attached a few pages."

"I thought you might," I said. "Let me see what you added, and I'll get back to you."

She reached into her briefcase, pulled out the big red file folder in which I had delivered to her the agreement. As I took hold of it, I glanced at Gullicksen. With his eyes still on the two of us, he was now speaking very quickly to his client.

"I put in language regarding Charlie's testimony and possible punishments concerning Chantal Adair," said Jenna.

"Were you unreasonable?"

"You might think so."

"Don't be upset if I have some changes of my own."

"You said you had something for me?"

I directed her attention to Bradley Hewitt, who was now staring at us with quiet alarm. I pointed at him, subtly enough so it wasn't obvious, obvious enough so he couldn't miss that I was pointing. "Do you know who that is?"

"No," she said.

"His name is Bradley Hewitt. Your office is investigating him in that pay-to-play investigation where you guys bugged the mayor's office and got caught. He's one of the go-betweens the mayor uses, and he's testifying today. You might want to listen in on what he says."

"It's not my case."

"I'm sure the U.S. Attorney would appreciate knowing what he testifies to today."

"Anything interesting?"

"Could be," I said.

She looked at the courtroom door, checked her watch. "Okay, sure. Thanks, Victor."

I waved the file. "And thanks for bringing this."

With the big red file folder clutched to my chest, I walked back down the aisle, pulled out the chair at counsel table, started to sit. Gullicksen was at my side before my butt could settle.

"What is she doing here?" he said.

"It's a public courtroom," I said. "Here for the show, I suppose."

"What's in the file?"

"Stuff," I said. "Odds and ends."

"I won't let you ask about anything involving his business."

"If his business is illegal and he is under investigation, don't you think that could impact the custody decision?"

"This is totally out of bounds."

"I practice law the way I play golf. Do me a favor, Arthur, and ask your client how he likes the veal chop at La Famiglia."

At that moment Judge Sistine decided to grace us with her presence. "All rise." We all rose. She brusquely made her way to the bench. "Be seated." We all sat.

"Wellman v. Hewitt," said the clerk.

"Where are we, people?" said the judge. "I seem to remember we were going to hear from Mr. Hewitt today. Are you ready, Mr. Gullicksen?"

"Can we have a moment, Your Honor?" said Gullicksen.

"I've already given you a half hour by my unavoidable tardiness. How much more could you need?"

Gullicksen glanced at me and then said, "Certain statements made by Mr. Carl seem to indicate there is room for a settlement to this dispute. I think it might be in everyone's interest to explore the matter."

"How long will it take?" said the judge.

"Can you give us fifteen minutes?" said Gullicksen.

"Fine. And I must say, Mr. Gullicksen, it warms my heart to see the parties trying to work together for the benefit of their child. You have your fifteen minutes."

"What does this all mean, Mr. Carl?" said Theresa Wellman as we waited in the hallway for Gullicksen to continue to hammer sense into his client's perfectly groomed skull.

"It means we're going to come to some sort of an agreement," I said, "as long as you don't get greedy."

"What about weekends, Theresa?" said Beth. "That's what Bradley's attorney is trying to convince Bradley to agree to. Let Belle stay with Bradley during the week and continue going to the private school she attends."

"I want her all the time," said Theresa. "She's my daughter."

"And she's Bradley's daughter, too," said Beth. "Taking care of her during the week might compromise your job. This way you'll have her back in your life and you can continue to build on the progress you've made. But if we push too hard, and Bradley says no, you could end up with nothing. Take this as a gift and see how it works out."

"I don't know."

"Think about it," said Beth. She checked her watch. "You have another ten minutes to decide to say yes."

As we watched Theresa Wellman walk away, a slight slide of victory in her step, Beth said, "What was in that red file folder?"

"Charlie Kalakos's cooperation agreement."

"Remind me never to get sued by you," she said. "I had the house inspection yesterday."

"How'd it go?"

"The boiler is a ruin, the water pipes need replacing, there's a leak in the roof."

"So you're nixing the deal?"

"Of course not. Sheila was with me and was thrilled. She's getting the price reduced."

"Beth, the house is a wreck."

"The inspector said its bones were good."

"It's a house, not a supermodel."

"My mortgage was approved, we're having the closing next week. Will you come and be my lawyer?"

"Isn't this whole thing a little hasty?"

"Sheila says it's a great opportunity."

"Sheila's a Realtor, she has the scruples of a mollusk."

"I like her."

"So do I, actually, but that's not the point."

"Then what is the point?"

"Do you really think a house is going to solve whatever it is you need to solve?"

"Did you see how happy Theresa was? She really did change her life, didn't she?"

"Let's hope so for her daughter's sake."

"She's an inspiration. If she can do it, I can do it."

"And a house is the ticket?"

"It's a start. During the inspection I was walking through all the rooms, imagining the way they'll look after I settle in. The way, during parties, everyone will be hanging out in my new kitchen."

"You don't have parties."

"But I will, with a house."

"And the kitchen is a pit."

"It gets morning light."

"In April."

"I was imagining the way my friends will stay over in the guest bedroom. I was imagining the way, whenever I wanted, I could work from home in the home office."

"Any fantasies about the nursery?"

"Do you have a problem with my buying a house, Victor?"

Did I? Good question. Was I really worried that she was looking to real estate to solve an existential dilemma and bound to be disappointed? Or was I simply jealous that she was getting a house and starting a life when I seemed incapable of doing that for myself? And why had it suddenly gotten so difficult between us?

"No, Beth," I said. "No problem. It's a great fit."

"What about the closing?"

"I'll be there," I said. "I promise."

46

We return now to the curious case of Sammy Glick.

Why, you're a regular Sammy Glick, had said Agnes LeComte during our little tête-à-tête on the edge of Rittenhouse Square. I had an idea of what the old buzzard had in mind, the slow, acid drip of condescension in her tone pretty much said it all. I hadn't reacted much at the time, one thing I had learned over the years was to measure my responses to the insults that came my way, but it registered, yes it did. And I figured I'd go right to the source to get the full measure of her slight. So after running the name through my computer, I picked up a copy of *What Makes Sammy Run?* from the bookstore on my way to the airport. I was flying to Rochester. Business or pleasure?

It was Rochester. What the hell do you think?

"I told you on the phone I had nothing to say to you," said Serena Chicos. She was a small dark woman, fifty-some years of age, pretty and slim, with the sharp eyes and tense mouth of someone who had become used to giving directions and having them followed.

"I hoped if I came in person," I said, "you'd appreciate the seriousness of my inquiry."

"You hoped in vain," she said. "Now, if you'll excuse me, I have much work."

"I can assure you, Ms. Chicos, that everything you say to me will be held in strictest confidence."

"But I don't choose to be in your confidence. As I told you repeatedly, I am simply not willing to discuss my tenure at the Randolph Trust."

"Is there a reason?"

"It is ancient history. It is a part of my past that I have chosen to put behind me."

"Do they know about it?" I said, gesturing toward the hallway. "Do they know what happened while you were there?"

I was standing in the doorway of her rather small office. We were on the second floor of an impressive granite building with a huge bell tower, the Memorial Art Gallery of the University of Rochester. She was in the curatorial department. Just down the hall was the director's office, which was noticeably larger.

She smiled a tense smile. "I have been at this museum for twenty years, Mr. Carl. The administration here is no longer concerned about my qualifications."

"So the answer is no."

"I'm sorry to disappoint, but you will not be able to blackmail me into talking with you. My job as associate curator at the Randolph Trust was my first after I left school. It is clearly indicated on my curriculum vitae. In fact, it was Mr. Randolph himself who helped me attain this position just shortly before he died."

"That's interesting, since I heard you were a suspect in the robbery at his trust."

"Who told you that?" she said sharply, but not before involuntarily glancing behind me to see if anyone was listening in.

"Maybe we could discuss this whole situation somewhere more private?"

She narrowed her eyes at me for a moment and then shook her head. "No, Mr. Carl. I will not talk about the Randolph Trust no matter what vile rumors are being spread about me. I'm sorry you wasted your time. If you want, I can give you a pass for the gallery. The collection is actually quite good."

"But not as good as at the Randolph."

"No. The collection at the Randolph is . . . astounding." She sat quietly for a moment, as if remembering it painting by painting. "Is that all," she said finally, "because I really do have work."

"It was Mrs. LeComte who implicated you in the robbery."

An eyebrow rose. "Oh, was it, now? And how is the old bat?"

"Old. But still frisky and still there, on her throne. She said you had checked out certain blueprints just before the crime."

"It wasn't true."

"She said there were fingerprints."

"A mistake was made."

"She also said your tastes were slightly vulgar."

"My tastes? Have you seen the height of her heels?"

"And that your neck was too long."

"There are thirteen masterworks by Modigliani at the Randolph."

"What you're telling me, I suppose, is that Mr. Randolph admired long necks."

Her hand started to rise involuntarily to her throat, and then she caught herself. A man and a woman, deep in some conversation, both peered into the office as they passed in the hallway. Serena Chicos fiddled with her hands and then sighed.

"Where are you staying, Mr. Carl?"

"The Airport Holiday Inn."

"I can give you a few minutes after work."

"Splendid," I said. "I'll be waiting."

His given name was Samuel Glickstein. Jewish, of course, which was certainly a significant part of Mrs. LeComte's little dig. She was still rooted in that musty age in Philadelphia when to be a Jew was considered something sordid, like being a sloppy drunk or having a predilection for young boys, nothing to lose your job over, but still. *Why, you're a regular Sammy Glick.* Yes, I was, wasn't I? Little Shmelka Glickstein of the Lower East Side, whom we first spy as a copyboy at the fictional *New York Record*. "Always ran," writes the narrator. "Always looked thirsty." Sammy Glick.

What Makes Sammy Run? by Budd Schulberg was quite the celebrated novel when it appeared in 1941. You know Schulberg, he's the guy who wrote *On the Waterfront* as a justification for naming names to the House Un-American Affairs Committee in the fifties. "I could have had class. I could have been a contender." Sammy Glick's shady maneuverings as he claws his way to the top made Sammy rich and Budd Schulberg famous.

While I was waiting for Serena Chicos at my hotel, I followed Sammy's meteoric rise from copyboy to columnist, from columnist to Hollywood screenwriter, from screenwriter to producer to head of the movie studio, married to a rich redhead with flawless beauty. You go, brother. Sure he had to cross a few lines and step on a few toes, screw a few writers out of credits and help smash the union, but nothing he did through the whole of the book was worse than what your basic U.S. congressman commits before breakfast. And Sammy had better taste in shoes.

And yet I found the novel troubling. The problem wasn't that I identified with Sammy Glick, the problem was that I didn't, at least not enough, and not in the way I wanted. All my life his was the path I had expected to tread, the ruthless march to wealth and success, not to mention the redhead. But somehow I couldn't pull it off. There was a weakness in my soul where in Sammy Glick's there was only steel. If there was a curse in my life, it was that I didn't have what it took to take what I wanted in this world. The great men and women in history all had that steel. If you think Gandhi was a pushover, you never tried to give him a ham sandwich.

And here again, in that crummy hotel room in Rochester, it was playing out. In my desk drawer back at the office there was a pile of gold and jewels just waiting to be appraised and sold. And Lavender Hill was offering a king's ransom if I could just convince Charlie to sell the Rembrandt and sail off into the sunset. I was in the golden land of either/or, where I couldn't lose, but instead of taking care of business, I was off on some quixotic quest to find a missing girl. You know what I was? I was a sap, pure and simple, and I felt it all the more keenly as I read about Sammy Glick's rise up the Hollywood ladder toward a success that I would never match.

But I wasn't reading the novel only to make myself feel blue, or to suss out the depth of Mrs. LeComte's insult, or even just to pass the time, though I was accomplishing all three. No, I was reading the novel because Mrs. LeComte's comment hadn't been as offhand as she made it seem, and I couldn't help feeling that maybe, just maybe, somewhere in the book was a clue that would help me discover what really happened to Chantal Adair twenty-eight years ago.

And damn if I wasn't right.

*   *   *

"I was framed, Mr. Carl," said Serena Chicos, and perhaps she heard the inevitable sigh I sigh whenever anyone tells me he has been framed, because she added, as if compelled by that very sagging of my shoulders, "No, but I was. Really."

"By whom?"

"I don't know for certain, and I am not one to cast aspersions."

"As they were cast upon you."

"Precisely."

"But why would this person want to frame you?"

"To divert attention, to scuttle a career. When Mr. Randolph was alive, the Randolph Trust was like Versailles, a snake pit full of courtiers vying for the king's attention."

"And you were young and beautiful and long-necked, is that it?"

She stared at me without responding, her fingers tapping impatiently on the little round table in the hotel's café. But then a half smile turned her thin, tense lips, and I saw it all, the young art academic, the old millionaire art collector, the shared passion, the mutual admiration, lust among the Monets and the Matisses, the Modiglianis, his old bony hands on her long lovely neck.

"It's not something I'm comfortable talking about," she said.

"Do you have any children?"

"Three. Two boys and a girl. And they are waiting for me at home."

"I'm looking into the Randolph Trust robbery because something happened about the same time. A little girl disappeared. The detective involved in the disappearance thirty years ago believed that the robbery and the missing girl were somehow connected. On behalf of the family, I'm trying to find out if that's so. Anything I can learn about the robbery would be a big help."

"I told you, I had nothing to do with it."

"I believe you, but you might be able to point me in the right direction."

"I doubt it."

"She was six when she went missing. Do you want to see a picture?"

"No," she said. She sat back, crossed her arms, thought for a moment. "Mr. Randolph and I were together until I was forced to leave after the robbery," she said finally. "There were suspicions that there was some insider help. An insider had to go. I was chosen to take the fall."

"By Mr. Randolph?"

"No, by others."

"And Mr. Randolph didn't try to keep you?"

"There were two people who held sway over Wilfred, at least while I was there. One was his wife, a quite formidable woman. Their marriage had become something of a museum piece itself, more mummified than alive. But she had been with him when he was still poor and had helped him amass the collection. Whatever secrets he had, she knew them."

"Even you?"

"I wasn't aware of it at the time, but from what I later learned, they discussed everything. They lived their lives in the spirit of their times, Kinsey, Masters and Johnson. It was in many ways a time of greater personal freedom than we have now. But Wilfred was always a little terrified of his wife. And also of Agnes LeComte."

"Mrs. LeComte? How did she get such power?"

"She had became a close friend of Mrs. Randolph's, for one. And before Wilfred and I began our . . . personal relationship, he was very much with her. They had been having an affair for a decade."

"Until he dumped her for you."

"That's right. The two women convinced him that, for the protection of the trust, I had to be let go."

"It seems LeComte had a pretty good motive for framing you."

"Obviously, yes. We were never close, and at first her resentment was palpable, but when she came back, things were very different."

"Came back? From where?"

"From her sabbatical. After Wilfred made it clear to her that he had found someone new, and after Mrs. Randolph refused to come to her defense, she left the trust. She was gone for more than six months."

"What did she do?"

"Traveled, from what I heard, though she didn't talk much about it. But when she returned, things were very different. There was something changed about her, she had found a certain peace, which I didn't understand then, but now I think I do. I think she met someone during her travels, I think she fell in love. She would never admit to anything, but when she returned, she poured herself into the working of the trust, remained close with Mrs. Randolph, and began to take an active interest in my career. Maybe too active. Of course there was always an edge to our relationship, but she tried to become something of a mentor."

"How'd that work out?"

"Not well. I already had a mentor in Wilfred. He was a brilliant man. He had so much to teach about so many things, and he was never boring. That is a rare quality in men, I've found, rarer even in lawyers."

"Tell me about the robbery itself."

"There's not much to tell. That day we were closed, no visitors or classes. Wilfred was working with Mrs. LeComte in the gardens. The trust keeps a fascinating garden, full of rare specimens collected from all over the world. That whole day I was reviewing some records with Mrs. Randolph. After the night guards showed up, we all went home. No one knew anything had happened until we opened up the next morning and found the guards bound and gagged."

"How did the crooks get in?"

"Apparently someone was inside. No one knows how he got there."

"Any ideas?"

"None. It has remained a mystery."

"Anything unusual about the guards that night?"

"The crew had been working together for ages. The supervisor was an old friend of the Randolphs'. The police naturally focused on them, but they all came up clean. Everyone came up clean except for me."

"The fingerprints and files."

"It wouldn't have been so hard to fabricate the evidence, which was why no charges were ever filed. The file jacket could have come from anywhere. I handled many. And my signature on the sign-out sheet must have been forged. Really, if I was stealing the blueprints, would I have signed them out?"

"Not likely."

"I had enough freedom to take home what files I needed without a signature. But it was quite convenient for me to be blamed. Wilfred had been making noise about marrying me. I didn't want that, but still, I heard later that Mrs. Randolph was horrified that he might divorce her. And Mrs. LeComte was growing concerned about my influence over the trust. Wilfred was giving me more and more responsibility."

"And with you gone, Mrs. Randolph's marriage and Mrs. LeComte's place at the trust were both secure."

"Yes. But even after I was forced to leave, Wilfred took care of me. Gave me money when I needed it and then got me a position at the gallery here. He was really very sweet. Is there anything else?"

"Where did she go?"

"Who?"

"Mrs. LeComte. On her sabbatical. Where did she go?"

"Europe, Asia, Australia. She came back through the West Coast."

"California."

"That's right."

"Hollywood."

"I suppose."

"Stayed there awhile."

"I think so, yes."

"Took a lover."

"That's what I believed, yes."

"I bet I know who it was."

"Really?" She leaned forward, captured for a moment by a piece of gossip from decades in her past. "Who?"

"Sammy Glick."

47

The brown building of the Randolph Trust, with its great red door, stood once again before me.

I couldn't look at it now without thinking of its sordid history. The philandering Wilfred Randolph, his long-suffering wife, the catfights between the two mistresses in Randolph's life. And then the robbery of jewels and golden figurines and two priceless paintings that was carried off by a quintet of neighborhood mooks, aided by someone inside. The investigation, the accusations, the missing girl, the lovely young curator who shared Randolph's bed and was framed for the crime. All of that past was as much a part of the building as the stones and mortar.

But now Randolph was dead and his wife was dead, Serena Chicos was raising a family in Rochester, and Agnes LeComte was shriveling by the day as she searched for a young man to sexually mentor. Chantal Adair was still missing, and Charlie Kalakos was in exile, and Ralph Ciulla was murdered, and Joey Pride was on the run. To top it all off, the forces of power and money were trying their mightiest to wrest the fabulous art collection from this very site, and it looked very much like they were going to succeed.

It was sad in its way that the collection was bound for another location, it was part and parcel of this very building and its history—sad, but not tragic. The Randolph Trust

was a monument to a man and his money, but what does
a great Cézanne canvas or a Matisse portrait care about
such a monument? Put the works in a museum, put them
in a brothel, it wouldn't make a difference, they still would
shine. In the end the paintings Randolph collected were too
luminous, too perfect to be controlled; mediocrity could be
contained, but the greatness of the art Randolph bought had
now transcended the cage he built around it.

I was tempted to bang on the door and go inside, to see
them all once again, but this wasn't the second Monday of
the month or the alternate Wednesday or Good Friday, and I
wasn't there for the art.

I found her around the back. I had called first, been told
that she was working today in the gardens. Did I want to
leave a message? "No," I said, "no message." What I needed
to ask, I needed to ask in person.

"So you've come to me at last, my darling," said Mrs.
LeComte. "Are you here to take me up on my offer?"

She was sitting on a small green cart, leaning over and
weeding a bed of bright flowers as red as her lipstick. She
glanced up at me as my footsteps approached and then
turned her attention back to her work. She was wearing a
smock, gloves, a wide-brimmed hat, and she looked every
inch the suburban dowager tending her garden, except that
she was still wearing her improbable high heels and this
garden was spectacular, with brilliant beds and marble statues and lovely stone paths. Each tree and bush and patch
of flowers was carefully labeled with a neat green sign
inscribed in Latin. Around her a crew of gardeners in their
blue overalls pruned and raked while she tended her own
small plot.

"No, thank you," I said. "I'm afraid I have to pass."

"That is rather a shame. In these sorts of mentor-protégé
relationships, I've found that even with very little sexual

desire at the start, through time and intimacy the sexual attraction can grow positively voracious."

"They say the world will be destroyed in five billion years."

"Oh, don't worry, Victor, I'm sure whatever repulsion I feel for you now can eventually be turned around, if you are ardent enough."

"Is that what happened between you and Mr. Randolph, your repulsion for him was turned around?"

"To whom have you been talking?"

"I just came back from Rochester."

"How is the little tramp?"

"Older, with children."

"Serves her right. Whatever she told you was a lie. Wilfred and I were violently attracted to one another from the start. Our passion was a force of nature."

"As long as it lasted."

"But while it lasted, it was glorious. I wouldn't trade our time together, I wouldn't trade all he gave me, for anything in the world. It was the most precious period in my life."

"Until the end."

"Endings are always a problem. Have you seen a film lately? Wilfred, especially in his later years, was attracted to youth. Mine was going, hers was in full bloom. And she wore that tacky turquoise jewelry around her neck like an invitation to rut. But we reconciled after everything, Wilfred and I, so at the end we were simply the best of friends with a delicate shared past. We would sit here in this garden, Wilfred and Mrs. Randolph and myself, sit and drink wine and talk. We talked about everything."

"About your love life?"

"The Randolphs were quite liberated about those things, and Mrs. Randolph especially liked to hear the details. She much preferred to listen than to participate."

"But my guess is you never talked about the lover you took between your ending with Randolph and your reconciliation. Was that another mentor-protégé relationship?"

"He was so young, he had so much to learn. And I had all this experience, this wealth of knowledge passed on to me by Wilfred. I was bursting with it all, it needed an outlet."

"And so you found your Sammy Glick. Ambitious, ruthless, a willing pupil."

"A mutual friend from Philadelphia made the introduction. Talk about an ardent lover. Wilfred was passionate but somewhat soft where it counted, if you catch my drift. A bit like you, I'm certain. But Teddy was something else entirely. Violent and stirring, filled with a need to devour. Whoosh. I can still feel the tingle in my loins."

"Yuck," I said.

"Squeamish, Victor?"

"Absolutely. So who came up with the idea of robbing the trust and taking your revenge on the lover who had jilted you?"

"It just came up. We were on the beach, at night, in each other's arms, and it just came up."

"Oh, I bet it did."

She laughed. "That, too. And then, on the beach, with a fire blazing and our naked bodies up against each other, covered with sweat and between two blankets, with the soft sand beneath us and the velvet sky above, we worked it out."

"Love is a many-splendored art heist. How did you pull it off?"

"Oh, Victor, some secrets must remain, don't you think?"

"I'm surprised you've told me as much as you have."

"I don't respond well to rudeness."

"I've tried to be polite."

"Not you. I care as much about your manner as I care about the manner of the worm that burrows in my soil."

"So you've heard from him in the past few days."

"Not directly, but yes. You must be worrying him. For some reason he thought it opportune to send me a message."

"Let me guess. It was hide the Monet and keep your mouth shut."

"Don't get too clever, Victor, you'll end up in therapy."

"And you're disobeying. Aren't you afraid of what he'll do to you?"

"I'm tougher than I look, dear. I love him still, but if ever we came face-to-face again I'd pluck his eyes out quick as a raven." She took hold of one of the flowers she had been tending and, with a quick tug, yanked it from the ground. "Such brilliant crimson. Aren't they a vision?"

"Where is he?"

"I don't know."

"You must have an idea."

"No. None. Not anymore."

"When was the last time you saw him?"

"The day after. He said he'd send for me."

"And you're still waiting."

"I think of him in the late hours when the wind blows gently outside my window. There is always one that comes to you in the middle of the night, like a ghost, and for me it is he."

"Do you know anything about the girl?"

"What girl? Oh, the one in the picture. Why do you keep asking about her?"

"Let me ask one other thing. Who passed along his message? Was it a little man with a sweet scent and a Southern accent?"

"Don't be silly. What would I be doing with such a creature?"

"Then who?"

"You know what time it is, Victor?"

"About noon?"

"No, dear. It's that time when dusk approaches and the dark night beckons. A good time to settle old scores."

"That's what I'm here for," I said cheerfully.

"He asked a favor. This is many years ago, when I was no longer waiting like Falstaff for the summons. 'I shall be sent for in private to him.' For a while after, we were still in touch. A few phone calls, idle talk about our life together. Australia was the plan. I had been, he said he wanted to go. But he couldn't yet leave, he said. It would be too suspicious, he said. In those days he was back in California, where we had first met. I wanted to rush out, but I heeded his warning. What else was I to do? Years passed, the urge died. And then he called, a voice out of my past, asking a favor. A young lawyer was looking to hook up with a large, prosperous firm. It would help if there was a prestigious client he could bring along with him. Could I perhaps convince Mr. Randolph to give him a look? When he appeared at the trust, freshly scrubbed for the interview, I recognized him at once, and yet I put in the word."

"What do you mean, you recognized him?"

"He was one of them, one of the thieves."

There was only one possibility. "Hugo Farr?"

"That's not the name he goes by now. I thought I was helping a young man traverse the difficult road of life. He was handsome enough and young enough and, like a fool, I believed there was a chance for something new in my life. But instead of a lover, I was bringing into the trust a spy whose purpose, I soon learned, was to keep me quiet and under his thumb."

"Who?" I said.

"Oh, Victor, don't be so slow."

"Be quick, is that it?"

"I think my job here is done. Thank you for coming. I've so enjoyed our chat. Time to start packing, I believe."

"Taking another trip?"

"I've waited long enough. If ever you make it to the other side of the world, please don't look me up."

"What was he going to do with the money?"

"What everybody wants to do with their money out there. It was what the whole thing was really about. He was going to make a movie."

It went off in my head like a camera shutter. Click, click, Sammy Glick.

48

    I drove right back to the city, parked on the street by my office, and without stopping in to check my mail, I headed for One Liberty Place. I took the elevator to the fifty-fourth floor. The doors opened onto a huge lobby with shiny wood floors and antique furniture. Talbott, Kittredge and Chase. Oh, my.

"I'm here to see Mr. Quick," I said to the receptionist.

"Do you have an appointment?" she asked.

"No, but he'll see me," I said. "Tell him Victor Carl is here."

A few minutes later, a slim young woman in a blue suit appeared in the lobby looking very grim. I was thinking that whoever she was coming for was in for a nasty surprise, when I realized she was coming for me.

"Mr. Carl?" she said.

I abruptly stood. "Yes?"

"You're here to see Mr. Quick?"

"That's right." I recognized her suddenly, the paralegal from my earlier visit. Jennifer.

Jennifer gestured me to a spot away from the center of the lobby, beside the great wall of windows gazing down over the eastern edge of the city. Her hair was pulled back primly, and her lips were only discreetly painted, but even so her raw, youthful beauty shone through. As we stood there, she moved in close and lowered her voice.

"What did you wish to see Mr. Quick about?"

"We have an ongoing matter involving the Randolph Trust," I said. "Why, is there a problem?"

"Did that matter involve any emergency travel?"

"Not that I know of."

A swift glance away. "I'm sorry, Mr. Carl, but Mr. Quick isn't in today."

"Do you know where he is?"

"No. That's the thing. He didn't call in and he always calls in." A nervous laugh. "Every ten minutes if he's away from the office. He can't stand to be out of touch. We are in constant contact." Hands playing one with the other. "But I haven't heard from him in two days."

"Maybe he's at home?"

"He's not answering his cell phone, and his wife said he wasn't there, but I'm not sure if I believe her. She's not the most reliable source." Lips pressed together. "What with the drinking. Frankly, I'm worried."

"Maybe there's a reason he doesn't want the office to know where he is. Maybe he's sick or out playing golf. Does he belong to a club?"

"Philadelphia Country Club."

"Of course he does. If you give me his home address, I could run over and check if he's at the house for you."

"I'm not supposed to give that out."

"Stanford and I are old friends, Jennifer. And I'm sure he wouldn't want you to worry like this." She nodded in agreement. "And as soon as I find out something I'll give you a call."

"Would you, Mr. Carl?" Her hand on my forearm. "I really am desperate to know he's okay, and I'm afraid, for some reason, Mrs. Quick isn't so cordial to me."

Funny how that works, I thought as she leaned forward

and gave me her cell phone number and Stanford Quick's address.

"Can I ask a question, Jennifer?" I said.

"Sure."

"How old are you?"

"Twenty-one." Her shoulders squared. "I just graduated from Penn."

"Let me say Stanford's very lucky to have you."

Driving back into the suburbs, I had the wheel in my left hand and the cell phone in my right.

"Philadelphia Country Club," came the voice over the phone.

"Can I talk to the starter, please?"

"Hold on one moment?"

Merion might have the highest-rated golf course in the city and its suburbs, but Philadelphia Country Club's is rated almost as highly, and it has the distinction of being an even snootier place. You want to play golf, you join Merion; you want to hob with the nobs and flaunt your social connections, you join the Philadelphia Country Club. But despite their differences, there is one towering concept on which all the members of both clubs violently agree: They would never have me as a member. Truth be told, I couldn't get into either joint as a caddy.

"Starter shed, here. Chris speaking."

"Hello, Chris. I was tentatively scheduled to play with Mr. Quick this afternoon, but I haven't heard from him, and I wondered if he was already on the course."

"Nah, Mr. Quick hasn't been in all day."

"Has he called in to set up a tee time for us?"

"You must have gotten the days mixed up. We have a

ladies' shotgun going out in forty-five minutes. The course won't open up until something like five."

"It must be my mistake, then. Thanks."

"If I see him, do you have a message?"

"Sure. Tell him to call Carl if he can to reschedule, because I am aching to get out there and punish those links."

I had always imagined myself in a massive stone Tudor with a wide front lawn and a willow tree in front. There would be a pale dog sleeping in the shade of that willow tree, just beside the hammock swaying gently in the wind. A basketball hoop would be attached to the detached stone garage at the end of the long, looping driveway and a pitch-back would stand beside the tall hedges so my kids could throw high pops to themselves. The lawn would be mowed, the trees trimmed, the sun shining. And parked right beneath that basketball hoop would be some behemoth of an SUV, and beside it, neat and black, a BMW, nothing too grand, let's not be too ostentatious, maybe something out of the 5 series.

The good news was that if ever I came into a boatload of cash, I now knew where to find it.

The dog woke up as I pulled into the driveway. When I slipped out of my car, it jumped to its feet beneath the tall willow and scampered over. I reached out my hand, palm up. It sniffed and licked and let me rub the folds at the bottom of its neck.

"How you doing, fella?" I said.

It stepped back and barked loudly.

"Yeah," I said. "Me, too."

The door to the massive stone Tudor was red, the same red as the door at the Randolph Trust. Fitting, no? I dropped the heavy knocker once and then again. The dog barked. I held myself back from yelling out, "Honey, I'm home."

The door swung wide, a woman stood in the opening, the dog slid past me and rubbed its side against her leg. Lucky dog.

"Hello?" she said.

"Mrs. Quick?"

"Yes." She was tall and lovely and about thirty years younger than her husband. I wondered if her name was Jennifer, too. She wore jeans, a white oxford shirt, her hair was blond and cut short. She smiled nervously as she took hold of the dog's collar. "Can I help you?"

"Yes, I think you can. My name is Victor Carl. I'm a lawyer, and I'm looking for your husband."

She tilted her head and stared at me with unfocused eyes, as if I were a puzzle which she really didn't care to solve. "I'm sorry, I don't understand. Why do you need to see my husband at his residence?"

"It's something important that really can't wait. Is he at home now?"

"If you have a summons or such to deliver, you should really deliver it at his office. He doesn't bring his work home with him."

"Well, you see, he's not at the office."

Her lack of reaction told me she knew this already. "I'm sorry, I can't help you."

"You don't know where he is, Mrs. Quick, is that it?"

A voice came from behind her. "Mom, I'm going to be late."

She stepped aside. Behind her I could see a young boy, about eight, dressed in his baseball uniform: maroon shirt, maroon socks, baseball cap with a big LM on it.

"In a minute, Sean."

"But I'm going to be late."

"In a minute." She turned back to me. "I'm sorry, but I have to go."

"How long has he been gone?"

Her eyes slowly came into focus, and she looked me over as if I had just materialized in front of her. Then she stepped forward with the dog and closed the door behind her. "You were the one on television, the one with the client that has the painting."

"That's right."

"Stanford was very upset about what was happening."

"I'd bet he was."

"Leave him alone. Leave us alone."

"It's not me you should be worried about, Mrs. Quick. Do you know where he is?"

"No. I don't."

"When did you see him last?"

She looked at me again, then turned her gaze toward the perfect expanse of her perfect front lawn with its graceful willow tree. "Yesterday morning. He left early. He was upset."

"Did he say anything about where he was going?"

"He just said he might be away for a while. He said he had heard from an old friend who was in trouble."

"Has he called at all?"

"No."

"Have you tried his cell phone?"

"All I get is his voice mail. I've left four messages."

"What kind of car did he take?"

"We have a Volvo station wagon. Green."

"Okay. Thank you."

"Will you find him for me?"

"I'll try."

"And if you do, will you tell him I forgive him?"

"Yes, ma'am, I will."

* * *

At first I didn't know where I was heading. I was behind the wheel of my cramped gray car, and I was driving for sure, stopping at red lights and going on greens, but I wasn't concentrating on the road. Instead I was swatting away the bluebirds of happiness that were flitting around my shoulders and crapping on my head. Why were they crapping on my head? Because they weren't the bluebirds of my happiness, they belonged to Stanford Quick, who had somehow stolen the life to which I had always aspired.

He had the house, the wife, the job, the country club, even the little piece on the side—*oh, Jennifer*—which, while maybe not part of my original plan, certainly didn't help the envy any. And how he had gotten it all was what really gouged my heart. He had simply up and taken it. Hugo Farr had been offered a chance by Teddy Pravitz to leap the abyss and become someone new, and he had seized his destiny. And if he had to cross the line of legality, and if he had to change his name, and if he had to pretend to be something he wasn't, so what? He hadn't let niggling details get in the way of what he wanted from his life.

Hugo Farr. Stanford Quick. Success on a stick. Sammy Glick. Son of a bitch.

And I guess what was bothering me the most was that he had blasted away the fiction with which I had justified the weakness in myself that seemed to stay my hand whenever I was finally reaching for the life I so desired. Sure I always had my reasons, failure always does, but underlying the hesitancy was a belief I somehow couldn't shake. We are what we are, we can't transform ourselves, the die is cast and we play out our fates. I might hit upon the million-dollar case, I might stumble upon the love of my life, something hard and clean might fall into my lap and change everything, but it really wouldn't change anything. I'd still be Victor Carl, I'd still be second tier and second class, I'd still be less than I ever hoped to be.

But now, in the short span of just a few hours, Stanford Quick had shown me the lie that underlay my blighted state. Transformation was possible, absolutely, he was living proof, and my failure to transform was failure indeed. It wasn't just bad luck, it wasn't just a sorry twist of fate; I simply wasn't man enough to take hold of my destiny and steer it myself. So I bobbed and floated and meandered to where the currents of my life led me, which was very much like the way I was driving right now, heading in whatever direction the road turned.

Except I wasn't heading just anywhere, I was heading someplace very specific. And when I recognized the direction in which I was driving, I knew where and why. He had heard from an old friend in trouble, had said his wife, which meant he was heading back into his past. And I knew enough now to know where that lay.

I was looking for a green Volvo wagon, the kind you'd see at horse shows and suburban soccer games in Gladwyne, not the usual ride for the Northeast row-house set. I first checked Hugo Farr's old street. Nothing. Then Teddy Pravitz's old street. Nothing. Then Ralph Ciulla's street. Nothing. I was about to head toward Mrs. Kalakos's house when I remembered, despite my suburban heritage, that every row house in the city has an alley behind it. And there it was, parked in the spot right behind Ralphie Meat's house.

Beside a door on the level of the alleyway, a wooden stairway led up to a small, rickety deck. There was police tape, wrapped around the banisters of the stairway, blocking the way up. And there was more of the yellow tape lying flaccid on the ground beside the door, yet the door itself was clear. Nothing too tricky to figure out there. The knob turned easily in my hand, but the door wouldn't open right off. A push with my shoulder shoved it a few inches, and another shoved it open enough for me to slip through.

I entered a narrow passageway that led to a cluttered, musty basement, ragged cement floor, strange stacked boxes, old furniture piled haphazardly, legs and arms rising menacingly out of the shadows. It smelled damp, airless, it smelled of spilled laundry soap. With the help of the light coming through the open door and a mottled window, I could see the bulky cubes of an old washer and dryer in the corner, copper tubing leaning against one wall and casting twisting shadows, a heap of bizarre implements on a makeshift worktable fashioned from thick cast-iron pipes.

"Mr. Quick?" I yelled out.

The sound died swiftly in the darkness of the basement. There was no answer.

I took a step forward. I heard something creak. I spun and saw nothing and I knew right away. I think I had known as soon as grim-faced Jennifer approached me in the lobby of Talbott, Kittredge and Chase.

A narrow wooden stairway rose from the left side of the basement. I followed it up, sagging wooden steps groaning, to a closed door. I pushed it open and stepped into the kitchen, bright with sunlight. The room was wide, the appliances were avocado green and from the era before my childhood, the yellow linoleum floor was stained and badly scuffed.

"Mr. Quick? Stanford?"

No answer. But I smelled something I didn't like, something familiar enough and yet too strange for words. I had smelled it before, not too long ago, in this very house. The homey aromas of decades of gravy stewing in the kitchen, of garlic and sausage and spices that clung to the very walls, along with the fetid coppery scent of death. Of an unnatural, murderous death. Ralph Ciulla's death. His body had been found in this very house, which the police had closed down pending further investigation. And now I was inside, smelling it again.

And yes, it was fresher than I remembered, if the scent of death can ever be described as fresh.

I turned on the lights. The lights of the kitchen, the old pewter chandelier in the green-walled dining room. I turned on the lights to protect me from what I now was certain I would find.

I scanned the living room from the dining room archway and saw nothing, and relief frizzled up my spine, and then I saw the leg with its khaki pants sticking out from the edge of the easy chair, the shiny brown loafer resting flat on the floor, as if someone were sitting in that chair calmly waiting for me to come around and say hey.

"Hello," I said. "Mr. Quick?"

No answer.

49

Stanford Quick was sitting in the easy chair, the same chair I had sat on when I tried not to throw up on my shoes. Khaki pants, plaid shirt, blue blazer, a drink in his hand, something brown and watery. He was leaning back comfortably, and there was in his expression something of a man telling a humorous story, who had been rudely interrupted. Interrupted with a bullet in his skull. I guess it wasn't such a humorous story after all.

A flash whited out the entire scene, and then it came back, just as strange. Just as bloody. Flash flash.

"Can we go over this one more time?" said McDeiss, grabbing my lapel and pulling my attention away from the blood-spattered chair and the corpse of Stanford Quick as the photographer worked. Police were swarming once again in the Ciulla household, dusting for fingerprints, searching for blood. Outside, the carnival was in full swing—the boisterous crowd, the reporters, the television trucks with their microwave dishes pointed high. It's funny how fast a murder brightens a slow news night.

"You were driving around looking for this Stanford Quick," said McDeiss.

"That's right," I said.

"And you came up with the bright idea of looking for him here."

"I thought there might be a connection."

"And lo and behold you found the car that Mr. Quick's wife had described."

"It's funny how when you tell a story ten times, the details stick, isn't it, Detective?"

"And so, quite in character, you stepped right inside what was still a sealed crime scene."

"The tape was gone, the door was open."

"And you climbed the stairs and turned on every light in the place."

"I'm afraid of the dark."

"Leaving a trail of your fingerprints."

"My little gift to the crime-scene search unit. At least I didn't throw up, I know how much they love that."

"And then you found him sitting on that chair, just like that, and called the police."

"I poured him a drink first."

"Excuse me?"

"He looked thirsty."

"And you didn't touch a thing when you found him."

"Not a thing," I said, which wasn't exactly true, because before I called the cops, I had searched for something and I had found it and I had checked it out and then wiped off my prints and put it back.

"You want to tell me now about the connection you mentioned between Stanford Quick of Gladwyne and Ralph Ciulla of Tacony?"

"I thought I'd wait for Slocum and Jenna Hathaway. You know how I hate telling the same story over and over and— Oh, look, they've arrived."

Slocum strode into the house like a captain striding onto the quarterdeck, his eyes behind his glasses alert, his beige raincoat swirling dramatically around him. It wasn't chilly out and it wasn't rainy, which sort of dampened the effect of the swirling coat, but still, you could tell that a crime scene had become a natural part of his habitat. Not so, however, with Jenna Hathaway, who walked hesitantly inside and stopped cold at the door when she saw the corpse. She stared at it for a long moment and then turned away as she put a hand up to her nose. Her father had been a regular at such scenes, but I suppose you don't get to see too many dead guys on the tax-avoidance circuit.

"I'll be back," said McDeiss. "Wait here and don't move." He started walking toward the prosecutors, stopped and swiveled his head toward me to check that I had listened.

"What?" I said.

"Don't even twitch," he said before continuing on his way.

When I had placed the call about the dead man in the easy chair, I placed it directly to McDeiss. Whatever we felt one for the other, my feelings were charged with a professional respect. And I had asked McDeiss to call both Slocum and Hathaway to the crime scene, because with two corpses, a killer on the loose, and my client still trying to come home, it was time to stop dicking around.

"Any idea what happened?" said Slocum when the four of us were finally together in the kitchen and I had gone through the whole finding-the-corpse business for the eleventh time.

"I'd guess murder," I said.

"You think?" said Jenna Hathaway. "What was it that gave it away? The bullet in the forehead?"

"Any ideas on who did it?" said Slocum.

"Same guy who killed Ralph," I said.

"Why?"

"Well, it's the same room and the same house and, from what McDeiss has told me, it looks like the same caliber of bullet coming from the left side."

"No, I mean why would the same guy want to kill two characters so different? Ralph Ciulla was a blue-collar guy from Tacony, and Stanford Quick was a high-powered corporate lawyer from Gladwyne. Where's the connection?"

"The Randolph Trust."

"Stanford Quick was the trust's lawyer. Ralph Ciulla was maybe involved in the robbery twenty-eight years ago. That's a pretty tenuous connection."

"It goes deeper than that, and farther back into the past," I said.

"No more dancing, Carl," said McDeiss. "You're going to tell us everything you know."

I checked my watch. "It's a little late for a story, don't you think?"

"You can do it here and now," said McDeiss calmly, "or later from a jail cell."

"Now's good," I said quickly. And with that, I relayed to them the whole story, as much as I knew, about the Randolph Trust robbery, the five neighborhood losers who planned it, and what happened to four of them after they pulled it off.

"So what you're saying," said McDeiss once I had laid it out as best I could, "is that Ralph Ciulla, Joey Pride, your client, and this Stanford Quick were all part of the crew that pulled the heist?"

"That's right."

"So why are some of them showing up dead?"

"To keep them quiet. To keep the whole thing quiet. To keep Charlie away, to keep the painting hidden, to break any link that still existed between the Randolph heist and the one guy out of the original five who is still not identified. It was this final guy who arranged for Stanford Quick to show up at Ralph's old house for some reason and then had him killed right here, in the very same room as Ralph."

"Teddy Pravitz," said Jenna Hathaway.

"So you think he's back, killing all his old friends like Jason with his ski mask?" said McDeiss.

"Something like that, yeah," I said. "Or he hired someone to do it for him."

"But the statute of limitations on the robbery has long passed. Why does he care so much to drop a couple of corpses and make it all matter again?"

"Because it's not just a robbery, is it, Jenna?"

"No," she said.

I turned to her. "He was with her. Her brother told us what he told your father, that he had seen them together. And after the robbery that bastard took her, I'm sure of it."

"You think he still has her?"

"I don't know."

"It's been twenty-eight years."

"I know. But we need to find out."

"How?"

"Enough already with cooperation agreements being tossed back and forth like a football," I said. "Two men are dead, and more will die if you and I and Slocum don't get together right now to make a deal."

"Can someone tell me what the hell you two are talking about?" said McDeiss.

"She will," I said. "After we make a deal."

Slocum stared at me for a moment, trying to figure out how much of what I had just said was the truth and how much was utter bullshit, and then he turned to Jenna and nodded.

"What do you need?" she said to me.

"Immunity," I said. "And witness protection. Someplace hot, but with a dry heat, for his sinuses. You give us that, he'll tell you everything about the mob, the heist, and the girl."

"And the painting, too," said Slocum. "Don't forget that little detail."

"Has he agreed to your offer?" said Hathaway.

"I'll get him to."

"And what will he tell us?"

"I don't know yet, but I'm going to find out, I promise you."

"Okay. We'll give him immunity on everything not having to do with the girl. And if he cooperates on her and we end up with the true story and an arrest, depending on what actually happened and his role in it, I promise nothing more than a couple of years in protective custody and then relocation."

Slocum turned back to me. "Will that do it?"

"That will do it."

"And who will bring him in?"

"I will," I said.

"You?" said Slocum with a derisive edge to his voice.

"Yeah, me."

"You got any body armor?"

"No."

"Better get some."

"This is all very pleasant and cordial," said McDeiss, "and you better tell me what the hell you're talking about, and soon. But first can you answer two questions for me? One: Who the hell is going around killing these guys?"

"Did you check that note Joey Pride gave me for fingerprints?" I said.

"Two matches," said McDeiss. "Yours and prints from the phone where the 911 on Ralph Ciulla was called in."

"That would be Joey, who is not the killer but instead is in line to be the next victim. The guy who did this is most likely an old hit man from Allentown, a Korean War vet with a buzz cut and gnarled hands, hired through and getting help from the remnants of the Warrick gang. Two hoods from that gang, named Fred and Louie, have been following me tighter than my shadow."

"You see them around again, will you kindly give me a call?"

"With pleasure."

"And question two," said McDeiss. "What the hell was Stanford Quick doing with a pickax in the back of his Volvo?"

CHAPTER

50

To avoid the crowds and reporters waiting outside, they let me sneak out the back of the Ciulla house while Slocum was on the front steps making a statement and saying nothing. Sure, I wanted to avoid the snap, snap of cameras and shouted questions that make even the pope look guilty of something, but I also wanted a moment to check out the basement on my way from the house. I had hoped I'd be unescorted, but they sent a uniform named Ernie along to make sure I found my way out. Nice of them, don't you think?

With the light on, the basement was an altogether less ominous place. The shadowy boxes were now just cartons of stuff. The heap of bizarre implements on the makeshift worktable were welder's tools, a torch, a mask, an igniter, spools of solder, all covered with a layer of dust and debris. The sad remnants of Ralph Ciulla's failed dream.

When McDeiss had asked about the pickax in Stanford Quick's Volvo, I had simply shrugged and mentioned something about the gardens at Quick's Gladwyne estate. I purposely hadn't told McDeiss about the equipment, clothes, and guns buried in Ralph Ciulla's basement, and I had my reasons. Sheila the Realtor was doing me a favor and keeping tabs on any potential buyers for the Ciulla house. There was surprising interest in the property, she said. I didn't want word to get out that the cops were digging up the basement before I discovered from where the interest was emanating.

I had hoped the uniform would point me to the door and then head back upstairs, giving me time to explore, but it didn't seem to be happening.

"Out this way, Mr. Carl."

"Thanks, Ernie," I said. "You can go on up if you want. I can get out from here."

"That's all right," said Ernie as he led me forward and pulled open the door for me. "I'm glad to help."

Ernie stood in the rear entryway and watched as I opened my car door and waved. He was still watching as I started the car and pulled out of the parking spot beside Stanford Quick's Volvo and into the alley. They seem to be training them better these days.

I was just reaching the end of the alley when a shadowy figure jumped in front of my car. I slammed on the breaks and just avoided slamming into the intrepid Rhonda Harris.

I rolled down my window, she came around the side and leaned on the sill.

"Can you give me a ride?"

"You're missing Mr. Slocum's statement," I said.

"Is he saying anything?"

"No."

"Then I'd rather talk to you."

"I don't think so, Rhonda. I have nothing to say to the press."

She gave me a sly smile. "I felt bad about walking out on you that night."

"It was a bit abrupt."

"The business I had to deal with was completed sooner than I thought. I slipped over to your apartment, but you weren't there."

"You really came over?"

"Yeah. Where were you?"

Screwing Sheila the Realtor, I thought but didn't say. "I called a friend."

"Someone I should be jealous of?"

"No," I said.

"Good. What about that ride?"

I thought about it for a moment. Everything told me it was a mistake to put a reporter in my car, but she had come to my apartment looking for me, she had sought me out. The old weakness started shaking my knees.

"Sure," I said, and her smile was bright enough to hurt.

She said she was living in the Loews Hotel on Market Street while she was working on the story. As I headed for I-95 and then drove south into Center City, I could feel her sitting next to me, her heat, her spicy red scent, the sensuality that she seemed to broadcast into the very air about her.

"What was it like in that house?" she said.

"Let's just say you have a nicer fragrance than the dead man."

"You want to tell me who he was?"

"Have the police announced his name yet?"

"No. They say they're waiting until the family is notified."

"Then I'll wait, too."

"Is this also about the painting?"

"No comment, Rhonda, really. I thought this was just a ride."

"It is, but I am a reporter. Why don't I make a few statements? If I'm completely off base, you'll tell me. If I'm not, you won't say anything."

"Is this a trick you learned in journalism school?"

"No, from Robert Redford. You ready?"

"Go ahead."

"The dead man was somehow associated with Ralph Ciulla."

"No comment."

"And he, too, was somehow involved with the painting."

"Still no comment."

"And the rumor swirling around the press corps was that he was some prominent lawyer."

"I have nothing to say."

"And other people are at risk, including your client."

"Can we stop now?"

"And it's all about someone who is desperate to get the painting for himself."

"I don't think that's it," I said. "I don't think it has anything to do with the painting."

"No? Then what is it about?"

"I'm not answering questions, remember?"

"But it is all somehow related, the robbery and the painting and your client and the two dead men, right?"

"No comment."

"Okay, that's great. Wait a moment, I have to make a call." She took out a cell phone, pressed a button on her speed dial, waited for someone on the other end. "Jim? Rhonda. It's just like I told you. . . . Right, it's all connected. So along with the Rembrandt and the hood on the lam who wants to get home, there are two dead guys already and probably more on the way. . . . Yes, wonderful, isn't it? I don't think we need to wait and see if I can get the interview anymore, let's get it done. . . . Great. Let me know. . . . Ciao."

"Who was that?" I said. "Your editor?"

"No, my agent."

"Your agent?"

"We're packaging this whole thing as a true-crime book: art, death, sex."

"Sex?"

"There's always sex," she said as her hand distractedly fell on my knee, as if she were going to put sex in her book right then and there. "A couple publishers have already bid, but the offers have been limited because they all thought the scope was too small and they were waiting to see if I could get access to Charlie. With another body they won't care about that anymore. I should have an advance by tomorrow afternoon."

"There's a man dead in that house. He had a wife and kids."

"Yeah. That's a shame, isn't it?"

"How'd you get so hard on the art beat?"

"Artists are a bitch. Okay, no more business, I promise. How are you?"

"A bit rattled, actually."

"Oh, Victor, I'm sorry," she said. She lifted her hand from my leg, put her palm on my cheek. "I forget that you have a weak stomach."

"It's just that I was feeling really envious of him for the whole day until I found him dead. It was like he had the life I always wanted, the house, the job, the family life."

"And now it's available."

I laughed. "Oh, so I should give the wife a call?"

"After a suitable mourning period."

"And what is that?"

"Depends. Was she good-looking?"

"Yes, actually."

"Then don't wait too long."

"You are hard, aren't you?"

"It's a hard world, Victor. You have to take what you want."

"Do you think I'm tough enough to do that?"

"Victor, are you okay?"

"I'm just asking. What do you think?"

"No comment," she said.

"I guess that's my answer."

When I pulled up in front of her hotel, she sat quiet in the car for a long moment. The Loews was in the old PSFS Building, a classic of modern design. The building was sleek and spare, with clean lines and big windows. I couldn't help but think that making love in the Loews would be like making love in a Swedish movie. And Rhonda actually did look a little like Liv Ullmann.

"Do you want to come up?" she said finally.

"I don't know. Maybe not tonight. I can still see him sitting there. He was in a chair. He still had a drink in his hand."

"A drink in his hand? Oh, that is terrific. I have to call back and tell my agent that. It's the details that make a story. When the book comes out, Victor, I'm going to make you a star, I promise."

"I don't feel like a star."

"Not yet, you don't. And an interview with your client would really seal the deal. Will you ask him?"

"Yes, I'll ask him."

"Thank you," she said. She leaned over and gave me a kiss. It started out like a little peck, but it evolved. Her lips on mine were hard, angular. She leaned her upper body toward me so that her breast pressed into my chest, and when she opened her mouth, our teeth clacked. Her tongue was strong and rough. You could almost hear the sproing of arousal in my pants.

"Come on up," she said, her voice suddenly husky. "We could order room service. Champagne and strawberries, what do you say? To celebrate my pending book deal."

"I don't think I should."

"Oh, Victor, don't think so much."

"I can't help it. It's been my lifelong curse. So I'm sorry, really, but I have to decline. Besides, I have to pack. I'm heading out of town."

"Where are you going?"

"I don't know yet," I said. "But I'm finding out tonight."

CHAPTER

51

It turned out to be Los Angeles, which was absolutely not a surprise. If you're chasing Sammy Glick, you don't head off to Moline.

Driving north on the 405, or at least pointing north, I had the strange feeling that I'd found my place in the world. I had sprung for a convertible, bright red and cheap—characteristics I find incredibly sexy in both convertibles and women's lipstick—and I had the top down. The wind wasn't quite blowing through my hair, since the 405 was more parking lot than thoroughfare, and, to tell the truth, with the sun uncomfortably hot on my shoulders and the nauseating scent of hot pavement and exhaust, I wasn't feeling all that swell, but still, something felt so right about the place. And look, down there, well beyond the highway, on one of the streets heading off to the left, wasn't that a palm tree?

I wondered if the other motorists saw a young man on the make, come west to stake out his future, or just a pathetically pale tourist in a cheap suit, kiosk sunglasses, and a rent-a-car convertible trying to act L.A. and failing miserably. Well, really now, who the hell cared what anyone else thought? I was here, I was in a convertible, I had a beautiful woman by my side, I was ready for my close-up. And yes, to top off the picture, I was heading for a meeting with a mogul. Life in the fast lane, baby.

Now, if only traffic would start moving.

After I had dropped Rhonda Harris off at her hotel and bitten my lip in frustration as I saw her sashay into the lobby, I placed a call to Skink. We met in his dust-up of an office and tried to figure out where the hell was that bastard Teddy Pravitz. All it took to find him, finally, was a little triangulation.

"What do we got to go on, mate?" said Skink, lying on the leather couch with his shoes off. Skink did his best work with his shoes off.

"Not much," I said. "He probably changed his name. At one point he was in California. He wanted to make a movie."

"Who doesn't?" said Skink. "I got this idea myself. It's about a private dick in Fresno what brings down a motorcycle gang to help a damsel in distress. Turns out the damsel ain't so much in distress and ain't so much a damsel. All I needs to do is write the screenplay. What's it take to write a screenplay anyway?"

"Just a few free hours, I'm sure," I said. "You spent some time in Fresno, didn't you, Phil?"

"So he's out west, is that it?" said Skink, quickly changing the subject.

"That's my best bet right now."

"It's a big country."

"I might have something else." I took a piece of paper out of my jacket pocket and handed it to Skink.

"What's that?"

"A list of phone calls made or received by a dead man."

"Come again?"

"These are all the incoming, outgoing, and missed phone calls for the last week from Stanford Quick's cell phone."

"Cops give you that?"

"Not exactly."

"Oh, I get it. Frisked a corpse." Skink grinned in admiration.

"My guess is, one of the numbers is connected somehow to the guy we're looking for. We should concentrate on the West Coast for starters."

"I'll see if I can rustle up a name for each number with the right area code," said Skink, sitting up in interest. "I'll also run a name what I've picked up about that Lavender Hill fellow, see if anything matches."

"Great," I said. "Meanwhile I might be able to find us another lead."

"From where, mate?"

"A woman I know," I said.

"Business or pleasure?"

"She's a Realtor."

"That's the answer, isn't it? With a Realtor it's always business."

"You never told me the plan," said Monica as she sat beside me in my rental red convertible. She near shouted to be heard over the bleat of L.A. traffic and the loud hum of the wind racing over our heads now that we were moving again.

"Plan?"

"You don't have a plan?"

"Plans fall apart," I said. "A strategy is a mode of operation infinitely adaptable to the truth of the situation as we find it. I prefer strategies."

"Okay. So you never told me your strategy."

"Strategy?"

"You don't have a strategy either?"

"That, I'm working on," I said.

Monica turned to me and frowned, and I must say it was a lovely frown. Her black hair was pulled back in a tight ponytail, her sunglasses were big and round. To the other drivers peering into the cabin of our convertible, she must have looked like a starlet on the way to the set. I probably looked like her accountant.

"It will be all right," I said. "Hey, we're getting close to the Pacific Ocean. Can you smell it?"

"We have to take a right somewhere."

"I know. But it is so cool, isn't it? Sit back and take a sniff. The Pacific Ocean, the Santa Monica Pier, Muscle Beach." I had gotten off the blocked stream of traffic on the 405 at Venice Boulevard, heading west toward the Pacific Coast Highway. Not the most direct route, maybe, but scenic, sure, and, dude, like, what's the rush? "Maybe I should pop my biceps for the locals."

"You'll need to give out magnifying glasses."

"Be nice," I said.

"Really, Victor. What's the plan? We're just going to march up and demand the truth?"

"Pretty much," I said. "He'll be prepared for us. I don't know if we'll be shut out or charmed to death, but whatever game he plays, we'll adjust. Sometimes the best strategy is to just blunder forward and make a mess. It's how I found him, I riled things up enough so that he knew I was coming, and he got nervous. That's why Mrs. LeComte was rudely warned to keep quiet and why Stanford Quick ended up dead."

"And from that you found his new name?"

"Well, I had some help," I said.

*   *   *

The Lakeside Chinese Deli was not by a lake and not a deli, and with its bare tables, busted sign, and the hand-scrawled Chinese posters in the window, the joint screamed botulism. But if you wanted dim sum in Philadelphia, if you weren't looking for linen tablecloths and silver candlesticks, and if you didn't mind being the only Occidentals in the place or being treated like family, which included rude service and a lot of yelling, then there was no better place than the Lakeside.

"You're not eating," I said to Sheila.

"I'm not really hungry."

"But I ordered all this for us," I said, gesturing at the metal steamers and small round plates sitting before us, a tempting array of dumplings on each.

"Oh, I'm sure you'll find a good use for it."

And she was right, I would. I was suddenly starving, ravenous, as if my brush with death had fed my hunger. Eat while you can, because you never know when it will be you in that chair with an unfinished drink and a bullet in your head while some skeevy interloper gropes through your clothes for a cell phone. I pinched a dumpling with my sticks, dipped it in the dipping sauce, popped it in my mouth. Shrimp. Nice.

"So if you're not hungry," I said, "why did you come?"

"Because you called."

"It's that simple?"

"Why not?"

"How's your fiancé?"

"Lovely. Thank you for asking."

Her smile was sly, her lips were coral, her eyes were bright, and I liked the way her false blond hair rested lightly on her cheek. Sheila was one of those women who got better-looking every time you saw them. How did she do that? I wondered.

"You sell that condo yet?" I said.

"Are you interested?"

"Not in buying the condo."

"Good, because I don't think it is a good fit." She looked down, traced a Chinese letter on the tabletop with her fingertip. "But if you want another look, just to be sure, that can be arranged."

"Not tonight, thank you. I've had a tough day."

"Too bad. I'm feeling frisky."

"Are you going to keep dating while you're married?"

"I don't know. Give me a call after the wedding and we'll see."

"He's a lucky guy."

"You don't know the half of it."

"Investment banker?"

"Of course. But I have something special just for you, Victor. A name."

I put down my chopsticks. "Go ahead."

"That house you wanted me to keep tabs on? The Ciulla property? There is another Realtor who is showing surprising interest. His name is Darryl. I had lunch with Darryl just yesterday. We chatted, we laughed, we drank too much. It was quite chummy."

"I can imagine."

"Darryl is short and sweaty and wears a toupee, yet still he thought just the thing I wanted in my ear was his tongue."

"Men are funny like that."

"In the course of our rather wet lunch, we decided to work together and form a syndicate to purchase the Ciulla property for ourselves. It's unethical and illegal, which is why it's so delicious. Instead of bidding against each other to make the seller rich, two Realtors buy the property for themselves and then let the clients bid to buy it from the syndicate. It costs the clients no more, but the Realtors end up splitting the profit."

"Sweet."

"Of course, even in a syndicate, the name of the buyers always stays confidential. No Realtor wants another Realtor to poach a client."

"You would never do something like that."

"I'm a Realtor, Victor. But in the course of our conversation, after our fifth drink, while I was trying to keep my eardrum from drowning, Darryl let slip a bit of his client's name. Reggie, he called him."

"Reggie as in Reginald?"

"There you go."

"Reggie."

"Yes, and he's on the West Coast. Darryl was very pleased to have a client on the West Coast. He mentioned it repeatedly. 'My client on the West Coast.' "

"Reggie from the West Coast."

"Does that help?"

"Yes, yes it does. You're beautiful, do you know that?"

"It was nothing."

"No, it was definitely something, but that's not what I mean. You really are beautiful."

"Oh." She almost blushed. "Then thank you."

"I was trying to figure out why every time I see you, you seem more beautiful, and now I know."

"And why is that, Victor?"

"Because against all appearances and against all odds, despite your Escalade and your bracelets and your rather frightening profession, and despite all your attempts to appear otherwise, inside you are actually a doll. I asked a favor without telling you why, and you endured a drunken lunch with the likes of Darryl just to see it through. You are too sweet for words, and I think the more I see of you, the more it shows."

She lowered her chin and stayed quiet for a moment. "If you tell anyone," she said finally, "I'll rip out your lungs."

"I don't doubt that you would."

"Nobody wants a sweet Realtor."

"Just promise me one thing."

"Go ahead."

"If things don't work out with your investment banker," I said, "you'll give me a call."

She fought a smile for a moment and then picked up her fork. "Maybe I will have one," she said as she speared a dumpling.

Triangulation is as easy as one, two, three. We had the numbers from Stanford Quick's cell phone, we had the name from Sheila the Realtor, and we had an intriguing piece of information picked up from Skink's contacts in Savannah. Our friend Lavender Hill had mentioned something to one of his more sinister associates. Lavender had said he was thinking of getting into the film business. He had a screenplay he'd been working on, about an art dealer and a precious urn and old money gone bad, and now, thanks to a stroke of luck, he had a client to sell it to.

"Everyone thinks they have a movie in them," I said to Skink. "What was the name of the company?"

"Sara Something Productions. The guy didn't catch the whole thing, but he said it sounded like a name. Sara something."

"Does it exist?"

"Couldn't find it. Found me a registry of production companies, and there wasn't a Sara Something or a Sara Anything in the whole list."

"Sara," I said. "Sara something." I thought about it for a moment. "What about Zarathustra?"

"Say what?"

"Zarathustra, with a *Z*, not an *S*. It's a Nietzsche thing, and our boy had a thing for Nietzsche."

"Wasn't he the bald guy what played for the Packers?"

"Sure he was. Check it out. Zarathustra Productions."

And that was it, exactly. With an office in North Hollywood. There wasn't much about it on the Web, just a few contact numbers, but one of them was for a Reginald Winters. Reggie from the West Coast. I laughed when I saw it. What a perfect name for an upwardly striving Jewish kid from Tacony to adopt, as if he played tennis in his whites growing up, summered on Mount Desert Island, had cousins at Andover. Reginald Winters. The more I rolled it over my tongue, the more I was certain it was a phony. It's the kind of name that would be picked by a kid who had read one too many *Archie*s and decided he was more a Veronica than a Betty kind of guy. Reginald Winters. How fake could you get? Except it wasn't.

"I found out what I could about him," said Skink after a few minutes checking out his databases. "Born in Ohio, graduate of Northwestern, started off as a reader for Paramount before latching onto his current position."

"How old is he?"

"Mid-twenties."

Ouch. Not the right guy, not the right guy at all. So much for my phony-name theory. "What's his job?"

"Vice president."

"Vice president of what?"

"Acquisitions, apparently."

"Oh, I bet. Just the job for a kid in his twenties. The new Irving Thalberg. He's an errand boy. That's why he was dealing with Darryl the Realtor. Who does he work for?"

"The big boss at Zarathustra is a guy named Purcell," said Skink. "Theodore Purcell."

"Theodore, huh?"

"It's his place. Apparently he's been in the business for decades."

"How's the company doing?"

"Used to be big. Remember *Tony in Love,* huge hit back in the early eighties?"

"That sentimental piece of garbage about two doomed lovers where everyone ends up in tears?"

"It made me cry, too, mate. I'm not ashamed to admit it. That was Theodore Purcell. And *Piscataway* with Gene Hackman, the one with the car chase. And then *The Dancing Shoes.*"

"*The Dancing Shoes*?"

"Apparently things have gone a bit downhill since."

"Not a surprise with those turkeys. What's his background?"

"Can't tell. All I get are filmographies, and they all start with him buying the book and then producing *Tony in Love.*"

"How'd he get the dough to buy the book?"

"Don't know."

"I bet I do. And he was even too cocky to change his first name. Do you have an address?"

"I've been looking. Nothing. He doesn't want to be found."

"How about on Stanford Quick's phone? Any numbers match up with Purcell?"

"Nothing directly. But there does happen to be a number what came in to his phone a few times and what is seriously unlisted. Can't get a thing on it. And when I calls it, the voice what answers won't give me any info. Just wants to know who the hell I am and tells me not to call again. Quite rude, actually. Chinese guy, by the sound of it."

"Give it another call. Tell the guy who answers that you

have a package for Mr. Purcell. A gift basket from Universal, but you're having a hard time finding the house. Try to get specific instructions on how to get there. Maybe he'll give up the street and the number."

"You think he'll fall for it?"

"One thing I know about Hollywood, they love their gift baskets."

The house was high in the Santa Monica Mountains, overlooking the ritzy compound of Malibu. The ride was winding and steep, switching back here and there as we rose ever higher alongside the ravine, brown desert spotted with green. I stopped by the squawk box in front of the rusted gate. Beneath the intercom was a mailbox without a name or a number, and atop the gate, off to the right, sat a camera, pointed directly at our car. I leaned over to press the squawk-box button.

Nothing.

I pressed it again and then again.

Still nothing.

"Are you sure this is it?" said Monica. "Maybe we passed it already."

"This is it," I said, and pressed it again.

"What you pressing so much for?" came a voice from the box, the voice tinny and from the East, not the Northeast but the Far East. Not quite Chinese, but something. "We not deaf. We hear you. Now, what you want?"

"We're here for Mr. Purcell," I said.

"You have appointment?"

"No, sir."

"Then what you pressing button for? Go away. Mr. Purcell not here for you."

"I think he's expecting me."

"No he's not. Mr. Purcell resting. Mr. Purcell ill. Mr. Purcell in New York. Mr. Purcell not here for you. What you got, script? We don't take script unless we ask for script, and we never ask for script. Put in box, and we won't get back to you. Go away now. Mr. Purcell has headache and cannot be disturbed."

"You must have a law degree."

"Why you want to insult me, when I just do my job?"

"Tell Mr. Purcell that Victor Carl is here to see him."

"Victor Carl?"

"That's right."

"You Victor Carl?"

"That I am."

"Ah, Mr. Carl. About time."

"Excuse me?"

"We been expecting you for days. Hurry, hurry. Mr. Purcell waiting for you."

"I bet he is," I said as the gate swung slowly open.

When it had opened wide enough to pass through, I drove slowly forward. The drive headed up and then around, through a rising, overgrown landscape of thick flowers and shade tress and weed-strewn patches of sun-dappled lawn.

"I guess he's going the charm route," I said as we made our way up the drive.

"I think I'll be immune to Mr. Purcell's charms," said Monica.

"Don't be so sure. He'll lay it on thick. But however charming he might be, don't ever forget."

"Forget what?"

"That he's a liar. If the secret to success in Hollywood is to never say an honest word, then he's found his perfect place. He'll be convincing, his sincerity will flow free and threaten to drown us in its earnestness, he'll peer into our eyes with the most unaffected gaze, and every instinct will tell us to trust him. We'll end up liking him and we'll want to believe every word he says. That's how good a liar he'll be. But don't ever forget that he's a liar, pure and simple, born to it, like the snake is born to crawl and the tiger is born to kill."

"So why are we here in the first place, Victor, if all we'll get is lies?"

"Because a great liar doesn't make up his lies out of thin air. In every effective lie will be a kernel of truth, and that's what we're looking for. The kernel of truth about what that bastard did to your sister."

CHAPTER

52

The man from the squawk box was waiting for us at the front entrance of the house. He was short and thin, with a shock of very black, very false hair perched uneasily atop his wrinkled skull. He wore sandals and a scowl, white pants, a loose flowered shirt. He had to be at least ninety, maybe more. The oldest Filipino houseboy in the world.

"You Victor Carl?" said the man, clearly not impressed with what he was seeing.

"That's me."

"And your lady friend?"

"A friend."

"I think Mr. Purcell happier to see lady friend than you. I know I am. Leave car in front and come with me."

The entranceway of the house looked like something from an upscale boutique, or a very upscale bordello, a circular portico floored with marble covered by a maroon awning. It would have been impressive if not for the thick clumps of weeds growing between the marble slabs.

We were led through the double wooden doors, into an empty central hallway, and then to a wide parlor that was bare of all carpeting, with only a single white couch sitting before a fireplace. A wooden crate served as a coffee table. The walls were dark, with patches of unfaded paint where paintings had once hung. Lined along the edge of the floor were photographs in silver frames, photographs of lovely tan men with gleaming teeth and women with deep cleavage.

"Where is everything?" I said.

"Out for cleaning," said the man.

From another room we heard an affected voice call out, "Lou, is that Anglethorp?"

"Not Anglethorp," said Lou with a barking laugh. "Victor Carl."

"What the hell?"

We heard a chair scrape and something fall to the floor before a man appeared, a young man in cream-colored slacks. He was thin and blond, very tan, and his face was weirdly devoid of personality.

"You're Victor Carl?" said the man in the blazer, drawing out my name as if I were a great disappointment.

"That's right."

"I thought you'd be different. Bigger, maybe. And with a hat. How'd you get here?"

"We flew in from the coast, and, boy, are our arms—"

"I told you he come, Mr. Winters," said Lou. "You owe Lou another hundred. Pretty soon I own your car."

"Try collecting, you little lemur." Reggie Winters turned to Monica with a dispassionate gaze. "And you are?"

"My associate," I said.

"The Derringer of Derringer and Carl?"

"Close enough."

"The whole firm has come to us for a visit. How pleasant. But you've come at a bad time. Where are you both staying?"

"We got a couple rooms by the airport. Why?"

"Mr. Purcell is in the middle of something right now and can't be disturbed," said Reggie. "I'm sure you understand. Why don't you give us the number of your hotel, and he'll get in touch with you when he can."

"Are you serious?" I said. "Lou, is he serious?"

"Oh, Mr. Winters, he very serious young man. Always. No kid in him."

Reggie Winters sniffed. "You just can't barge in here like a herd of—"

"But I already have, haven't I, Reg? Where's the boss man, Lou? He out back?"

"By the pool," said Lou. "I show you."

Reggie Winters glared for a moment and then stalked past us, to a stairwell at the end of the room. Lou shook his head and led us in the same direction.

Down the dark set of steps, across a large room emptied of furniture except for a dying tree in a pot, dried leaves scattered across the wooden floor. Past a billiards room with mahogany walls, Lou turned right and led us outside, through a passageway covered by a wooden pergola overgrown with roses and lilacs. Just beyond was a large swimming pool, its water murky and green. Weeds grew through cracks in the stone surrounding the pool, a few deck chairs, straps hanging loose, sat forlornly by the edge of the water, a hot tub was set off to the side, its water becalmed. And in the distance, far below, the desolate expanse of the Pacific Ocean.

"Ahh, you don't have a week to read it," came a growly mumble from off to the left. "I need to know tomorrow."

A small man in a terry cloth robe was sitting with a woman at a wrought-iron table beneath a green umbrella. The man sat with his back to us, talking into a headset. A wreath of smoke rose around him. The woman, who was quite pretty, was taking notes and holding a phone. The presence of Reggie Winters standing at the edge of the table identified the man exactly.

"Ahh, trust me. Best script I read in years," the man said. "Brilliant. And I gave it to you first, kid. Remember that at Oscar time."

He prefaced almost every sentence with a guttural stutter, as if his voice were gearing up to release a flock of words into the sky, and when they finally did come out, they came out fast and skittish.

"Ahh, but I need to know ASAP. Come on over tomorrow night, we're screening my latest. Big party. Tell me what you think then. . . . That's right. . . . Okay. Ahh, do me a favor and fuck that new wife of yours for me." Laughter. "You know I am. Ahh, we're going to make a flick, baby. . . . Right. Tomorrow."

The man waved his hand, the woman pressed a button. The man stuck a thick cigar in his mouth and said to the woman, "He's going to screw me, I know it. Ahh, get in touch with George and tell him I have a script for him."

"We have a problem," said Reggie.

The man took off his headset and turned to Reggie. "Ahh, can't you deal with it, kid? I don't have time right now. What kind of problem?"

"I think he means me," I said.

The man in terry cloth swiveled in his chair and fixed me with a startled expression. He wore big round glasses that magnified his blue eyes, his hair was black and slicked back, a gold medallion hung on his bare chest. The skin of his face was dark with sun and as shiny and taut as plastic wrap stretched across a bowl of fruit.

"Who the hell are you?" he said.

"Victor Carl," I said.

He took the cigar out of his teeth and looked me over. "Lena," he said, "go on up and get ready for Anglethorp."

The woman at the table stood, smiled at us before heading into the house.

When she was gone, Purcell said to me, "Ahh, what the hell took you so long?"

"You weren't so easy to find."

"Easy enough, apparently, for a Philly kid. Didn't I tell you, Reggie? There's nothing a Philly kid can't do so long as you get him out of Philly."

"You told him, Mr. Purcell," said Lou. "And now he owe me hundred dollar."

"Pay up, kid. That's the way we do it around here. We always pay our debts."

"I'll pay, all right," said Reggie.

"Next it be your car," said Lou.

Purcell's eyes latched onto Monica and gave her the up and down and up again. "Who's the dish?"

"Her name's Monica," I said. "Monica Adair."

"Adair, huh?" I thought the name would land like a punch in the solar plexus, but it fazed him not at all. "Cousin?" he said.

"Sister," she said.

"I didn't know she had a sister."

"I was born after Chantal disappeared."

"Interesting. But it looks like you made out okay. Ahh, more than okay. What do you do, Monica Adair?"

"I work in a law office."

"What a waste. You ever make a movie?"

"No."

"You ought to test. You got a look. Healthy. Like Connelly before she went anorexic. The teeth, we can fix. Did you two bring your swim trunks?"

"We're not here for recreation," I said.

"This is L.A., kid. Everything here is recreation. But I got no time now. Anglethorp's on his way. We'll talk later. Just the three of us."

"We need to talk now," I said.

"I'd like to, really would, got lots to say, but I can't. Just can't. Ahh, Lou, set these two up with towels and suits. Make sure hers is nice and tight. And give them something to drink. You drink, Victor?"

"Not well," I said.

"Then learn. You going to make it in this town, kid, you got to be able to drink the money boys under the table and then steal them blind. Fix them something hard, Lou. We'll chatter later, I promise. But right now I'm in the middle of something big. When was Anglethorp due?"

"An hour ago," said Reggie.

"Bastard. Hey, Victor, while you're waiting, take a gander at this." He picked up a set of bound pages and tossed them at me. "Just came in. Brilliant. Genius. Let's see if you got an eye."

He stood up from his chair and walked swiftly past us, toward the pergola and the house. He was shorter than I thought, almost a foot shorter than me. Reggie walked behind him and to the side, like a subservient wife.

"Did you call twice?" said Purcell.

"Twice," said Reggie.

"What did he say?"

"No answer."

"Ahh, the son of a bitch would be late to his own orgasm."

"What happened to my sister?" said Monica loudly.

Purcell stopped, turned around, stared at her for a moment with those big eyes. "I didn't have to let you in, kid," he said finally. "I'll get to it in time, you have my word, but in this business, business comes first."

"We're not going away," I said.

"I'd be disappointed if you did. That tattoo Lavender told me about, was that painted on or is it the real thing?"

"The real thing."

"Is there a story behind it?"

"I'm still trying to find out."

"I bet you are. You're a bulldog, kid. I admire the type. Philly boys are tough enough to make noise in this town."

He waved to the pool and the ocean beyond. "But just because you got your teeth in a bone doesn't mean you can't enjoy the scenery."

He put the cigar in his mouth, sucked it for a moment, then turned around again and kept on walking until the two men disappeared under the pergola. Quick as that, in a puff of smoke, the astonishing Theodore Purcell was gone.

"I take care both of you," said Lou, "find bathing things that fit." He gestured us toward a small, low cabana by the side of the pool. "This way. In here you change."

53

You might think that I told Lou where to stick his bathing suits, that I charged after the inscrutable Theodore Purcell demanding answers, that I determined then and there to get to the bottom of the whole rotten mess, but you'd be wrong. I could give you all the strategic reasons for biding my time, but strategy would only be part of the reason. The other part was that it was hot and my suit jacket was sweaty and the idea of a swim, even in the murky waters of Teddy Purcell's pool, didn't seem such a terrible idea. It was L.A., baby, and if this wasn't the pool at the Beverly Hills Hotel, it was as close as I was ever going to get.

With a borrowed swimsuit, a terry cloth robe tied tight like a trench coat, sunglasses on and the script in my hand, I stepped out of the cabana to the edge of the pool. The sun was hanging hot and fat over the Pacific. In the torpor of the afternoon, with the weeds and the heat and the color of the water, the deserted deck felt like the pool of a second-rate hotel in a Third World country. I looked down. My feet glowed in the sunshine like startled albino mice.

"Why is the water green?" said Monica, sidling up next to me.

"Maybe the pool boy has been taken out for cleaning, along with everything else in the house," I said.

"Didn't this Purcell in effect just admit that he did something to my sister?"

"He pretty much admitted that he was Teddy Pravitz and that he knew your sister. Beyond that, it's hard to say."

"But whatever he did, he's not racked with guilt, is he?"

"No, not at all, though he doesn't seem the racked-with-guilt type of guy. But he also doesn't seem like someone who has been murdering his old pals to keep his secrets."

"Maybe you're wrong about him," she said.

"I doubt it."

"What are we going to do?"

"Swim."

I glanced at her and couldn't help but glance again and then to stare. Monica Adair was born to wear the little two-piece nothing Lou had given her. There was something American about her body, healthy, abundant, maybe too much of a good thing, but then what's a little excess among friends?

"I don't think it's right accepting his hospitality," said Monica. "It makes me feel dirty."

"He seems to have a story he wants to tell. I figure we should accept his hospitality to the fullest, put him at ease, and let him tell it."

"So this whole lounge-by-the-pool thing is part of our strategy?"

"Of course it is, Monica. Do you think I'm enjoying this?"

Just then Lou appeared, a sweating glass with an umbrella standing tall on his tray. "I bring your colada," he said. "Made it fresh, right out of can."

"I'll be sitting there, Lou," I said, pointing to a lounge chair in the shade of a canopy. "And could you put these things over there, too?" I unbelted my robe, slipped it off, and handed it to him, along with the script.

"Why not? Lou has nothing better to do than to serve you foot and mouth?"

"Thank you so much. Can you bring one of these concoctions for my friend? And, Lou, keep them coming."

Lou huffed. I smiled broadly at Monica. She put her hand up as if blinded by the white of my smile. Or was it the white of my sun-starved skin?

"I didn't know you were German," she said, taking in the little Speedo that Lou had given me to wear. "I've worn G-strings with more material than that."

"It's all Lou had in stock."

"Teddy Purcell's hand-me-downs."

"When you put it that way, yuck."

"And with the color of the water, I wouldn't go in that pool if you paid me. It's like colonies of mutated life-forms are swimming in there. I expect the blob to crawl out of it at any moment."

"Where is Steve McQueen when you need him?" I said as I peered into the water. I couldn't see the bottom of the pool. Instead of diving, I lowered myself carefully until I was sitting on the edge, my legs dangling in the murk.

While I was sitting there, a young girl came out of the house, climbed onto the diving board, and leaped into the water like a graceful slip of light. She swam the length with perfect form. When she got to the end, she effortlessly lifted herself out of the pool. Clean enough for her, it was clean enough for me. I lowered myself in, keeping my head above the water as I paddled around. The water was cool and silky, more like lake water than the usual chlorinated pool.

When I pulled myself out, I walked over to my lounge chair in the shade of the canopy and toweled myself off with the robe. The white toweling took on a strange green tint. I sat down, drank a deep draft from the piña colada, and then lay back with a strange sense of contentment. Just yesterday

I was in an old Philly row house, stuck with a dead man. Today I was poolside in the mountain retreat of a big-time Hollywood producer. That the two places were related, I had no doubt, but still I savored the pleasure of the juxtaposition. And then something caught my eye. It was the young girl who had been swimming in the pool. She was standing again on the diving board, her back straight, arms outstretched.

She wore a bikini, blue with yellow flowers that matched her yellow hair. Long legs, high breasts, just a smattering of acne across her prominent cheekbones. There was a radiance to her, a youthful exuberance, and yet you could see in her the woman she would soon become. For an instant I wondered if maybe she was the missing Chantal, but then I did the calculation. Chantal would have been in her mid-thirties, this girl was all of fourteen. Still, she frolicked in the afternoon sun as if the pool and patio were her own backyard. Maybe they were. Maybe she was Theodore Purcell's daughter.

I watched her perform a graceful jackknife into the water and thought about what I might end up doing to her comfortable life, and then I stopped thinking and took another long sip of my drink. For lack of something better to do, I opened the script.

Fade in.

It wasn't very good, you could tell it right off, with its hackneyed title and too-cute dialogue that went nowhere, and it wasn't long before I started fading out.

"Who is Chantal?"

I woke with a start when I heard the voice. It was the young girl, standing right next to my lounge chair, looking down at me. "Excuse me?" I said.

"Chantal. The name on your tattoo. Is she your mother? That's the kind of tattoo that usually has 'Mom' on it."

"It's not my mother," I said. "It's just the name of a girl. I'm Victor."

"I'm Bryce. Is she Chantal?" she said, pointing to Monica, who was asleep in the sun beside me. In the heat, and with a few of Lou's piña coladas between us, the jet lag had taken us both down.

"No, her name's Monica. She's just a friend. We're working together."

"Do you make movies, too?"

"Hardly."

"Then why is there a script open on your stomach?"

"Oh, this?" I sat up, put the script to the side. "Mr. Purcell gave it to me to read."

"Uncle Theodore always has a new script he needs you to read. They're all"—and here she roughed up her voice in an imitation—"brilliant, genius. Take a look and tell me what you think."

"So he's your uncle?"

"Friend uncle, not uncle uncle. I like your tattoo. The colors are still bright, and you don't see too many hearts except on old men."

"Thank you, I think."

"Your friend Monica has a nice flower on her ankle. And I like the dove on her shoulder. I wanted to get a tattoo of a fish on my back, but my mom wouldn't let me. She said I was too young."

"Well, Bryce, I think that's very sensible. A tattoo is easy to get and easy to regret."

"But it was a nice fish, blue with yellow stripes. I saw it when I went scuba diving in Cabo San Lucas with Uncle Theodore."

"Is your mother here?"

"She's working inside," said Bryce. "Her name's Lena. She's Uncle Theodore's secretary. She's worked for him from before I was born. Do you regret your tattoo?"

I thought about it for a moment. "I'm not sure," I said.

"I won't regret mine, it was a pretty fish." She smiled at me brightly before spinning away and heading toward the hot tub. I watched as she turned on the jets and slipped into the bubbling water. She tossed back her head in the water as if the jets were giving her a deep-muscle massage.

"Who was that?" said Monica, groggily lifting herself onto her elbows and opening her eyes.

"That was Bryce," I said.

"Who's Bryce?"

"I don't know," I said. "But there's something about her that worries me."

"How's the script?"

"Awful."

"Too bad. I have an idea for a movie."

"Why shouldn't you? Everyone else does."

"It's about a girl who goes missing."

"Why am I not surprised?"

"And she reappears decades later. But here's the thing: She's the same age as when she disappeared. And she wears white robes, and she glows."

"And then she saves the world."

"How did you know?"

"Lucky guess. So why did she go missing?"

"I'm not sure yet. Aliens, maybe, but good aliens, not bad aliens."

"That's a relief."

"Or maybe there was, like, a saint involved."

"Or a clown."

Just then I spied Theodore Purcell charging out of his house, followed by the nastily servile Reggie and just-plain-servile Lou. Theodore Purcell was chomping on his cigar, obviously upset, when he glanced at us, stopped for a moment, and then said something out of the side of his mouth. Lou nodded and hustled our way as Theodore shucked off his robe. He sported a Speedo of his own, stretched beneath a round, sagging belly. Purcell handed his robe to Reggie as he climbed into the tub with Bryce. I could hear Theodore Purcell's guttural mumble followed by a squeal of laughter from the girl.

"You like quail?" said Lou, who had now appeared behind my chair.

"That's not very politically correct of you, Lou."

"I mean bird. Roasted. With pine nuts and pineapple."

"Sounds delicious."

"I make special for you and pretty lady friend, you stay for dinner."

"Is that an invitation?"

"What you think, I run restaurant?"

"Will Mr. Purcell be there?"

"Oh, yes, just three of you. He say he want private dinner. Everyone gone. Staff go home. Just Lou to cook and clean like slave."

"I suppose he has a story to tell."

"Either that or he want to have hot hot sex with you."

I looked over at Theodore Purcell in the hot tub. "Let's hope it's a story."

"So you stay?"

In the hot tub, in a quiet moment, Theodore Purcell patted young Bryce on the neck. Bryce edged toward his touch. Reggie looked away.

"I wouldn't miss it," I said.

CHAPTER

54

"**What did you** think of the script, kid?" said Theodore Purcell.

"Not much," I said as I cut into my quail. "It didn't grab me."

He tilted his head as if I had insulted his mother.

"It reminded me of the way I used to run in Little League," I said. "A lot of up-and-down without much forward movement."

"How would you fix it, then, smart guy?"

"I'd hire a writer and tell him to start on page one."

Theodore Purcell stared at me for a moment with a deep anger brewing in his eyes, and then, suddenly, he broke into laughter, loud and guttural. We were in a large room, big enough to hold a king's banquet, but completely empty except for the small round table by the window where we were sitting. There was crisp linen on the table, the china was fine, and the cutlery was silver, but the table shuddered with each stroke of the knife, as if it were about to collapse under the weight of everything upon it.

Still, our skin was nicely crisped, the quail was gently roasted. Lou, in his tuxedo, was filling and refilling our wineglasses with something very old and very white. Quite charming, actually, with hints of peach and oak. No white zinfandel for Theodore Purcell. It was all so lovely it was almost possible to forget why we were there, which might have been the point of the whole exercise.

"Think you could make it in this town, kid?" Purcell said when his laughter subsided. "Think you could have a run at the producer's table?"

"What's so hard? Read a little Nietzsche, steal a little art, screw over your pals. Nothing to it."

"Give it a try, punk, and see where you come out. L.A. can be a tough town if you're from out of town. Even though everyone's from out of town. I spent years trying to get my foot in the door. Was it hard? You bet. I was like you, kid. I didn't have Harvard, I didn't have a rich daddy. All I had was the eye of a hunter. And the determination to pay the price."

"And what price was that?"

"To bet my life in the hope of becoming something new and better. You want to hear how it happened?"

"We want to hear about Chantal," said Monica.

"Oh, she's part of it, all right. The best part. So listen up and take notes, kid. You might even have a chance yourself."

"I was tending bar in Del Rey. Tending bar was what I did till I found my way into the business. Why did I want into the business? The same reason everyone else wants in. You want to live high and fat in L.A., you got to be in the flicks. But it wasn't happening, and I was getting too damn good at mixing drinks.

"So one night I get to talking to one of the regular drunks, and he tells me he's a writer. He wrote a book. The book came out and it tanked and so now he drinks. Old story. I ask for a copy, I give it a read. I know right away why it never flew, it was empty at the core. Still, there was a hook in the premise. We come to an agreement. I wipe out his tab for the rights to the thing. Suddenly, just like that, I'm a producer.

"I set up meetings at every studio in town. I got a property, so suddenly the bigwigs are willing to sit with me. I go in, I pitch the thing, and no one bites. Doesn't earn me a penny, but it's an education. I'll be back, sure I will, as soon as another book comes walking into my bar.

"And then it does. Not a writer this time, but a dame with nice legs and her mascara running. I ask her what's wrong. She says nothing's wrong, she's just been reading. Must be a hell of a book, I say. 'It touched my soul,' she says. I ask her to tell me about it, and she does. All night. Hell, she's got me crying the way she's telling it. Next morning, without even reading the thing, I call the author. The son of a bitch has an agent, which means it won't be the price of a bar tab. And the agent, he tells me all I need is fifty thou.

"The book's name? You bet it was. *Tony in Love.*

"The opportunity I had been waiting for. And I knew how to pitch it, I knew who to pitch it to, but only if I could buy it first. In this town you control either the money or the property. Anything else, you get it up the ass. I wasn't going in without the property. It was like a poker game that I knew I could win, but with a fifty-thousand-dollar buy-in.

"Hopeless, except I had an idea to get the dough as old as the town itself. I was going to find a woman, older, rich, ready to fall in love and pay my way. Happens every day in the big city. But one thing I knew, she wasn't going to step in that stinking bar in Del Rey.

"And then I caught a break. One of the studio guys was from Philly, a Main Line guy, but he took a shine to me because I was city. Invited me to one of his parties at the house. Lots of stars, studio honchos, a hippie band playing. And there I spotted her. She fit my profile perfectly. A woman, older, visiting from Philadelphia, with her hair up and the best clothes and a twitchy mouth that let me know she was looking for something herself, looking for me.

"I took out two cigarettes, put them both in my mouth. She took out a lighter. I cupped her hand as the fire reached the tips. I gave her a cigarette, she gave me the lighter. As simple as that.

"She wanted to educate me, and I was willing to learn. We both were full of a desire that had nothing to do with each other. Was it more than mercenary? Truth is, she tasted like ashes in my mouth. But I tasted worse in my time, and you got to eat your vegetables before you get dessert. One night, on the beach, I took that twitch right off of her lips, and after, as we stared up at the stars, I told her I loved her. It's Hollywood, kid, a factory of dreams, and I was giving her the grandest one of all. And when she bought it, I told her what I needed. She said she didn't have the money, which was like a blow to the gut. But she had an idea. Out of left field. A heist. Why a heist? I asked, and she told me she had her reasons. But it would work, she said, and the money would be beyond my richest dreams.

"That night, with the stars in my eyes and the taste of ashes filling my mouth, with my hope distant and my future dimming by the minute, I thought it through. The risks were huge, but playing safe hadn't gotten me anywhere.

"During one of my pitch meetings, a studio VP had given me a book. It was his thing, to give it as a gift. He thought it made him seem literary and hip. That's right. Nietzsche. By the end of the year, the VP was back in Waukegan, but the book stayed with me, along with its most important lesson: that we could will ourselves to power. 'Man is a rope stretched between the animal and the Superman—a rope over an abyss.' And I wanted to believe it. On one side of the abyss was Teddy Pravitz, a bartender from the streets of Philadelphia sinking slowly into his failure. On the other side was a stranger I could only dimly glimpse: Theodore Purcell, a man with a name I had invented to use in the business, the great man I always wanted to be. The question was whether I was strong enough to make the leap and become something new.

"What about you, kid? Do you think you have the balls for it?"

....

It was an impressive experience, listening to Theodore Purcell justify the choices in his life. He relished the opportunity to tell it to someone who knew where he came from and what he did to get where now he sat. He wasn't apologetic, he was proud and confrontational. As he told us about how he contacted Hugo, brought in the rest of his old gang, how he orchestrated everything, he could barely keep the self-satisfied half smirk off his face. He leaned forward at the table as he talked. Each sentence was like a fighter's jab, quick and bloody. This is what I did, this is how I became a big-time mogul. Who the hell are you to judge what I made of my life?

"You must have put on some show in that bar," I said, "convincing Charlie and Joey and Ralphie Meat to go along with your crazy plan."

"I convinced them with what convinced me. Nietzsche. I pitched it like I was pitching a flick, and they put it in development right there in that bar. Setting up that operation was like setting up a movie. Working out the three-act plot, with its subtle character arcs, the big action scene, the getaway and payoff, picking the cast, getting everything ready for the shoot. Even with all the success I've had, it was the greatest achievement of my life. I took the risk, made the leap, watched it all work out. And it did work out, like a dream, kid. You ever do something so perfect it changed everything?"

"No," I said.

"It ain't easy, trust me."

"How did you guys get someone in the building?"

"It was her idea," said Purcell. "As soon as she saw Hugo, she realized how to do it. He was the same size as the old man, same build and coloring. And the old man was the only one who didn't have to sign in and out of the building. She swiped a suit and hat, did the makeup herself, taught him how to walk, how to stoop, how to ignore the guards like the old man ignored the guards. While she was out with the old man in the garden, Hugo went in a different exit and then went straight to a closet and hid until the time was right to let the rest of us in."

"And you made off with a fortune."

"Not quite a fortune. She had been overoptimistic, and some of the jewels we were counting on had been out that night. And then, of course, we knew from the start that the paintings couldn't be sold. They were too famous to be worth anything."

"So why did you take them?"

"One for her, all she wanted from the deal, a sentimental gesture she said. And one for us, our ace in the hole to deal our way out of trouble if it turned bad. Always have a backup plan, kid, or the vultures here will eat you alive."

"And you left your ace in the hole with Charlie?"

"Yeah, that's right. With Charlie."

"Why with him?"

"Had to be somebody. Look, I didn't have much choice. After Ralph melted down the gold and I had a fence look over everything, we were picking up only about seventy thou. Enough for me to make my start, but not enough for an even split. So I took it all and ran. The others would have pissed it away in any event, I knew that. Ralph on girls, Joey on cars, Charlie in a futile attempt to run from his mother. They were trapped. I still had a chance. So I took it all and bought my opportunity."

"Tony in Love."

"It was a big hit, kid. It put me on the map. I didn't just sell the property, though they wanted to buy me out. Instead I bargained my way into a three-picture deal, my own production company, an office on the studio lot, my place at the table. I been eating there ever since."

I pushed my quail away, the meat stripped from the fragile array of bones. "Eating on the carcass of your old friendships."

"Eating on the carcass of my old life. Teddy Pravitz didn't have it in him to screw his pals like that. But Teddy Pravitz was nothing but a bartender in some cheap Del Rey dive. I ate his corpse and grew into someone new. I had my name legally changed, just in case the old crowd started looking for me, and I became what I dreamed. That's what it takes in this world, kid. You put everything on the line and see where it ends up."

"And that's why you got scared it was all going up in smoke when word reached you that Charlie wanted to barter the painting for a get-out-of-jail card."

"Scared is not the word."

"Terrified?"

"No, you don't get it. I saw an opportunity to help out my old pals. I had already put Hugo through law school, helped him change his name, set him up at that big firm of his. I figured buying the painting and letting the others split the proceeds was an easy way to give the three of them the payoff they had been waiting for without tipping my hand. Let them all retire in high style."

"So you sent in Lavender Hill to make a deal."

"That's right."

"And you were going to buy the painting."

"You got it."

"With what? I look around here and I see rooms empty of furniture, I see a pool without a pool boy, a yard gone wild, I see a man on the edge of financial ruin."

"It's an up-and-down business, kid. I'm down right now, sure, but I've had more comebacks than Lazarus. And I got a new film coming out that's going to make a bundle."

"But if you're down now, how were you going to pay the money you were promising Charlie?"

"I worked it out. There's a Swiss banker who dabbles in the movies and the arts. He'll be putting the painting above his fireplace."

"And you'll get your cut."

"God bless America."

"What about the murders?"

"Yeah, what about them? Who's doing the killing?"

"You."

He shook his head. "Not my doing, kid. They were once my friends, all of them. I only wanted to help. Best I can figure it, the killings are all about Charlie. He fell into some bad company after our little deal. His old gang doesn't want him to come home and talk, that's the story. It's why I want him to take Lavender's offer and stay away. That's why I let you into my house, to convince you to convince him to take the offer and save his life."

"That's what you want?"

"You got it. Make the deal, send him to some far-off place. Belize, maybe. You ever been to Belize?"

"Yes, actually."

"Nice place to retire, I hear."

"Not really," I said. "And why do I have the feeling, Theodore, that as soon as you find my client, he's going to end up as limber as Ralph and Hugo?"

"Don't be a fool. They were my friends. Why on earth would I want to kill my friends?"

"Because of Chantal."

He sat back, stared at me for a moment with those big blue eyes framed by his oversized glasses. "It's a little insane to tattoo on your chest the name of a girl you never met, don't you think?"

"Absolutely."

"I admire the hell out of that. You might have the makings of a producer after all. But tell me, kid, what's the point?"

"I guess it's so I don't forget." I lifted my wineglass and waved it about. "So I don't get swayed by luxury and recreation."

"You're her avenging angel, is that it?"

"That's why I'm here."

He laughed. "It's almost romantic, kid, except you got the wrong idea about everything."

"You said Chantal was the best part of your story," said Monica. "What did you mean by that?"

"Just what I said. You think I created my new life only on a crime, but you're wrong. There was something heroic, too. I didn't hurt your sister, I saved her. Gave her the life she always dreamed of."

"We're supposed to believe that?" I said.

"Lou," he called out, "let's get on with dessert. I got a date tonight. She's twenty-four. The jaw of a wrestler, but twenty-four. And she wants to be in the movies. Imagine that."

"You don't really think you can just brush us off with your bland assurances, do you?" I said.

"If I thought that, you wouldn't be here, kid."

"Then tell us what happened to Chantal."

"Why ask me? Why don't you ask her?"

"Chantal?" said Monica.

"Sure, kid. How about tomorrow? Afternoon good? I'll set it up. About time you met your sister, don't you think?"

"I think I'm going to throw up," said Monica Adair.

"That's my line," I said.

"No, really. Stop the car. I need to get out. Please."

"We're on an L.A. freeway, Monica. If we stop the car in the middle of the highway, someone will shoot us."

"Oh my God, oh my God, oh my God."

"Calm down."

"I can't calm down. I'm having a heart attack right here in this crappy rent-a-car."

"But I got the premium model. It set me back an extra seventy-five bucks a day."

"My arm. I'm seeing lights."

"That's the sun glinting off all the bumpers. You're having a panic attack, Monica. You're going to be fine."

"How are you so certain? Are you a doctor?"

"If I were a doctor, I'd be better at golf. I like golf. Not so much the game, which is actually a little silly, but the outfits. Sweater vests, white gloves, plaid pants."

"Shut up, Victor."

"You don't approve of plaid pants?"

"There should be a law against plaid pants."

"It's the state pant of Connecticut, did you know that?"

"Why are we talking about plaid pants?"

"Because you're having a panic attack, and nothing cures a panic attack as quickly as garish men's attire."

"Is that why you wear that tie?"

"Keeps my anxiety level low."

"Well, if I am having a panic attack, can you blame me?"

"No, not really," I said. "Panic away."

"It just, I think this might be the most important moment in my life."

"Or not."

"I'm meeting Chantal. Finally, after all these years. I'm meeting my sister."

"Or not."

"I am," she said. "It's her. I can feel it. All this time she's been silently communicating with me. And through the tattoo and the missing painting and all the mess in Philadelphia, she's been drawing me to her."

"Wouldn't it have been simpler if she called?"

"Don't be silly, Victor. That's not the way saints work. They don't just pick up the telephone or send e-mail. They give mysterious messages, they place barriers in your way, they require you to move toward them on faith and faith alone."

"And your sister's a saint?"

"Why not?"

"If you have such faith, then why are you so nervous?"

"What if I'm not good enough? What if she rejects me? Victor, don't tell her what I do. Promise me you won't."

"I promise."

"I work in a law office. I'm dating a nice young man. I have a dog."

"But you do have a dog."

"Victor."

"Monica, tell her whatever you want to tell her. That's between you and her. I'm just there to listen."

"You don't believe in her. Still."

"What did I tell you about him?"

"But maybe he's telling the truth?"

"And maybe fish fly and birds swim."

"But they do, don't they? It's a matter of faith, Victor. Do you believe in anything?"

"Pain and money. Everything else has disappointed me."

"That's sad. Really. No, really. You should get some help, something to change your outlook on your life. Maybe a tan, for starters."

"What do you believe in, Monica?"

"Chantal."

"You want to know something strange? In my own way, so do I."

The address Purcell gave us was in West Hollywood, just north of Hollywood Boulevard. It was one of those beige apartment complexes they don't have on the East Coast, places with names too fancy for the building, with two levels of bland apartments surrounding a small, cloudy swimming pool, with a tattooed super and rusted wrought-iron railings and the old, pale-faced lady in apartment 22 who clutches her housecoat as she answers the door for the liquor-delivery boy and tells him she was once in a movie with Jean Harlow, yes, Jean Harlow, a real star, not like these skinny little waifs they have today. The place was called the Fairway Arms, though the nearest golf course was twelve blocks south.

The two visitor spots in the underground lot were taken, so we parked where we could, space 22 to be exact. No harm, I figure, since the old lady's car had probably been re-possessed in 1959. At the complex's front entrance, Monica danced around a bit and then finally pressed the button for apartment 17.

Monica was about to press it again when a voice came

from the speaker. "Who's there?" A female voice, strangely familiar.

Monica froze, unable to respond, her hand still reaching for the button like the hand of Michelangelo's Adam reaching toward the white-haired guy.

"Mr. Purcell sent us," I said into the speaker. "We're here to see Chantal?"

"There's only the two of you?"

"That's right."

"Come on in, then," said the voice as the buzzer buzzed. "And don't worry about Cecil. If you keep your hands in your pockets, he won't bite them off."

Cecil turned out to be a dog, white with one spotted ear, a blunt nose, and a body like a single clenched muscle. He silently rose from his spot on a chaise by the pool, jumped down, aimed himself at us, and trotted our way. He wasn't big, his back was the height of our knees, but it only took a second look to realize that this torpedo-shaped thing could take me apart with a leisurely snap of its jaw and jerk of its neck. I put my hands in my pockets. Cecil took that as a sign to close upon us even faster.

I stepped back, Monica stooped down. She reached out her hand, palm up. Cecil swerved toward her, stopped suddenly, sniffed Monica's fingers, tilted his head as if confused by something, and then rubbed her hand with the muzzle of his nose.

"That's a nice boy, that's a sweet boy," said Monica. "He's just like Luke, all he wants is to be hugged."

"Cecil, come here," came a voice from the side of us.

The dog gave Monica's hand a quick lick and then trotted over to a now-open door and rubbed his nose against the leg of a tall young girl in jeans and a T-shirt. She was pretty and blond and stared at us with a flat, unself-conscious gaze. Bryce. How could I have been surprised?

"He doesn't usually take to strangers," said Bryce.

"Is he yours?" said Monica, standing.

"He belongs to the super. But I take care of him."

"How are you, Bryce?" I said.

"Fine. I figured it was going to be you, what with the tattoo and all."

"Do you know Chantal?" said Monica.

"I guess, if that's what you're calling her."

"What do you call her?" I said.

"Mom."

"Oh, sweetie," said Monica, stepping toward her. "Look at you. Look how lovely you are. Do you know who I am?"

"No."

"I thought you said your mother's name was Lena," I said.

"It is. Or was. Or something, I don't know. It's L.A., right?"

"How about your father? Who's your father, Bryce?"

"He lives in Texas. His name is Scott."

"Scott, huh? You see him much?"

"Holidays and stuff."

Just then from behind Bryce appeared her mother, no more the competent poolside secretary. She was wearing jeans, a loose white shirt, her blond hair was pulled into a ponytail, her hands clutched nervously together.

Monica took a step forward. "Are you Chantal?"

The woman nodded.

"Oh my God, oh my God, oh my God. Hi. I'm your sister. Monica. How are you? Oh my God, I can't believe I finally found you."

And with that, Monica burst into tears and lunged forward, reaching out to embrace her long-lost sister and her niece. Blinded by love and longing, by a need that was raw and unyielding, swept away within the obsession that had taken hold of her life from its earliest dawning, she didn't notice how Bryce shied away, she didn't notice Cecil sneering as he scurried back to his spot on the chaise by the pool, didn't notice the expression of panic and fear on Lena's face. She didn't notice any of it, because for a moment the gaping hole in her life had been filled with something rich and full, something loving and warm, something close to hope.

CHAPTER

56

We'll call her Lena, because that's the name she called herself. Lena sat primly on the edge of her sofa, her hands clasped together on a knee, her lips tense. Lena had been in a few movies many years ago. Theodore had been able to help her get the roles when she was still in high school. She had been Girl Number Three in a Chevy Chase film, she had been Sue Ellen in a slasher flick that actually made a ripple at the box office. She wasn't one to blow these accomplishments out of proportion. With a shrug she told us there were thousands just like her, pretty girls who made a little money and had a little fun but never had the talent or fierce determination to make a career of it.

"Mom, do you know where that shirt is?" called out Bryce.

"Which shirt?"

"The one with the things on the you-knows."

"It's hanging in the bathroom, on the shower rod."

"Thank you."

We were sitting in the living room of Lena's small apartment at the Fairway Arms. The sofa was faded, the chair slightly greasy from age, but the paint on the walls was fresh, and the pictures were bright, and the television was a wide-screen LCD hooked up to all kinds of electronic contraptions. Compared with the wreck I had waiting for me back in Philadelphia, Lena had done pretty well for herself, and for Bryce, too.

Lena had been married, she told us. Her husband's name was Scott. He was a cowboy, who had traded in his horse for a limo. He had driven Theodore and Lena to a premiere one night. Scott hit on her, they hit it off, and the hits just kept on coming. He was older than Lena, and drastically good-looking, with an edge of anger that both scared and attracted her. He was a mistake from the start, but at the time she was nineteen and desperate to get out of the house. Theodore was strict about her hours, her life. No drinking, no late-night dates, no clubbing. She was young enough still to enjoy her life, she thought, and certainly young enough to ruin it on her own, so she ran off with Scott. They lived in Texas for a while, came back here after she had the baby. Scott thought it was the perfect time to hit up Theodore for some money and a job. But Theodore, who was still angry at the whole elopement thing and knew how to hold a grudge, told him to hit the pavement. After a while, as their debts grew and taking care of the baby got so hard, Scott finally hit the road. That's when Theodore came once again to her rescue.

"Mom?"

"What, honey?"

"Can you come here a moment, please?"

A look of sweet exasperation. "What is it, Bryce?"

"I need something, I don't know what."

"Can you give me a moment, please?" said Lena.

"Of course," said Monica. "Go."

Lena went. I looked at Monica. She was overcome with some sort of unbearable emotion. She straightened her shirt, wiped at her eyes.

"She's borrowing my jewelry," said Lena when she returned. "She has plenty of her own, Theodore's so generous, but she feels more mature wearing mine. I don't know, I can't remember ever being that young."

"I can," said Monica. "And it was brutal."

"Oh, you didn't have much trouble, I'm sure, a girl as pretty as you," said Lena.

"I filled out a bit later," Monica said, "but I was quite the gawky adolescent."

"How did Theodore save you?" I said.

"He gave me a job, made sure my money problems were handled, made sure I finished school. It wasn't handouts he was giving, it was better. He was giving me myself back. What I am now I guess I owe to him. And the way Bryce has grown up has been because of him, too. He took responsibility for her from the start. As soon as Scott left, Theodore sort of became the father figure in her life."

"When's the car coming?" called out Bryce.

Lena looked at her watch. "Any minute."

"Egad. Do you have that barrette?"

"On the bureau. And not too much makeup. You know Uncle Theodore doesn't like too much makeup."

"I know, I know. But I need something."

"Where's she heading?" I said. "A date?"

"No, thank God," Lena said. "Bryce is only fourteen. She's going to a screening. At the house. Theodore makes a big party out of it."

"You're not going?" said Monica.

Lena looked at Monica and smiled. "I'd rather get to know my sister."

Monica glowed from the light of the compliment, her eyes watered.

Lena said that she now worked for Theodore. In the company. She was listed as an executive producer on some of the movies, but all she did, really, was answer the phones, manage the office, handle crises on the sets. It was a little stressful, working for Theodore was always stressful, but the pay was enough to keep the apartment and take care of Bryce. She dated some and had a few steady boyfriends in the last couple of years, but mostly she spent her time at the office, at Theodore's house, or with Bryce. It was not the life she always dreamed of, but it was a good life. The mistakes she made had been her own, and everything good, besides Bryce, had come from Theodore.

"He's been very kind to me," she said. "You wouldn't know it by looking at him, but he has a heart of gold."

"You're right," I said. "I wouldn't know it by looking at him."

Lena gave me a pained expression just as the buzzer buzzed. She stood. Bryce ran into the room. Tight jeans, silk cowboy shirt, hair straight, makeup bright. She didn't look fourteen, she looked weirdly adult, older than her mother.

"I'll be right down," said Bryce into the intercom before coming over to hug her mother. She said good-bye to Monica and then turned to me and gave me a puzzled look before saying, "I guess I'll be seeing you."

"Sure," I said.

"I won't be late," she told her mother, then skipped out the door.

"Nice kid," I said.

"She's my heart," said Lena. "My life. I'd do anything for her. Everything that ever happened is worth it because of her." She paused for a moment, clutched at her hands again. "I suppose you have questions."

"Yes, of course we do," said Monica. "But it's okay. You can talk about it later if you want."

"I haven't even thought about it in years and years. It's all like a dim memory of a movie I saw a long time ago, that starred someone I can't quite remember."

"Let's talk about it later, then," said Monica. "When you feel more ready."

"Do you have a good life, Monica?"

"I suppose."

"What do you do?"

"I work in an office. I have a boyfriend."

"I'm glad," said Lena. "I'm glad it worked out for you. How's Mom and Dad?"

"Fine. Sad. They never got over your going missing."

"It would have been worse if I stayed. I was sad when I left, but I had to go. The way Theodore explained it, I didn't have a choice. It was the only way."

"The only way to do what?" I said.

"To save everyone," said Lena. "To save the family."

This is what Lena said she remembered. The details that slipped through her repressed memory of those days were vague. She had a hazy picture of her mother's face. Her father, she remembered, was big, so big. And she liked to dance. She especially loved the concerts and the recitals. And her red shoes. She remembered being both so excited and so scared when she appeared on that television show. She had some memory of the joy of her childhood, but what she remembered even more was the terror.

"Terror?" said Monica.

"I could never escape it," said Lena.

He was always there, bigger than she, stronger than she, reaching for her, hitting her, grabbing her, hurting her. Touching her. Touching her where he shouldn't have been touching her. Making her do terrible things. She didn't understand, she was too young to understand, and even so she knew it was all too terrible to tell anyone. Everything that he did to her and made her do to him.

"Who did this to you?" I said. "Was it Teddy? Teddy Pravitz?"

"Who is that?"

"Theodore."

"What are you thinking, and why do you call him Teddy Pravitz?"

"That was his name then."

"I don't remember that. But no, of course not. He never touched me, ever. But he listened. He was the only one who listened. He was nice, and he gave me candy and gifts, and he listened. I told everyone, and no one believed me, no one did anything. I told Mom, I told our priest. No one."

"What about Ronnie?" said Monica.

"No. He thought I was making it up, too. But Theodore believed me. And he saved me. He took me away."

"Who knew Theodore was taking you?" I said. "Who did Theodore tell?"

"No one. Not Mom or Dad, not his friends. No one knew. It was all a secret. If anyone was told, Theodore said, I would be put back into the house, and nothing would happen, and I would be at his mercy again, for the rest of my life. Or, if I *was* believed, I would be taken out of the house, and he would go to jail, and the family would be torn apart. I didn't want him to go to jail, I just wanted it to stop."

"Was it Daddy who was hurting you?" said Monica.

"Don't you know, Monica? Don't you know?"

"No, I don't," she said.

"Thank God. Then it stopped before you were born. Or it was only about me, which is what I always thought anyway. The thing that scared me when I thought about it was that it would keep happening with someone else. But Theodore told me that the only way to stop it and to protect me, to protect everyone, to keep the family from tearing itself apart, was for me to go away. That it would stop if he took me away, took me away to safety."

"Who was it, Chantal?" said Monica. "Who was touching you? Who was hurting you?"

"You really don't know."

"No, I don't. Who?"

"Which means it did stop. For everyone. Which is such a relief. Which means what I did was right. That leaving was right. For everyone."

"Who was it?"

"My brother," she said. "Our brother. It was Richard."

"Richard?"

"And no one would stop him. It might have been jealousy, it might have been something he was born with, but no one would stop him. I wanted to kill him, to kill myself, until Theodore came along."

"I don't understand," said Monica. "Richard?"

"He was so much bigger than me, so strong, and so angry. I couldn't stop him, I just couldn't."

"Oh, you poor thing," said Monica, slipping closer to Lena on the couch. "You poor, poor thing."

She reached for her sister, she put her arms around her, pulled her close. The two women broke into tears together. The lights dimmed, the camera pulled back, the music swelled.

57

"You keep pressing button, it very annoying," came Lou's voice over the squawk box beside the closed gate at the Purcell estate. "I have headache already. What you want?"

"To see the new movie, to talk to the boss."

"He invite you back?"

"Sure he did. Told me to come around whenever I wanted. Any good-looking women there tonight?"

"Always good-looking women at screening party. You think you get lucky tonight, Victor Carl?"

"Why not?"

"My English not good enough to tell you why not."

"Oh, Lou, my guess is you could give Shakespeare a run for his money if you wanted."

"Okay, you smarter than you look, which maybe not so hard in your case. I let you in, but don't eat all my canapés. They for invited guests only."

"Deal," I said. A moment later the gate slowly opened.

The winding, unkempt drive, the clutch of cars parked off to the side, the guy in a red jacket standing at the front entrance.

"Beat the hell out of it, I don't care," I said as I handed over the-keys. "It's rented."

I expected the bare living room to be crowded with the

rich and the beautiful, but it was mostly empty, a couple sitting on the floor off in the corner making out, a man standing by the window with a drink in his hand, looking dazed and confused. There was a tray of canapés on the coffee-table crate and Bryce on the couch, legs curled beneath her, paging through a magazine.

"Where's the party?" I said.

Bryce looked up and smiled. Somehow her smile immediately brightened my day. I had the strange sensation that I was being smiled at by Chantal, the real Chantal.

"I didn't know you were coming," she said.

"Neither did I."

"Did you bring my mother?"

"She decided to stay and talk with Monica."

Bryce seemed a little disappointed. "I guess that's nice."

"It looks like Monica's sleeping over."

"Like a pajama party," said Bryce.

"Just like," I said. "What did your mother tell you about the name Chantal?"

"Nothing. She told me today that some people would come by and call her Chantal and that she'd explain everything to me later."

"And you had no problem with that?"

"My mom's an actress, she's always playing a part."

"And she acts for Uncle Theodore?"

"When she's not too busy at the office."

"I see. Where is everybody?"

"In the screening room. Downstairs, just across from the billiards room. Theodore's showing his newest film."

"Why aren't you there?"

"I'm not allowed. Theodore's very strict."

I took a step forward, stooped down to speak with her at eye level. "How is he strict?"

"He takes care of me, he looks out for me. I don't know.

He's very nice to me and all, but he's just strict. He likes to have me around but he doesn't let me do anything. No boyfriends, makes me watch my language. He's like an ornery grandfather or something, you know? I don't know. He's old-school about a lot of things."

"Okay," I said, standing. "Good."

"When are you and Monica leaving?"

"Tomorrow."

"Don't be late for the plane."

"Don't worry. That way?"

She nodded in the direction of the stairs. I popped a canapé in my mouth and climbed down the stairs, following the sound to the screening room. An uncomfortably primal sound.

It was a large room, larger than the living room, with all kinds of easy chairs and couches facing a huge screen. A video projector was attached to the ceiling, and the sound was being blasted out of a set of speakers hung fore and aft on the walls. The chairs and couches were mostly filled, the air was thick with smoke, the picture was bright, the dialogue was loud and sparklingly clear.

Although how clear it needed to be to make out the *"Ooh, baby, yeah, that's the way I like it, do it again and again and again"* is a little beyond me.

I guess I shouldn't have been surprised. Sometimes, even though my experiences as a lawyer have hardened me to the hard facts of the world, I still find myself inexplicably clinging to a hope that all is not as foul as I imagine it to be. And inevitably that's when I tumble into the cesspool.

Yes, the movie on that giant screen, Theodore's newest film production, was baldly pornographic. Not pornographic the way some in this country would call a square sponge with buckteeth and tight briefs pornographic, I mean out-and-out, too-hard-core-for-late-night-hotel-television pornographic. I mean pornographic enough to shock me into almost swallowing my tongue and lead me into a coughing spasm that had many in the room turning around to stare at the disturbance.

And one of the stares came from Theodore Purcell himself, with his ubiquitous thick cigar. He was sitting on a couch next to a tall lovely with elegant posture and a strong jaw. She had one arm over his shoulder, one hand on his knee, and she was whispering in his ear even as he stared at me.

Purcell said something to the woman, she turned to look at me. Then Purcell struggled to his feet. Without saying a word, he passed by me and stalked into the billiards room.

When I followed him inside, he closed the door behind us. The room was bright, quiet except for the moans slipping in from the screening. The tip of the cigar glowed. The cue ball made a lonely comment on the long brown table. From the window I could see the murky pool, glowing strangely in the night. I almost expected to see a body floating facedown, but then I remembered that only shows up in act 3.

"Ahh, surprised to see you here, kid," said Theodore Purcell.

"I thought I'd check out your new movie," I said. "I didn't know you were making such fine family entertainment these days. How long have you been making porn?"

"Not so long. It's like guerrilla filming, in, out, and lots of dough. A few flops in this town and you're on your back, but I'm building up my stake again, getting ready to return to the fray. I got a script that can't miss. Best script I've read in years. Not a porn script, legit."

"The thing you showed me yesterday?"

"Not that crap, that was just a test. What I got is the real deal. It's genius, brilliant. Another *Tony in Love,* but better than *Tony in Love*. It'll put me right back on top. You want a look?"

"No thanks."

"I might need a line producer on the project."

"What about Reggie?"

"He's in over his head. I need a different kind of smarts, street smarts. Earn yourself a credit, get a start in the business. Hell, everyone wants to be in the business. You interested?"

"Not a whit."

"Think about it. The offer's open. But I'm surprised to see you here." Purcell rolled the white ball hard against the far bumper and, when it shot back, he stopped it deftly. "I thought you'd still be with Chantal."

"She's not Chantal. She's a hoax, and not a very good one at that."

"She's the real deal, kid."

"As real as anything in this town, I suppose, but she's not Chantal."

"What does your friend Monica think?"

"She wants to believe, she's trying hard, but that doesn't make Lena any less a fraud."

"And how are you so certain?"

"Oh, it's a little bit of everything," I said. "She knew nothing about Chantal's family life, her friends or uncles. When Monica mentioned Chantal's cousin Ronnie, the cousin who was like a sister to Chantal, she didn't know who that was. She tried to fake it, but Ronnie's not a he, she's a cute little blond girl who might have been the most important person in Chantal's life."

"She's repressed most of her early memories."

"Give it a rest, Teddy. She didn't know anything that you couldn't have known to tell her. And then you had her blame the wrong guy. Richard is not the beast type, it's not in him.

He's a coward, always was. He was more sinned upon than sinner when it came to his sister, you ask me. But the biggest tip-off was that Lena said none of your friends knew that you had taken her. But we know that's a lie. Charlie knew what happened to Chantal, didn't he?"

"He tell you that?"

"Nope."

He rolled the cue ball against the far bumper again, caught it with a quick, violent snatch. "Then you're guessing."

"Sure I am. That's what lawyers do, but I'm right."

"If you have all the answers, kid, then what do you need from me? What are you doing here?"

"I originally came to bring Bryce home," I said.

His blue eyes startled, his jaw slackened, his head tilted to the side. He was the very image of a man trying to figure out the impenetrable mystery of another man's thoughts. He stuck his cigar in his mouth, sucked in a mouthful of smoke, and then he got it, all my worst suspicions, in one quick revelation he got it. And in that instant I could sense not the nervousness of guilt but the relaxation of someone who knows that his adversary doesn't yet know enough to hurt him.

"So you don't got all the answers do you, kid?"

"Some, but not all."

"Information's power, kid. What you don't know will ruin you every time. You got me all wrong. I'm no pervert."

"I wouldn't go that far," I said. "But I no longer think Bryce is in danger. Which means I still don't understand what happened to Chantal. I thought for sure you were abusing her, and it got out of hand, and you killed her, but I don't think that anymore."

"Course not. I just like kids, like having them around. And Chantal, she had something special about her. A toughness."

"So why did she go missing?"

"Maybe she ran away."

"She was too young."

"Maybe you're wrong about Lena."

"No, not that either, because something bad happened. I know that for sure."

"How do you know anything, you punk?"

"Because Charlie has the painting, which tells me all I need to know. You stole it as an insurance policy, as something to barter in case something went wrong, but somehow Charlie ended up with it. I asked you point-blank why Charlie, and you didn't have an answer, but I do. You gave him the painting to keep him quiet. It's why you want to keep him away from Philly now, buy him off, make sure he won't talk. Because he knows."

"What does he know, kid?"

"He knows all you did to create your new life. You said what you did with Chantal was heroic, and I bet you think of it that way still. You crossed the final line with her, didn't you? First you decided to whore yourself to Mrs. LeComte. Then you decided to steal your way to a new life and to screw over your friends in the process. But all that wasn't searing enough. The one act that sealed it all, the one heroic gesture that made it all happen, was Chantal. You killed her, I know you did. The only question was why. Why did you do it?"

Purcell rolled the ball one more time against the bumper, caught it when it bounced back, lifted it quickly and threw it at my head.

It would have dented my skull for sure, if he wasn't a feeble old man with a paunch. I ducked, the ball slammed into a fancy wooden dartboard, darts went flying as the board tumbled to the ground.

The door sprang open, and both Reggie and Lou burst into the billiards room, Lou with his hands in some sort of martial-arts pose, Reggie with a pistol in his fist. It was meant to inspire fear in me, this grand show of force, except Lou's toupee had slipped forward to cover his eyes, and Reggie, frankly, seemed more afraid of the gun than was I.

"What do you know about changing your life?" said Theodore Purcell. "Nothing. You're a punk, adrift in the wind, and you always will be. You're weak. You're normal. You end up with nothing because that's what you deserve."

"We all end up getting what we deserve," I said. "You mind, Reggie, pointing the gun in some other direction? The way you're shaking, the gun is liable to slip out of your hand and fall on my foot."

"Put the gun away, Reggie," said Purcell. "Victor here is too small to kill."

Reggie pointed the gun at me for a moment more before sticking it back into his jacket pocket.

"So what are you going to do now, kid?"

"I'm going back east," I said. "I'm going to bring Charlie home. I'm going to get out the truth."

"You don't know what the hell the truth is."

"He'll tell me."

"Maybe he will," said Purcell. "If I don't find him first. You should think about what I offered you. I'm giving you a chance to make something of yourself."

"To take Reggie's job, to follow you around like a toady and pull cheap pistols on your enemies?"

"I'm no toady," said Reggie.

"Sure you are, kid," said Theodore. "And don't you forget it."

"I'm a vice president," said Reggie.

"A vice president in charge of toadying," said Purcell. "But you're still more than Victor here will ever be. Because Victor is a failure, born to it, sinking in it, doomed to end exactly as he started."

"Let me ask you something, Theodore," I said. "What's it like to take that leap to become someone new and then find out the new you is a decrepit old monster?"

"You want to know how it feels, kid? When the wine is old and the food rich and a broad with fake tits has her face in my lap, let me tell you, it feels pretty damn good."

58

Did it rankle? You bet it did.

What do you know about changing your life? had said Theodore Purcell. *Nothing. You're a punk, adrift in the wind, and you always will be. You're weak. You're normal. You end up with nothing because that's what you deserve.* Consider the source, I told myself. What lessons did I want to learn from a pornographer with a homicidal past and a crippled soul? But still it rankled. Why? I'll tell you why. Because he was right, and I knew it in my gut.

The whole flight home from L.A., while Monica sat silent and morose beside me, I ruminated on the words Theodore Purcell had spit at me. Monica had met me at the airport with a silent nod and a poignant sadness in her moist eyes. What was I to tell her? How do you convince a believer that her faith is misplaced?

"How are you holding up?" I said to her as we waited to board.

"Let's not talk, okay, Victor?"

"You got the right guy for that, Monica. If you want quiet, that's what you'll get. I can be as tight-lipped as the—"

"Ssssh," she said, and I got the idea.

So we sat together in silence on the plane as Monica stared blankly out the window at the silver wing of the plane and I thought about all I hadn't yet achieved in my life.

My entire career I had been whining about my lack of opportunity. Clients weren't paying bills, opponents were judgment-proof, the million-dollar case had not come walking in my door. Boohoo. I had become a sob sister of defeat as my legal practice collapsed, my love life grew ever more pathetic, my apartment lay in ruins. But it wasn't my fault, I told myself. Boohoo-hoo. Teddy Pravitz had taken control of his life and turned himself into Theodore Purcell, and whatever the results, at least he hadn't sat back and whined. And the same with Stanford Quick, who had made his move and taken all that to which I had aspired, my job, my house, my dog, my SUV, my pretty blond wife, my life. My life. They had seized their opportunities, I had let mine wallow.

Finally, too angry at myself not to want to hurt someone else, I said to Monica, "It's not her, you know."

"I know," she said.

I was frankly shocked. "When did you figure it out? When she referred to Ronnie as a he?"

"Before then. I knew it right away."

"How?"

"I just knew."

"So why did you stay the night?"

"I liked her," she said. "And I wanted to know why I had been led to her."

"Because that lying bastard was trying to set you up," I said.

"No, something else was behind it, I'm certain. Lena asked me to come back and visit. Maybe to stay with her for a while."

"You're not thinking of actually taking her up on it?"

"She was nice."

"It was all an act."

"Not all of it. Everything has a purpose, Victor. There's a message here, if I just listen hard enough."

"The message is to get help."

"You're being mean again."

"The lie didn't shake your faith?"

"Only the truth can do that."

"Well, that's what we're going to find back in Philly. Are you ready for the truth, Monica?"

"I've been ready all my life."

"We'll see, won't we?"

"What are you going to do?"

"I'm going to find your sister," I said, "and maybe change my life in the process."

"How?"

"That's what I'm trying to figure out."

And that's what I tried to figure out the rest of the long trip home. Maybe it was time to take to heart the lessons I had been learning from Teddy and Stanford Quick. Sure, I knew that Purcell was a total creep and Quick was a total corpse, but still, they had known more than I ever would about taking hold of the reins of life and forcing it to do your will. And sure, Nietzsche was an incestuous nut job with acute gynophobia and the mustache of a porn star, but maybe the guy had a point. Leap the abyss or stay on the wrong side of life for all eternity.

Enough with the law of either/or, enough with letting the richest fields lie fallow for matters of decorum or quaint moral qualms. It was time to seize my opportunities. To seize my destiny. To follow the lead of Sammy Glick and create my own damn success. It was time, damn it, to get some cable in my life.

And son of a bitch if I didn't come up with a plan.

CHAPTER

59

"I'm bringing him home, Mrs. Kalakos."

In the scented darkness, she rose unsteadily from her deathbed, reached her palsied hand to my face. "You good boy," she said as she brushed my cheek gently with her gnarled finger. "You good boy." And then, abruptly, she slapped my face. Hard. It rang like a shepherd's crook snapping over a knee.

"What was that for?" I said.

"A warning," she said. "You no play fool and lead them to him like last time. You almost got him skewered like lamb."

"I thought I had taken precautions."

"I spit on your precautions. Precautions are for timid men with girls they can't handle. You, you be certain."

"I'll do my best."

"Your best, it better be good enough, Victor."

"Is that a threat, Mrs. Kalakos?"

"I am Greek, Victor. I don't threaten. I slice. Thinly, you know? Makes the meat very tender."

"Are we talking about lamb again?"

"Yes, of course. Thalassa makes very nice lamb, with garlic and coffee. Special recipe. You want see my slicing knife?"

"No thank you, the sight of your gun was enough."

"That little thing?"

"I will be very careful, Mrs. Kalakos."

"Good. I choose then to trust you, and also will my son, because I tell him to. You'll meet him where I say, and you bring him right here, to me."

"Someplace more neutral might be more secure. I was thinking that it would be best if I met up with the police at—"

"Don't tell me what is best for my son. His whole life I know what is best for my son. You bring him here, to me."

"This is the one place they'll be certain to be waiting, Mrs. Kalakos. It won't be safe to bring him here."

"You make it safe. You bring him here. I don't know how many days I have left, how many hours. I waited long enough. You bring him straight to me."

"I don't think that's a very wise—"

"Are we still discussing this? No more discussion, Victor. You do what I say."

"Okay," I said. "My client told me to let you call the shots. But on two conditions. First, this will clean our family's debt to you. We are even, forever. No more favors."

"As you say."

"Speaking of which, I have a question. My grandmother, when you found her with that man, was she happy?"

"What is happy, Victor? Who is happy in this life?"

"Ballplayers," I said. "Supermodels. Ballplayers married to supermodels. But my grandmother, before you dragged her back, was she happy?"

"You want truth?"

"Yes, I do."

"She was crying every night in the small apartment of that strange man, your poor grandmother. She saw she made terrible mistake. But she was afraid her husband not accept her back. I didn't take her home for your grandfather, I take her home because it was what she wanted."

"And she was grateful?"

"For the rest of her life, my boys they never paid for shoes. 'Give it to them for free,' she told your grandfather."

"I bet he hated that."

"He was grateful, too. They had good life together. She thought she wanted more and ended up with nothing. Life can turn to tears when you want more, always more."

"Speaking of more," I said, "this brings me to the second condition. We need to talk about the final payment for my legal work on behalf of your son."

"What you mean, final payment?"

"At our first meeting, I told you I needed a retainer. But a retainer is just enough for me to agree to take the case."

"You want more."

"Since that meeting I've done a significant amount of legal work."

"Is that what you call it? What kind of legal work have you done, Victor Carl?"

"Meetings, negotiations, investigations. If you want, I can give you an itemized bill showing my work down to the last detail, in six-minute increments, and then you can pay me in cash. If you're short of cash, I could find you a finance company that would be quite willing to take out another mortgage on the house. Thalassa wouldn't mind, I'm sure."

"It's good you sure, Victor, because that makes one of us."

"Or maybe, if you choose, we can work something else out."

"You have idea, of course you do."

"When you gave me those jewels and chains at our first meeting, I couldn't help but notice there was more in the drawer."

"And you want rest, is that it, Victor Carl?"

"That's it," I said.

"You would leave me with nothing? You would take the last bauble from an old, dying woman?"

"I'm a lawyer, Mrs. Kalakos."

"You sure you not Greek?"

"Pretty sure, but to tell you the truth, I seem to be getting more Greek every day."

"I'm bringing him home, Dad," I said over the phone, "but I'm going to need some help."

"What can I do?" said my father. "I can barely get up the stairs."

"Not you. I want you to take a little trip out of town. Maybe down to the shore."

"I hate the shore."

"Get a little seaside rental for a week. Hit the beach."

"I hate the beach."

"Foot-long hot dogs, barefoot girls in bikinis, frozen custard."

"Now I know you're trying to kill me."

"My treat."

"Stop it, my heart can't take the shock."

"Look, Dad, there's a man in California who is going to do everything he can to stop me from bringing Charlie home, violence no object. I don't want him to go after you to go after me."

"Why me?"

"Because he knows you."

"Who is this supposedly frightening man?"

"Teddy Pravitz."

Pause. "I always liked Stone Harbor."

"I know a Realtor. I'll let her handle it. She'll be in touch."

"Make sure it's on the first floor."

"Will do. But there's something else you have to do for me. To do what I need to do, I'm going to need some help."

"What kind of help?"

"I'm going to need a driver."

"I'm bringing him home," I said. "But before I do, I need the deal in writing."

We were in Slocum's office, McDeiss, Slocum, Jenna Hathaway, and myself. The three were not happy with me right at that moment. With two murders and a host of questions, they had been trying to reach a material witness for days and were angry as hell that he had left the jurisdiction and couldn't be reached. One of the great joys in life, I have found, is turning off the cell phone.

"You have the answers you were looking for?" said Hathaway.

"That I do."

"You found her?"

"Not exactly, but I found him."

"My God. Where?"

"I'll let you know after the deal is signed and I bring my client in."

"And Charlie is ready to testify against him?"

"When I show him the written deal, he'll talk. And not just Charlie. Joey Pride, whom you've been looking for and haven't been able to find? He'll talk also, about the Ralph Ciulla killing and the events surrounding the Randolph Trust robbery, so long as you have a deal for him, too."

"What kind of deal does Joey want?" said Jenna.

"Flat immunity."

"Do you represent him?"

"By the time you get hold of him, I will."

"And there is something we can prosecute after all this time?" said Slocum.

"Absolutely. You should be able to bang him away for the rest of his pathetic life. And trust me, Larry, your boss will be quite pleased with all the publicity. *Time* and *Newsweek* will be calling, and the bestselling book is being written as we speak."

"This isn't about publicity," said Jenna.

"With politicians it's always about publicity. And your father, Jenna, will finally be able to close that case."

She turned her head, thought a moment, and then nodded.

"Sounds good," said Slocum. "Where should we pick him up?"

"At his mother's house."

"Don't be silly," said McDeiss. "Too hot, too obvious, too damn dangerous."

"It's not negotiable," I said. "His mother's house. I'll let you know the when. And he has to have the chance to spend some time with his mother, no interference, before you take him away."

"You're going to get him killed," said McDeiss.

"No I won't, Detective, because you'll be there to protect him. I have total faith in your abilities."

"Don't even try to sweet-talk me," said McDeiss. "And how are you going to get him there?"

"I'll figure that out." I nodded toward Slocum. "And when I do, I'll call Larry on the cell with the exact time and day. He'll relay it on."

"So that's it?" said Slocum. "Everything's settled?"

"Well, almost everything," I said.

"Here it comes," said McDeiss.

"Why so cynical, Detective?" I said.

"I've dealt with you before, and I'm still looking for my wallet."

"Remember that painting? The Rembrandt? Well, Charlie might have been a little mistaken about the painting. He did have it, once, but he's not sure that he has it anymore. It might have up and disappeared on him. Bit of a mistake on my part there."

"No painting," said Slocum.

"Sorry."

"Are you kidding me?"

"Wish I was, but no. Too bad, really. I always like pictures of guys in funny hats, but it seems bringing up the painting was just Charlie's way of getting attention."

"But the Rembrandt was the point of the whole thing from the start," said Slocum.

"Maybe at the start, but the key to this deal now is Charlie's testimony about the Warrick gang and the missing girl. Best I can tell, none of you gives a damn about the painting, and neither do I. The Randolph Trust is just going to have to make do with its other five hundred masterworks."

"You know it is a crime to sell a stolen artwork," said Slocum.

"Maybe I missed the meaning of immunity."

"We can't countenance a crime."

"Remember what I said about there being no painting."

"And if we don't agree?"

"The story's going to come out anyway, I'm going to see to that. My client's truest ally all along has been the press, and we're going to use it this one last time. So after the story comes out, either you'll have cooperative witnesses that can pretty much make your case or everyone will know about the murderer you let go free because of your abiding love of the fine arts."

"I'm bringing him home, Lav," I said into the phone.

"You silly wabbit," said Lavender Hill. "You silly, silly wabbit."

"I knew you'd be pleased. Did your client enjoy our visit?"

"He was entranced."

"He's going down."

"Not without a fight, I assure you."

"And you, Lav, are you his designated champion?"

"All I am is a procurer."

"It's good that you found your rightful place in the universe. So he's got someone else to do the hard work, is that it?"

"The way you run around like a fatted goose without its head, it will not be so hard. Is this still about that girl whose photograph you showed me?"

"Yes it is."

"Did you discover the truth?"

"Yes I did, and let me assure you, he's going down. What were your financial arrangements with your client?"

"None of your sweet business, darling."

"I assume he paid you something up front, because an operative of your caliber doesn't work on credit. But has he, as of yet, paid for the object in question?"

"Arrangements have been made."

"Escrow?"

"Not exactly. Why?"

"What would happen if, as a condition of procuring this little doodle, I insisted it not go to your client in L.A.?"

"Are the negotiations back on track?"

"With my added condition."

"You are a font of surprises, aren't you? I am not an idle man, Victor. I anticipated possible financial problems with my original client and I have made arrangements with other collectors whom I have worked for in the past."

"So even if the painting doesn't go to L.A., payments would be forthcoming."

"That would be correct."

"Tell your other collectors to get out their checkbooks. Maybe we'll open it up to bids, boost those commissions."

"What a delicious possibility."

"Be available."

"Oh, Victor, trust me on this, I will be more than available. But let me ask, are we getting a tad greedy, dear boy?"

"Lav, let's just say it's about time I took the leap."

CHAPTER

60

"**And what exactly** do you want from me?" said Beth as we walked toward a small row house in an old neighborhood just off the Cobbs Creek Parkway in West Philly.

"I need you to test the security arrangements put in place by McDeiss, maybe direct them away from where I intend to go."

"So I'll be your decoy."

"Decoy is such a loaded term."

"Not as loaded as their guns will be."

"You can stay out of it if you want."

"No, Victor. Of course I want to help. It's just that you studiously kept me out of everything involving the Kalakos case, including the boondoggle to L.A. that left you all fat and sunburned, and suddenly you want me to run around with a target on my back."

"I kept you out to protect you."

"And I feel so safe now as your decoy. When are you going?"

"Tomorrow."

"What do you want me to do?"

"Stay by your cell and be ready to ride when I call."

"Okay."

"You might have to rent a car. I'll let you know the model as soon as I know."

"Okay."

"You're fabulous."

"I'm a fool."

"That, too. Do we have to stay long?"

"No," she said as we reached the right address. "Just go in, get a few congratulatory hurrahs, drink a beer or two."

"I hate these things."

"It was a big victory for Theresa. She got her daughter back in her life. Now she wants to celebrate and thank us."

"If it wasn't for the honor, I'd just as soon drink alone."

We were heading up the stoop to Theresa Wellman's new place. There was music coming through the open door, loud and rhythmic, there were people hanging out on the porch. We edged our way through the small crowd and inside.

"Hello, both of you," said an exuberant Theresa Wellman over the pounding of the music. She was wearing a print dress and a bit too much jewelry, and she had a drink in her hand. "Thank you so much for coming. You're the heroes of the hour."

"Oh, we just put on the evidence," said Beth. "The hero of the hour is you."

"Don't be slighting yourselves. You saved my life, got me my girl back. Thank you. Both of you."

"What's that you're drinking?" I said.

She looked down at the glass, back up at me. "Ginger ale. There's more soda in the kitchen and a cooler of beer in the dining room. Loosen up, Victor. Why are you wearing a suit to a party anyway?"

"I wear a suit to the beach," I said.

"We'll find the cooler, Theresa," said Beth. "Thanks."

"Victor, Beth. Really, I'm so glad you came. Thank you. For everything."

She gave Beth a hug, gave me a smile. Sometimes the job almost seems worth it. Maybe clerks at 7-Eleven get paid better, but no one hugs you when you get them that pack of cigarettes from behind the counter.

It was a pretty loud and happening party. The music was ripe, there was laughter and dancing, women enough to loosen my tie. I pushed through a crowd to find the cooler. While I checked out the beers, picking out a Rolling Rock, Beth checked out the wainscoting.

"Nice," she said. "Maybe I should get some."

"I think wainscoting becomes you."

"I think so, too. And look at these floors."

"Yep, they're floors, all right."

"No, the wood, the finish. I think the first thing after closing on my house I'll get the floors done. Sand them smooth, lighten them up. Maybe a nice blond."

"Funny, I'm looking for the same thing. But I find this new-homeowner thing you have going on a bit disturbing."

"You're just jealous that I'm joining a club you're not a part of."

"The world is filled with clubs I'm not a part of. The homeowner club is the least of my worries."

"I'm just excited. It's like I'm ready to open a new chapter in my life."

"We'll entitle it 'Thirty Years of Indebtedness for a Glimpse of Morning Light.'"

"Can't you be excited for me?"

"Oh, I am. Really. Really."

"I want a soda," said Beth.

The kitchen was narrow and utilitarian but clean. *Spacious and modern,* would say Sheila the Realtor. *Ergonomically laid out, but with an old-fashioned charm.* Lined up on the small table were bottles of soda, bottles of liquor, a large ice bucket, highball glasses. Beth poured herself a diet soda. I took a long draft of my beer and looked around. People were crowding the doorway, leaning on the counter-tops. I wondered where all these people came from. Theresa Wellman seemed to have more friends than she let on in our discussions, but that's the way of it, I suppose.

"Let's go upstairs," said Beth. "I wonder how many bed-rooms and baths this place has."

It's a disease, I thought as I climbed the stairs behind Beth, this real-estate thing. Owning a house is worse than owning a boat. There's always a boat out there that's bigger and shinier and faster. There's always a house with more modern appliances. That's why I rent, to stay out of the whole thing. And I was feeling both miserable and self-satisfied when I smelled it.

Something burning, sweet and musty all at once, the scent of a college dorm on a Thursday night.

"What's that?" I said to Beth.

"What?" she said.

"That?"

"Oh," she said.

"Yeah," I said.

"Is it really?"

"Yeah."

"What should we do?"

"As much as I'd like to flee, I don't think we can."

"It's not her, I'm sure of it," said Beth.

"As sure as her ginger ale was just a ginger ale?"

"We can't just snoop around, can we?"

"I don't know," I said, "but I think maybe we ought to look into the bedrooms just to satisfy our real-estate lust."

"That we can do," said Beth.

The scent grew stronger as we climbed the stairs. There were four doors on the upper hallway, all closed. One had a sign that said Bathroom. Beside the bathroom was another door. I looked around, leaned into the wood, heard nothing. I turned the knob, peeked in. Linen closet.

"Nice storage space," I said.

"Oh, storage space is very important."

I leaned close to another door, listened in. There was a conversation going on, animated. An animated television conversation. I slowly twisted the knob, opened the door. No cloud of smoke billowed out. I peeked in, saw the television tuned in to some cartoon, and then the bed, and then, when I opened the door wider, a huge pair of pretty brown eyes.

"Hi," I said.

"Hello," said the girl.

"You must be Belle," I said.

"That's right."

"What's on?"

"Cartoon Network. Do you want to watch?"

"If you don't mind."

"As long as you don't talk too much."

"I promise," I said.

"That'll be a first," said Beth.

"I have an idea," I said to Beth. "Why don't you check out those other bedrooms and look for Theresa. I think maybe we ought to have a talk."

After Beth closed the door behind her, I turned to Belle and put out my hand.

"I'm Victor," I said.

"Ssshhh."

"Okay," I said.

Isn't it fun how clever we lawyers can be, with our clever questions and our clever tricks? We use our cleverness to spin everything on its head for the benefit of our clients, and the clever lawyer on the other side does the same, and the judge, in the middle, simply makes the decision. It's such a clever system, because it cleanses all responsibility from the participants. We are merely cogs in the great wheel of justice. Be as clever as you can and hope for the best, that's the job description. And just then, sitting next to Belle, now in the custody and care of her mother, I felt oh, so clever.

Two cartoon kids were being chased by some skeleton in a big black cape, and they were all singing a fun jazzy song. I had never seen it before. These are the kinds of things you miss when you don't have cable, which was a shame, really. Although you also miss Pat Burrell swinging and missing at sliders down and away, so it evens out. I couldn't tell if Belle was enjoying herself—she had the fixed, blank expression on her face of someone who was trying very hard not to cry. I wanted to ask her how long she'd been there, or if she missed her daddy, or what she thought about clever lawyers, but I had promised her I wouldn't talk too much, and that was one promise I was going to keep.

About ten minutes later, Beth opened the door. She had grown suddenly pale, her jaw was locked as if some sad specter had risen from the blond wooden floors, grabbed her arms, and shaken her until her faith came loose.

"Do you know Bradley Hewitt's telephone number?" she said.

"I can get it."

"Then maybe you ought to give him a call."

61

I took the expressway to I-95 and followed it south, through Chester, around Wilmington, continuing on the way to Baltimore and Washington, D.C. I kept careful watch on my rearview mirror and spotted nothing, which meant not a whole lot. It was becoming pretty damn clear that I had no idea for the life of me how to spot a tail.

I sped up, slowed down, I pulled over and stopped, started again and wove my way through traffic. They were there, I had no doubt, Fred and thick little Louie, in their Impala or boxy Buick or two-tone Chevy with whitewall tires. They were there because I had told everyone and his brother that I was bringing Charlie home. They were there, but they were hidden from my gaze. Still I kept looking. Why? Because they would expect me to keep looking.

I paid my toll into Maryland and kept on driving, south, south. Whatever I-95 is, it is not the scenic route. I jiggled around in my seat, fiddled with the radio. Sports talk, news, classic rock. What is up with classic rock? Get your own damn music, why don't you? Oh, yeah, they did and they didn't like it, so they come after ours. I jiggled some more in my seat, as if my bladder were bursting. Oh, good, a rest stop. I swerved right, cut off a van, and headed in.

I slammed into a parking spot, hopped out, looked behind me a couple times as I hustled into the building. It had the usual crap: a Burger King, a Mrs. Fields Cookies, Pizza Hut Express, Popeye's Fried Chicken, and then, to salve your conscience, a TCBY. Worth a visit all on its own, wouldn't you say? But it also had Starbucks to keep you awake and a bathroom to pass all the coffee that was keeping you awake. I headed straight to the bathroom, to the left of the entrance. Looked around and then entered one of the stalls, second from the end. It was occupied.

"Here you go, mate," said Skink in a whisper as he handed me a set of blue overalls and a hat. He was wearing a suit exactly like mine, same tie and shoes.

"You look good, Skink."

"You want me to dress like you again, you gots to start dressing better. Hurry."

"I sort of need to pee," I said.

"No time."

I tossed him my keys and started to climb into the overalls. "I'm parked third row back, right in front of the entrance."

"Swell."

"You don't look anything like me."

"Can't be helped. I'll hang here for a bit and then put a hand to my face. By the time they cotton that I'm not you, you should be long gone."

"If my ride shows."

"That was up to you, mate."

"Be careful when you go out there. They won't be so pleased to see you."

"They's the ones ought to be careful. Out you go."

I tugged on the hat, shook my head a couple of times, and then settled into a bent slouch, like I'd been steering an eighteen-wheeler for twelve hours straight. I gave Skink a good-old-boy bang in the shoulder before I left the stall.

Keeping the slouch, I looked around the bathroom as I rinsed my hands. One old guy stood at a urinal, a young kid was washing up. Nothing there to worry about. I grimaced into the mirror, set the hat just so, and headed out of the bathroom.

The entrance I had come in was to the left, I darted right and ducked into a little shop selling candy and books. At the end of the shop was a door that led to the gas station. As soon as I stepped through the door, a white-and-green cab shot out of a parking spot and came right at me, swerving at the last second so that the front passenger door stopped right at my hip. I opened the door, looked in, and hesitated a moment before jumping inside. Off we went, hitting the northbound exit of the highway.

"Why the hell is she here?" I said, thumbing toward the backseat.

"The lady insisted on coming," said Joey Pride.

"We have to drop her somewhere."

"Don't think she'll be dropped."

"Monica," I said angrily. "What the hell are you doing here?"

"You told me to meet Joey," she said.

"And give him the message and then let him go off without you."

"That second part sort of slipped my mind."

"Monica."

"Charlie is going to tell you what he knows about my sister."

"That's right."

"Then I need to be there. I told you I waited long enough for the truth."

"You couldn't get rid of her, Joey?"

"I had about as much success as you're having. But it makes the view in my rearview a hell of a lot nicer, I'll tell you that."

"And why are we in a cab? I told my father to tell you to borrow something different."

"I did. From my friend Hookie."

"But it's still a cab."

"Not my cab. So where are we headed?"

"To a morgue, most likely. This is a foul-up. This is a complete mess. Were you followed?"

"Nope."

"You sure?"

"I got the eyes of a falcon. We're clean."

"For the time being. We're not going to be able to get rid of you, Monica?"

"No," said Monica.

"Crap. Okay, I have to make a call. Joey, keep going north until we reach 295 East, then go over the Delaware Memorial Bridge. We're heading into the Garden State."

CHAPTER

62

We were traveling east, toward familiar turf. If all was going as planned, by now Skink would have led my tail through Baltimore and toward Washington, D.C. I figured two more thugs in the nation's capital wouldn't make much difference. Elect them to the Senate, turn them into whips, we might actually get something done.

"It would be quicker if we take the expressway," said Joey.

"No, this road is perfect," I said, and it was, a two-lane jobber heading through small towns and farmers' fields, past small produce markets selling tomatoes and leeks. We went slowly, and every now and then we pulled over to the side of the road and let people pass. No one seemed to be hanging back with us.

"I ain't seen Charlie for fifteen, twenty years," said Joey. "He's been more memory than real, a wisp of smoke. Don't know if I should hug him or slug him in the face."

"A little of both, I expect," I said. "I talked to the prosecutors about you, Joey."

"And what did them little darlings say?"

"They agreed to a deal. They'll give you immunity if you tell them everything you know about the robbery."

"Just the robbery?"

"And the girl."

"Yeah, I figured she would be involved. What does immunity mean?"

"They can't do anything to you."

"Then maybe, after all is said and done, I don't deserve no immunity."

"There's a lot of ways you can make amends for whatever happened, other than going to jail."

"Oh, yeah? Tell me how, Reverend."

I thought about it for a moment. "Thirty years ago you tried to save your life through a crime. That didn't work out so well. Maybe this time you can save it by looking clear-eyed at what you are and what you did. Maybe you can make amends by becoming something better based on the truth."

"I'd rather do the time."

"You know what it's like inside better than I do."

"You made that deal for me?"

"Yes."

"What do I owe you?"

"You're paying it off as we drive. Pull in over there."

"It's empty."

"Perfect," I said.

We were at an abandoned farmer's stand on the left side of the road. Schmidty's Farmer's Market was long deserted, the stand falling in on itself, the signs advertising summer corn and vine-ripened tomatoes weathered and worn. I got out of the taxi and did a quick inspection. The weeds and trees on either side of the lot had encroached upon the center, leaving it like an oasis within the middle of an overgrown woods. Between the collapsing structure and the road was a gravel lot, and behind the stand was another parking area, this second lot overgrown with high grasses and stalky weeds. To the side of the stand was a picnic table that was still in decent shape. Apparently the place was now used as a rest stop for travelers caught in Sunday-evening traffic driving home from the shore.

"About how far are we from the ocean?" I asked Joey.

"Maybe twenty," said Joey.

"Okay, I have to make a call."

"Does he know I'm with you?" said Joey.

"He will," I said.

I went off to the side of the stand, looked around again and flipped open my phone.

"Let's go," I said when I had climbed back into the cab. "Keep heading east and follow the signs to Ocean City."

Charlie was sitting on a bench on the boardwalk. He was wearing a baseball hat and sunglasses and his usual socks in sandals. His idea of a disguise. After what happened last time, this would not have been my first pick for a meeting place, or my second or my third, but Mrs. Kalakos told me to find Charlie at the same location and hadn't given me much choice about it, so here I was.

"Nice costume," I said as I sat beside him and handed over a vanilla custard I had bought him.

"I look like I drive NASCAR. Do I look like I drive NAS-CAR?"

"The sandals cinch it. Couldn't you have picked some-place different?"

"Who would think we'd be dumb enough to meet at the same corner of the boardwalk?"

"Not I," I said.

"Everything arranged?"

"Yes, it is."

"What's the deal?"

"You answer all their questions, don't hold anything back, tell them everything you know about the Warrick gang and the robbery, especially about your old friend Teddy Pravitz, and you'll be given protective custody with no more than a couple of years. After that, if you want witness protection, you can get it."

"Can they back out once I show up?"

"Not really. I have the offer in writing, and I'm going to take a precaution to make sure they keep their word."

"I have to tell them everything?"

"Yes."

"Even about the girl?"

"That's the most important part."

"I don't want to."

"You've been holding it in for a long time now, haven't you, Charlie?"

"I don't want to talk about it."

"You once told me your life had turned to crap. I think it's because of what happened to the girl and the way it's twisted you around, the way it twisted all of you. You wanted to do that robbery to start a new life, but look at the life you ended up with, more crime, more filth. And then flight, turning yourself into a vagabond. It's all because of the girl. You can't start anew without coming to grips with the crimes of your past."

"What does my mom say?"

"She just wants you home. To say good-bye."

"How's she doing?"

"She looks pretty chipper, actually. She wanted to show me her knife."

"I told you from the start she'd outlive us both. What about that guy you set me up with? What was his name? Lilac?"

"Lavender."

"Right."

"Here's the story. I set it up so that your agreement with the government does not require that you give them the painting. The only thing that can screw up your deal with the government is if you don't tell them the entire truth. Selling the painting to Lavender Hill could constitute a crime not covered by the agreement. Lying about selling the painting could screw up your plea deal. But the amount of money realized could be enormous. I can't make the decision for you, but I can relay any message you want to send to Mr. Hill. Put it in an envelope without showing it to me, and I'll get it to him. What's in the message and how it works out after that is up to you."

"So you're saying I could tell him where the painting is and not tell you and then lie to the cops."

"That would put your plea agreement at risk, but it could be done."

"How many years could I get for selling the painting?"

"A few more."

"It might be worth it."

"That's your decision."

"What do you think I should do?"

"It's a lot of money, Charlie. There's a lot you could do with that money."

"Let me think on it."

"Okay. We have to make one stop, and then we'll see your mother."

"I'm shaking."

"Happiness or fear?"

"What do you think?"

"I think you didn't eat your ice cream cone."

He looked down at the vanilla cone in his fist, with its dripping frozen custard and its smear of sprinkles. He stood and tossed it into the trash can by the bench.

"You ready?" I said.

"No."

"Good, then let's go and start your life all over again."

63

It was a strange reunion, two old friends with a long-buried secret who hadn't seen each other in decades. Joey Pride and Charlie Kalakos.

The cab was parked on a side street just off the boardwalk, and when we reached it, Joey was outside, leaning on the fender, giving Charlie a hard look. There was a shake and then an awkward reticence, with shoes kicking at the asphalt. I introduced Charlie to Monica. Charlie's head cocked when he heard her last name.

"That's the same as the girl," he said.

"Yes it is."

"You related?"

"I'm her sister," said Monica.

The two looked at each other and kept their distance. And then, cutting through the tension, Joey loosed a shot of anger.

"You were trying to dick us out of our share, you little Greek snake," said Joey. "You were leaving your oldest friends out on the side of your highway to happiness."

"I wouldn't have done that, Joey. I wouldn't have done that."

"We all deserved a taste."

"I know that, Joey. I do."

"You heard about Ralphie?"

"Yeah."

"It was your old running buddies who did it to him. They was looking for you."

"They aren't my friends no more, not for a long time."

"If you just kept your mouth shut and stayed away, none of this would have happened."

"It was my mother."

"What you say?"

"It was just that my mother—"

"Still the same, ain't you, Charlie? When you going to break away?"

"I thought I had."

"Fool. She'll be dead and buried, and you'll still be tugging at her apron. 'Mama, Mama, what am I going to do?' What are we going to do, Charlie?"

"I guess we're going to tell them what happened."

"I guess we are. What about the painting?"

"I don't know?"

"You still got it?"

"I know where I put it."

"You going to sell it?"

"Maybe."

"Well, let me tell you this, you Greek snake." He stepped forward, stuck a finger in Charlie's chest. "I don't want nothing from it no more."

"What?"

"Don't include me."

"You sure?"

"It still haunts me."

"Yeah, I think I understand."

"What do you understand?"

"I think about her, too. A lot more lately, after Victor showed me the picture."

"Well, then, maybe you do."

"Guys," I said, breaking in. "This is sweet and all, quite the tender moment, but can we get moving? We still have a lot to do, and there are people trying to kill us."

"Kill him," said Joey, jerking his thumb at Charlie.

"I don't think they care about the body count, do you? Let's go."

We piled into the cab, Joey and I in the front seat, Charlie sitting in the back next to Monica, and headed out of Ocean City. We drove around the traffic circle at Somers Point, with its bars and liquor stores. Signs pointed toward the Garden State Parkway, which led to the Atlantic City Expressway and straight to the heart of Philadelphia.

"Let's go back the way we came," I said.

"That's way the hell out of the way," said Joey.

"So it is, but we have another stop to make."

"Where?"

"To buy some tomatoes. Nothing better than a Jersey tomato fresh off the vine."

"We're not hungry," said Joey.

Charlie said, "I could use a little—"

"Let's just get on with this," said Joey. "We're not hungry."

"That's good," I said, "because they might be a little out of stock."

We headed back, through traffic and past strip malls, toward the long two-lane road on which we'd come east. I had Joey keep careful check on his rearview mirror to see if he caught anything in the least suspicious, but he said it looked clean. About ten miles along, there it was on our side of the road. The broken-down shed of Schmidty's Farmer's Market.

Parked in front was a generic silver midsize rental. On the table to the side was a large picnic basket, red-checked tablecloth festively sticking out one of its sides. And sitting on the bench in front of the basket, her pretty legs crossed, her eyes crinkled in welcome and her hand waving hello, was Rhonda Harris.

I told Joey to park the cab in the weed-strewn lot behind the shed. A cab might attract some unwanted attention, while a single car and a few picnickers would look totally in place. Rhonda had taken verisimilitude to a new level. After a few moments of setup, we were all seated at the table with the tablecloth spread, our paper plates loaded with fried chicken and potato salad, our paper cups topped up with soda or wine. A few citronella candles burned in their clear plastic shades.

Rhonda started to ask Charlie a question, but I cut her right off. "Before you do anything, you have to promise to hold the story until I give the okay," I said.

"I promise," said Rhonda Harris.

"I don't want the bastard behind it all to lam out before the cops can nab him. But I also want to give Charlie a chance to get his story on the record before the feds get hold of him."

"To keep the prosecutors honest or your client honest?"

"Both," I said. "And to make sure our friend in L.A. pays the full price for what he did." I looked at Charlie. "Are we ready?"

Charlie nodded.

"Okay, Rhonda," I said. "Go ahead."

"Hello, Charlie," she said with a bright smile. "I've been looking for you for a long time."

"Ain't you the lucky one, then?" said Charlie.

And right there, as cars whizzed by on their way to or from the shore, she conducted her interview, with both Charlie Kalakos and Joey Pride pitching in to tell the whole sad and fabulous story of the greatest art heist in the history of a city known for its robberies and rip-offs.

"What about your life on the run, Charlie?" said Rhonda once the old men had finished telling her the details of the robbery. "Tell me what you've been up to after skipping bail fifteen years ago."

"What's there to tell?" said Charlie. "It was a whole lotta crap." And then he proceeded to give us a sad recitation about the long period of his exile: the mean apartments he was able to rent without identification, the menial jobs that kept him afloat, his inability, without his mother's influence, to create any kind of meaningful life for himself. As he spoke, I kept changing my mind about Mrs. Kalakos. Was she a monster, an eater of dreams, or the rock of reality that kept those around her from floating into the ether and expanding into nothingness?

"Okay," said Rhonda after Charlie arrived at the part about his first meeting with me and his decision to come home, "I think that's everything except for the Rembrandt. What happened to the Rembrandt?"

"That's involved with the girl," said Charlie.

"Girl?"

"The girl's the point of this whole thing," I said. "It's why you're here. To write about the girl."

Rhonda looked at me a little startled. In the darkening evening, with the red of the sky behind her and the yellow of the candles on her face, she had a weird, demonic glow. "No one told me about a girl," she said. "What girl?"

"Her name was Chantal Adair," said Monica. "She was my sister, and that's why I'm here, too. To hear Charlie tell me about Chantal."

"Joey knows what happened to her, same as me," said Charlie. "We all did. We were all a part."

"But you the one that was there," said Joey. "You the one that was handed the painting. It's your story, Charlie boy. You tell it."

Charlie sat quietly for a long while.

"Go ahead, Charlie, and tell us about the girl," said Rhonda Harris as she fiddled with her tape player. And after another long moment, as we slipped into the gloaming, Charlie did.

CHAPTER

64

The whole night of the robbery, Charlie had been seized with terror, terror that they would be caught, terror that the guards would come out shooting, terror that his mother would have to bail him out from the police station and what she'd do to him when she finally got him home. In his entire life, nothing had worked out like it was supposed to, and he was sure this crazy scheme would be no different. But it was different. Teddy's plan fell into place like the parts of a delicate lock, and the world clicked open for them.

As they headed back to the neighborhood in Ralph's van, Joey driving, the rest of them hunkered down in the back, amidst a welter of metalworking tools and the plunder of a lifetime, a thrilling euphoria overtook Charlie, overtook them all. He could see it in the smiles and flushed faces, in the pumped fists and nerves. They felt powerful, sly, young and frisky, renewed, special, invincible. They felt like they had actually leaped Teddy's abyss and reinvented themselves. And, more than anything else, they felt love, yes love, one for the other, each for all, as they made their way in that van toward their suddenly limitless futures.

Ralph's mother was deaf and an invalid, and so his house was the perfect place to put into play the final pieces of the operation. In Ralphie's basement, using his lock-picking tools, Charlie carefully removed the jewels from their fittings in the bracelets and necklaces and rings they had taken from the safe. Ralph and Hugo worked together with the precious metals. Gold figurines, silver medallions, platinum settings were melted and recast into simple bars of precious metals to be sold. Joey spent all day and night listening to the police radio, monitoring reports of suspicions and raids as the police worked desperately to find out who had pulled off the crime of the century. And Teddy was making arrangements to sell everything but the paintings. There had been some cash in the safe, a few thousand that had already been split up, with promises not to spend a cent of it until the heat cooled, but the bulk of the proceeds was going to come from the metal and the jewels.

It wasn't going to bring in as much as they had hoped, though. The haul was less than they had been promised by their inside source, although it was more than they had ever seen before. Still, to be truthful, it wasn't really about the money, it was about them all making the decision and taking the chance and pulling it off. Suddenly the sweet possibilities of life that once seemed as far away as the moon now loomed large and bright and close enough to touch.

And then, just a few days after the heist, while the papers were still blasting headlines about "The Great Randolph Robbery" and the police were still turning over every stone, Teddy pulled in to the alleyway with a little red sports car Charlie had never seen before and parked it right under the deck. Ralph was at work, keeping up appearances, Joey was home with the radio, and Hugo was out, somewhere, so it was only Charlie in the basement, with the stash of valuables and the two paintings and the big hole in the floor that they had already dug up to bury the evidence in case the police came searching, when Teddy arrived with that car.

"I need the stuff," said Teddy as he grabbed some wooden crates out of the car.

"Which stuff?" said Charlie.

"All of it. I got a guy who's talking about buying the whole shooting match for more than we thought."

"But isn't it dangerous to take it all to him?"

"No more dangerous than to keep it here," he said, and then he lifted his shirt to show a gun in his belt. "Don't worry, Charlie, I got it covered. Give me a hand. I need to take everything."

"Everything?"

"Yeah, the paintings, too. I got to give the one up to my contact."

"Okay, but why the other one? I thought you said that was our insurance policy?"

"We don't want to leave anything here," said Teddy. "This place is getting too hot. I'll take it all someplace safe."

"Do the guys know about this?"

"Absolutely, I cleared it with them all. Just help me load up, okay?"

"Sure," said Charlie, even though he wasn't sure, wasn't sure at all. There was something wrong with Teddy, something off. Charlie thought about calling Ralph at work or going to get Joey, but Teddy brushed through the door and started reaching for the stuff that was scattered about, the jewels and bars of metal. Uncertain about what else to do, Charlie pitched in to help put everything in the boxes. They were halfway finished when the girl slipped through the open door and into the basement.

They hadn't noticed her at first, they kept on loading the stuff into the boxes as she watched. They even talked about it, the paintings and the jewels, the whole operation. They spilled it all as she stood, motionless, just to the side of the doorway.

And then she stirred, and they both turned their heads, and there she was, the girl, staring at them with her wide eyes.

She was no stranger, this girl, dark-haired and pretty and impossibly young. She was one of the children who had been drawn by Teddy to the alleyway with candy and little gifts. First there was the boy, her older brother, and then he brought the girl, and then others showed up, like pigeons drawn to crumbs. Teddy liked having them around, their laughter, their unalloyed greed, the way as soon as they got some candy in their mouths they asked for more, and he liked this girl most of all. There wasn't anything more to it, nothing sexual or weird, but even when the others suggested it might not be the best idea to have them around, Teddy persisted. He said the kids gave them all a cover, made Ralph's place a more integral part of the neighborhood, but that wasn't the real reason, they could tell. Teddy had some desperate need to be worshipped, and these kids were his congregation.

And now one of his flock, his favorite, was in the basement, wide-eyed and innocent, but not as innocent as she'd been just a moment before.

"Hi, Chantal," said Teddy.

"Hi."

"What are you doing in here?"

"I came to say hello. I heard voices."

"You didn't knock. You should always knock."

"Okay. I will. Next time. I promise."

"As long as you promise. We're just packing up some stuff. Come on over, I want to show you something."

"What?"

"Come on."

She did. She stepped forward.

"Look at this," said Teddy, holding out something big and glistening. "You know what this is?"

She shook her head.

"It's a diamond," he said. "Isn't that something? Isn't that cool? You want to touch it?"

"Okay."

"Here, touch it."

"Teddy," said Charlie. "What the hell are you doing?"

"Shut up, Charlie. Here, Chantal. Touch it."

She reached out her hand, petted the diamond as if petting a cat, even let out a little purr, and as she did, her eyes sparkled.

"Do you want one?"

"Oh, yes," she said.

"Remember I gave you that lighter you liked? I could also give you a diamond. Just a little one. If you make a promise. Can you make a promise, Chantal?"

"Yes."

"Will you promise not to tell anyone what you saw in here today?"

"How little?"

"About as big as your fingernail."

"Really?"

"Sure. But can you promise?"

"Okay. Why is there a hole in the floor?"

"Just a plumbing thing. But you promise, right?"

"I promise."

"Good, Chantal. Now Charlie and I are going to put some stuff in the car, and then I'll give you your diamond, okay? Can you sit on that box and wait?"

"Okay."

"Good. Let's go, Charlie, let's load it up."

And they did, put everything in the car. It was heavy, but the volume was surprisingly small after Ralph and Hugo had melted down the metal, and the whole stash fit in the small trunk of the sports car.

"All right, Charlie," said Teddy when it was all packed up. "Go take a test drive, nice and slow. Maybe buy some gas. I'll walk Chantal home and meet you back here in about half an hour."

"She knows," said Charlie.

"She won't tell anyone."

"Of course she will, she's a kid."

"She won't," said Teddy. "Let me give her the diamond, walk her home. Be back here in half an hour."

"Maybe I should just stay."

And there it was, in Teddy's eyes, something hard and cold, a look not of anger but of shared understanding of what was going to happen. Charlie tried to shake his head, but he couldn't, he was frozen. And he felt, in that moment, all the euphoria and good feeling and hope, most of all the hope, bleed out of him as if a vein had been slashed.

"Go on, Charlie," said Teddy.

"I don't think I should."

"Stop thinking, then, and go."

"Teddy?"

"Just go."

"I don't want to."

"Hey, Charlie, you know the painting, the one we took for insurance, in case something went wrong? I think maybe you should hold on to it for us all."

"Where will I put it?"

"I don't know, you'll figure it out. But go on now, go for a drive. I'll meet you here in half an hour."

And he did just that, Charlie. He got in the car, and he drove away, and he filled up the tank, and he drove around, and when he came back, Teddy was waiting for him under the deck. He told Charlie he took the girl home. He told Charlie it was all right, that he could guarantee she wouldn't say a word. He told Charlie that he'd meet them all back at the house that night with the money, and they'd divide it up, and they'd have a party. And then as Charlie stood under the small deck, with the rolled-up painting in a carton tube in his hand, Teddy Pravitz drove away with all the fruits of their great and noble act of self-creation.

And Charlie never saw him again.

65

It was dark now, with only the flickering of the citronella candles and the intermittent headlights sweeping across the landscape illuminating our faces. But even in that strange, uneven light, I could see the tears, on Charlie's face, on Monica's cheeks, welling in Joey's hard eyes. Only Rhonda seemed distracted, keeping watch on her tape player, taking notes by candlelight.

"How come you didn't look for him?" said Rhonda.

"We thought he'd contact us," said Joey. "At first we was scared something happened. But when there was nothing in the papers, we figured he'd give us a call sometime."

"He said something before about going to Australia," said Charlie, wiping at his nose with his wrist. "What was we going to do, head off to Australia? But in the end I'm not sure we really wanted to find the bastard. He didn't flash that gun just to show he was prepared. It was a warning, too."

"Australia was just a feint," I said. "He was planning to rip you off from the start."

"What about Chantal?" said Monica. "What else do you know? What did he do with her?"

Charlie looked at Joey, who glanced back and then down.

"What is it?" said Monica. "Tell me."

"We was burying everything connected to the crime in the basement, our clothes, the guns, the equipment we used to melt the metal," said Joey. "Everything they could use to identify us. We thought it was safer than chucking it into a landfill. Early on, we had bought the cement and some sand and gravel to mix up with it to slather on top. The day after Teddy disappeared, when we started filling in the hole, we saw it."

"What?" said Monica. "What did you see? Exactly."

"The edge of a sheet. Holding something, covered by chunks of cement and piled-on dirt. I knew what it was right off."

"Oh my God," said Monica, breaking into tears. "All this time. But I would have known. I would have felt it."

"What did you do, Charlie?" I said.

"What could we do? The four of us, we buried everything and tried to forget."

"That's really why we didn't hunt so hard for Teddy," said Joey. "Would you?"

"But it ruined everything," said Charlie. "All the dreams, they died with her. Hugo left a few weeks later, Ralphie and Joey just hung on. I knew someone who knew someone, and I figured I was only good for one thing anymore, so I passed the word about locks and safes, and soon I was doing it all again and again with them Warrick brothers, but it never felt the same."

I was sure it didn't. There was something so ecstatic about the story of five neighborhood guys pulling off the crime of the century that the aftermath had never made much sense. Teddy and Hugo had altered their names in an attempt to obliterate their pasts, and now I knew why. Ralph and Joey hadn't moved forward at all in their lives, and now I knew why. Charlie's life had turned into an absolute wreck, and now I knew why. At the heart of their effort to reinvent themselves was the worst of all crimes, the murder of a child, and how could anything bright and shiny come from that?

I lifted my arm to the candlelight, checked my watch. "We have to go. Do you have what you need, Rhonda?"

"Sure. Thank you. It's quite a story."

"Hold it like you promised," I said. "And when I'm ready, I'll tell you who Teddy Pravitz became in his new life after the robbery."

"Will it be interesting?" she said.

"It will be on the front page, is what it will be, and get you your full-time gig. Now can you do me a favor and take Monica home?"

Rhonda turned to Monica, who was still in tears and who seemed lost in some strange emptiness. "Of course."

"No," said Monica. "I'm staying with Victor."

"It's going to be dangerous. I don't want you around."

"Are they going to dig up that basement tonight?"

"Probably," I said.

"Then I'm going."

"Monica—"

"Don't even, Victor," she said. "It's my sister. Someone from her family should be there."

I thought about it for a moment, realized there was nothing I could do to change her mind, and nodded.

"Go on ahead," said Rhonda. "I'll clean up."

And so we left her at the table as the four of us made our way slowly to the back of the ruined shed and climbed into the borrowed green taxicab. Monica sat in the back, leaning against the door and as far away from Charlie as she could. Charlie leaned forward, wringing his hands. Joey nervously tapped the wheel with his fingers. I pulled out my cell phone.

"Where to now, Victor?"

"Home," I said as I pressed the button for Beth's cell. Just as we were about to pull away, I saw Rhonda, clutching her pocketbook and coming toward the car. "Hold up," I said to Joey as I closed the phone.

Rhonda leaned into my car window, her elbows on the ill. "Can I ask one more question?" she said. "Something I orgot to bring up?"

"Go ahead," I said.

"Charlie. You said that Teddy gave you the Rembrandt, ut you never said what you did with it."

I turned to look at Charlie, shook my head. "He doesn't now what happened to the painting," I said. "It disap-eared."

"Really?" said Rhonda. "No idea?"

"I have an idea," said Charlie. "A pretty damn good dea."

"Charlie, be quiet."

"No, Victor. Joey don't want nothing more to do with that ainting, and neither does I."

"Are you sure?"

"Let it go back to the damn museum. Every penny would nly make me sick. You told me I can't start new without aying for my past. How could I start new with a wallet full f cash from what happened?"

I thought for a moment, let the familiar disappointment oll through me, and then I realized how right he was. "Okay, Charlie. Go ahead and tell her."

"So where is it?" said Rhonda.

"Is Ralphie's workbench still in the basement?" said Charlie.

"Yes, it is," I said.

"It was made up of plumber's cast-iron pipes and wooden eams. I pried up a beam, slipped it in one of them pipes, and ammered the beam back down. It should still be there."

"How fabulous," said Rhonda.

"That doesn't get printed until I give the okay."

"I promise," said Rhonda.

Just then she leaned forward into the window, leaned in

and faced me as if to give me a huge kiss. I felt a little awk
ward about kissing her in front of everyone after everything
we had heard, but then her face kept moving until it was pas
me. She reached out, grabbed the car keys with her righ
hand, killed the engine, pulled back with the keys in he
hand until she was once again leaning on the car window.

"What are you doing?" I said.

"I'm sorry, Victor, but I can't let you go."

"Why not?"

"Because that's not what I get paid for, sweetie," she
said as she reached her left hand into her purse, pulled ou
a neat automatic, and placed the tip of the muzzle right a
my head.

66

I figured it out right away, exactly what was happening. As Charlie cursed at the sight of the gun and Monica gasped and Joey laughed, the truth of it clicked in my head, left, right, left, oh, crap. I might not be the sharpest spade, but put a gun to my head and I sharpen considerably.

He had sent her from the start, Teddy had. She was the friend from Allentown. Rhonda, not some old grizzled vet, she was the left-handed dispatcher of both Ralphie Meat and Stanford Quick, now here to wipe out Charlie, and Joey, and then me. Monica had met Teddy in California, so she'd have to go, too. Who's next? We were next, the four of us, and I had delivered us all to her like sacrificial lambs on the altar of my stupidity.

It wasn't like I hadn't checked her out. I had called *Newsday,* I had asked if there was a Rhonda Harris who reported for them on the art beat, they assured me there was. But I hadn't asked for a description, and how hard is it for a clever hit girl to steal an identity for as long as it takes to get the job done? And I should never have doubted, for even an instant, that someone was out there to wipe away Teddy's problems in his old hometown. The one thing I had learned about him was that he never went with just a single option. *Always have a backup plan, kid, or the vultures here will eat you alive,* had said Theodore Purcell, and now his backup plan was pointing a gun at my face.

"Does this mean you're not writing a book?" I said as I frantically tried to figure out what the hell to do.

"Why would I worry over words when this is so much simpler?" she said.

"No agent? No proposal? No advance? I thought we had a future together."

"Oh, Victor," she said as she waggled the gun at me. "We do. It's just going to be very short."

"What's going on?" said Monica. "Victor?"

"She's going to kill us."

"Of course she's going to kill us. But why?"

"It's payback for what we done to your sister," said Joey. "Karma with a gun."

"Chantal wouldn't have wanted that."

"But it's what she's getting," said Rhonda. "And after what I heard, I think I'm doing everyone a favor."

"You look good for a Korean War vet," I said.

"That's my father," she said. "But with two false hips, he doesn't get around so well anymore, so I took over the family business. One step up from animal control."

"You led them to me again, you idiot," said Charlie.

"I guess I did."

"As a lawyer you might be okay, Victor," said Charlie, "but as a bodyguard, you're the—"

Before he could finish, I jerked up the door latch and slammed the door with all the strength in my shoulder. I expected to feel the weight of her bang away from the taxi, but she did a graceful sidestep as the door swung wildly open. I almost tumbled to the ground, held up only by my seat belt, when the door swung back and smacked me in the head.

She pulled the door away from me and kicked me in the chest, so I was flung back into the taxi.

"Let's not make too big a mess," she said. "The cleaners are already on their way."

With her side to the now-open door, she pointed her gun toward Charlie in the backseat. And then we heard it.

An engine revving nearby, a rustle of weeds behind us.

Rhonda looked up just as a small, dark car burst out of the vegetation and headed right for us.

Rhonda's gun arm swiveled.

The onrushing car's high beams burst on.

She threw up an arm.

The car jumped forward.

There was an explosion near my head. And then, with a blast of hot air on my face, with a jumble of red hair and white limbs, with an aborted cry and the dying scream of torn metal, the car came upon us and beside us and rushed past us.

And just like that, the gun, the open car door, and Rhonda Harris had all disappeared.

CHAPTER
67

Well, not quite disappeared. They lay about fifteen yards away, in a jumble of blood and bone and metal, all the elements mercifully indistinct one from the other in the darkness. To the side of the mess was the little car, its motor still running, its lights now washing across the weeds at the far side as it slowly started turning around.

I unbelted and stumbled out of the now-doorless entrance-way of the cab. My knees were shaking so hard I lost my balance and fell to the ground, ripping my pants, before I climbed to my feet again. The night smelled of exhaust and cordite and terror, coppery and hard. And something else, too, something vaguely sweet and vaguely familiar. I looked around. The others were now out of the taxi also, looking as dazed and confused as did I. The three stared at me. I shrugged. Slowly, we approached the little car. We approached hesitantly, with undue care, as if it were a wild animal, turning so that it could gather us into its sight and leap ferociously at our throats.

I tried to peer inside the little car, but the headlights were now shining brightly in my eyes, and even with my hand up to shield me from the sharp light, I could see nothing but the dented bumper, the bullet hole in the windshield, and the cracked glazing over the twin beams that were coming ever closer.

Then the car stopped, the door opened. Out climbed a silhouette, small, dainty. It stepped forward into the light.

Lavender Hill.

"Toodle-oo, Victor. Isn't it a beautiful night? Reminds me of the bayou, not that I am a habitué of the bayou, mind you, I have all my teeth, and I have never had leech stew, but this little stretch of New Jersey does have that unpredictable scent of violence about it, doesn't it?"

"Lav, dude" was all I could muster.

"Yes, well, always one with the quip, aren't you, Victor? You must tell me all about your trip west. Did you see any stars? Alan Ladd, now, that was a star. Is he still alive, do you know?"

"What are you doing here, Lav?"

"You told me you were bringing your client home so he could sell me the painting. I thought I better make sure you all arrived safely. Is that him there?"

"Charlie Kalakos," I said, "let me introduce you to Lavender Hill."

"Yo," said Charlie. "Thanks for—"

"Saving your life? Oh, it was nothing." He turned to look at the remains of Rhonda Harris. "Well, maybe not nothing."

"But how did you get here?" I said. "How did you follow me, with all the precautions I took?"

"I'm sure your precautions were stunning in their design, though, of course, seeing that you ended with a gun in your face, not quite as effective as you might have hoped. But no, I didn't follow you, dear Victor."

"Then how?"

"I followed her," he said, indicating the mass of bone and blood on the ground. "From the start I sensed she was trouble. I know the type. I am the type. Didn't I tell you she was a killer?"

"I thought you were speaking metaphorically."

"I'm a very literal person, Victor. You should know that by now. I followed her to this spot. I realized she was setting up a rendezvous. I slipped my car into a clearing in the woods and waited. Just me, my car, and my long-distance microphone. Quite the clever gadget, but one I would never use out in the open. The headphones make me look like Princess Leia."

"So you heard about the girl," I said.

"Yes, I heard. Too sad for words, actually, so why even try to speak of it?" He glanced at his watch. "But the woman with the gun mentioned something about cleaners coming. I assume she means Charles's friends from the Warrick gang, hurrying this way as we speak to dispose of your bodies. So maybe we should cut our little gabfest short. Charles, are you ready now to sell?"

"No," he said. "I'm sorry, and I think I owe you, what with you saving our lives and all, but I'm not going to sell it. I just want to give it back."

"Are you sure? I've already made arrangements to dispose of the item without its going to your old friend."

"I don't want nothing good to come from what happened, 'cause it'll only turn out bad, you know what I mean?"

"Not really, no. And what about you, Joseph? Are you willing to let such a payday disappear after all these years?"

"Good riddance, I say," said Joey.

"Ah, the disappointment, but it seems there is little I can do. A wave of cheap sentimentality has seemed to overcome you both and I wouldn't dream of crashing the party, though I'm quite shocked that you, Victor, have not endeavored to change their minds. But it would have been a pretty thing to gaze at before I delivered it on, don't you think? All right, then, take my advice, all of you, and flee, madly. I too need to rush off. There is a Fabergé egg available in a trailer park in Toledo. Imagine that. Toledo. The provenance is not quite clear, but with a Fabergé egg it never is, don't you know. I mean, the last true owner was killed by Lenin in a pit. After that, it's open season, don't you think? Ciao, friends."

We watched as he climbed back into his dented car, flicked his lights as if in farewell, and pulled around the taxi, past the picnic table and the collapsing shed, and onto the narrow two-lane road, heading west, toward Ohio, I assumed. He'd swept into my life, threatened it, saved it, swept out of it again. Funny the kind of people you meet in this business. I'd almost miss him.

"We have to get out of here," I said.

"Back in the cab," said Joey.

"There's no door," I said.

"I can drive without a door."

"Maybe you can," I said, "but how far we'd get before the cops stop us is another thing entirely. And then she probably told the cleaners what kind of car we had. If we pass them on the road, they'll figure it out and spin around after us."

"But it's Hookie's car. I can't just leave it here."

"We'll retrieve it later, patch it up, I promise."

"It's a piece of crap anyway," he said.

"Then how do we get out of here?" said Monica.

"We'll take her car," I said, gesturing toward the pulpy mass on the ground. "Let's find her bag."

"Is this a time to be rummaging for spare change?" said Charlie.

"We need the keys," I said. "And her phone. Joey, check her car and see if the keys are there. The rest of us will comb the area, the bag should be somewhere around."

The gun was off to the side. I picked it up carefully by the trigger guard and placed it in a jacket pocket. Joey came back, reporting that the car was locked, and we continued our search, moving slowly toward the heap of metal and flesh.

"She had nice hair," said Monica, as we passed the corpse. "I always wanted red hair."

Beyond the body, beyond the door, almost to the edge of the gravel lot, where the woods had already encroached, we found the bag. Phone, wallet, but no keys.

"They must have spun out in the crash, flying somewhere into the woods," I said. It could take us another hour to find them.

"I could just pick the lock of her car," said Charlie.

"Don't they have electronic gizmos?"

"I can get around them," said Joey.

I turned to stare at them.

"Hey, you were the man with the plan," said Joey. "We was following you."

"Let's get the hell out of here," I said.

A minute and a half later, we were in Rhonda's rental car, the engine humming, Joey Pride pulling us out of the lot.

"Go east," I said.

"Back to the shore?"

"Back to the parkway and then the Atlantic City Expressway," I said. "It might take a little longer, but I don't want to pass any goons on this little road on our way back to Philly."

He did as I said, and then I made my calls.

68

I didn't know I was in a race.

I should have known, of course, it was all there in front of my face. But at the time I was a little preoccupied with staying alive. So we took the roundabout route to Philadelphia as I called McDeiss. I gave him the last phone number Rhonda had called, so he could track down her accomplices, and a description of Fred and Louie. He promised to have a squadron of New Jersey state troopers converge on the site of Schmidty's deserted farmer's market and pick up whoever showed in response to Rhonda's call.

"And when the cops finally arrive," I said, "there will be a little treat waiting for them. A dead body."

"Damn it, Carl, what the hell is going on?"

"You know the guy who you think killed both Ralph Ciulla and Stanford Quick?"

"The guy from Allentown?"

"Well, you were right about him doing the killings, except he wasn't a guy."

"Get the hell out of here."

"I cleared two of your cases, you should be thrilled. I even have the murder weapon sitting in my pocket. And when you figure out who she really is, pick up her father. He was in the business before her. Now, are you ready for us?"

"We have a cordon around Mrs. Kalakos's house, and we

have a phalanx of black-and-whites ready to pick you up at the mouth of the Tacony-Palmyra Bridge and escort you to her street. You're still in that green-and-white taxi?"

"Not anymore," I said.

"What happened?"

"We had a little accident. We're driving something new."

"Just picked it up off the street?"

"That's right," I said.

"Mind telling me what it is?"

"Yes, I do. Last thing I want is a phalanx of police cars pointing out to everyone in the city exactly where we are. How many in a phalanx anyway? Can two be a phalanx if they're really, really big?"

"Don't be a hero, Carl," said McDeiss.

"Little chance of that. But don't worry, there will be a green-and-white cab meeting your phalanx."

"Come again?"

"Just have your phalanx meet the cab and flash its lights and escort the cab to the Kalakos house. Have it pause there for a moment, and then lead it back to the Roundhouse. That should be safe enough. But the Kalakos house is not where you and I are going to meet up."

"Then where?" said McDeiss.

"Someplace else. I want you to show up quietly, no black-and-whites, no commotion or press. Wait until the noisy procession begins and then slip in unnoticed. Just you and Slocum and Hathaway and a team from your CSI unit to process a body. Can you do that?"

"We can do that. Where?"

"Ralph Ciulla's basement. And remember that pickax you found in Stanford Quick's car?"

"We still have it."

"Maybe you should bring it along."

"What the hell's down there?"

"Unfinished business," I said.

It was Monica who drove us into the city. I didn't know who'd be looking for us, but I figured, even in the rental car, they'd be less likely to identify us with a pretty woman at the wheel.

When we reached the Walt Whitman Bridge, I called Beth on her cell. It was time for her to play decoy. Earlier she had gone to the railroad station, picked up a green-and-white cab, and been cruising around the city. The driver didn't know what he was in for, but I figured the police protection and the hundred Beth slipped him would cover it. Now, while we headed over the Delaware, she headed to the western mouth of the Tacony-Palmyra Bridge.

As we drove north on I-95, Beth phoned in her reports. It was like a parade, she said, with the police cars, the lights and sirens. McDeiss had even put in a few motorcycle cops for effect. The man knew how to build a phalanx. But there was no effort to stop her, no opposing army of thugs, no shots, no danger. Apparently Rhonda Harris had called off those dogs before Lavender Hill had silenced her but good.

We got off I-95 at the Cottman Avenue exit, took a nice calm drive into the Northeast, circled counterclockwise to the back alley behind Ralph Ciulla's house. Nothing looked strange, nothing looked out of place. Monica pulled the gray rental car into the spot beneath the little backyard deck.

I got out, patted the heavy metal thing in my pocket as I looked around. Nothing. I stepped to the closed basement door and slowly pushed it open. It was dark inside.

"Hello," I said softly.

"Hello yourself," came McDeiss's whisper.

"Any news from New Jersey?"

"They found the body and picked up four suspects at the scene, including two that matched the descriptions you gave me over the phone."

"Terrific. All right, give us a second."

I stepped back, waved to Monica. She climbed out. Then I tapped the windshield, and two figures popped up from hiding low in the backseat. I motioned them out. They scrambled quickly out of the car, as quickly as two old guys bent stiffly at the waist can scramble out of a car, and then slipped through the basement door. Monica and I followed.

When the door closed, the lights suddenly clicked on and we could see the whole setup. Two CSI technicians, with their briefcases. Two uniforms, pump-action shotguns at the ready. Slocum and Hathaway together off to the side. And McDeiss, leaning on the handle of a rusted old pickax, standing smack in the center of the room.

"Welcome home, Charlie Kalakos," said McDeiss in a booming voice. "We've been looking for you for quite a while."

"I been away," said Charlie.

"We're going to have ourselves a chat," said McDeiss.

"In due time, Detective," I said. "In due time. But first we have some serious matters to take care of."

I turned to take a peek at the workbench and then did a double take. Slowly, I walked toward it. The first of the wooden boards that made up the tabletop had been pried off the pipe frame. The front pipes on either side had been yanked forward. I looked inside each. Both were empty.

"How long have you guys been here?" I said.

"About ten minutes," said Slocum.

"Was the basement door locked or unlocked?"

"Unlocked."

"Crap," I said. "Now we know why he was in such a hurry to get to Toledo."

"Who are we talking about, Carl?" said McDeiss.

"I'm talking about a little guy who goes by the name of Lavender Hill. I didn't know we were in a race, but he did.

He was the one who took care of our friend from Allentown, Detective, and after he did that, and after listening in on his microphone to everything Charlie had to say, he rushed up here to seize the painting. The Rembrandt has been stolen once again."

"We'll find him," said McDeiss.

"I doubt it," I said. "But the painting all along has been just a sideshow. Hasn't it, Jenna?"

"All along," she said.

"Time to take care of the main event? Are all the terms of our agreement still in place?"

"They are," said Slocum.

"Okay, then. Joey Pride, do you remember where the pit was?"

Joey looked at me and nodded.

"Go ahead," I said.

He looked around the basement and stepped toward the rear. He cleared some boxes and pointed at a cracked portion of the uneven cement floor. "There," he said.

McDeiss lifted the pickax and held it toward the CSI guys in the corner. One of them stood and started toward McDeiss when Charlie spoke up.

"Can I do it?" he said. "It's been haunting me for half my life, that hole in the ground. Can I open it up?"

"Like lancing a boil?" I said.

"Something like that."

I looked at McDeiss. He thought about it some, looked at the CSIs, who shrugged. McDeiss turned to offer the pickax to Charlie.

"I'll help, too," said Joey Pride, pushing away some cartons that were piled around the spot he had pointed to.

Then we all stood back as Charlie Kalakos hoisted the pickax in the air and let its sharpened point drop into the floor. The cement was thin, brittle, it cracked easily under the weight of the heavy metal tool. Charlie pulled it loose and hoisted it again. When he started breathing heavily, Joey took hold of the pickax. One of the CSIs stooped down to lift up the loose chunks of concrete. Then Joey raised the pickax high in the air and let it fall.

Slowly they worked, Charlie Kalakos and Joey Pride, clearing the cement that covered the crimes of their past, blow by blow, bit by bit, as Slocum and McDeiss, Jenna Hathaway and Monica Adair, as all of us looked on, some with stoic faces, some with tears, looked on knowing exactly what we'd find and dreading it all the while.

69

"I've brought him home to you, Mrs. Kalakos," I said.

"You good boy, Victor," she said to me. "I knew you do just as I say."

"I appreciate your confidence," I said.

The room was dark, the air thick with incense, I was back in the chair, by the bed, where Mrs. Kalakos, as usual, lay stiff and still. And yet there was something very different about her appearance. Where normally her hair was wild and unkempt, this night it was combed and teased and set in place with bobby pins, the twirls at her temples taped to her flesh. Her cheeks held red circles, her lips were brightly painted, with two peaks in the middle of the upper one, and there was lace in her bodice. Miss Havisham waiting for her groom. Yikes.

"So where he is? Where my boy?" she said.

"He's just outside the room, but I wanted to talk to you about him first."

"Don't make me wait, Victor. I'm old woman, without much breath left. Bring him to me. Now."

"Charlie is very anxious to see you, Mrs. Kalakos. Both excited and scared."

"What he need to be scared about from such pitiful bag of bones?"

"Because you're his mother," I said. "That's enough terror for anyone. And then, also, because he knows you so well."

"You try to flatter old woman, Victor?"

"That's not my intent, ma'am. I just wanted to tell you that your son has been through a lot in the last couple of weeks, especially today. There was another attempt on his life just a few hours ago. And, even more significant, he was forced to dig up something very dark from his past. Something that happened as a result of the robbery thirty years ago."

"What you trying to tell me, Victor?"

"There was a girl killed."

"A girl?"

"The Adair child, the one that went missing."

"I remember."

"She was murdered by Teddy because she saw them with their stuff from the robbery. Charlie didn't do the killing, but he knew about it. It was why things turned rotten for your son, why he ended up with the Warrick brothers and ended up on the run. And it is why he's going to be spending some time in jail now. He knows you'll find out about it, and he wanted me to tell you first."

"And for this my Charlie spoiled his life?"

"That's right, ma'am."

"He's even bigger fool than I thought."

"What I'm asking, Mrs. Kalakos, is that you be especially gentle with your son."

"What you think I am, Victor, monster?"

"No, ma'am, just a mother."

"Okay, you told me. Now, Victor. No more delay. Let me see my boy."

I stood up from the chair, went to the door, opened it, and nodded to the little group standing outside.

Thalassa, gray and tense and stooped, came in first. "Mama," she said. Mrs. Kalakos lay unmoving on the bed,

her eyes now closed as if she had been unconscious for days
instead of talking to me just an instant before. "Mama, can
you awaken? Mama? Are you still with us?"

"Yes," said Mrs. Kalakos with a voice weak yet rich with
the drama of the grave. "I am still here. What have you for
me, my child?"

"It is Charles," said Thalassa, speaking her words as if
speaking to the mezzanine far in the distance. "My brother,
your son, Charles. He has come home to say good-bye."

"Charlie? Here? My Charlie? My baby? Bring him, dear
Thalassa, bring him to me."

Thalassa stepped back, the door opened wider, and Charlie Kalakos, his hands cuffed in front of him and McDeiss
close behind him, entered the room. He stepped hesitantly
forward, knelt before his dying mother, clasped his cuffed
hands together and laid them on the bed.

"Mama?" he said.

Without opening her eyes, she raised her hand toward
Charlie. When it reached the top of his bald head, it dropped
there and then moved down to feel his forehead, his eyes and
nose, down and around his chin, and then up to his mouth.

"Is that my Charlie?" she said.

"Yes, Mama."

"You've come back to me."

"Yes, Mama."

"To say good-bye as I requested."

"Yes, Mama."

"Come closer, my child."

"Yes, Mama," said Charlie as he leaned forward so that
his lips were almost touching his mother's cheek.

Her left hand rose from his face, reared back, and slapped
him. Hard. The sound was as loud as a shot in that room.

"What kind terrible fool you?" she said, her eyes now
open and trained on her son. "How you run away so long?

How you leave us scrape to save the house? How you let your friend kill that girl? You weak, you always weak. When will you stand up, Charlie, and be a man?"

"Mama," he said, his cuffed hands rubbing away the tears from his cheek.

"Why wait for them to kill you? I ought kill you myself."

"Mama. I came to say good-bye."

She sat up in her bed. "Why good-bye? Where am I going? You never good enough, Charlie, that was problem. You were never smart enough, never strong enough."

"Mama?"

"Your life nothing but failure."

"I'm sorry, Mama," said Charlie, bursting out in sobs.

"Now you cry for all you've done to me? Now you cry? You think crying, it help? Come here, you failed little fool," she said, raising both her hands. "Come to your mother, come to me, my little one."

"I'm sorry," said Charlie.

"I know you are."

"Mommy."

"Yes, my son. Yes. Shush now and come to me."

And Charlie, weeping unabashedly now, lay his head on her thin, withered breasts, and she enveloped him with her arms, hugged him and held him close and squeezed him to her as if squeezing the life out of him. Charlie was crying, and Thalassa, off to the side, was crying, and Mrs. Kalakos, with her son now at her breast, was crying, too.

This whole sordid story had started with a plea from a mother to bring her son home, and now the Kalakos family was together again, the scary old woman with her vile, grasping power, the old man who never grew up, the sister off to the side as she seemed always off to the side. I had brought them together, and I was glad. Despite the Kabuki drama we had just passed through, I couldn't stay dry-eyed at the scene before me. Whatever lay between this family, lines of attraction and repulsion and betrayal that would strangle Freud if he tried to untangle them, the emotion on display right then in that strange, dark room was shockingly pure. I don't know if there is such a thing as redemption, but when I see something that pure come from a history that rotten, I begin to have greater hope for the fate of the world.

70

They buried Chantal Adair beneath a bright summer sun on a sparklingly clear day. The papers said the family wanted a small, intimate ceremony at the cemetery, but the Adairs' wishes were ignored. The neighborhoods of the Northeast turned out, Frankford and Mayfair, Bridesburg and Oxford Circle, Rhawnhurst and Tacony, all races, all religions, those too young to have heard the story and those old enough to have forgotten, they all came out to bury a child of the city, one of their own.

Philadelphia has always been better at mourning a child than caring for one.

I stood on the outskirts of the crowd while a priest spoke, and then some guy that looked like Ulysses S. Grant spoke, and then Monica Adair spoke. I was too far away to catch everything, just the rising and the falling of the voices and the occasional punctuated word, but the sense was as clear as the sky that day. Chantal was a gift from God, what had happened to her was a crime that affected the whole of humanity, and now God, who had already wrapped her in his warm embrace, had sent her body home to her family.

I suppose there were oblique references to her murderer in those speeches, but nothing more was necessary. The photographs of Theodore Purcell being led from his Hollywood home in handcuffs were in all the papers and all the tabloids.

The producer of *Tony in Love* and *The Dancing Shoes* had hired a famous lawyer and was getting the full celebrity-on-trial treatment. His spokesman, one Reginald Winters, stated that Mr. Purcell expected to be acquitted and to produce a fabulous script he had recently acquired. You could almost see the glee in Teddy's face as the paparazzi snapped his photograph. Was he in trouble? You bet he was. But he was also back in the game, baby.

Charlie Kalakos couldn't attend the funeral because he was in protective custody. Joey Pride decided against attending, saying that after what he had done, and the quiet he had kept, he wasn't entitled to mourn with the family. But I wasn't alone among the crowd as they lowered the tiny coffin into the ground. Zanita Kalakos had insisted on coming with me. She had risen like a specter from her bed, had been carried down the stairs by her surprisingly strong daughter, and was now in a wheelchair by my side.

"Take me to the family," she said when the ceremony was over.

I glanced at my watch. "I can't, I'm late," I said. "This took longer than I thought."

"You be good boy and take me, now. I need speak to family of that girl. It is obligation."

I tried to protest, but she shut off my protestations with a wave of her hand. I didn't even pretend to be strong enough to stand up to that old lady and her obligations. Slowly, I pushed her wheelchair down the path toward the tent.

There was a line, of course there was. I glanced again at my watch and tried to push my way ahead—cripple coming through—but it didn't work. We were forced to wait as young and old and strangers and friends, as a cascade of mourners paid their respects.

Finally we were under the tent, crossing between the still-open grave and the row where sat the Adairs. I had expected to see dark glasses and reddened noses, I had expected to see the faces of a family deep in mourning, but that's not what I saw. The Adairs seemed calm, almost cheerful, as if the cloud of sadness and uncertainty they had been living with for more than a quarter of a century had suddenly dissipated and let the sun inside. Mrs. Adair seemed calmer, with some bloom to her cheeks; Mr. Adair's posture had changed, as if his shoulders had suddenly grown lighter.

"Oh, Victor, there you are," said Mrs. Adair, standing to greet me and give me a bright hug. "We're so glad you came. Thank you for everything. Monica just keeps talking and talking about you."

"I bet she does," I said.

"It's going to be hard maintaining a long-distance relationship," said Mr. Adair as he shook my hand, "but I'm sure you kids will work it out."

"Long-distance?"

"Introduce me," said Mrs. Kalakos, interrupting our conversation.

I stepped back at the order. "Mrs. Adair, Mr. Adair," I said. "I'd like you to meet Zanita Kalakos. This is Charlie Kalakos's mother."

Mrs. Adair looked down at the withered crone, and her face went slack as it decided which emotion to display. After a long moment of indecision, she smiled warmly and bent to take the old woman's hand.

"I wanted to say," said Mrs. Kalakos, "that I am so sorry that my son, he was part of what happened to your lovely daughter."

"How long was your son away, Mrs. Kalakos?"

"Fifteen years I not see my boy."

"I know how hard that was."

"I know you do, my darling."

"I'm glad for you he's back."

"Yes, I can see that. But I want you should know, part of my son, maybe best part, is in grave with your daughter."

"I think I understand, Mrs. Kalakos," said Mrs. Adair. "And thank you for coming, it means more than you might know."

"Be at peace, both of you," said Mrs. Kalakos.

When they were finished, I slowly pushed Mrs. Kalakos down the line of family. Richard Adair was sitting next to his father, his face set in some strange fixed expression while his eyes bounced like Superballs in his skull. He was pale and out of place in a suit way too tight, but he was out of the house, which I suppose was a start.

"Richard," I said with a nod.

"Yo, Victor."

"How you doing?"

"How you think?"

"It gets easier."

"What the hell do you know about it?"

"Only that it gets easier."

"Well, doesn't that just make it all worthwhile," he said.

When we reached Monica, she threw her arms around my neck and whispered, "Thank you, thank you, thank you," in my ear. She was dressed that day in her scrubbed, college-girl look, and I must say it felt entirely too good to feel her so close.

"This is Mrs. Kalakos," I said. "Charlie's mom."

"Thank you for coming," said Monica.

"Of course, dear. You pretty one, aren't you? You have house for Victor?"

"No, ma'am. Just a dog."

"Too bad, though it means Thalassa still has chance."

"What's this about our fake relationship becoming a long-distance one?" I said.

"I'm moving. Going out west."

"Hollywood?"

"Why not? You keep on saying I need a change. Maybe I do. And there was a vibe out there that felt right for me."

"You have a place to stay?"

"Lena said I could stay with her and Bryce for a while."

"Lena?"

"Yeah."

"Lena?"

"I know, it's weird, but we've been in touch. Even after I knew, we somehow felt like sisters. I really needed that. So did Lena, and I think so did Chantal. And Lena said she could help me get a job out there. Maybe with a law firm for real. And maybe, while I'm out there, I could do some auditions."

"Dancing?"

"Acting. Commercials and stuff."

"You're going to be an actress?"

"Why not? You know me, I'm never one to shy from attention. And I feel, in a strange way, suddenly light, as if I can just float away and do anything. Victor, it's like this whole thing, you, the tattoo, the trip to California to meet Lena, Charlie and that horrible woman with the gun, everything was Chantal's way to show me the truth. When they dug up my sister, they buried a chain that had been wrapped around my neck. What do you do when the whole point of your life disappears?"

"You go to L.A. and make soap commercials," I said. "You'll be a smash, Monica, I know it. Like Teddy said, there's no telling what a Philly kid can accomplish so long as you get her out of Philly."

"You'll keep in touch?"

"Of course I will," I said.

"Victor, have you ever met my Uncle Rupert and my cousin Ronnie?"

She gestured over to Ulysses S. Grant in the front of the line. Put him in a blue uniform, give him a bottle of whiskey, and he could have led the charge at Cold Harbor. But it wasn't Uncle Rupert who caught my interest, it was the woman who had been by his side but was now slinking away. I hadn't noticed her before, but when she glanced back worriedly, I caught her face and my heart seized.

I had seen her before. We had shared drinks. I had made an awkward pass. Son of a bitch. It was the woman in Chaucer's the night I ended up with my tattoo. The motorcycle blonde with the ponytail and the eau-de-Harley had been Chantal's cousin Ronnie.

"Son of a bitch," I said.

"What?" said Monica.

"I'll be right back," I said as I left Mrs. Kalakos at the graveside and headed sprightly after Ronnie.

When she saw me coming, Ronnie started rushing off faster, and then she stopped and wheeled and faced me down. She was cute and was wearing a skirt, but her eyes were suddenly hard and I had no doubt but that she could have pounded me into the dirt with one hand.

"What did you do?" I said to her. "Drug my drink and then waylay my ass to a tattoo parlor to scrawl your cousin's name on my scrawny chest for all eternity?"

"Something like that, yeah," she said.

"Why?"

"So someone would remember," she said. "Detective Hathaway had told my father long ago that he believed there was a connection between those five guys and Chantal. And then there you were, on the television, looking so smug and clever as you tried to get Charlie the Greek a sweetheart deal. I thought someone needed to remember the little girl who disappeared. My friend Tim runs a parlor on Arch. He agreed to do it."

"And you couldn't have sent me a letter?"

A smile crossed her wide, pretty face. "I thought this would be more effective. And with that stupid smile of yours on the television, you looked like you deserved it." She dropped her chin. "But Monica's been saying nice things about you, and I sort of feel bad."

"You should. I could have you arrested for assault."

"I know."

"And I could sue you for everything."

"All I've got is a motorcycle."

"Harley?"

"You think you're man enough to ride it?"

"It was a really rotten thing to do."

"I know. I'll pay for the laser to get it removed if you want."

"You bet you will," I said. I glanced back at the grave site, the family together under the little tent, the small hole in the ground in which the tiny coffin had been lowered. "If I do remove it."

She tilted her head at me.

"Well, he did a nice job," I said. "And I've sort of gotten used to it."

"I've always liked a man with a tattoo," said Ronnie.

I looked at her, the wide, pretty face, the shoulders of a field-hockey player. "You want to maybe get a drink sometime and talk about it?"

Yeah, I know, I am so pathetic it hurts.

71

Due to the funeral, I was late for Beth's closing, obviously later than I thought, because when I charged into our conference room, expecting to see the sellers and the real-estate agents, the title guy with his stamps and stacks, all I saw was Beth, sitting alone among a welter of paper.

"Did I miss it all?" I said.

"You didn't miss much," said Beth.

"How'd it go?"

"It didn't," said Beth. "I backed out."

"Excuse me?"

"I backed out. I didn't buy. I remain unencumbered, unmortgaged, utterly homeless."

"You decided you didn't like the house after all?"

"No, I loved it, really. It was perfect for me."

I sat down next to her, looked into her eyes. I thought she'd be upset or distraught or something, but she seemed happy, almost giddy. "Then why, Beth?"

"Do you think people can really change?"

"I don't know. Charlie gave up a boatload of cash to do the right thing with the painting, even though it didn't quite work out. That seems like a real change for him. But then again Theresa Wellman lapsed right back, didn't she?"

"I was devastated when I found her that night, drunk and

high, totally oblivious to the fact that her daughter was in the next room. I was so wrong to take her case."

"You saw a need in her and tried to fill it."

"I saw a need in myself and tried to use her to fill it. But when I saw her lolling and insensible, for the first time in a long time I saw my life clearly."

"What did you see?"

"I've been miserable to be with for the last couple of years, haven't I?"

"A little."

"More than a little. I've been whiny and dissatisfied and paralyzed, everything I never wanted to be. And buying a house with all my little plans to fill the little rooms would only make it worse. I love being your partner, Victor, but the firm has become something I never expected it to be. I think I need a break."

"Take a few weeks."

"I need more than that."

"I'll stop doing criminal law."

"But you love criminal law, and you've become great at it. You've found your place, I'm still looking for mine."

"We'll find it together."

"I don't think so. How long have I been talking about traveling the world? Khartoum. Cambodia. Kathmandu."

"I thought it was just talk."

"It was, but not anymore. I've always wanted to be the kind of woman who can find herself in Kathmandu. That's not what I am now, that's not what the house could ever change me into. But that's exactly what I'll be the moment I set foot in Nepal."

"So you're really going?"

"I can't wait."

"When will you come back?"

"When the money runs out, I suppose."

"I got a fee out of the Kalakos case. Give me a little time and I'll get you your share."

"A little time? What, is the check postdated?"

"Well, it wasn't quite a check. We were working the barter system."

"Victor."

"Don't worry, I know a guy who knows a guy who can take care of it for me. I think it's worth a lot."

"Keep it, all of it, I have enough for right now. The thing I feel most terrible about is leaving you in the lurch. Use my share to keep the firm going."

"Derringer and Carl."

"You'll have to take my name off the letterhead."

"Never. You'll be our foreign office."

"It's a shame, really, because I did love that house."

"It had ghosts. Sheila told me. There was a suicide that haunted the place."

"She didn't tell me."

"She didn't want to spook you."

"But I like ghosts."

We sat there for a moment, quiet, together and apart, thinking about our diverging futures. Then I started laughing.

"What?" she said.

"I'm imagining Sheila's expression when you told her you were backing out of the deal."

"She wasn't happy."

"Oh, I bet not. I can just see her throttling your neck."

"It wasn't that bad. She actually said she understood. Said she was thinking about backing out of a deal of her own."

I turned to Beth, thought that one out, started laughing again.

And that, right there, was how I became a sole practitioner. I'd been afraid of becoming just that for a long time now, left alone to my own pale devices, but when the news finally hit, it didn't feel so bad. I had an office, a career, a pile of swag in my desk drawer that I didn't have to share with anyone. I would miss Beth, absolutely, but I figured the cash would go a long way to assuage my bruised feelings.

Though not as long a way as I had hoped.

"Fake," said Brendan LaRouche in his small third-floor office above Jewelers' Row as he pawed through the pile of jewels and chains I had dumped on his desk. "Fake, fake, fake."

"What are you saying?"

"What do you think I'm saying, Victor? They are all fakes, and not very good fakes at that. Didn't you examine them closely?"

"I don't know enough to know what to look for."

"The chains are too heavy for gold. Lead, most likely, plated in some cheap brass. The diamonds are glass. No sparkle, no depth. I don't even need a loupe to tell. And the color, the rubies and sapphires, bad imitations. With the technology now, you can fake color so that only the most sophisticated gemologists can tell the real from the manufactured, but we don't need a gemologist for these. Fake, fake, fake, fake."

"What are they worth?"

"Trinkets like these are sold by the pound."

"Yikes."

"You were maybe expecting better news?"

"I was hoping."

"From where did you ever receive such junk?"

"From a Greek shark," I said, "with teeth like razors."

"Perhaps you should introduce me. I like dealing with ruthless businessmen."

"Brendan, even as hard as you are, this woman is out of your league."

And so that was that, the payment for my adventures with Charlie the Greek turned out to be no more valuable, pound for pound, than a chunk of prime chuck. And with Beth readying to hop a plane east and my boondoggle turned to ash, I was left alone in my dingy little office, with the rent to pay and the utilities to pay and my secretary's salary to pay and the bar fees to pay and the copier lease to pay, left alone with nothing but a tattoo on my chest and my prospects dimming by the minute. I figured I had enough for a month, two at the most, before I had to fold the tent. Failure was staring me in the face when a tall, lugubrious man with a black suit and black fedora stepped into my office.

"I am ashamed to admit, Mr. Carl, that I am in need of a lawyer," said the man. He had introduced himself as Samuel Beauregard.

I asked him what kind of trouble he had found.

"In the course of my travels, I have been involved in certain activities in this city that have drawn the attention of the authorities."

I asked him what kind of activities.

"I'd rather not specify," said Beauregard, "but they are unsavory to say the least. Quite enjoyable to a man of my temperament, but unsavory."

I said that I bet they were.

"What I need," said Beauregard, "is to have an attorney in this very city I can consult with. Someone who knows the rules, who knows the players, someone I can call on at a moment's notice, anytime, day or night, to deal with my situation should the need arise."

I asked if he wanted me to make a recommendation.

"Oh, no, Mr. Carl. I want you. From what I hear, you are

the one. No, sir, I have done my research and have chosen you for this rather delicate assignment."

I told him I was flattered.

"And of course, Mr. Carl, in order to have you on board, and at my beck and my call, should the need arise, I would be willing to pay a generous retainer." Beauregard reached into his long black jacket, pulled out a check. "I hope this is sufficient."

I took the check, examined it, almost swallowed my tongue.

It didn't require much brainpower to realize what was happening here. Lavender Hill, that strangely honorable man, was keeping his part of a bargain I had never agreed to. This was my finder's fee for the Rembrandt, which he had swiped from Ralphie Meat's house and sold to his private collector. To accept such an improper fee for an illegal transaction would violate every precept of the bar association, along with a myriad of sections contained in the Penal Code of the Commonwealth of Pennsylvania. Beth had been the conscience of our firm, and I knew what she would have done, but Beth was no longer here to advise. It was up to me, on my own, to make the decisions now.

This whole story of Charlie and Chantal and Monica and my tattoo was about change. After my visit to Hollywood, I thought I knew what kind of man I wanted to change into. I thought I would step up and turn ruthless, morph into a Sammy Glick as I grabbed hold of my success. But that hadn't worked out, not for Teddy Pravitz or Hugo Farr, not for Charlie or Joey or Ralphie Meat. Not even for my grandmother, Gilda. And not for me. The lesson, I suppose, is that change may be possible, but with a dangerous caveat: How you change goes a long way to determine what you change into.

So maybe I should find a different route. Maybe I should

follow Charlie's lead and become a simpler, more trustworthy person. Maybe I should become a man of admirable virtues. I liked the way that sounded. A man of admirable virtues. I could be that. I could. Really. Why not? And who knew, it might change my life in ways I never imagined. Maybe good flows from good, maybe karma rules. Change for the better, that was the ticket. While Samuel Beauregard waited for my response, I examined the check one more time.

Did I cash it?

You tell me.

WILLIAM

NEW YORK TIMES BESTSELLING AUTHOR

LASHNER

Her name is Julia. She's ridiculously lovely. Women like her date athletes and marry tycoons. They don't hang out with second-rate lawyers on the edge of insolvency. But back in the day, Julia had agreed to marry Victor Carl. Then she deserted him, running off to marry a doctor. Now she's back, and she's trouble with a capital T. Her husband has been murdered, Julia's incriminated, and there are big bucks at stake. Naturally, Victor is on the case.

WILLIAM LASHNER

A KILLER'S KISS

A Killer's Kiss

978-0-06-114346-5 • $24.95/$29.95 Can.

ON SALE IN HARDCOVER: 8/21/07

Available wherever books are sold or please call 1-800-331-3761 to order.

wm WILLIAM MORROW
An Imprint of HarperCollins*Publishers*
www.harpercollins.com

Visit www.AuthorTracker.com for exclusive information on your favorite HarperCollins authors.

AKK 0607

NEW YORK TIMES BESTSELLING AUTHOR

WILLIAM
LASHNER

OSTILE WITNESS

8-0-06-100988-4/$7.99/10.99 Can.

blue-blood attorney wants hard-luck Philadelphia lawyer
ctor Carl to represent a councilman's aide and his boss,
ho are on trial for extortion, arson, and murder.

BITTER TRUTH

978-0-06-056038-6/$7.99/10.99 Can.

The desperate scion of a prominent family, Caroline Shaw
wants Carl to prove that her sister's recent suicide was, in
fact, murder before Caroline suffers a similar fate.

FATAL FLAW

978-0-06-050818-0/$7.50/$9.99 Can.

When an old law school classmate is accused of murdering
his beautiful lover, Carl agrees to represent him—while keeping silent about his own prior romantic involvement with the
victim.

PAST DUE

978-0-06-050819-7 /$7.50 US/9.99 Can.

A determination to do the right thing, albeit for the wrong
reasons, is leading Victor Carl deep into the murkiest corners
of his murdered client's history.

FALLS THE SHADOW

978-0-06-072160-2/$7.99/10.99 Can.

ictor Carl wakes up with his suit in tatters, his socks missing,
d a tattoo on his chest of a heart inscribed with the name
tal Adair.

Visit www.AuthorTracker.com for exclusive
information on your favorite HarperCollins authors.

WL 0307

Available wherever books are sold or please call 1-800-331-3761 to order.

Athleta. Com
/.